Sisters and Brothers

Judith Glover

CORONET BOOKS
Hodder and Stoughton

Copyright © 1984 by Judith Glover

First published in Great Britain in 1984
by Hodder & Stoughton Ltd

Coronet edition 1986

British Library C.I.P.

Glover, Judith
    Sisters and brothers.
    I. Title
    823'.914[F]   PR6057.L64

    ISBN 0-340-37765-8

Printed and bound in Great Britain for
Hodder and Stoughton Paperbacks, a
division of Hodder and Stoughton Ltd.,
Mill Road, Dunton Green, Sevenoaks,
Kent (Editorial Office: 47 Bedford
Square, London, WC1 3DP) by
Hunt Barnard Printing Ltd.,
Aylesbury, Bucks.

Sisters and Brothers

Frank Flynn adjusted the oil lamp hanging from a beam above the stall. Its flickering light cast his shadow across the brick floor to the bottom step of the loft ladder, where it just touched the edge of Lizzie's skirts.

'And you didn't give him his answer?' She remained silent. He tossed a blanket over the back of the groomed horse and came across from the stall to her. She was sitting on the wooden step, her arms hugging her body, her head bent. It was an attitude of defeat, and it angered him.

'He'd no right to talk to you that way. No right at all. Who's he to say what'll be? I've half a mind to go and fetch him out and ask him, I have. It's nothing to do wi' him and I'll thank him to keep his damn' nose clear o' my business!'

Lizzie shifted uneasily. 'Hush . . . they'll hear you if you don't keep your voice down. I'm not supposed to be here still. That Mr Weldrake gi' me orders to clear off, didn't he? His sister — '

'To hell with his sister! I'm not wed to the silly slut yet. You'll stay if I say so.'

About the author

Judith Glover has had a career as a journalist, a freelance writer and a book reviewer. Living in Tunbridge Wells, Kent, she has gained an expert knowledge of Kent and Sussex, and is the author of a number of books on the two counties.

Her first novel, THE STALLION MAN, also published by Coronet Books, was highly acclaimed, and SISTERS AND BROTHERS continues the story of some of the characters introduced in that novel.

'SISTERS AND BROTHERS is as crisp as an apple, full of bracing scenes and characters . . . Miss Glover keeps the pace cracking along with never a wasted word, using witty and authentic dialogue to good effect'

Jessica Stirling

There is a tide in the affairs of women,
Which, taken at the flood, leads — God knows where.

Byron, *Don Juan*

1

"No . . . I won't listen to you! I won't, I won't!"

The auburn-haired girl clapped both hands to her ears and hunched her shoulders.

"Why not?" jeered the youth with her. "Does the truth upset you?"

Without answering, she swung round and walked quickly away from him along the narrow field track; but in a few strides her companion overtook her and stood blocking the way so that she was forced to stop again.

"Well, does it?" he repeated.

Isabelle Flynn lowered her hands and stared resentfully at him.

He stared back, tossing the coarse brown hair from his eyes.

"You're ashamed, aren't you. Ashamed o' being a bastard – "

"Don't use that word!"

"Well . . . chance-born, then. Chance-born, same as me. Why pretend different?"

"I don't pretend. I'd soonest not be reminded of it, that's all."

Reaching out, she snatched away the sketch-book Joel Adams had been carrying for her and hugged it to her breast, arms crossed over it in a gesture of defiance.

"Let me go by, why won't you. It'll be dark afore long and they'll wonder at home where I've got to."

Young Joel moved reluctantly aside, his boots sinking into the wet clay of the plough furrow beside the track.

"And don't go following me, neither," Isabelle flung over her shoulder.

"I'll follow you if I've a mind to. Or isn't your own half-brother nice enough company for you these days?"

He dragged his feet out of the sticky clay and began walking after her, stepping deliberately on the faint outline cast by her figure, a sulky expression turning down the corners of his mouth.

Away in the far distance, the smooth flanks of the Sussex Downs were stained red by the dying rays of sunset streaming from the west. Nearer, the wealden valleys lay veiled in a thin gauze of twilight, their open fields shadowed, stands of trees showing black against the skyline. In the dip beyond the sheep pasture a glow of oil lamps would soon be reflected in the cottage windows of Weatherfield.

The two went on in silence, leaving the village behind as they crossed the top of a second field to where a solitary hawthorn marked the opening to a steep holloway. Dusk had already thickened between its gorse-dotted banks and Isabelle slowed her step as she began the descent, lifting her long skirts clear of the mud underfoot.

She was no more than a short way down when she slipped suddenly on a stone, and in trying to keep her balance let her sketch-book fall to the ground.

Joel put out a hand to steady her.

"Careful – you nearly legged yourself over."

She struggled to free herself from his grip; but he only held her the tighter and gave her a little shake.

"And don't you push me off like that, neither. What's the matter wi' you? Can't you even bear to be touched no more, eh?"

"I don't know what you mean. Let go o' me. You're hurting."

He thrust her away and said bitterly, "You've grown very high and mighty since you come back from staying wi' your fine friends at Bonningale. Going about wi' your nose in the air like Lady Muck. It would have done no harm to treat me civil this afternoon."

"I would have treated you civil," Isabelle threw back at him, "but you had to go making fun o' the way I spoke, saying I was putting on airs."

She bent to retrieve her sketch-book; then, seeing the splashes of mud staining its cover, exclaimed in vexation, "Now look what you've made me do, Joel Adams."

"What? Me? It was *you* as dropped it. Oh, give it here – " He snatched the book from her and started rubbing at it with the sleeve of his shirt.

"It was a new book, an' all. Aunt Rachael Bashford only give it me the day afore I left. Oh, leave go of it – you're making it worse wi' your dirty sleeve."

She made to pull the book away but he held obstinately on, and a tussle developed as they began tugging it this way and that between them.

"Do as you're bid, blast you!" came a sudden sharp voice.

Before Joel realised what was happening, a hand had gripped him by the shoulder and pushed him roughly away so that he almost lost his footing and half-fell backwards into the gorse at the bankside.

"Frank? Frank – !" Isabelle turned, and with a glad cry hastened to fling her arms about the neck of the newcomer, a well-dressed young man of powerful build whose good looks were marred just now by a surly cast of feature.

"Oh, Frank – you're back!"

Frank Flynn, coming up the holloway to meet his sister, had caught sight of the struggling pair silhouetted ahead of him on the rise; and not liking what he saw, had approached in silence, moving on the balls of his feet with the light step of the trained prize fighter.

He jerked his head.

"What's this? He's pestering you, is he?"

"I was seeing her safe home, that's all." Joel Adams faced his half-brother warily a short way up the track. "There's nothing wrong wi' that, is there? Or are you Flynns so swelled now wi' notions of your own importance you've forgot we come from the self-same stock?"

Frank Flynn's dark eyes narrowed slightly.

"Seems to me," the other went on, prudently widening his distance, "what they're saying in the village is true. That you've had your heads turned, the pair o' you. Our Belle wi' her rich relations at Bonningale taking her in out o' charity and learning her their fancy ways – ''

"It's not out o' charity!" Isabelle protested, releasing her brother from her embrace.

Joel ignored her. "And you, Frank, wi' your crowd o' fair-weather friends in Lewes mopping and mowing about your heels, inflating your self-conceit wi' their talk, and for why – on account you make money wi' your fists . . . money to buy yourself good boots and a silver-topped cane. It don't count wi' us in Weatherfield, all that. You're Frank Morgan's come-by-chance, same as me. Born out o' wedlock. So it's no use you coming here acting the gentleman and making out you're quality.''

Frank looked at him in silence. When finally he spoke, his voice was thick with disgust.

"You're piping that tune again, are you? I'd have thought you'd be wearied of it by now. Lord knows, you've wearied me enough. Aye, mebbe he did get us out o' wedlock – even so, he was one o' the best men ever bred, was Frank Morgan. And by God, you should be proud to be of the same blood.''

"Proud? Proud o' that 'un?'' Joel flung back. "What did he ever do that I should be proud of him? A stallion man – a common gipsy horse man! Why should I be so proud to have that 'un for a father when half o' Sussex is filled wi' his bastards?''

"I've never been ashamed to count myself one o' them – ''

"No, you wouldn't be. You're cast in Morgan's mould all right. You're the spit o' the old devil.''

"A pity you couldn't have favoured him more yourself, you miserable runt.''

"Please . . .'' Isabelle laid a hand on her brother's arm, sensing his aggression. Hurt though she was by Joel's words, she had no wish to see him harmed. "Leave it. It's not worth a quarrel.''

"It's worth a damn' sight more than quarrelling if he's been using you abusively, Belle.''

"He vexed me earlier, but he meant nothing by it. I was sketching up near Stillborne's and he come along and started on about me ignoring folk since I've been back. That's all.''

She picked up the sketch-book lying where Joel had discarded it among the gorse, and went on, "Please, Frank. Let's go on home. Mam'll wonder what's become o' me. I don't like to worry her when she's ailing."

Her brother glanced down at her; and after a moment, nodded.

"Aye. We'll not mention this business, though. She'll only fret the more. And you – " he swung menacingly back towards Joel – "you mind your step, d'you hear? Because if I catch you ill-speaking us again, I promise you, you'll be sorry. And leave our sister alone. If you must tag along at women's skirts to vex 'em, go and find yourself some easy wench in the village to cut your puppy teeth on."

"Don't you puppy me, Frank Flynn," Joel retorted hotly. "I've had all the easy wenches I want round here."

"Is that so?" his half-brother sneered back. "Then you've savoured my leavings, haven't you."

The man who had sired Frank and Isabelle Flynn, and their half-brother Joel Adams, had in his day pursued the occupation of stallion leader: procuring a livelihood by his champion Shire horse, leading the stud around the country farms to cover the breeding mares. Eighteen years ago, in 1852, he had met with an untimely death; and the woman he had promised at last to marry, red-haired Dinah Flynn from the alehouse at Weatherfield, had been left to bring up their young son and infant daughter alone.

Frank Morgan had been a handsome, virile man of gipsy stock. His lusty nature and the dangerously potent allure of his work had together proved irresistible to the weaker sex; and proof of his passage was to be found stamped on the features of a number of bastard offspring – most of them sons – around the farming communities of the wealden and downland countryside.

Weatherfield, on the edge of the Ashdown Forest, had expanded itself since the stallion man's time, pushing outwards along its by-ways and boundaries as the three young lives he had fathered here left their years of infancy behind. The alehouse no longer stood alone beside the lane running

11

through fields and woodland to Troy Town: the way was now broadened to a road, and cottages had been built along it to accommodate the families of farmworkers brought into the area by new landowners.

Nor had the alehouse itself remained untouched by the change going on around it. Its old name of "The Man in the Moon" had been revived and a painted sign hung out above the road, bearing a crude representation of a bent figure against a silvered crescent for those who could not read the lettering. Inside, the ale-room had been altered to take a handsome mahogany counter with brass pump handles, and what had formerly been the storeroom behind was now a snug for the wives and children of customers.

Dinah Flynn was busy at the counter when Frank and Isabelle came in together; but as soon as she could get away she left a helper in charge and followed them down the passage to the living quarters at the back of the house.

"Belle's gone up to her room," Frank remarked as she came through into the kitchen. "It was slippy underfoot in the holloway. She took a bit of a fall."

"She's not hurt herself?"

"No, no. Just muddied her skirts, that's all."

He began leafing idly through the pages of his sister's sketch-book left lying on the kitchen table; and after a moment or two observed with a touch of satisfaction, "She's come on well since I was here last. Getting quite a hand at making a picture. Look at this one. She must've done it today. The old barn, isn't it?"

"What's that? What d'you say?" His mother looked at him sharply, then at the drawing held up for her to see.

"Stillborne's old barn. I recognise the – Here! What d'you think you're doing, mam? There's no need to snatch at the damn' thing."

Before he could move to prevent her, Mrs Flynn had seized the book from his hand and pulled the page out of it.

"What did you want to do that for?"

"I won't have her drawing that place," she said loudly. "Not that place . . . not where your father got hisself killed.

12

You tell her, Frank. Much note she takes of anything I say to her. Tell her to keep off Stillborne's in future."

"Now don't go working yourself up over it. Sit down for a bit and stop ripping at that picture. I thought the doctor said you're not to be agitated?"

"Don't talk to me o' no doctor! There's naun that 'un can do save charge the earth for his service. I'm sick o' paying his bills, I am. I don't know which makes me feel worse – them, or the rubbish he keeps making me swallow. There's only one thing cures this dratted pain o' mine, our Frank. Laudanum and brandy – neat."

She put a hand to her chest and shook her head, the peppery-grey hair falling untidily from its pins; and after a moment reached out to pick up the torn pieces of her daughter's drawing.

"Here, we'd best put these to the back o' the fire, afore she comes down. We'll say there was lamp oil spilt on the page. She was pleased to see you, was she, when you went out to meet her?"

"Aye."

"I'm sure she was. She misses you nigh on sorely as me when you're not here. Oh, but it does my heart good to have the pair o' you both home again. The place is never the same when you're gone – you always so busy in Lewes, and our Belle over at Bonningale. She wrote to you, did she, while she was there?"

Frank nodded.

"She's a good girl," his mother went on, getting up to unfasten the long white pinafore she had been wearing in the ale-room and hanging it on a hook behind the kitchen door. "I'm glad Mr and Mrs Bashford take such a kindly interest in her as godparents. They've had her to stay nigh on a month this time, did you know?"

He nodded again and picked a piece of gorse from the cuff of his well-cut Norfolk jacket.

"She's done nicely there," he said, "getting herself so close in with 'em. It's an advantage to know the right folk."

"To be sure. And you, our Frank, you'll be staying a good while this visit? I'm that glad to see your face again.'

"Two or three days. No more."

"Two or three days? Oh, son! When we haven't set eyes on you for Lord knows how long?"

"What's that?" Isabelle came from the staircase door into the kitchen. "What's that, mam?"

"Would you credit it. He's stopping no more'n a couple o' days. Hardly in the house five minutes afore he's off again. I know what the excuse'll be. Same as it always is. Training. Always blessed training. That Boaz Palmer has him leaping up and down like a monkey on a stick, he does."

"Now you know he's got to do it. If he doesn't keep hisself properly fit he'll lose his fights," Isabelle said philosophically, seating herself beside the range. She had brushed her hair out so that it hung in loose curls over her shoulders and the soft light of the oil lamp above her on the mantelpiece glowed in its rich auburn depths.

"What's he want to go and fight at all for, that's what I'd like to know," her mother grumbled. "You tell me, our Frank. Why d'you do it? You had a good enough job, working as groom to that Mr Weldrake. Why couldn't you stay content wi' that, instead o' getting yourself mauled about in them fisty-fights?"

Frank Flynn pulled a leather purse from his jacket pocket and threw it down on the table.

"Here's your answer . . . thirty pounds of it."

"Thirty – ?"

"Aye. Go on. Count it. There's thirty pounds in sovereigns there."

"Frank! You won that much wi' fighting?"

"I did. By getting myself mauled about, as you put it."

Mrs Flynn stared at the purse. Cautiously, she leaned over and stretched out a hand until her fingers touched the soft leather shape.

"Well, go on. Open it and count it. It's yours, all of it."

"What – for me?"

Frank reached out impatiently and pulled at the purse strings. Holding his mother's hand open within his own, he poured out the golden coins into her palm.

"For you, mam. You and our Belle. And d'you know how

long it took me to earn that much in a fist-fight? I'll tell you. Just eighteen minutes."

"But . . . why all for us, Frank?" Isabelle looked up at her brother. "You don't usually bring home your prize purse. What's behind it?"

He shook his head and smiled at her, his teeth showing white in the swarthy clean-shaven features.

"Why not? I can make you a gift if I want, can't I?"

She stared at him, wondering whether she had imagined the note of condescension.

"I've got some'at to tell you both," he continued, glancing away towards his mother. "Are you listening, mam? Good. Now, that money's to be used to buy the pair o' you new clothing. So don't go hoarding it away in the old tin box behind the brick, d'you hear? You're to spend all of it – every last shilling of it – on fitting yourselves out to come to Lewes."

"To Lewes? Whyever for? What's Lewes got to do wi' it?"

"I'm to be married there Saturday week."

"Lord above!" Dinah Flynn snatched her hand to her mouth and sat down in amazement, her eyes fixed on her son's face.

"But – who to? Who is she?" Isabelle immediately wanted to know. "Who are you marrying? Why haven't you said anything to us afore this? You've not mentioned any girl in your letters, has he, mam?"

"It'll be that 'un he's been keeping a secret. I knew it! What's her name, now? Oh – what is it, our Belle, can you think? He did tell us the once. Don't you remember? He wrote as how he'd met this young woman at Midhurst . . . Elizabeth somebody, wasn't it?"

Frank Flynn's expression altered instantly. The smile left his lips and his dark brows drew together in a scowl.

"I don't recall any o' that name," he said, a curious edge to his voice.

"But you do, surely, son? You said as how you'd – "

"I said nothing."

"You said Elizabeth – "

"Let it be, mam," Isabelle interrupted gently. "We've misremembered the name, evidently." She looked across

15

at her brother again. "Well? So who is she? Come on, don't leave us to guess. Who is it we're having into the family?"

Frank let the question hang in the air for a second or two, savouring the coming surprise.

"Miss Rosannah Weldrake," he said at last.

And was duly gratified by the reaction.

"Miss Rosannah – ? Rosannah Weldrake?" His mother's face was a study. "*Her*? No! Go on wi' you. You're having us on a string!"

Isabelle echoed her disbelief. "Not Miss Weldrake . . . It can't be."

"Why not? Why can't it be?"

"Well – " She looked about her, shrugging her shoulders. "Because she's Mr Weldrake's sister, that's why. She's a lady."

For some reason, this made Frank Flynn laugh.

"Lady or no, she's the one I'm marrying, right enough."

His mother clutched her hand on the money he had given her.

"Oh . . . our Frank! Oh, but you've done yourself proud there, son. Just think. Miss Rosannah! Well I never . . . who'd have believed it." Recovering from her astonishment she was full of admiration. "Only the best for you, eh? You've ever been the same. Never satisfied wi' second-rate, always wanting to get on in the world. Just imagine it, though, my daughter-in-law a lady o' quality. All that money of her own, an' all. You've fallen on your feet this time, an' no mistake. You'll be a gentleman now!"

Then another thought struck her.

"But where will you live, the pair o' you?"

"At the house in Tea Garden Lane."

"She shares that with her brother, surely?" Isabelle asked, a little uncertain.

"Aye. But Harry keeps to his own apartments."

"Oh, so it's Harry now, is it? No more Mr Weldrake, I suppose. Does he approve o' the match?"

Frank looked away. "No," he said bluntly after a moment. "He doesn't."

16

"Oh? So . . . so Miss Rosannah doesn't have his permission to wed you?"

"She's of age, and her money's her own. Even so, if she needed it he'd have to give it."

"But, then . . . I don't understand – "

Her mother interrupted. "No more do I, our Belle. What's this, Frank? He'd gi' his permission, but not his approval? How's that come about?"

Frank Flynn smiled drily. "Because I've got his sister in the family way, that's how."

2

Rosannah Weldrake stood on a low stool regarding herself in the rosewood cheval glass in her dressing room. Her beautiful face wore an expression of discontent.

"It still isn't fitting properly at the waist," she told the woman kneeling to pin the hem. "Can't you do anything better?"

The dressmaker got to her feet and took a few paces backwards among the clutter of garments and shoes, examining the heavy white silk wedding gown anxiously.

"See how it pulls?" Rosannah twisted herself about. "No, it won't do at all, Miss Perrins. You'll simply have to undo the band and make it up again."

Miss Perrins removed the pins from her mouth.

"But – "

"No! I dare say the town biddies are hinting already behind their hands about my condition. But I'm damned if I'll give them proof positive by going to the altar in something that makes me look like a bow window."

"But Miss Weldrake – "

Rosannah stepped down from the stool.

"Get me out of the wretched thing."

There were thirty tiny pearl buttons to be unfastened one by one from the crocheted loops at the back of the bodice. The dressmaker worked at them nervously with a button-hook.

"If I might make a suggestion, ma'am?" She eased the tight-fitting sleeves over her client's arms. "An extra gusset, perhaps? It won't do any good unpicking the waistband, not again."

"Why not?"

"Well . . ."

"I'm growing larger?"

Miss Perrins nodded.

"Nonsense. I'm three months into my time, that's all. It hardly shows."

"It shows on my measure, ma'am."

"Oh, don't be tiresome. Have a little gratitude for the work. I could just as easily have taken my custom to Miss Martin."

Rosannah stepped out of the layers of skirts and petti-coats and stood bare-foot in silk-embroidered drawers and camisole.

"Except that she lacks your discretion. They'll know about the child quite soon enough once I'm wed, but I dislike giving the tea-party circle the satisfaction of a gossip in the meanwhile. Let them be content wagging their silly tongues over my choice of husband."

Miss Perrins said nothing. It was the talk of Lewes that Rosannah Weldrake was marrying in unseemly haste. And not the man she had been virtually engaged to, either, but to her brother's own groom, a common young brute who fought for money and, to cap it all, was fully five years her junior.

Public speculation had been rife ever since the wedding was announced; and those loudest in voicing disapproval had hastened to accept their invitations to the ceremony for fear of missing a single moment's enjoyment. But then, what could one expect? The Weldrakes, after all, had rather come down in the world, and the reputation of the family name was hardly one of the best, being already more than a little tarnished by the scandalous behaviour of its bearers.

Miss Perrins produced a tape measure from her workbox and held it out.

"If you'd raise your arms a moment, ma'am?"

Rosannah complied, catching back the heavy golden-blonde hair that fell in waves to her waist. Later in the day she might wear it in a chignon, ringlets covering the nape of her neck, or plaited in braided loops to frame the oval of her face; or whatever other style might appeal to her fickle fancy. At twenty-six she was at the full bloom of her beauty, a spirited, headstrong young woman who delighted in scorning the rigid social conventions of her time, and in so doing had alienated many who clung to the belief that the church, convention and class were the triple pillars of Victorian society.

Regarding herself in the cheval glass, she made a critical examination of her figure and was reassured that the rounding abdomen was still not pronounced enough to spoil her shapely outline.

Though men admired her greatly among themselves, there had been few suitors of the right background to pay her court: when a man is making his way up in the world, it is more to his advantage to select a wife for the virtues of respectability and prudence, however plain her looks, than for what others might regard as the vices of sensuality and pleasure.

At the time she first became acquainted with Frank Flynn, Rosannah had as good as accepted the proposal of one of her brother's gambling companions, a Frenchman working as agent for a Parisian firm of wine importers. Adolphe de Retz had asked for her hand in marriage on several occasions; and she had been disposed to give it – not because she loved her suitor enough, but because he loved her far more than enough, and being the object of such utter and absolute devotion appealed to her capricious vanity.

Even here, though, society held her at fault: being a foreigner, de Retz was accounted no more than a second-rate gentleman, and his courtship of Rosannah was viewed as but a further example of her flouting of the acceptable standards of her class.

She turned away from the reflection, tossing her hair back over her shoulders.

"I'll lace myself. That will do, don't you think? If I were to pull in my waist tightly enough we might get it down to twenty inches."

Miss Perrins's red-rimmed eyes held a look of doubt.

"You'll only harm yourself doing that, ma'am. I wouldn't advise it."

"Oh, but not for long. Only during the service. I'll let the stays out in the vestry afterwards, and wear something comfortably loose for the wedding breakfast."

The dressmaker shook her head, and made the necessary adjustment to the figures in her book. This was intended to be one of those premature infants, of course. Plump, lusty and the picture of good health, for all that the mother's confinement had not been expected for another ten weeks.

There was a knock at the door.

"Oh . . . there, that will be my brother on his way. Quickly, my wrapper. No, not that one. The other – the mauve."

The dressing room door opened and a lace-capped maid appeared.

"Beg pardon, Miss Rosannah – "

"Yes, thank you, Minnie."

She turned, tying the wrapper about her, and looked across at the young man in riding attire who had followed in behind the maid.

"Well, Harry?"

Harry Weldrake returned her look and seated himself in a chair, throwing aside a discarded underbodice before swinging a booted leg casually over the worn brocade of the arm. He ignored Miss Perrins, hastily tidying her workbox, and occupied himself studying his fingernails until the maid had seen her out.

Then he raised a languid eyebrow.

"Well?"

He had his sister's pale complexion and blue eyes, but there the resemblance between them ended. Weldrake's eyes were heavy-lidded above a strong nose, giving him a faintly predatory appearance. The fair hair was parted at the centre

20

and brushed back above the ears, and a thin, neat moustache outlined his upper lip.

"Did you make the killing you intended last night?" Rosannah went across to the window embrasure and sat down at her cluttered dressing-table.

"Scarcely a killing. I took two hundred guineas from Cross and fifty from young Jermyn."

She made a face. "I thought Jermyn's father had threatened you with prosecution if you encouraged the boy to gamble any more of his money?"

"What's fifty guineas? A bagatelle. But it was sufficient to salve my pride – "

"And pay some of your creditors."

" – not to mention keep up appearances for a few weeks more. Though God knows, Rosannah, you make it deuced difficult to keep up appearances of any sort with this outrageous marriage of yours."

She picked up a silver-backed hairbrush and gazed at her reflection in the looking-glass, choosing to ignore her brother's remark.

"You still mean to sacrifice yourself at Miss Adelaide Winter's altar?"

"One more assembly ball and two German bands and I think I have her. Lord help me."

"Ah, but will she have *you*, there's the question."

"She's a fool if she doesn't." Weldrake smoothed his moustache with a forefinger. "Look what she's getting in exchange for her fortune."

"Not so hasty, dear brother. There are married women's property acts now, remember. Miss Winter may decide to hold firm to her fortune."

He made a sound of contempt. "What do maiden ladies like her know about property acts? There's only one kind of act they understand. And Adelaide Winter will have little cause to complain about my ability to consummate that."

"I don't doubt it. But have a care, Harry, or you may find yourself married to the old dear and still no better off than before. It's no longer a case of what's yours is mine, wife, and what's mine is my own. All that has been changed now."

21

Rosannah cast her brother a sidelong look over her shoulder. "Otherwise I'd never have gained your grudging permission to marry Frank."

The handsome features darkened at once and he said angrily, "The devil you wouldn't! I curse the very day I first heard the name of Flynn mentioned!"

Weldrake's rancour was directed partly against himself: it had been he who, little more than a year earlier, had introduced Frank Flynn into Rosannah's life. At the time, he had been seeking a young man for second groom and, impressed by Frank's knowledge of horses and learning something of his background, that his father had been a stallion leader of gipsy stock, had been happy to offer employment.

It was not only Frank's instinctive way with animals that had favoured his selection, but the powerful muscular physique which had carried him from schoolroom brawling and rowdy juvenile fisticuffs to the violent pursuit of prize fighting. As an exponent of that bloody and ignoble art he had already made a name and a reputation for himself throughout the neighbouring district when he came to Tea Garden Lane as Harry Weldrake's groom.

Within a short time the new master had realised his man's worth and become his patron, viewing the expenditure of money on his training and management a good investment against future return from professional bouts. Nor were his gambling instincts proved at fault: during the first few months of fighting, Frank's winnings had more than covered expenses and put his patron, his trainer and himself nicely in pocket.

Those viewing these events did not let it pass without comment that Rosannah Weldrake attended many of the fights; and there was some talk about the familiarity with which she allowed her brother's cocksure young bruiser to treat her.

"At least," Harry Weldrake went on tersely, "he can't touch the money Father left to you, no more than I. That's yours entirely and Flynn has no claim to it."

"Now you're being a hypocrite," Rosannah flung at him.

"How so?"

"You intend making Adelaide Winter your wife purely to

get at her fortune. Yet you resent the notion of Frank marrying me in order to get at mine."

"It isn't the same thing at all. And you know it." Weldrake removed his leg from the chair arm and sat up. "Flynn has a duty to marry you. A responsibility. You carry his child. Though I wish to God it were otherwise and you had not been in such a confounded hurry to get him into your bed –"

"Oh, Harry, *must* you start on that again? How often must I tell you. It was the only way."

"You deliberately became pregnant to force him to wed you."

She looked defiantly back at him from the looking-glass. "Yes."

No one was sure where the rumours had started, but soon after Frank Flynn had moved into the servants' quarters in Tea Garden Lane, a whisper began to go the round of the afternoon parties and soirées, passed on behind a flutter of fans and dainty lace-edged mouchoirs, that Rosannah Weldrake had formed a most undesirable attachment for her brother's young groom.

It was true; and had they but known the strength of that attachment, the whisperers would have been doubly scandalised, for within a month of their first meeting, she had taken him for her lover. Neither was inexperienced. Both shared the same unbridled physical appetites; and it had needed only a glance or two and a few words for her to communicate her willingness.

This, though, had been only the prelude to what was to follow. However much Frank might brag in the privacy of his mother's alehouse that he had "got her in the family way", it would be more accurate to say that the responsibility for Rosannah's condition was solely her own, since she had deliberately planned the conception of this child in a reckless and desperate attempt to retain her lover's cooling affections.

"And you believe you've won, don't you?" There was a note of bitterness in Weldrake's voice.

"What do you mean?"

"You fondly hope that once you're his wife he'll no longer

associate with this woman . . . this female he's lately been keeping company with."

"Of course. What can she offer him that I can't. And more?"

The answer was a shrug.

"I haven't pressed Frank to talk about her," Rosannah went on after a moment. "Why should I? She's of no interest. I know only this – he could never marry *her*. She has a husband already."

"So? Do you suppose it's marriage he's after her for? Use your sense. He's young, just starting his way in life. He hardly wants to be encumbered with a wife and child so soon – "

"He seems happy enough to be *my* husband!"

Weldrake gave a short laugh. "You delude yourself, dear sister, if you imagine that. It's an entrée into society he's after. The cloak of a gentleman to cover his peasant hide. No – sit down and don't interrupt. I'm against this misalliance. Most strongly against it, as I trust I've made perfectly plain. The fellow's not even bourgeois! Damn it, the lower orders should be kept buttoned down, not encouraged to get above their class."

Rosannah flung the hairbrush aside in a sudden temper.

"How dare you be so smug! Remember at whose expense you yourself are able to play the gentleman. So long as you continue living off the crumbs from my table you'd do well to have a care how you criticise my conduct, Harry! Must you be reminded who it is saved you from bankruptcy scarce a year ago? Paid off your creditors? Recompensed your friends? Must you be reminded who it is that feeds you, provides your wardrobe – the very roof above your head?"

She rose to her feet, the mauve wrapper swinging loosely about her, her beautiful face distorted with anger.

"Rosannah . . . Rosannah, calm yourself – " her brother began; but was ignored.

Leaning towards him she continued loudly, "Must you be reminded that I needn't have taken you into this house when you were forced to sell your own? I could have left you lying in the gutter – yes, in the gutter, where your own feckless gambling had thrown you. But I didn't. You're my brother, I told myself – all the family I have. Who else is there but me, your sister, to offer help and support? And now, what do you offer in return? Smug, hypocritical criticism! After everything I've done, you have the gall to sneer at Frank Flynn – Frank, whose winnings you don't scorn to take for pocket-money!"

Weldrake chewed on his lip and stared down at the carpet. It stung his pride to be reminded how much he owed his comfortable existence to Rosannah's generosity. And much though it irked him to acknowledge the truth of her accusations, it was wiser not to provoke her with argument when she was working herself up like this.

He waited in silence.

After a while she reseated herself in a chair among the disarray of crumpled clothing flung carelessly over its back. In a more rational tone of voice she went on, "I know what it is. You're afraid. Afraid my marriage to Frank will lose you Adelaide Winter and her fortune. The gamble, as ever, is yours – to tell her the facts, or else fob her off with half-truths. For I mean to have him, Harry, and convention can go hang. I've come too far to turn back now."

"But – why?" he demanded to know. "What is it that makes you debase yourself in this fashion? Good God, you've always been such a proud-stomached creature. Will nothing deter you from your folly? To see you throw yourself away upon a brute – "

"Yes – a brute! That's what he is. A brute. Coarse, ill-bred, uncouth . . ." Rosannah stared at her brother, her eyes darkening. "That's where he's so different from the rest. Oh, Harry, what do I want with genteel men. Except for poor Dolly de Retz, I despise them . . . despise their soft manners, soft looks, soft caresses. They're like slugs. Each time one of them so much as touches me I want to scream. I need the kind of man who'll abuse me, hurt me, exact my submission by violence. It's what makes me want Frank Flynn so desperately. His passion is an act of hatred, almost. Raw, naked – oh, how I love it when he mistreats me . . . love to feel his rough hands bruising my body."

Weldrake shook his head and looked away. He was not

shocked by the frankness of his sister's confession. He had known for years what kind of appetites she had. Their mother had been the same; but she had married a man who was too good-natured to chastise her, however much she goaded and tormented him. And so she had turned to others to provide the physical violence she craved.

One night, when his father was away at a Midland race meeting, young Harry had been awakened by his mother's cries and had come down from the nursery to her room. A man was there – a stranger – using a dog-whip on her naked flesh. And though she was screaming, there had been something in her face that frightened the child far, far more.

It was not long after this that her body was found in a derelict house among the riverside slums. The circumstances were hushed up, of course; but years later he had learned the truth from one of the servants. She had not died of accidental injury, as the coroner's inquest found. She had been beaten to death.

Harry Weldrake got to his feet, brushing the creases from his immaculately cut riding breeches. The long cheval glass at the further end of the room caught the movement of his figure and he shifted round to see himself better, admiring the elegance of the mirrored reflection.

Without taking his eyes from his image he smoothed back the fair hair above his ears and said, "Well, now that you've put yourself in a position where marriage seems a necessity, have you considered the alternative? Adolphe de Retz is prepared to take you still, you know. Despite your condition. Though it may damn his papist soul to hell, he is quite ready to marry you in a private civil ceremony."

Rosannah bowed her head; then shrugged and gave a little laugh.

"Dear, faithful Dolly. He's far too noble. I'd destroy him within a year . . . and I like him much too much for that."

"But he loves you – "

"Exactly. He worships me. But no, Harry. I am not a damsel in distress to be rescued. Better I continue to hurt my devoted French knight by refusing him, than hurt him far worse by becoming his wife."

"You're a difficult creature. If only you'd go away and have the wretched child quietly somewhere!" Weldrake kicked aside a footstool in his irritation. "Oh, very well – cover your ears! Don't listen to me."

"I won't. We've had all these arguments before."

"If I could – " he went on after a moment, "if it were possible – I'd force you to marry my own choice."

"And what choice is that?"

"Jacob Marshalsey."

"Good God! Are you serious?"

"Never more so. Jacob Marshalsey would make an ideal husband. He's one of the richest men in the county."

"Which would suit you admirably, of course. A wealthy brother-in-law to dangle before your latest collection of creditors."

"To dangle before Adelaide Winter, my dear. That's what suits me. And you would be marrying into your own class. He's very well connected."

"He's also in his dotage, half-blind and more than a little mad."

"All the better. He's easily to be persuaded the child's his doing if you play clever."

"Stop it, Harry." Rosannah stood up.

"But you should consider him."

"Why him? Why not Thomas, his poor ugly cripple of a son? At least he's sane – "

"Oh, come now. One has to draw the line somewhere."

"And mine is drawn at any beyond Frank."

She was suddenly tired of the conversation. Dragging her wrapper about her, she moved past her brother to the open door of her bedroom. There she paused, turning for a moment to look back at him from behind the veil of her hair.

"It's no use, you know. All the talk in the world cannot change things now. I intend to take Frank Flynn for my husband, come what may . . . and damn the consequences."

3

Isabelle Flynn rose from her knees and brushed away the grass and earth of Weatherfield churchyard clinging to the coarse material of her skirts. The grave she had been tending was marked by a sombre headstone bearing the legend

SACRED TO THE MEMORY OF ESMOND JEZRAHEL BATES
RECTOR OF THIS PARISH
WHO DEPARTED THIS LIFE SEPTEMBER 6TH 1852
IN HIS FORTY-THIRD YEAR
"THEN SHALL THE DUST RETURN TO THE EARTH AS IT WAS:
AND THE SPIRIT SHALL RETURN UNTO GOD WHO GAVE IT."

On the day before his demise eighteen years before, the Reverend Bates had baptised the infant Isabelle here at St Anne's church. He had been the first husband of her godmother, who was now Mrs George Bashford; and he had died in the same mishap which killed her father, Frank Morgan, when both men were trampled by Morgan's stallion.

That, seemingly, was all there was to know about him. He had not been a popular minister and his name was rarely mentioned in the village, and then only in connection with the stallion man. Even when she went to stay with the Bashfords across the country at Bonningale where they farmed, no one made reference to Mr Bates; and Isabelle had consequently grown to feel pity for the shunned remains and took it upon herself as an act of charity to care for his neglected grave.

Today she had thought to plant the grassy plot with flower bulbs to give it the colour and sweetness of blossom in the coming spring. The task had taken longer than she anticipated, the frost-hard earth defying her efforts to dig it, and now her hands in the fingerless mittens were almost numb with cold and the needle-sharp November wind was beginning to make her ears ache, despite the woollen muffler tied round her bonnet.

Even so, she still had one other grave to visit before starting the three-mile walk back to the alehouse. This other lay beside the wall on the far side of the churchyard, shadowed by the naked branches of a copse of alder and hazel. No headstone marked it. Instead, there was a sturdy wooden cross whose inscription read simply

FRANCIS MORGAN 1820–1852 R.I.P.

A tangle of relationships lay behind the making of that memorial. It had been carved by Isabelle's uncle, Jack Adams. In that same fateful year of 1852 Jack had salvaged the honour of a girl Morgan had seduced, marrying her and giving her bastard son, Joel, his own family name. He was never a strong man: by 1866, when he was little more than thirty years old, consumption had wasted him away. It was one of the little ironies of life that his last months should be eked out fulfilling a promise to his cousin Dinah Flynn, to make a lasting marker for the resting-place of her footloose, faithless stallion man.

Jack had always been a fine carver, and the cross which he had borne in silent pain during the days of his dying was, when completed, as much a memorial to himself as to the deceased Frank Morgan. He never saw it in place: he was dead before its erection, and his own grave marked by a small neat stone which some uncaring mason in a distant yard had chiselled in a single morning's work.

Isabelle paused as she went by; then, hugging her cape closer round her chilly shoulders, continued on towards her father's plot. It had been edged with cockleshells, painted white with lime to keep the moss from them, and rosemary bushes grew at head and foot as an evergreen token of remembrance.

Despite the keenness of the wind, the girl stood there by the wall for several minutes without moving, her eyes downcast, her thoughts upon this father she had never known: a stranger who had not given her or her brother Frank so much as his name to bear, only the stigma of his paternity. It was open knowledge in Weatherfield and beyond that the pair of them were of the stallion man's begetting; and until young Frank grew ready enough with his fists to be feared, many were the tears Isabelle had shed from her playmates' taunts, and many were the nights she had lain awake pretending to herself that their true father had been a gentleman born, married in secret to their mother before dying bravely for the honour of his country in some foreign land.

Even the name they had, Flynn, was not really their own. It had belonged to their great-grandfather, an Irishman who had purchased the licence to the alehouse in the time of George the Fourth. His unmarried daughter Molly had started calling herself Mrs Flynn when she became licencee after the old man's death; and *her* daughter, Dinah, had continued the custom when she, similarly unwed, had in turn assumed proprietorship in 1861.

Isabelle had once asked Frank what he thought their family name should rightly be. He had told her Morgan. But there were no papers to prove their paternity, and the baptismal entries in the parish register gave them both as Flynn.

And now there was to be another Mrs Flynn. Rosannah. The only one of them with any legal right to use the title.

Isabelle blew on her frozen fingers, the wind whipping away the white breath-cloud. Reaching inside her cloak she withdrew an envelope from the seam pocket of her skirts. It had arrived from Lewes that morning and already she had read its card sufficient times to be able to recite the wording by heart.

Miss Rosannah Weldrake presents her compliments to . . . and requests the honour of their company to a wedding breakfast upon the occasion of her marriage to Mr Francis Flynn at All Souls Church.
Tea Garden Lane, Lewes,
Saturday noon, November 19th 1870.

Frank, who had sent the card to his sister, had scribbled in pencil on the reverse – "For your scrap-book. Tell mam I've got you lodgings. R. wants you both to take tea on the Wednesday."

That would be the Wednesday before the wedding, in a fortnight's time. Before then Isabelle and her mother had arranged that Joel Adams take them by waggon into Tunbridge Wells for a day, to spend Frank's prize-money on new outfits at Weekes and Paine's. This was by far the best store in the whole district, with a reputation for expensive taste, and ordinary folk seldom felt encouraged to penetrate much beyond the row of potted palms by the front counter. Mrs Flynn had agreed to this visit only with the greatest reluctance, saying it was wrong to spend their money in such a showy fashion, and the outfitters at Buckfield would do them just as well.

But Isabelle had been insistent. Only the best, Frank had said; and no one could do better than Weekes and Paine's.

She replaced the card carefully within its envelope. Then, seized with a sudden rush of excited elation, she kissed her hand to the cockleshelled grave and ran off along the church-yard path to the lychgate and out into the lane. By the time she reached home the frosty air had whipped the colour to her cheeks and her limbs tingled with warmth.

"Oh, our Belle, wherever have you been?" her mother greeted her plaintively as she entered the alehouse kitchen through the back door. And before she could answer, went on, "The bar's been open this half hour past and there's customers calling for their ale to be warmed wi' hot iron, the wind's that bitter up on the fields. I'm short-handed as it is, wi' your aunt Lottie laid abed still wi' screwmattics. And this pain in the chest's playing me up again terrible. Get your cloak off, do, and tend to them pokers."

She jerked her head towards the black-leaded range where a fire was blazing brightly. Several long rods, their handles wrapped around with pieces of rag, had been thrust between the bars of the grate to heat in the glowing coals before being doused in the pots of ale standing ready on the kitchen table. This method of taking the chill off was believed to

31

strengthen the liquor with iron and thus be doubly efficacious in inclement weather.

"It's rheumatism," Isabelle said, removing her mittens to untie the muffler from under her chin and hang it up with her bonnet and cloak. "Rheumatism. Not screwmattics. I wish you wouldn't talk so quaint, mam. You'll make a regular boffle o' things in Lewes. They'll never be able to understand you."

"They can please theirselves how they like," Mrs Flynn answered sharply. "I can't abide folk talking tip-tongued as if their mother-speech were some'at to be shamed of. Now you just watch them pokers, my girl, afore the rags catches alight, and never you mind so much how others be thinking of you. There's a saying I was told as a child – manners maketh man – meaning fine words don't always go to make fine ways. You'd do well to remember that in life if you don't want others to advantage theirselves o' your young nature."

"I didn't mean to rile you, mam," her daughter said regretfully, taking up one of the pots from the table. "I'm sorry I mis-spoke."

Mrs Flynn gave a shake of the head. "It's my own fault . . . don't take no note, our Belle. I'm easily riled these days – "

She was about to add something more when there came a swelling chorus of shouts for attention from the direction of the ale-room.

"There, hark at 'em – not a minute's blessed peace!" she exclaimed; and seizing a tray of ale already warmed, hastened away with answering shouts through the kitchen door, the heels of her boots clattering on the flagstones of the passage.

Isabelle carried the remaining pots across to the range and set them down. Grasping each rod in turn by its rag-bound handle, she drew it from the fire and plunged the red-hot end into the brimming ale. There was a series of frothing hisses and a plume of steam rose about her and clung to the auburn hair.

In the short time it took to complete this task, Mrs Flynn had served her noisy customers and was back again.

"This 'un's ready now, is it?" She indicated the second tray. Then, pausing at the table, she gave a loud sniff and announced suddenly, "I wish our Frank hadn't set his cap at that Miss Weldrake. I don't fancy traipsing all the way to Lewes to be looked over by a lot of strangers."

"Oh . . . mam!"

Isabelle's face was flushed now from the heat of the fire. Pushing back wisps of damp hair clinging to her forehead, she stared at her mother in dismayed perplexity.

"But I thought you were pleased for him to be marrying so well!"

"Aye. Better, though, if he'd kept to the village for his courting. There's girls aplenty would've had him. Tod Oliver's youngest, now she's a pleasant soul. And that 'un from next to Izzards."

"He's never liked any o' them sufficient to wed . . . and why have you taken against Miss Weldrake so sudden? When Frank told us his news, you said yourself how proud you were he'd chose a lady."

"Lady!" Mrs Flynn leaned forward and gripped the handles of the tray. "Seems to me she's no more a lady than the rest of us poor mortal females."

"But, mam, you said – "

"I know what I said, Belle. That was afore Frank told us *all* his news. You mark my words and learn by 'em. Gentry-born she may be, but Miss Weldrake can't be that much the lady, not if she's quickened wi' child afore she's wed."

Harry Weldrake reined his horse to a walk at the end of the long gallop and sat back in the saddle, the reins slack between his fingers, gazing moodily across the green slope of the Downs towards Lewes. From here the whole town lay spread out along the length of its castle crest, the high street its backbone, its ribs the crowded narrow streets and twittens sloping away on either side.

Below him the River Ouse parted course with the railway line and flowed south past wharves and warehouses, past the gasworks and iron foundries whose effluence streaked the dark waters with ribbons of metallic scum and swirled round the hulls of barges moored against the banks.

The horse jerked its head and pranced sideways across the

springy turf, impatient to be off again. Weldrake checked it; then altered his mind and spurred it forward into a trot. It was a handsome animal, a bay, bred from the line his grandfather had built up during the last decades of the old century.

The first Harry Weldrake had had a natural instinct for bloodstock and his racing stables prospered so well that by the time of the Regency the family name had become synonymous with winners. His son, Norris Weldrake, had in due course taken over the management of what was recognised as the finest string of race-horses in the southern counties, boasting champions such as Bosphorus, Allentown, and the steeplechaser Janzy d'Or.

But of all that old glory, only this one bay remained. The rest of the stock had been sold off long ago. After Norris's death the estate had been administered by negligent trustees; and in the few years since young Harry came into his inheritance, he had squandered what remained of the family fortune in pursuit of pleasure, pouring his wealth away down the twin drains of gambling and debauchery.

It was fortunate that Norris Weldrake had had the foresight to make a separate settlement on his daughter, Rosannah. The house in Tea Garden Lane was hers alone; and as she had so recently had cause to remind Harry, he could touch neither her property nor her independent income.

Since he had not been bred to work, he had only one means of supporting himself as a gentleman. Though the green baize tables, the race tracks and bare-knuckle rings enabled him to keep up appearances, it was a precarious livelihood, dependent too often upon the whims of chance; and when his luck ran low he had been forced periodically to turn to courtship.

But even this, like everything else, was a game with him: a gamble to see how far he might edge along the road to matrimony with some rich, plain, love-silly woman before fortune smiled on him once more at the tables or tracks and he could – with charming apology – make his escape back to the unfettered life of a bachelor man-about-town.

Not that Harry Weldrake was averse to marrying. It was something he meant to try if only for the satisfaction of begetting heirs, the vanity of seeing himself reproduced in sons. But he could wait awhile yet. The desires of the flesh were better gratified for the present by certain women at a house in Star Street, where gentlemen might enjoy artfully lit *tableaux vivants* and *poses plastiques* while sampling expensive champagne in the red plush comfort of a private room.

The wind, racing up the open spaces of the Downs, caught him in the face as his horse breasted the top of the rise, bringing a warm, sour smell from the breweries on the river bank beyond the bridge. He circled there; then urged the powerful bay forward again with his whip and cantered towards a line of stunted hawthorns, where a flinty track gradually widened as it curved away into a belt of trees.

The house Weldrake shared now with his sister stood at the end of the steep lane further down, off the Downs on the southern edge of the town. It was an elegant residence dating from the time of George I, its imposingly columned entrance porch opening directly off the lane and separated from the horse traffic by a flight of stone steps.

An archway led to the stables and outbuildings behind.

Weldrake walked the bay through into the cobbled yard and dismounted. The place seemed deserted. Now that he no longer had the service of his future brother-in-law, he was using one of his sister's house servants as a temporary groom.

"Osborne?" he called. "Hallo! Anyone about?"

There was a quick movement from within the store-room above the stables, and a sound as though someone were whispering. Weldrake waited; but no one appeared.

"Hallo! Osborne! Jenkins!"

The door at the foot of the storeroom stairs swung back and a man came out into the yard. Not Osborne or any of the others, but Frank Flynn himself, rolling down the sleeves of his shirt, his coat thrown carelessly over one shoulder. There were pieces of straw caught in the black curly hair and dust streaks on the knees of his corduroy breeches.

Behind him, her face a pale oval in the shadow of the unlit stairs, a young woman was hastily buttoning the neck of her high-collared gown.

35

4

As the woman moved from the shadow into the clear afternoon light Harry Weldrake had a better view of her; and recognised her immediately. He had seen her only once before, but she was the kind of bewitching creature a man does not easily forget.

Early that spring he and his friends had attended a prize fight between Frank Flynn and a West Sussex butcher in the yard of an inn at Midhurst. This dark young beauty had been there that day, standing on the back of a waggon with two others, engaged in high-spirited banter with the men around.

The contestants had been called out to the ring. Frank Flynn came across the yard past the waggon. He looked up at her; and paused.

Weldrake had been in a position to observe both their faces, and it was the most extraordinary encounter he had ever witnessed between a man and a woman who, only a moment before, had been total strangers to one another. Something unspoken passed between them in that instant and like twin mirrors their eyes had reflected the same surprised recognition, the same hungry desire.

Frank had said something to her, and she had leaned down from the waggon and kissed him boldly on the mouth. Then, as he wore no colours for the fight, she raised her skirts and ripped a length of scarlet cambric from the petticoat beneath, revealing a smooth curve of leg to the noisily appreciative onlookers.

He had worn her colours, and won his fight. And since that day, so far as Harry Weldrake knew, the pair of them had been meeting whenever she had a chance to slip away from her husband, a Midhurst farmer.

36

The affaire could not long be kept a secret from Rosannah. Despite Frank's discretion, she had soon begun to suspect her young lover of straying, and like most women who fear they are losing a man before they themselves have grown sufficiently bored to let him go, she became quite desperate in her efforts to win back his attention and hysterically abusive each time she thought he was neglecting her. When, to everyone's dismay but her own, she found she was pregnant, Frank had at first refused to marry her, saying the whole business would be a farce; but then – again to everyone's dismay but Rosannah's – he had suddenly had a change of mind.

Harry Weldrake wondered how much this decision may have been influenced by the young woman he was looking at here in the yard, whether the fact that she herself was not free to marry had had anything to do with it.

She returned his look, the full lips parted slightly as though she were unsure whether to smile at him or not. Her sloe-black eyes held an expression that robbed him for a moment of his anger at Frank Flynn for bringing her here; for taking his pleasure so blatantly beneath the very windows of his future wife.

Without being too uncivil he said, "I don't know your name."

"It's Mrs Newbrook, sir. Elizabeth Newbrook."

Even the voice was warm and inviting; not a hint of embarrassment at being discovered in such indiscreet circumstances.

Weldrake glanced beyond her to the storeroom door and back again, waiting for an explanation. She gave him none. Instead, it was Frank who spoke.

"I'll take the horse along to the stables for a rub down. You've ridden him hard. And standing out in this wind won't help him, the sweat he's in."

He took up the reins, looping them over his arm, then added, "Oh – I'm sorry I wasn't able to let you know I'd be back a day earlier than we arranged."

Weldrake ignored the apology. "You'll oblige me by not bringing Mrs Newbrook here again," he said curtly. "Remember whose property this is."

"I hadn't forgotten."

"Then don't press your luck too far, man. Once you're married to Rosannah she'll hardly tolerate this kind of behaviour. Not on her own doorstep."

"Once we're married –"

The other checked himself. After a pause he went on, "It wasn't what you think. I didn't bring Lizzie here for that."

"No?"

"No. Well . . . it wasn't the intention, leastways. She only come by to collect some'at, that's all. Didn't you, girl? Nobody's seen us except Osborne, and he'll keep his mouth shut if he knows what's good for him."

"So my sister isn't aware of your return?"

"Does it look like it?"

Frank started slackening the bay's girth-band, and motioned with his head in the direction of the house.

"She's got the curate in to see her, Osborne said. That chap Bethway from All Souls. Come to put the finishing touches to Saturday's execution."

He smiled thinly, and drew a forefinger across his throat in a snatched gesture.

"You know. The wedding ceremony. When I get turned off. Topped. Sent across the great divide."

Weldrake's retort came smartly. "There's such a thing as a last-minute reprieve. A free pardon, even. You've only to say the word."

Frank laughed. "But I'm already committed, aren't I. The evidence is lying snug in its mother's belly."

Turning the bay's head he led it off towards the stables, calling back over his shoulder, "So you'll understand if I don't apply for any reprieve. But then, I always was a great believer in the afterlife . . . all that milk and honey and idling about on clouds. Come Saturday I'm going to be in regular bloomin' paradise, aren't I, Lizzie?"

The young woman made no answer. Her eyes were still fixed on Weldrake's face.

He looked back at her, slapping his riding crop irritably against the side of his boot; and when Frank had moved out of earshot, said abruptly, "You have influence with him, surely?"

"Influence, sir?"

"To make him alter his confounded plan. To put it bluntly, ma'am, I don't want him marrying into my family."

"Ah. He did say as how you weren't best pleased about it." She cast a quick glance behind her. "But he's got to do the right thing by her, hasn't he?"

"That depends rather on how you look at it. My sister backed him into this corner quite deliberately, you know. She's labouring under some kind of emotional delusion that seems to have robbed her of all sense."

Lizzie Newbrook smiled faintly.

Weldrake gave his boot another slap. "You seem remarkably complacent about this marriage, if I may say so, Mrs Newbrook. Surely you can't be any more happy than I am."

She lowered her eyes and he saw the generous mouth compress itself a little.

Deliberately he went on, "This relationship you have . . . I am aware of its nature, of course. But things will have to be very different now. You do see that, I hope? Whatever has passed between you and Frank Flynn must end, and that must be causing you some distress. Oh – don't think I mean to pry, please, but it is something of my business. And I must point out that there can be no question of things going on as they have in the past if my sister becomes your . . . well, your lover's wife. I mean you no ill will, ma'am, but unless you can bring influence to bear which will alter the course of events, I neither wish to see you nor hear of you in connection with my family again."

"That's what he told you?"

Frank Flynn adjusted the oil lamp hanging from a beam above the stall. Its flickering light cast his shadow across the brick floor to the bottom step of the loft ladder, where it just touched the edge of Lizzie's skirts.

"And you didn't give him his answer?"

She remained silent.

He tossed a blanket over the back of the groomed horse

and came across from the stall to her. She was sitting on the wooden step, her arms hugging her body, her head bent. It was an attitude of defeat, and it angered him.

"He'd no right to talk to you that way. No right at all. Who's he to say what'll be? I've half a mind to go and fetch him out and ask him, I have. It's nothing to do wi' him, and I'll thank him to keep his damn' nose clear o' my business!"

Lizzie shifted uneasily. "Hush . . . they'll hear you if you don't keep your voice down. I'm not supposed to be here still. That Mr Weldrake gi' me orders to clear off, didn't he? His sister – "

"To hell with his sister! I'm not wed to the silly slut yet. You'll stay if I say so."

She got to her feet and pulled the paisley-patterned shawl up over her dark hair, crossing the long ends over her breast to tie them behind.

"It's no good, Frank, love. I'd best be away. I'm meant to be back in Midhurst tonight. Tom thinks I'm visiting wi' friends."

"You can't go just now." He reached out and caught her by the arm. "We haven't settled anything. Look . . . come up into the loft, won't you. It's warmer there and we can talk easier."

"No, Frank. I mustn't. I can't stay."

"A few minutes more won't hurt."

"Somebody might come in."

"They won't. And if they do, we shan't be seen up there."

He moved away from her and reached across the stall for the lamp chain. The blue flame inside the smoked glass chimney flared for a moment, then guttered away, leaving the place in near-darkness. The only illumination came from the lights of the house, reflected palely through the open doorway from the other side of the stable yard.

"Come on. Give us your hand."

Lizzie hesitated. But desire was stronger than prudence and she reached out and let him lead her up the steps to the loft, to the mustiness of straw and mildewed leather and saddle soap.

Frank dragged some pieces of sacking over the bales and stretched himself out, pulling her down beside him.

"How's that, now? Rest yourself along by me for a bit. That's better, eh? Hold up a minute, let's get my arm comfortable."

"Frank—" she began, holding away from him. But his firm lips found hers and silenced her.

She put up a token struggle, pushing at his shoulders and trying to turn her head away; then made a soft low sound and began returning his kisses, holding his face between her hands, pressing herself against his hard-muscled body.

His fingers moved lightly, skilfully, from the nape of her neck down the arch of her back to her waist; and up again across the swell of the bodice to the laces fastening the front of her gown. For the second time that day he undid them, his movements slow and deliberate; and this time there was no Harry Weldrake below to interrupt him.

In the dimness he smiled down at her; and when his hands began caressing the warm nakedness of her body, felt her tremble beneath him. He bent his head to kiss her again. There was the taste of salt tears on her lips.

"Lizzie?"

She did not answer immediately, but only pressed herself more urgently against him.

"Lizzie, what is it?"

After a moment she whispered, "Us. This."

"Shall I stop?"

"Oh, no . . . no."

"What, then?"

She buried her face against his shoulder and her trembling grew stronger. When she spoke again, the words were so low he could barely make them out.

"I . . . I can't bear to lose you, Frank. That's all. I need you. Need to be like this wi' you, together like we are now. It's the only thing I live for, being wi' you this way. Oh, Frank, what am I going to do wi'out you?"

Gently he kissed her again, on her mouth and eyes, stroking the waves of hair back from her face. She was his woman completely, in body, heart and soul; his in every movement

41

she made and every thought of her mind. Since the day they met at Midhurst she had cleaved to him utterly, forsaking all others, willing even to abandon her marriage bed and keep herself for him alone, constant and faithful. Never once in the time they'd been together had she failed or disappointed him. And though their meetings were often no more than a snatched hour after weeks apart, she never complained as another woman might, never questioned him nor made demands upon him, never bored him with the sweet familiarity of love.

He kissed her mouth less gently this time and thrust the full weight of his body against her, crushing her beneath him into the yielding straw.

Hoarsely he said, "I'm not giving you up, damn it. Don't ever think that. You're mine, Lizzie, my woman, you and me together. Nothing's going to change that. Not the law, not the church – not that bitch across the yard. It's going to be just like we said it'd be. I'll marry her to help me get on, gi' me a leg up in the world, but I swear to God she'll never be my wife. She's got all she's getting from me, my name and my child. It's you that's my true wife in the eyes of heaven, Lizzie. You and no other."

"I, Rosannah Beatrice, take thee, Francis Patrick, to my wedded husband, to have and to hold from this day forward, for better for worse, for richer for poorer, in sickness and in health, to love, cherish and obey, till death us do part, according to God's holy ordinance."

Rosannah Weldrake turned in the darkened frame of the drawing-room window and cast a backward glance over her shoulder at the slim young man in clerical black seated on the edge of the horse-hair sofa.

"And thereto I plight thee my troth. There, Mr Bethway. I have the words by heart."

He smiled faintly. "There was no need to go to such trouble, ma'am."

"Oh, but I've said them over to myself so often I have them perfectly. There's such a reassuring ring to them. Wedded husband . . . cherish . . . obey . . ."

She turned back again to the window and stood for several moments gazing out across the roofline of the darkened outbuildings to where the last red bars of sunset were paling in an iron-grey evening sky. Someone came from the stable door below and moved quickly away in the shadow of the wall. For a second she thought it was Frank, but the light was too poor to be certain.

She touched her fingertips to her cheek. "Of them all, I think I like best the line that says with my body I thee worship. Why is it, do you suppose, only the groom vows that?"

"I beg your pardon?"

"That line. With my body I thee worship. Surely such a vow applies as much to the bride?"

Alec Bethway raised his eyebrows a fraction. He was no prude, but he was not normally called upon to answer such forthright questions from females in the course of his parochial duties.

He cleared his throat.

"The main purpose of matrimony is to bring forth children into the world," he began briskly. "And to that end the union between man and woman . . . husband and wife . . . must be consummated. When the groom vows to worship his bride with his body, he is promising to . . . that is to say, ma'am, promising to . . ."

He came to an awkward stop.

"Yes?"

"He is promising to do precisely that."

"Precisely what?"

"Well . . . to consummate the union."

"I see." Rosannah moved slowly from the window, a curious half-smile giving the beautiful face a look of guile. "Thank you, Mr Bethway. You explained that quite charmingly. But I hope the naivety of my question hasn't discommoded you?"

"Not at all."

He glanced away towards the fireplace with its overcrowded marble mantelpiece. Clearing his throat again he said carefully, "Perhaps we might settle the choice of hymns for the service, Miss Weldrake? I'd like to suggest if I may 'How Welcome Was the Call'. It's quite a recent piece, composed especially for the ceremony of marriage, and I think you and your future husband would find the words most apposite. Or perhaps 'The Voice that Breathed o'er Eden'? That's become popular with couples over the past few years. Henry Gauntlett's words again, set to the tune St Alphege –"

"I *have* discommoded you," Rosannah interrupted, coming to sit at the other end of the sofa. The afternoon gown was cut immodestly low and the swell of her breasts was revealed by the soft light of the gasolier. "But of course – you're a bachelor still, are you not? I'd quite forgotten. Do forgive me."

There was a subtle, mocking note to her voice.

"The hymns, ma'am?" he reminded her politely. "Do you have any personal preference?"

"Not especially. Either of those will do. Or both. I really don't mind. You choose. You've had far more practice, and I'm sure whatever you select will do perfectly well."

"As you wish. But your husband-to-be may like to be consulted –"

"Frank? Lord, he knows nothing of music! Left to him, we'd come away from the altar singing 'Jan Cladpole's Trip to 'Merricur in Search o' Dollar Trees'. Does that sound terribly unkind of me? I didn't mean it to. Are you yourself planning to be married, Mr Bethway?"

The directness of the question caught him off guard.

"Not – not in the foreseeable future, no."

"No? But you're paying court, surely?"

"No."

"No again?" She smiled at the curate, enjoying the look of embarrassment on his young face. "You disappoint me, sir. You're much too handsome to keep yourself from the ladies. I wonder half the town haven't thrown themselves at you already. Or perhaps they have, and there's not a single one of them you admire?"

"Miss Weldrake –"

"Oh, there. Now I've trespassed too far altogether."

She was like a cat with a mouse, a game that delighted her;

and the more her victim struggled, the more pleasure she derived from her teasing.

"But it's entirely your own fault, you know. Have you no notion at all what ferment you've been causing among the females of my acquaintance? No idea of the passions you've aroused in the time you've been in Lewes? The talk is of nothing else! And no wonder. You look so splendidly manly riding past on your penny-farthing bicycle – "

"I think we will not pursue this conversation, if you please."

Alec Bethway got to his feet. His sensitive features betrayed an ill-mastered annoyance. He was quite aware that a number of younger parishioners found him more interesting as a man than as a minister; that the reason they sought his attendance at their social functions was not so much respect for his cloth as a desire to claim his personal attention for an hour or two, simpering and blushing behind their fans; and that when he addressed them as part of the congregation, the look of dreamy devotion upon their faces was possibly not solely induced by the inspiration of his oratory.

Last St Valentine's Day he had received no less than three separate messages, two proclaiming the anonymous senders' undying affection, the other containing verses praising his physiognomy in disconcertingly fulsome detail.

It was not that the curate of All Souls was averse to receiving the admiration of young women. On the contrary, he was a man who fully appreciated feminine beauty and took as much delight in a pretty face or charming manner as any other healthy, normal male of twenty-five. Nor was he the type of cleric who was over-studious or retiring: he enjoyed ice-skating, bicycling, rowing, cricket, equally as much as music, art and good literature.

He had formed several friendships during his years as a student of theology at Durham University, but no woman yet had made any great impression upon his heart; and his discomfiture at Rosannah Weldrake's teasing was more impatience than modesty. She was, in his opinion, a female who wore her physical attractions like a mask, like the lid of a Pandora's Box, concealing a very different creature within.

"Now I've frightened you away, I fear." She rose languorously from the sofa and went to the bell-pull beside the fireplace. "How very remiss of me."

Her visitor made no response as he followed politely to his feet.

She looked back at him, her eyes moving slowly over his face, expressionless above clerical band and black stock. There was something about him – the neatness of his thick brown hair and side-whiskers, the classically regular features, the faint air of romantic melancholy – that suddenly irritated her. He was altogether too nice for her taste. Despite his mature appearance there was not the slightest whiff of carnality or tainted experience, but rather something of the innocent boy still.

When his hat had been brought and the maid was about to show him downstairs, a sudden quirk of humour seized Rosannah and she said casually, "You'll remember me in your prayers won't you, Mr Bethway? Who knows, it may do us both some good."

5

As Frank Flynn had arranged, his mother and sister arrived in Lewes several days before the wedding ceremony. There would be plenty to keep them both occupied, he said, what with seeing the sights of the town and looking inside the shops; not forgetting Rosannah's invitation to take tea one afternoon to make her acquaintance.

"There's no point in you all meeting as strangers for the wedding breakfast, even though you'll likely be living as good as strangers after it."

"But Miss Weldrake'll be visiting Weatherfield, surely? When she's your wife?" Isabelle had said at once.

"Not her! Visit Weatherfield?"

"What's wrong wi' that? She could stay wi' us at the alehouse. We've the room."

"Aye – and so has a hen-coop, but you won't find peacocks roosting there."

No more was said on the subject.

On the day of their departure, Isabelle and Mrs Flynn left the village riding with their baggage on the top of Joel Adams's carrier waggon; but at Buckfield, where he set them down, they transferred to the comparative grandeur of the London, Brighton & South Coast Railway, travelling in the third-class open carriage at the rear of the train.

Frank was waiting to meet them at the crowded terminal in Friars Walk.

"I've taken rooms for the three of us at The White Hart," he informed them, cutting short his sister's exclamations of vexation at the sooty streaks deposited on her new shawl from the engine stack. "It's the best hotel in Lewes, so you can't say I'm not doing you proud."

Dinah Flynn looked doubtful as she followed out after him to the carriage stand by the railway bridge.

"You didn't need to go to such trouble on our account, son."

He assisted her up after Isabelle into the back of the trap and loaded their baggage.

"It's no trouble. It'll look better if I'm married from there."

"But I'm not sure I want to be put up at any hotel. What's wrong wi' a lodging house?"

Frank climbed into the driving seat and flicked the whip impatiently at the horse's flank, rousing it into a walk. Over his shoulder he said, "You'll do as you're bid, mam. I'm not giving no lodging house as my address. It's got to go in the church register, remember, where folks'll see it."

"Can't you give where you're living now, in Tea Garden Lane?" his sister asked. "That's grand enough, surely?"

"Oh, our Belle . . . he's got to observe the decencies!" Mrs Flynn reproached her.

"Decencies? What decencies?"

47

Frank gave a short laugh. "Well, it wouldn't look right if I was to share the same address as the bride, now would it?"

The White Hart Hotel overwhelmed Dinah Flynn. She had never stayed away from Weatherfield before, and had certainly never imagined herself in a place as elegant as this, with its red, flocked wallpapered rooms, its profusion of paintings and marble statuary and sweeping staircases.

"It's like living in a big hall," she said nervously, standing in the middle of the high-ceilinged bedroom whose windows looked across to the porticoed majesty of the town hall opposite.

Nor was she used to dining in public and being waited upon at table; and there was some embarrassment on their first evening in the dining-room when she got up, and before Frank could prevent her, began helping the maid to clear away their emptied supper plates.

Those at the nearest tables had looked on, supercilious amusement in their faces; but if they hoped for similar entertainment the following evening, they were disappointed. Mrs Flynn did not reappear.

Immediately adjacent to the hotel stood a double-fronted beershop called The Unicorn, catering for a rather less distinguished clientele. Passing its window the next morning, she had persuaded Frank to take her inside for a glass of stout; and she was still there at midday when Isabelle came looking for her, the stout having been succeeded by several glasses of port and a veal pie.

"Oh, this'll do me better than all that fuss and feeding they gi' you next door," she said when her daughter remonstrated with her. "I'll make use o' the bed, since our Frank's paid his money for it. But you can tell 'em I'll be taking my meals here at The Unicorn from now on."

Isabelle made no offer to join her, much preferring to stay in her room at The White Hart. Unlike her mother, she was not in the least intimidated by the grandeur of the surroundings. Rather, it excited her, and in her fresh young innocence she derived the greatest satisfaction from imagining herself a lady of wealth and leisure, needing only to raise a hand to the bell-pull to summon a servant to press her linen or replenish the fire.

Everything around her was food to this fancy: the soft, thick Turkey carpets underfoot, the heavy velvet curtains swathing the windows, the lush ferns in brass bowls, the starched table napery, the fine china, the pervasive atmosphere of affluence and good taste. It was a similar atmosphere that she had sensed in the Weldrake house in Tea Garden Lane when they went to make their brief social call upon the bride-to-be.

That had proved a somewhat stiff little ceremony: Rosannah brittly polite in her conversation, Frank inclined to be boorish, Mrs Flynn over-anxious to please and in her nervousness lapsing into the ungrammatical idioms of Sussex speech. Only Isabelle herself had behaved naturally.

"I do envy you, Frank." she told her brother when they were together that evening in her room. "Just think, you'll be able to live like a lord, married to Miss Weldrake! How I wish I was her, having the money to buy whatever you want as the fancy takes you."

"That's idle spending, that is. Throwing money away for the sake of a minute or two's satisfaction. Don't wish yourself like her, our Belle. She's a discontented creature for all her fine possessions."

"Oh, but I do . . . It's spoiled me, it has, coming to stay at a fine place like this. It's give me a taste for some'at better in life than I've had so far."

She paused; and after a moment said with a smile, "D'you know what I was thinking just now?"

Frank shook his head.

"Well . . . you won't laugh at me, will you? Promise? It's about your Mr Weldrake. The notion come into my head how nice it would be if he took a liking to me at the wedding breakfast."

Her brother's eyes narrowed slightly.

She went blithely on, "Oh, you know . . . I feel acquainted wi' him already, the number o' times you've talked about him. What a shame he couldn't be there today. I was that

49

looking forward to meeting him. I thought if he liked me sufficient, behopes he'd marry me and then we could all live together up at the house – "

Frank got abruptly to his feet. "I'd rather see you dead!"

"What – ?"

"You heard me."

"But . . . why? What's wrong wi' wishing a thing like that?"

"You and Harry Weldrake? God help you, Belle, you don't know what you're saying."

His sister's artlessness roused feelings in which protective-ness mingled strongly with exasperation. She was a child still in many ways, he reminded himself. An innocent. The world of handsome young sophisticates such as Weldrake was as far outside her comprehension as it was possible to imagine. It was a world in which the pursuit of self-pleasure created a cynical indifference to finer human feelings, a world in which the outward trappings of breeding concealed a corruption of which her kind were all too often the hapless victims.

Isabelle bit her lip and said sullenly, "There was no call to answer me so sharp, Frank. I didn't mean anything by it. It was no more'n a foolish notion, that's all."

He glanced down at her, at the small head under its weight of thick hair bent forward over hands still reddened and rough from work.

In a gentler tone he said, "It's a notion best forgot if you've any sense. Swear you'll put it right from your mind?"

After a moment she nodded. "If it's what you want. I swear I won't think such a thing again."

For all that she meant it at the time, it was a promise made to be broken. The moment Isabelle set eyes on Harry Weldrake, she was drawn to him as surely as a moth is drawn towards the flame that will destroy it.

The day of the wedding started badly for them all.

Frank and Boaz Palmer, the squat, broken-nosed ex-pugilist who acted as his trainer and manager and who was to be groom's man at the ceremony, had spent the previous night going from one to another of the numerous public houses in the town. Arriving back at The White Hart Hotel in the early hours of the morning, both were so far gone in drink that the night porter was forced to summon assistance to get them up the stairs.

Roused from unconsciousness at daybreak, Frank had resumed his alcoholic assault; and by nine o'clock, when the hired carriage arrived at the hotel to convey the party to church, he had passed beyond the stages of inebriation and nausea to a total numbness of all physical sensation.

Her son's obvious inability to stand upright without support threw Mrs Flynn into a state of near-hysteria when she went to his room. After rounding on Boaz Palmer, who was doing his best to get the bridegroom clothed for his wedding, she broke into a noisy tirade.

"That I should live to see the day! You marrying a gentlewoman – and you have to go and get yourself into such a kelter. Here, let me sponge your face. Hold still! Drinking yourself to such a state, indeed. You done it on a purpose to vex me, I'll swear. All them fine folk waiting to see you wed, and you so mazed you can scarce put one foot afore another. Oh, Frank – I'm that ashamed o' you I don't know where to put myself. And what will Miss Rosannah have to say, I'd like to know!"

The reply was indistinct, but a great deal was conveyed by the force of its utterance.

Overwhelmed with nervous agitation, Mrs Flynn burst into sobs; and it was only after Isabelle had helped her back to her room and fanned her face while she sipped at a brandy restorative that the distraught woman was finally judged fit enough to leave for the church.

With the groom leaning heavily on the groom's man's shoulder and his mother steadying herself upon his arm, the party made a somewhat graceless procession down the lobby staircase to the waiting carriage. Isabelle followed at the rear, her eyes fixed steadily ahead of her so that she avoided having to see the expressions on the faces of their fellow guests who had assembled to watch the departure.

It was perhaps fortunate that the dull November morning was so sharp with frost, necessitating a slow progress through the streets. Straw had been laid down to keep the horses from slipping, but the ice-layered cobblestones were still a hazard to traffic and the carriage brake-shoe needed to be applied even on the gentlest slopes.

This snail-pace drive in the chilly air cleared some of the drunken haze from Frank's wits, enabling him to conduct himself with rather less noticeable difficulty once they had reached All Souls; and if Mr Kenward the vicar, a stooped, careworn figure with a bad cough and squeaking boots, was aware of the alcoholic fumes permeating his church porch, he gave no sign as he welcomed the groom's party.

Leading the way into the elegantly proportioned interior, dominated at the far end by a massive Italian painting of John the Baptist languishing in prison, Mr Kenward made brief introductions to his curate, Alec Bethway, who would be assisting him with the marriage ceremony.

"We've met already," the groom said ungraciously, ignoring the outstretched hand.

"Indeed, sir," Alec responded. "But it's a pleasure to renew your acquaintance. And may I wish you every felicitation upon this happiest of days."

The other looked at him in a glassy-eyed fashion; then, at the prompting of Boaz Palmer, turned unsteadily to follow the vicar along the centre aisle to await his bride at the chancel steps.

The pews were already starting to fill, and a number of people looked up in evident interest as he went by. Isabelle, ushered with her mother towards the front of the church, supposed they must all be friends of the Weldrakes. Certainly, they appeared very neighbourly, the ladies smiling across at each other and fluttering sheets of paper bearing the order of service, and the gentlemen exchanging murmured conversation and rising to acknowledge the greetings of newcomers.

As she took her seat, Isabelle's skirts brushed against the service sheet put out for her use and sent it gliding to the floor. Alec Bethway, following behind her, immediately knelt to retrieve it from beneath the pew where it had come to rest.

52

"Thank you."

She took the paper from him, returning his look gravely, and he smiled at her. They had been introduced at the porch, but the light had been too poor to discern her features properly and it was only here, in the glowing brightness of the newly installed gasoliers, that he was able to appreciate her fully and realise how very becoming was her appearance. The coppery hair had been drawn back from her face and gathered into a high knot of ringlets behind, and she wore tilted over her forehead a small hat of forget-me-not blue whose colour exactly matched that of her jacket and close-fitting gown.

Despite the fashionable outfit, Alec sensed a slight awkwardness in the stiff little set of her shoulders, as though she were more used to the plain homespun kersey and cambric of countrywear than the tussore and taffeta of town. He liked her at once. There was something about the clear, fresh beauty that reminded him of the girl in Holman Hunt's painting "The Hireling Shepherd", a print of which hung above the writing table in his room.

He continued to linger beside her pew; and when she glanced up again from the order of service he smiled a second time, wishing for a response. The wish was granted. For a moment, Isabelle's eyes softened and the full lips curved upward and parted, revealing small, regular teeth.

The effect upon the young curate was most pleasurable.

"I shall look forward to our meeting at the wedding break-fast, ma'am," he said, addressing himself to Mrs Flynn but still looking at her daughter.

The reply was drowned in a sudden discordant surge from the organ, swelling into the opening bars of Handel; and with a last appreciative glance at the girl in blue, Alec Bethway retired back down the aisle to prepare himself in the vestry for the solemnisation of her brother's marriage.

"Dearly beloved, we are gathered together here in the sight of God, and in the face of this congregation, to join together this man and this woman in holy matrimony . . ."

For all the flowers and fine music and accoutrements of

class, it proved a somehow unsatisfactory service. Robert Kenward, the vicar, was later to remark to his wife in the privacy of the vicarage parlour that he had seldom seen so many funereal faces at what should have been a most happy occasion; and he trusted to Providence that such an inauspicious beginning did not augur badly for the newly wed couple.

The groom and groom's man had appeared so dazed by the proceedings as to be virtually insensate . . . the bride was as white as wax and had gasped and sighed like a fish between every sentence of her responses . . . (little wonder, put in his wife, to whom Miss Perrins the dressmaker had confided Rosannah's condition) . . . and her brother, in giving her away in marriage, had looked as though he might be ready to do murder at the slightest provocation.

As for the groom's mother, continued Mr Kenward, warming to his grievance, that lady had disrupted the service at its most solemn moment by succumbing to an attack of the hiccoughs . . . and her daughter, instead of giving some assistance, seemed struck both deaf and dumb and incapable of doing anything more than sit staring at the bride's brother in the most witless manner imaginable.

Had she herself been required to describe the emotional effect of setting eyes upon Harry Weldrake for the first time, Isabelle would have said that the sensation was one of pain almost. As though all the blood in her body had rushed suddenly to her head, leaving her heart fluttering emptily; and then, a moment later, had rushed away again to leave her dizzy and weak, while her freshly flooded heart almost burst itself in beating against the cage of her ribs.

She had never in all her young life beheld anyone whose good breeding sat so elegantly upon them, whose air of self-assurance was so marked and whose features were so extraordinarily handsome.

Isabelle had always been a fanciful creature. Her imagination was peopled with the creations of her own wishfulness, characters she had made up since childhood to inhabit her day-dreams and in whose company she frequently escaped from reality to a private world where good-looking, well-mannered gentlemen surrounded her with their attention.

At home in Weatherfield she had already been courted by several of the village youths, but not one of them had ever roused her emotions beyond the level of friendship. For a day or two, perhaps, she thought of them fondly; but invariably, the brief attraction proved no more than a gilding upon human clay, and all too soon familiarity had rubbed off the gilt to expose the callowness beneath. Almost she preferred her dreams, where she could safely bestow her heart to its delight upon the figments of imagination.

And now, with delicious unexpectedness, those dreams had taken on mortal guise in the form of Harry Weldrake, from the moment he had turned on the chancel steps and swept the congregation with the arrogant indifference of his glance.

At the end of the service, as her brother Frank went woodenly down the aisle with his new wife upon his arm, the bridal attendants following, and the air throbbing with arpeggio vibrations from the organ, Isabelle remained deliberately seated until Weldrake was nearing her pew.

He paused as she rose to her feet, and the heavy-lidded blue eyes passed over her in quick examination, moved beyond to her mother, then back again. With a courteous motion of the hand he indicated that the two women should proceed ahead of him.

Colour flamed in Isabelle's cheeks. She hesitated; then gave a timid nod of acknowledgement. Taking her mother's arm, she went in front, walking slowly, nervously aware of his close proximity and careful to carry herself with as much grace as she could, praying that he might find her form and deportment pleasing.

A few yards further on, unable to resist the temptation to snatch one more glance, she turned on the pretext of admiring a carved wall memorial. His gaze flickered over her a second time, and she looked quickly away again lest her confusion show itself too openly.

Harry Weldrake permitted himself a dry smile. Women, old as well as young, always betrayed their interest in a man by a single look such as that: the eyes widening slightly, as though they could not drink in enough of what they saw.

He continued to study the girl as she moved ahead. From where they had been seated, in the place normally reserved for guests of honour, he surmised that the two women must be Frank Flynn's sister and mother. Mrs Flynn he had dismissed from his attention at once; but there was something about the daughter that might repay closer acquaintance at the wedding breakfast. He needed some amusement of the kind to lift him out of his present mood.

Weldrake had been in a soured frame of mind all through the ceremony, regarding it as an embarrassment to have to demean himself in such a public manner by giving his sister in marriage to a household servant; knowing that in the opinion of those who had gathered to witness this degrading spectacle, the Weldrakes had fallen yet lower, betraying their class by mixing their blood with that of inferiors.

And what an inferior the bridegroom had shown himself up to be! A red-faced brute in a loud set of clothes, reeking of drink and swaying on his feet, as perfect an example of uncouth peasantry as England had to offer.

But he was what Rosannah wanted, damn her; and as long as he did not seek to rise above his station and expect to be treated as an equal, then Harry Weldrake had perforce to swallow his pride and tolerate him, however reluctantly, at the same table as himself.

As to those who might sneer that such a *ménage à trois* was in rather poor taste – let them look to their own domestic arrangements, he thought savagely. Most of them kept a mistress or made use of whores, and there was hardly a man present at this service today but did not occasionally force himself upon his own maidservants to gratify the lust a cold or ailing wife denied him.

"Oh – I do beg your pardon!"

In his abstraction, he had walked too close to the two women in front and had stepped on the trailing hem of Mrs Flynn's skirts. Fortunately, little damage was done beyond a torn flounce; but the incident obliged Weldrake to introduce himself, and – an afterthought – make polite enquiry about what conveyance had been arranged to take them to the house in Tea Garden Lane, where the wedding breakfast was awaiting the bridal party.

The light pressure of his gloved hand upon hers and the trace of a smile accompanying his introduction had had the effect of rendering Isabelle mute. Eyes downcast, she allowed her mother to answer.

"Oh, don't you worry about us, sir," Dinah Flynn told him readily. "We come here to the church by hired carriage, and I dare say as how it'll be waiting still to take us on, along wi' the rest."

Weldrake nodded and went to turn away, glancing once more at the younger woman as he did so. The unconscious look of appeal on her face made him pause.

Upon consideration he said, "My carriage is at your disposal. May I convey you both myself?" And was immediately rewarded by a change of expression to one of disbelieving joy.

The bride and groom had already taken their seats in the open barouche standing beyond the lychgate, and as the white-ribboned horses were roused into a walk, a cheer went up from the small crowd gathered out in the street to watch their departure.

Standing on the steps of the church porch, Weldrake observed a young woman move forward and throw something into the vehicle. Her appearance struck a chord of memory; and as she glanced round he recognised her.

It was the bridegroom's black-haired mistress, Lizzie Newbrook.

6

Neither the new Mrs Francis Patrick Flynn nor her husband saw who had tossed the nosegay of dried flowers into the barouche. Now it lay where Rosannah had discarded it, a little token of another's heartbreak lost among the showy ornamental feather flowers which decorated the wedding breakfast.

The party gathered on that grey November morning in the Weldrake dining-room was a modest one by society's standards, but intentionally so. Apart from the Reverend Alec Bethway, Boaz Palmer, and the three bridal attendants, Letty and Maud Courthope and Cicely Mugridge, the only other non-family member present was Adolphe de Retz.

They had been privately astonished to find the young Frenchman among their number, even though he came by invitation as a friend of the bride's brother. It seemed not quite in taste, somehow, for the discarded admirer to help celebrate his rival's good fortune. He had been cast aside by Rosannah that she might wed another; and yet despite that cruel hurt, de Retz still regarded her with the greatest devotion.

His gift to the bride was typical of him, a symbol in which sentiment masked underlying anguish: a blinded linnet enclosed in a gilded cage.

"Now that I have lost you to another, *ma chère cocotte*," he had declared in dispirited tones, "the light has gone from my life just as the light has gone from this small bird's eyes. May its sad song remind you ever of the wound you have delivered to my heart."

Rosannah had laughed softly as she accepted the cage from him at the wedding table.

"A very pretty speech, Dolly. But you've left something out, I think."

"I leave nothing out. It is all for you."

She looked at him a little strangely; then smiled.

"Are you not still the captive of my love," she asked, mimicking his accented English, "just as this small bird is the captive of its cage?"

"It is true! Though you take away the bars, yet I sacrifice my liberty to remain the prisoner of your charms."

"How romantic you are," sighed Cicely Mugridge, a pale and rather plain young woman whose addiction to the popular novels of Miss Braddon, Ouida and Mrs Henry Wood was a compensation for her lack of looks and who fed upon Romance as other people might feed upon chocolate.

"I do declare, Mr de Retz, such sentiments might have fallen from the very lips of the noble, tormented suitor in Miss Ouida's *Chandos*."

She rested her clasped hands together on her breast and fluttered sparse eyelashes, her head tilted a little, striving to emulate her literary heroines in what she imagined to be a gesture of coquettish appeal.

Adolphe de Retz had barely glanced at her.

"I do think it's a cruelty to blind the poor things," Maud Courthope said, leaning forward at the table to poke a finger through the cage bars. "How do they manage it, do you suppose?"

Frank Flynn, seated opposite, had muttered something inaudible, and Maud looked across at him between the feather flowers, a questioning expression on her face.

"I said – they use a pin," Frank repeated, louder. "A long sharp pin."

He held up a hand and cupped it, as though holding something.

"Jab. Jab."

The index finger of the other hand made a quick stabbing motion.

Maud recoiled. "Oh . . . how horrid!"

"But, why?" demanded Letty, her sister and almost her twin in appearance, both young women being small and plump and round-featured.

"Makes 'em sing all the sweeter."

Rosannah gave a grimace, and pushed the cage away.

Adolphe de Retz caught the expression, and his gaze had moved to the man at her side, the man who was now her husband. No one looking at the Frenchman's calm, olivine features, a thin dark moustache enhancing the sensitive mouth, could have guessed at the bitter and corrosive hatred concealed there. Had it been required of him, he would willingly have laid down his very life for Rosannah Weldrake; and now she had wantonly thrown herself away on this coarse, ignorant fist-fighter who had not one single ounce of decent breeding anywhere in him.

"*Balance-le, si tu n'en veux pas*," he had said lightly. "Cast it out if you do not want it, as you have cast out my faithful poor heart."

"Oh, don't be so bloody dramatic, man," Frank said humourlessly.

Now the linnet was forgotten, its gilded cage removed to hang in the sunless window of the stairwell, where its mournful piping added a note of desolation to the distant sounds of the wedding feast.

Isabelle had hoped to find herself seated next to Harry Weldrake at the table, and was forced to hide her disappointment when she was placed instead beside the young curate, Alec Bethway. Politeness demanded that she give him her attention; but the meal passed with the two exchanging no more than a few sentences of conversation, stiff conventional phrases used by strangers seeking to uncover some common ground of interest.

"You draw, I believe you said, Miss Flynn?" Alec said at length, having exhausted his little stock of platitudes.

Isabelle reluctantly turned her gaze from the top of the table where Weldrake was sitting between the two Courthope girls.

She nodded.

"May I ask which subjects you like best?" he continued hopefully. "Portraiture, perhaps? Or still life?"

"I like to draw whatever takes my fancy, I suppose, sir. Not live things so much . . ."

"No?"

"No . . . they don't hold still long enough. But views. Wi' trees and old places . . . they're nice."

"And how long have you been doing this?"

"Oh, ever since I was little." Isabelle became more animated. "I disremember how old I was exactly, but I recall my grannam – she's dead now, rest her – I recall her once gi'ing me a real good larruping for scribbling over her clean flagstones wi' a bit o' charcoal I'd pulled from the grate."

Alec smiled. His companion's attraction for him was increased by the unselfconscious manner in which she expressed herself.

"But you've not received any formal tuition in the subject?"

"No, sir."

"I see." He paused. "What a pity you must return home so soon. Had you been staying longer in Lewes we might have arranged for you to take a few lessons at the academy."

"The academy?"

"Yes. Oh – but of course, you wouldn't know of it, I don't suppose. It's a private establishment for students of art, near The Turk's Head on School Hill. Mr Leopold de Retz is the proprietor."

"Dorrits?" Unfamiliar with a foreign name, Isabelle charmingly mispronounced it. Alec did not correct her. "Oh? Is he a relation of the Mr Dorrits here?"

She motioned with a hand towards Adolphe de Retz, seated further down on the opposite side of the table beyond her mother.

"I believe he is uncle, though I may be mistaken. Let me enquire."

The curate pushed aside the remains of his meal and leaned forward to attract de Retz's attention.

"Excuse me, sir! Miss Flynn and I are discussing the academy of art. Am I correct in saying it is your uncle who is proprietor?"

The other hesitated. He had been about to join Rosannah, who had left the table to show one of the Courthope girls something and was now standing alone at the other end of the room. Not wishing to seem ill-mannered, however, he thought he should acknowledge the question, and got up to move place to avoid having to reply across Mrs Flynn and Boaz Palmer, who were engaged in a sharply worded discussion of their own.

The gas-lamps had been lit to brighten the cheerless gloom of the day and their light was reflected in the sheen of blue-black hair sleeked with macassar oil as he bent his head and reseated himself opposite Alec Bethway.

"You wish to learn something of the academy, m'sieur?"

"If you would be so kind."

"But of course."

Declining an offer of more port, the Frenchman crossed one leg over the other and folded his arms.

"It was for young persons of good family wishing to study the art that the academy was commenced by my ancestor, Louis-Charles de Retz, at Paris in 1783."

Out of the corner of his eye he watched Rosannah return to the table and sit down beside her husband.

"When the Revolution happened, he was forced to close and remove his family from danger. Either that, or to feel the embrace of Madame Guillotine, you understand. *Eh bien*, he sought refuge in England, and made the home at Brighton. But already too many French persons were there, and in a while he could no longer earn money – "

"That I can well imagine," Alec interrupted. "From all the accounts I've read of the period, Brighton was filled to overflowing with penniless refugees. And most of them aristocrats trying to earn an honest coin by becoming teachers of the only things they'd ever been taught themselves . . . dancing, fencing, drawing, and the like."

De Retz appeared not to hear him. Rosannah had turned her head from her husband and was biting her lip as she did when upset.

He said something quietly under his breath; then, "*Alors*, m'sieur, my ancestor removed to Lewes and commenced a new academy. That was in 1801. When he died his firstborn son, Charles-Leopold, became proprietor in his place. The second son, Charles-Olivier, returned at the Restoration to live again in Paris. He was my grandfather, that one."

"Charles-Leopold?"

"No, no. Charles-Olivier."

"I see." The young curate's expression showed genuine interest. "This is all most fascinating, sir. And in what relationship, therefore, do you stand to the present proprietor?"

De Retz threw out his hands. "Deduce it for yourself, m'sieur. My father and the son of Charles-Leopold were cousins."

"The son of Charles-Leopold being – ?"

"M'sieur Leopold de Retz, *comme de bien entendu!*"

"Ah, now I have it." Alec smiled at Isabelle. "I misled you, after all. He is not an uncle but a cousin germane."

"Oh . . . I'm sorry. What did you say?" Her attention had wandered back to Harry Weldrake while de Retz was recounting his family history.

"The proprietor of the academy of art. A distant cousin."

"Ah." She made an effort to give the impression that she followed this elucidation.

"But you yourself have some connection with the academy, I believe, sir?" resumed the curate, helping himself to another small glass of port from the decanter.

"*Certainement*, but only for the place of living," de Retz answered. "It is to perfect my English, you understand, that I have left Paris last year. I am *facteur* in Newhaven for my father's company, which exports the wine of France to this country. But Newhaven, it is – " He made a dismissive gesture of the hand. "Lewes is more preferable for a gentleman. And since there is also the accommodation with Leopold, it is, how you would say . . ."

"A most convenient arrangement," Alec concluded.

Turning to speak once more to Isabelle, he saw that he had lost her attention again. She was gazing towards the other end of the table and there was an expression of such dreamy yearning on her young face that he looked immediately to see who it was could be the object of the girl's preoccupation.

His questing glance fell upon Harry Weldrake. The discovery nettled him. He should have guessed that such a man as that would prove a lure for this sweet and impressionable creature, he told himself resentfully. The fellow had the kind of well-bred good looks which the fair sex seemed so often to admire; but it was the curate's private opinion that "handsome is as handsome does", and from what he had heard Weldrake did very little that might in charity be considered handsome.

In an effort to distract Isabelle and win back her attention, he said briskly, "We must arrange for you to visit the academy when next you're in Lewes, ma'am. I'm certain you would find much there to interest you. And who knows, perhaps even spur you towards more creative studies of your own. What do you say, sir – " turning again across the table to de Retz – "might it be possible for Miss Flynn to spend an afternoon viewing the work of Mr Leopold's students?"

Rosannah had left her husband now and gone to sit beside Cicely Mugridge. Without taking his eyes from her, de Retz answered, "If that is mademoiselle's wish."

Had Isabelle been any other female, the Frenchman's inbred civility would have made his response a good deal more courteous. Already though, even at such short acquaintance, she was beginning to attract something of the enmity he harboured for her brother. She was a Flynn, however pretty her face; and that alone was more than sufficient to damn her in his eyes. He wished for no further contact with her.

Unless . . .

De Retz raised his clasped hands and tapped the extended forefingers reflectively against his lips. There was an old saying in his family: revenge is a dish enjoyed best when cold. It came to mind now, bringing with it the substance of an idea.

Instead of leaving his bitterness to fester in secret impotence against some unforeseen moment of retribution, might it not, he asked himself, prove a sweeter, sharper act of vengeance to make use of this girl – turn her into the instrument with which to strike at her brother where it would give the most injury? What could be more fitting than to make the sister's shame and dishonour the price Frank Flynn would have to pay for his pleasure in Rosannah's bed.

De Retz was suddenly animated. Unclasping his hands, he laid them palm down on the table and leaned forward.

"So, we must make the disposition! Let us go to it immediately. Without doubt, M'sieur Leopold will be most charmed to receive you, mademoiselle. Your returning to Lewes, it is soon?"

"Oh . . . I don't know, Mr Dorrits, sir. I don't think so."

Isabelle glanced towards her mother, but Mrs Flynn was

now listening to one of the Courthope girls and had her back to her.

"It's not likely I'll be coming back," she went on miserably. "There's nothing been mentioned of it."

De Retz gave a smile of encouragement. "*N'importe*. It makes no matter! You have now the sister-in-law to give you the invitation."

Hope at once brightened Isabelle's face. The thought of going home to Weatherfield not knowing how or if or when she would ever see Harry Weldrake again had been preying on her mind all through the wedding feast. He had so captivated her imagination that the dreams that had contented her for so long now seemed such poor, empty, unsatisfactory things compared to the reality of Harry.

Everything about him absorbed her fancy. The way he talked, drawling out his words as though they wearied him. The way he lounged in his seat, gazing languidly from under lowered eyelids. His manner of thoughtfully stroking his moustache with finger and thumb. And his laugh – not a sudden loud bray like Frank's, but a soft low sound, his lips curling a little at one side more than the other.

Isabelle was ready to clutch at any opportunity to remain here in Lewes, anything to delay the final terrible moment of separation.

Breathlessly she said, "I'd best ask my mother what she thinks."

"The idea is capital!"

Dinah Flynn, however, did not think the idea at all capital when she heard what was proposed. Not used to rich food, she was suffering the burning discomfort of indigestion, and inclined to be snappish.

"But where will you lodge, our Belle? Who's to keep an eye on you? What about your feeding, an' all? You can't expect Frank to be putting hisself out – can she, Frank?"

Frank was unhelpful. Several glasses of good wine and then of port on top of the alcohol already in his system had had the effect of reducing him to near-torpor and he was experiencing some difficulty in keeping his eyes open. If Belle wanted to stay here at the house, why shouldn't she? There was no harm in it. Mam always had to find something to work herself up into a fluster over.

He tried to say as much, but the words came out too thickly for anyone to make much sense of them.

It was Rosannah who answered for him.

Putting aside a book she had been showing Cicely Mugridge, she said, "Of course Isabelle must come to visit, Mrs Flynn. It will give us great pleasure. As soon as we return from the wedding tour we must correspond and settle upon an agreeable date. Better still perhaps, why not be with us for the Christmas season, both of you?"

"Oh, Lor', ma'am! You're very kind, I'm sure," Dinah Flynn cried, "but I durstn't be away from Weatherfield, not at Christmas-time. I've the alehouse to manage and my reg'lars won't take kindly to the place being closed up for the festivities. Our Belle can't be spared, neither. Why, she's not long come back from visiting at her godparents, and that's put me behind as it is."

The Courthope girls raised hands to mouths and lowered their heads to hide their smiles.

"And there's another thing," Mrs Flynn continued, oblivious to the amusement she was causing, "our takings're always up the latter end o' December, and we can ill afford to lose the profit as I'm sure you'll understand. Why, it'd be a folly and worse – "

Seeing her chances slipping away, Isabelle interrupted plaintively, "But you won't be needing me at the start o' the new year, mam. I could come away for a week or two then, surely?"

"Yes, surely!" Alec Bethway supported her, seeing his own chances of continuing friendship fading.

"Then it's settled," said Rosannah decisively, putting an end to any further argument. "We shall look forward to your visiting in the new year, when the wedding tour and the festivities are behind us."

She returned to the book, a slim leather-bound volume from which she had been about to read to Cicely before Mrs Flynn distracted her, and holding it up, indicated to her guests a marked section on one of the pages.

"It was this particular passage which decided us finally upon the place to make our tour. Would any of you care that I read it aloud?"

Apart from the bridegroom, whose head was slumped upon his chest, everyone at the table appeared to give her their full attention.

"Frank preferred that we remain in England and not travel abroad –"

"How very wise," Letty Courthope observed. "One practically always discovers the food abroad to be disagreeable and the hotels insanitary."

There was some agreement with this comment, and Rosannah had to raise her voice a little to begin reading.

"'Those married couples whose time is somewhat restricted we recommend to sojourn at Tunbridge Wells . . . Mount Ephraim is especially to be selected . . . and thence the most pleasing excursions may be made to different parts of coast and country. Those who care for sketching, botanising, and collecting sea-weeds will find ample opportunity for each. Those who like old ruins and time-hallowed places may reach them without difficulty' . . . And so it goes on."

"Excellent!" applauded Adolphe de Retz, who had been listening closely to her reading. "Sea-weeds. Old ruins. *Botanising*! Well can I imagine how much the dear husband will find to amuse him among so many rural delights."

7

The only illumination in the hotel bedroom came from a coal fire whose flames leapt up in almost violent fashion and flung long shadows across the moulded ceiling.

Frank Flynn unlaced his other boot and let it fall to the floor beside the brass bedstead, where his bride of little more than twelve hours lay in her nightgown under the single cover of a sheet. Standing up, he began unbuttoning his shirt and without looking at her said testily, "Don't expect anything from me tonight. I'm not in the mood for it."

Rosannah turned over on to her back and put an arm behind her head.

"You've become very dull these past months. What excuse is it this time? You've been drinking too much?"

"That's right. I have. All day."

She lay silent, watching him finish undressing until he stood naked in the firelight, his flesh tinged a dusky red, the muscles contoured by shadow. From the base of his throat a dark mat of hair spread across shoulders and chest and tapered to a thick line over the flat abdomen. It was a strong, hard body; and she wanted it still . . . even more, perhaps, now that the sham of love was over between them.

"This room's too hot," he said suddenly. "I'm sweating like a pig."

"I don't find it hot. Why don't you come into bed and warm me?"

"I told you. I'm not in the mood."

"This is our wedding night, Frank."

"You don't need to remind me, blast you," he answered roughly, going across to the ornate marble washstand against the wall. Taking up a flannel cloth he dipped it into the ewer of water and began wiping his face and chest, the drops leaving glistening lines on his skin.

When he had finished, he threw the cloth aside and turned back to look at the woman on the bed.

The honey-coloured hair had been braided into a thick plait, and for some reason this irritated him. Had she been Lizzie Newbrook she would have left her hair loose for him to run his hands through; and she would have unclothed herself for him, not smothered herself in several dozen yards of beribboned nightgown. But then, had she been Lizzie Newbrook he wouldn't be standing in some over-decorated room in the Mount Ephraim Hotel at Tunbridge Wells, finding excuses not to touch a woman to whose body he had every right of possession.

68

He went over to the window and pulled aside one of the heavy brocade curtains.

The night outside was clear, with a blue ring of frost round the moon, and in its pallid light he could see the humped line of an outcrop of rock a short distance away. When they arrived at the hotel earlier that evening they had walked across the road on to the Common – one of the features of the town, an area of wooded walks divided by open heathland – and inspected this isolated ridge of sandstone. Rosannah had wanted him to carve their names among the others engraved there; but he had refused.

There was silence within the room, broken only by the rustle of flames.

Then she said again, "Come into bed with me, Frank," and there was a note of pleading in her voice.

He let the curtain fall back into place and swung round.

"I'll sleep in the chair."

"The bed would be more comfortable." She drew aside the sheet; but the gesture was ignored. Instead, he moved across the room to the large mahogany wardrobe beside the door and began searching through it.

"What are you looking for?"

"My nightshirt. Damn it, why do they have to tidy everything where you can't find it?"

"It's laid out for you here." She reached over to where the garment had been placed ready for him on the pillow earlier by the chambermaid, and held it out. "But must you put it on just yet? You complained you were hot – "

"I'm not sleeping in a chair in nothing but my skin!"

"Then come into bed."

The repetitious invitation stung Frank into a burst of anger.

Snatching the nightshirt from her hand, he said savagely, "Let's have one thing settled, the pair of us. Now, afore we go any further. I didn't need to marry you. I didn't *want* to marry you – I'd soonest have married another if I could. But it's my child, my son, in that body o' yours, Rosannah. And for all that you got him on a purpose to snare me, he's the reason my ring's upon your finger. I've wed you, aye. And on

69

your terms. But by God, understand this – it'll be *me* as'll be setting the terms from now on!"

Softly she responded, "You're my husband. You have that right."

He stared at her. The harshness of his words had excited her. The look in her half-closed eyes, the full lips parted slightly, the rapid rise and fall of her breast . . . the familiar signs of growing desire were evident. In a minute or two if he let her touch him, she would start pawing at him, biting with her sharp teeth till she drew pricks of blood, raking the naked flesh of his back with her nails.

He felt suddenly sickened.

To judge by appearances, Frank Flynn had inherited very little of his mother's caring, compassionate nature. He was all his father's son. Along with the stallion man's swarthy gipsy handsomeness, he showed the same indifference to the feelings of any but his own; the same quick temper, the more dangerous because he lacked the self-discipline to keep it in check; and a swaggering cocksureness that easily turned to bullying.

And yet his affection for Lizzie Newbrook had revealed a deeply hidden streak beneath that hard veneer: the nervous tenderness of a sentimental lover.

At the start of his affair with Rosannah Weldrake, when she first began singling him out for her attention, watching him fight, buying him expensive gifts, filling his young head with notions of his own importance, Frank had found her brazen overtures to love-making a novel excitement. He had never known a woman like her. She was completely uninhibited, wanting him to satisfy her wherever and whenever the desire took her; and the more the likelihood of their discovery, the more this spurred her on.

Once, after one of his fights, she had even come into the canvas lean-to where he was changing and removed her skirts with people going by only a yard away; and another time, she had given herself on the backstairs of the house, while her cook Mrs Jenkins unwittingly provided the accompaniment of a music-hall song from beyond the open scullery door below.

It had been amusing, for a while; and their love-making an adventure. For a while. Then he had met Lizzie, and everything changed. For the first time in his life Frank was truly in love; and once he came to learn how tender and gentle a woman could be in his arms, Rosannah's insatiable passion had quickly palled.

He made a gesture of impatience and turned from the bed. Pulling his nightshirt on, he went and sat in the winged armchair by the window.

Rosannah raised herself on her elbows and stared after him in the flickering shadows of firelight.

"You don't want me."

It was a statement of fact, not a question; and he did not bother to reply.

When she spoke again her voice was louder, with an edge of hysteria to it.

"Very well . . . stay out of my bed. But don't expect me to pay for the privilege of your neglect. You can hardly hope to be kept by your wife in the manner of a gentleman if you refuse to honour your part of the bargain as husband."

"You'll do as you're bid," he snapped back. "You can't buy my favours any more like you did. It's me as holds the purse strings now."

"You think so? What a fool you are, Frank. Did you suppose our marriage would make you lord and master of my estate? Did you suppose it would give you a free hand to spend my income? It does nothing of the kind! My money remains my own . . . and you can't lay even so much as a finger on it."

"What's that? What's that you say?" Her husband gave a violent start and shoved himself to his feet.

"Ah, I thought that might ruffle you," Rosannah said snidely. "At least I have your attention now."

He sprang to the foot of the bed and seized hold of the brass rail, clutching it so tightly that his knuckles showed white to the bone.

"You've changed your mind, my darling?" she goaded him. "You'll come into bed after all?"

"Blast you," he said softly, and there was a dangerous

expression in his eyes. "If you've cheated me out o' what's legally mine, I'll . . ."

"Yes? You'll what?" She looked back at him, eagerly almost. "What will you do to me, Frank? Tell me."

And when he said nothing, but merely shook his head as though his wits were too dulled for comprehension, she gave a harsh laugh and went on, "You've not boxed so cleverly this time, my prize fighter. If you had used your brain half as much as your brawn, you might the sooner have discovered my income stays my own, husband or no. Parliament has seen to that with its Married Woman's Act."

She knelt up in bed. "So why not enjoy our wedding night? It would be in your best interest. You do have the choice, you know. I am a generous woman . . ."

In the grate at the other end of the room the incandescent mound of coals collapsed noisily inward upon itself, sending flames roaring into the gaping mouth of the chimney.

Still, Frank said nothing. His entire world had of a sudden been turned inside out. The plans he had made once Rosannah's money was his for the spending . . . the things he was going to buy for Lizzie . . . and do for Lizzie . . . find somewhere with her where they could live together . . . Was all this now being snatched away from him, each one of his dreams torn into shreds?

He gave an inarticulate cry of rage and lunged forward across the rail, grabbing Rosannah by the shoulders. Raising a hand, he struck her forcefully around the side of the head.

The blow was cushioned by the thick plait of hair.

She looked up at him sideways. Panting a little, she said, "That's better, Frank. But not so hard. Remember . . . I'm carrying your son."

This reminder of the trap she had sprung incensed him still further. He clutched at the yoke of her expensive nightgown, and holding the delicate tracery of ribbon and lace in his bunched fists, ripped the fabric apart to expose the pale soft flesh beneath.

Rosannah gave a low moan.

He stared down at her; then thrust her away from him in disgust, sending her sprawling backwards on the bed.

"No," he said thickly. "I'm not going to strike you again, you bitch. I wouldn't give you the pleasure."

Alec Bethway sat back in the armchair in his room at All Souls vicarage and rested his slippered feet up on the low fender. The cheerful crackle of the fire and the steady deep tick of the mantelpiece clock made comfortable companions on such a dank December night, and he was glad to be spending the evening indoors.

He lit his pipe with a taper and then leaned back again among the woolwork cushions. When he had closed the curtains just now after supper the fog seemed thicker than ever, almost smothering the bare branches of the lime trees outside his window, while the churchyard beyond was nothing but a wall of heavy greyness pierced by the blurred golden nimbus of street lamps at the far end.

He reached a hand to the small table beside his chair and picked up his book of the week, Trollope's *Framley Parsonage*; but after a page or so laid it down again and took up instead an envelope bearing a penny-black stamp. It had arrived over a week ago, and he had read its contents so often that the envelope was quite dog-eared.

Since the wedding of Isabelle Flynn's brother to Rosannah Weldrake, Alec had written several times to the alehouse at Weatherfield, and had almost despaired of a reply. Had he been too persistent, he wondered; was Isabelle reluctant to encourage their tenuous friendship? And yet, when he had asked at the end of the wedding breakfast whether he might correspond, she had not evaded the request with some excuse, but had seemed happy to accept.

Brushing tobacco sparks from the black clerical stock covering his chest, he drew the folded pages of her letter from their envelope and opened them. She had a good round hand and her style of writing, though carelessly punctuated, conveyed a fresh and lively mind.

"Dear Mr Bethway, here I am with three letters of yours and none to you in return," she began at once. "What will you think of me I don't know but weve been that rushed since coming home from Lewes I've been like a bee in a bottle.

73

Mams taken bad again so theres only been me and aunt lottie Adams and Joel but hes got his carrier's busness to run so can only help in the eveningtime. However I am well thank you and happy to know your own health is keeping good in spite of such weather as we're having . . ."

Alec looked up from the page.

Over his desk by the window hung the framed Holman Hunt print which so reminded him of Isabelle. It depicted a young shepherd kneeling beside a girl to show her a captured moth, leaving his sheep unattended to stray to their ruin. The girl of the picture, feeding unripe apples to a tame lamb in her lap, was intended to portray a type of those careless females who make neglectful wives and mothers; yet the face, though bolder in its expression, was entirely Isabelle Flynn's, the colour of hair the same, the rounded cheek, the full mouth, the large expressive eyes and well-shaped brow.

Alec had originally bought the print for its moral and spiritual message of the sinfulness of an idle pastor's dereliction of duty to his flock; but its appeal now lay much closer to his heart. In the three weeks since that meeting at her brother's wedding, he had thought of Isabelle with a constancy which no other girl before had ever inspired in him. To have her image there upon his wall somehow brought her closer still.

He returned to her letter.

"You dont say if youve seen our Frank and his wife since they come back from their tour to Tunbridge wells. We got a page of the hotel paper with its name printed very handsome at the top but there wasnt much of interest writ upon it . . ."

Yes, the curate had been to see the newly wedded couple. At least, he had called on them yesterday at the house in Tea Garden Lane to enquire after their visit, and found Frank already gone to Hampshire with his manager Mr Palmer to arrange a sporting engagement.

Rosannah Flynn had received Alec in the drawing-room, and he noticed at once how strained she looked. Untidy, too, with the bodice of her gown carelessly buttoned and her hair coming away from its pins. There was an acrid smell of vegetation in the room from numerous indoor ferns standing in brass bowls and jardinières, and this, together with the strong fragrance of Rosannah's tuberose scent, had made him feel slightly queasy.

"Your husband intends, I take it then, to pursue his career in the ring?" curiosity had prompted him to ask.

"Why not. He's fit for no other skill. How else is he to earn his living?"

It was a peculiar statement to make, and delivered in a flat voice as though she had not the slightest interest in either her husband or his actions.

Alec had not pursued the subject further, but turned instead to enquire how she had liked Tunbridge Wells. Even here, though, Rosannah was laconic almost to the point of indifference; and he had been relieved that other parochial duties obliged this visit to be no more than a brief one.

He laid Isabelle's letter aside for a moment and got up to adjust the gas jet in the lamp above the mantelpiece; then put a few more coals on the fire before resettling himself.

"We had a visiter here Saturday last," the final page began. "You will not be able to guess who it was, but Mr Harry Weldrake. I was never so surprised in my life as to see him on his horse outside our door. He was on the way to Eridge for the sundays hunting and broke his journey for no better reason than to call. Was not that kind of him. He is a real nice gentleman and paid many compliments on my appearance and also our best brandy as being very fine. Alas he stayed only the hour but he did promise his sister wont neglect to invite me to Lewes as soon as the new years weather allows . . ."

This behaviour of Harry Weldrake's had annoyed Alec considerably. There was no cause for the man to go out of his way merely for the sake of an hour, unless it were for some purpose of self-interest. The curate had observed him at the end of the wedding breakfast draw Isabelle aside from the rest of the company and commence flattering the girl with the kind of fulsome attention guaranteed to feed her young hopes; and Alec had had to look on with growing irritation as this drone of society proceeded to bask himself in the reflection of an admiration thus deliberately encouraged.

"Have a care not to wear your heart where it might be bruised," he had warned as they were making their farewells, a little hurt that his own unpolished compliments had failed to rouse the same warm looks from her.

His words had plainly fallen upon deaf ears.

"Hoping we shall meet when I make my visit and wishing you the compliments of the season I remain yours truly Isabelle R. Flynn."

The signature was underlined with a merry flourish ending in a sputter of ink.

Alec folded the pages together slowly and put them once more away inside their envelope; and for a while he sat with his chin on his hand, staring into the glowing coal-caverns of the fire, until All Souls chimes, muffled by the fog, roused him from his reverie.

Sighing, he laid the letter aside and leaned forward to tap out the bowl of his pipe on the grate bar, then got up and went over to his desk. Earlier in the day he had started writing a sermon for the weekend, but, failing inspiration, had abandoned it after a few paragraphs. Picking up the paper he cast an eye over it, then screwed it up and with a practised aim lobbed it into the fire.

"Love," he had written, "Love divine, who comes among us at this season as a helpless child . . ."

There was nothing wrong with the sentiment; yet how difficult it was to elevate the mind to thoughts of love divine while it was so utterly preoccupied with thoughts of love profane.

8

Rachael Bashford, wife of George Bashford esquire, gentle-man farmer of Bonningale, and formerly widow of the Reverend Esmond Bates, sometime rector of Weatherfield, lifted her youngest son on to the nursery window seat and steadied him gently against her.

Young Henry had been confined to bed with a chesty cough for the past few days, and had not been allowed out with his brothers and sisters to watch the travelling mummers perform their Christmas play.

"There . . . now you can see everything," his mother reassured him, drawing the blanket more snugly around his small body. "Why, you have a better view even than Mary."

Henry jutted his chin and peered out through the window bars to the lawn below, where the band of mummers (or "tipteers" as they were locally called) in their chimney-pot hats and gaudy rags of calico trimmed with fringes of ribbon and coloured tissue, were about to start their traditional play of St George and the Turk.

Standing round in a wide ring, well muffled against the winter chill, were a group of Mr Bashford's farmworkers, their wives and children, together with members of his own family. The youngest, Mary, was seated upon her father's shoulders clapping her hands in delight as the mustachioed Turkish Knight, resplendent in streamers of crimson and gold, galloped his hobby-horse around the circle of spectators and made mock-ferocious stabs with his wooden sword.

"If I don't cough for ten minutes, *then* may I go down to watch?" Henry asked hopefully. "Please?"

"And leave me all alone here, with no one to keep me company?" His mother put on a forlorn expression. "Oh

Henry, must I then ask one of the others to come and sit with me?"

"You won't be lonely if you come too, mamma."

"But the Turkish Knight looks so very fierce! I'd be frightened of him coming near."

"I'll take care of you. He won't fright you if you're with me. I'll hold your hand tightly."

The slate-blue eyes, identical to her own, were so beseeching that Rachael almost relented.

Then Henry coughed again.

"No, my darling," she said firmly, "you must stay here in the nursery. Tomorrow, perhaps, if you're better, you may come downstairs. But not today."

The small chin jutted further.

Rachael gave her son a comforting hug. "Oh, look – they've already begun! Look, Henry, you'll miss them. See? There's St George. Isn't he fine? He's going to fight a duel with the Turkish Knight."

"Will he kill him?"

"Only a little. Then the Doctor will quickly make him well again. Do you see the Doctor? There, by Richard and Phyllis?" She pointed out her second eldest son, holding his small sister's hand. Beside them a stout mummer in silver and black was waiting to play his part.

"Is he a clever Doctor?" Henry wanted to know.

"I'm sure he is. He is able to cure Hippsy, Pippsy, Peasy Palmsy and the Gout, pains within and pains without . . ." Rachael recited the lines.

"Can he cure my cough, mamma?"

"Oh, that I don't know, my pet."

"Belle could cure it. She did the last time, didn't she? I wish she was here now. Why isn't she here, mamma?"

"Because she must stay at her house to assist her own mamma."

"But couldn't pappa send one of our workers instead, so's Belle could be with us? Then she can make for me another heart of brown paper as she did before, to stick upon my chest with goose fat."

Rachael remembered that old country remedy. She had

seen her friend Dinah Flynn apply the same treatment to Isabelle herself years before in the alehouse kitchen at Weatherfield, against what Dinah called "the bronticle".

"Belle can't be with us, Henry. Not yet. Perhaps when spring comes. Now – do you see? The Doctor is bringing the Turkish Knight to life again with his magical Golden Lossey Drops! If you are a good boy, pappa will ask that we might have some, too, for the cure of your cough."

Watching the antics of the mummers and the noisy enjoyment of their audience, Rachael's thoughts stayed with her god-daughter. Normally a most diligent correspondent, Isabelle had written only once since her brother Frank's marriage a month ago; and that solitary letter, fretful, impatient, full of naive reference to a gentleman in Lewes, had left her godparents with a feeling of disquietude.

For some while now she had always come to spend a few weeks with them early in the year; but there had been no mention of any visit this spring.

Christmas-time at Weatherfield brought with it a spell of bitter cold, the ditches clogged with ice, the mud in the lanes frozen hard into furrows, the fields around the village lying empty and bleak beneath a leaden sky. At the alehouse, icicles several feet long hung from the eaves, and Joel Adams was sent with the orchard ladder to knock them down before they loosened with the next thaw and imperilled the unwary.

The dark midwinter evenings made the ale-room particularly inviting. Chilled to the marrow from a day's work in the stock-yards, the Weatherfield men hastened to the warmth of its haven; and seated on high-backed settles, the Yule Log blazing on the open hearth and the walls hung with mistletoe and holly, they eased away their stiffness with pots of mulled ale and sang together the carols of their childhood.

Christmas Eve was the happiest Isabelle could remember. After so many anxious weeks of waiting she had heard at last from Rosannah: a pretty card of seasonal greeting bearing the longed-for invitation to stay at Tea Garden Lane.

"Being now settled once more at our residence," Rosannah wrote, "my brother and I lose no time – "

79

"Surely she meant to put *your* brother?" Mrs Flynn had interrupted her daughter's reading. "Our Frank and not their Harry?"

"It says *my* brother plain enough here," Isabelle assured her; and continued aloud, ". . . lose no time in soliciting your company, and trust that you will make it convenient to pass some weeks with us. Do not doubt but that every thing will be done to render your stay with us agreeable. Pray favour us with an early answer, and let it be such as we may expect."

"No, don't be frightened. He won't bolt with you. He's too damn' lazy to move faster than a trot."

Harry Weldrake turned smoothly in his saddle and adjusted the leading rein which controlled the horse bearing Isabelle. He had thrown her into some confusion at breakfast by inviting her to ride with him; and upon hearing her halting confession that her experience had so far been limited to the bare backs of farm horses, he had offered to redress this at once and school her in the more ladylike accomplishment of the side-saddle.

Rosannah declined to accompany them. With her pregnancy now entering its fifth month, she had heeded her doctor's stricture and taken to the more sedate conveyance of a well-sprung carriage placed at her disposal by Adolphe de Retz.

"Loosen the reins a little. You're pulling at his mouth. Good. That's better. And keep your shoulders well back, otherwise your line of balance is thrown out."

Weldrake nudged his bay gelding to continue its walk and gave the leading rein a tug to encourage the second animal to follow. Here in the sheltered lee of the Downs above Lewes the wind was less bitingly sharp; but even so, Isabelle was glad of Rosannah's fur-lined cloak to protect her from the raw January cold.

"No, you're pointing your foot downward again. Hold it flat in the stirrup. And remember what I told you about gripping the pommel."

Riding side-saddle was the most uncomfortable experience she had ever been made to suffer, and the muscles of her right thigh ached unbearably from the constant strain of supporting herself in such an awkward posture. Yet not a word of complaint passed her lips. She would have endured all the torments of hell itself for Harry Weldrake's company.

"Are you ready now? We'll try a short trot along this next stretch."

The bay gelding increased its pace and Isabelle's horse was forced reluctantly to do likewise. The irregular gait proved more than she could manage. Feeling herself begin to slip sideways round the pommel, she cried out to Weldrake to stop . . . but too late.

Reining his horse in hard, her companion swung lithely from the saddle and ran back to where Isabelle lay stretched motionless on the frost-rimed turf.

"Are you hurt?" he asked anxiously, bending down.

It was a moment or two before she could answer.

"I – I don't think so."

"A little shaken, I expect. Can you stand?"

She raised herself, and nodded.

"Here, let me – " He reached out a hand and assisted her to her feet.

The cloak hood had fallen back from her face and a lock of auburn hair curled against one cheek. There was a fetchingly sweet helplessness about her, Harry Weldrake thought. Damned if she wasn't a most attractive little piece.

"Any bones broken?"

Isabelle shook her head. He was standing so close to her that the white cloud vapour of their breath mingled together. Hesitantly, she looked up into his eyes; and then, before she knew what was happening, he cupped her face in his gloved hands and kissed her lightly on the mouth.

"You're a brave girl, my dear. I'm proud of you."

He kissed her again, and felt the violent trembling of her soft lips against his. It had been some while since he last tasted such inexperience, and the sensation pleased him. Ever since the girl's visit began a week or more ago, he had been aware of her mute adoration betraying itself in the wistful expression whenever she glanced at him, the eager attention to his every word, the way she followed about at his heels.

Such artless devotion pandered to Weldrake's vanity, and he encouraged it.

Putting his arm about her shoulders he led her over to her horse.

"You're not frightened to re-mount, I hope?"

Isabelle shook her head, not trusting herself to speak. More than the fall, even, his kisses had left her breathless and her lips burned deliciously from the touch of his warm mouth.

"Good. It's the first thing you should do after taking a tumble."

Had he asked her to race an unbroken stallion she would have done so without a second's hesitation, willing to risk even life itself should he ask it. She was still in this heady state of half-believing joy when they returned to the house in Tea Garden Lane; and her inner radiance, combined with the flush of health in her cheeks and the sparkle in her eyes, so enlivened her appearance that Alec Bethway, calling to visit, thought when she entered the drawing-room what a perfectly enchanting picture of natural health she presented.

His own cheeks coloured a little with pleasure.

"You've obviously enjoyed your ride," he said, pressing the hand Isabelle had offered.

"Oh, I did! Mr Weldrake's been that kind and good to me. He's showing me how to use the side-saddle."

"Yes, so I understand from Mrs Flynn."

Alec turned to Rosannah, stretched listlessly on the day-bed by the fire, a tray of tea-things near at hand on a low table. He hoped that she might offer him more refreshment so that he would have an excuse to stay longer, but she appeared not to notice the empty cup he held.

Reseating himself, he looked again at Isabelle, who had taken a chair at the other side of the fire and was warming her hands, and said, "There is an exhibition of watercolour paintings to be viewed here in Lewes on Thursday of next week."

"Is there?"

"I wondered whether you might be interested to attend?"

She gave it her consideration.

"Perhaps Mr Weldrake would take me."

"Oh, Harry's not interested in art and exhibitions," Rosannah came in. "Why not let Mr Bethway be your escort? He's plainly about to ask if you would do him that honour."

Alec gave a slight frown. She made it sound as though he needed to be prompted.

Clearing his throat he said hurriedly, "Indeed, ma'am, the invitation was already in mind."

Isabelle's response was no more than half-hearted. The curate had a pleasant manner and appearance and she appreciated his kindness; but the notion of any other company than Harry Weldrake's did not rouse her to much enthusiasm.

"Well . . . thank you, sir. It's very thoughtful of you, I'm sure."

"You'll accompany me, then?"

She gave a silent nod.

"Good. Then we'll make our arrangements closer to the time. In the meanwhile, you have not forgotten, of course, that you're invited to visit the de Retz academy with me on Monday afternoon?"

"I haven't forgotten, no."

Rosannah stretched herself on the day-bed and yawned delicately, putting her fingertips to her parted lips.

"What a busy programme you have, Belle, dear."

Alec put aside his empty cup and saucer. He went to say something; hesitated. There was a short silence, broken by the sound of someone whistling in the lane outside, and a woman's voice calling plaintively.

Then he said, getting up from his seat, "Do you care for skating, Miss Flynn?"

"Skating, sir?"

"Yes. I must confess, I have a great fondness for it myself."

When she made no response, he went on quickly, "The lake in Pelbrook Fields is frozen several inches deep. I was there this morning to try it. I thought perhaps you might like to . . . that is, I wondered whether you would care to skate with me one afternoon? I have no duties on Friday. Would that suit?"

"I – I don't know."

If only it were Harry asking. He had said nothing when they left the stable yard just now, merely remarked that she'd ride with more confidence tomorrow; and no one would have suspected from their casual parting that he'd been kissing her such a short time before.

In any case, she knew less of skating even than of the side-saddle. True, she had played as a child on the frozen midwinter pond at the back of the alehouse orchard, sliding with her brother across its glassy surface; but a shallow, muddy horse-pond was not the same as venturing out on the deep, dark waters of an ice-bound lake.

She looked cautiously at her sister-in-law. "Shall I go, Rosannah?"

The other gave a little shrug of indifference. "Why not. Everyone else does."

"But isn't it dangerous?"

"That's half the fun!" said Alec. "No need to be afraid. I'll guard you with my life, you may be sure."

Still she hesitated.

"Friday?" he pressed her.

"Very well . . . Friday."

When he had gone, Rosannah remarked, "You're very discouraging, aren't you. Why treat the poor fellow so indifferently? He's obviously your admirer."

"My – ? Oh, he's not! Whatever makes you think a thing like that?"

"I'm a woman. I have eyes. And so have you, if only you'd use them instead of being so blind. Let me give you a word of advice. Don't lose your heart to my brother."

Isabelle gave a start.

"Don't think it's not been noticed how much you dote upon him," Rosannah went on. "But he won't return your affections, you know."

"How can you say that?"

The other smiled. "He is already planning to marry another."

There was a long pause. Then Isabelle said in a small voice, "He's to be married?"

"Yes. I wonder he hasn't mentioned it. Her name is Adelaide Winter. It will be a most prestigious match."

She smiled again, savouring the stricken expression on her young sister-in-law's face.

"So do heed my warning, Belle, dear. Don't go losing your heart to Harry. It's just the kind of plaything he will enjoy breaking."

Lizzie Newbrook walked quickly, her head down, her arms crossed, hands clutching at the shawl she had thrown round her shoulders as she ran from the farmhouse. It was dark in the lane and she wished she had thought to bring a lantern. No use in turning back now, though; she was late as it was.

The wind roared in the branches above, sending them threshing wildly and scattering the few remaining leaves still clinging from the autumn. It was a rough night, and Lizzie would never have ventured out but for Frank's note, delivered that afternoon by a travelling slaughterman, for her to meet him. Her husband, Tom, had seen the man with her in the yard and for a heart-stopping moment she thought he would ask what he'd come about. Thank God he'd gone into the cow stall instead. By the time he came out again the slaughterman had gone; and Tom, being an incurious man, had let the incident pass without questions.

Lizzie reached a five-bar gate set into the thickness of the hedge and paused there, looking over into the field beyond. In the cold light of the moon the silhouette of a row of elms showed like blackened fretwork against the skyline. She pressed herself into the shelter of the gate and waited.

After a while there came the sound she had been listening for: a faint whistling carried on the wind, growing gradually stronger as the whistler approached along the lane. She recognised the tune. It was "Sweet Lemeney".

"Frank?"

The hoarse whisper was snatched away from her lips. She tried again, louder.

There was an answer from the darkness. "Aye. You're there, Lizzie?"

She ran from her shelter and a moment later they were in each other's arms, pressed together in the wind's possession as though they could never bear to be separated again.

"How did you come here?" she wanted to know when the first urgency of their kisses had been slaked. "Didn't you ride?"

"No, I've got a trap. It's down at the crossroads. Boaz Palmer's along wi' me."

"Oh?"

"We've been across to Petersfield to see about next month's fight."

"You're going back to Lewes?"

"Aye. We'll put up at an inn further along for the night." He began kissing her again. "I wish you could be wi' me, Lizzie. It's been nigh on a month now."

"I know. I've counted every day."

"I've missed you."

"Have you? Truly? I thought . . . being on your wedding tour . . ."

"What?"

"Well, that you'd most like forget all about me."

"Forget you? I thought about you every single minute."

Hesitantly she said, "You still love me, then?"

"Love you – God above! As if I'd ever stop loving you. How many times do I have to say it. You and me, we're two for a pair. We belong together." He pressed her hard against him. "I wish you could've been wi' me in Tunbridge Wells. We'd have had a rare time of it."

Again she hesitated. "How did you get on . . . you and her? I was that jealous – "

"You don't need to be jealous, sweet-heart. She's a creature to be pitied, that 'un. I don't care for her a bit, and she knows it."

"So it's me you love still?" Lizzie urged, desperate for the reassurance of hearing him say it.

He covered her face with kisses, holding her head between his hands, touching his mouth to her eyes and lips,

86

murmuring endearments between each caress. The wind whipped her dark hair across her face and he kissed her through its strands before pushing it gently aside and pressing his cheek against hers.

"You're shivering," he said after a while. "I'd best not keep you out, not on such a raw night. When can we meet? Will you come into Lewes next week?"

"Yes. Thursday."

"That'll do. Same place as always?"

She nodded.

He left her then, walking quickly away into the darkness of the lane; and even after the sound of "Sweet Lemeney" had died, its echo haunted her still in the whistle of the wind across the emptiness of the winter fields.

9

The de Retz Academy of Art was situated in premises in a terrace of Georgian buildings at the foot of School Hill. The ground floor of the house was occupied by a bootmaker, whose products were advertised by a large top-boot suspended from a bracket to the left of the main entrance. On the right, counterbalancing it, an enormous human molar made of plaster drew the public's attention to the presence on the middle floor of a tooth-drawer.

The sign had originally been painted white, but exposure to the elements had darkened its plaster to bone yellow and pitted it with blackened crevices, giving the molar an alarmingly realistic appearance.

Inside the building, the tooth-drawer's occupation was further advertised by large wooden tubs of sawdust on the landing outside his door; but not all those requiring his ministrations made use of these spittoons before leaving and the ill-lit staircase was splashed in places with the blood they had spat out on their way down.

Following the Reverend Alec Bethway to the top floor, Isabelle had been obliged to raise the hem of her skirts to avoid these bloody puddles, and the raw smell permeating the unventilated stairwell made her feel slightly sick. She was glad to leave behind this unwholesome level and ascend a second flight of stairs, giving on to a landing lit by a skylight in the roof.

The door which her companion indicated bore a polished brass plate furnishing the information that this was the entrance to "*L'Académie de Retz. Salle des Beaux-arts. Fondée à Paris en 1783 pour les Enfants de la Noblesse et de la Haute Bourgeoisie. Seul Propriétaire: M. Leopold de Retz.*"

After such an impressive introduction, the room beyond the door proved most disappointingly shabby. Its floor had an unswept look, the bare boards worn into splinters from the constant scraping of easels and stools, and the walls beneath the two large dormitory windows were stained brown with patches of damp. In one corner a dutch stove gave out a feeble warmth and fouled the stale air with fumes that had seeped from its cracked chimney pipe.

There were no more than half a dozen pupils, none of whom gave the appearance of belonging either to the *noblesse* or to the *haute bourgeoisie*, but rather to the lower ranks of trade.

Even Leopold de Retz himself somehow failed to fulfil the promise of proprietorship, being a sparsely bearded figure with the yellowed eyes and mottled skin of a spirit-drinker, and whose accent when he greeted his visitors owed more to the thick burr of Sussex than the nasal intonations of France, giving his occasional use of his native tongue an almost comical incongruity.

"As you may perceive, *mam'selle et m'sieur*, we are drawing from life this morning."

He waved a hand towards the centre of the room, where a stout middle-aged woman draped in voluminous folds of green velvet maintained an awkward pose upon a raised dais.

"The class has ten minutes more in which to complete

their studies, and then I shall be delighted for you to inspect the drawings with me. In the meantime, if you would be so kind as to be seated – " indicating chairs beside a table strewn with papers and paintpots – "I will attend on you myself with a little refreshment."

Apart from one youth whose incessant cough was like the tearing of tissue, de Retz's pupils worked without sound. Their quiet industry prohibited Isabelle from making conversation, and in the silence her thoughts returned to the almost constant theme of Harry Weldrake.

Rosannah's news that he was to be married had cost her sleepless nights and many tears. It had never crossed her mind that he might be considering such a step; and it did little to ease her anguish that Adelaide Winter was older than he, and rather plain. Had she been as aged as Methuselah and as ugly as Medusa she would still have been the most enviable of women in Isabelle's eyes.

Why did he wish to marry her? For her wealth, said Rosannah – what other reason would he have? And in her misery, her resentment and jealousy, Isabelle had hated the unknown Miss Winter, heiress to a baronet's fortune, while she herself, illegitimate daughter of a country alehouse keeper, had nothing; not even a name to call her own.

Then, on Friday morning, Harry Weldrake had decided to accompany her with Alec Bethway to the skating on Pelbrook lake, and it was as though the sun had risen again in her deadened heart and brought with it the dawn of new hope.

To the curate's evident chagrin the other had proved himself the better skater, skimming effortlessly ahead over the ice and executing leaps and spins that had Isabelle applauding in delight. When Alec attempted a similar feat, he misjudged his landing and went sprawling clumsily on his back; and though he laughed with them, it had given hurt to his feelings as well as his body to see Weldrake standing so smugly with an arm about Isabelle's waist.

A muffled wail, breaking the silence of the studio, startled the girl from her reverie. A moment later the sound was repeated, louder this time, ending on a rising shriek of pain accompanied by a curious drumming noise.

"Poor souls." The stout woman on the dais spoke unexpectedly.

"The way he pulls 'em about, it's scand'lous, it is."

She uttered the words without moving, her face remaining as rigid as a china doll's, and Isabelle found this almost as unnerving as the distant sounds of agony.

"But what is it?" Alec asked.

The woman maintained her fixed gaze towards the far corner of the room.

"Him, down below. The tooth-puller. How them miserable creatures do suffer at his hands."

"Hand, Clara. Hand." One of the pupils corrected her laconically as the drumming quickened its pace and then, abruptly, ceased. "He has only the one, remember."

This anatomical detail stirred Alec's curiosity; and after they had taken refreshment and were looking at the finished studies he raised the subject again.

"Tell me, how can the fellow operate if he has but one hand?"

"Why, sir, he uses his stump," the same pupil informed him. "His left arm was taken off at the elbow, you see."

This explanation failed to satisfy.

"But in what manner exactly does he make use of it?"

"Oh, 'tis a most ingenious procedure. I've watched him at it myself. He sets the patient down in a chair, tips back their head, and uses the stump as a lever again their jaw to keep the mouth ajar while he pulls their teeth."

Isabelle shuddered at the image this description conjured.

"And the drumming we heard just now," Alec persisted, taking out his pipe. "What was that?"

"That? Oh, that was somebody's heels threshing upon the boards. Mind, some kick more'n others. Them's the ones he has to strap down in case they dislodge the bootmaker's ceiling plaster beneath 'em."

"Poor souls." The stout woman spoke again. She had got down from the dais and moved across to the corner, where she now stood with her back to the dutch stove to warm her calves, the voluminous velvet garment hoisted up behind her.

"It fair makes my innards a jelly, it does, having to listen to such as that all day."

"My wife has a tender heart," Leopold de Retz remarked fondly. "She cannot bear even to see the sufferings of a dog."

He had been leafing through Isabelle's book of sketches, brought along at Alec Bethway's suggestion; and with a sudden change of conversation, indicated the book where it lay open among the table's clutter and went on, "Your drawings, my dear mam'selle Flynn . . ."

"Yes, sir?"

"They tell me much. And yet nothing."

She looked at him blankly.

"You wished for my opinion, did you not? Very well. You shall have it."

He picked up the book and held it towards her.

"These drawings tell me that you have ability. The ability to see a subject and transpose it accurately to paper. The ability to make a reproduction faithful enough for others to behold that subject through your eyes, as it were. And yet, your work conveys no information. Ah, I see by your expression that still you do not follow. Let me attempt illumination."

He leafed through the pages.

"Yes. Here. This little landscape will serve admirably. You have drawn a building – a barn – and beside it, a tree. In the foreground, a path leads the beholder's eye across the scene to a gate and thence into the fields of your background. You have set down everything exactly as you saw it."

Isabelle nodded. It was one of her better sketches, drawn in the autumn at Stillborne's farm. There had been another one, an even nicer study, but that had been accidentally destroyed when her mother spilled lamp oil on it.

"The scene is well executed. Yet I ask, where is the life in it? Where is the feeling? There is nothing here to tell me that this is real. It is not real as you have drawn it, mam'selle. It is dead. Still you do not comprehend? Well, then . . . the stones of your building, I should be able to imagine them against my fingers rough, crumbling, warm still from the sun. Your tree, I should feel the coolness of its shade upon my skin, be sensible to the dying colours of its leaves. And your path . . . is it trodden earth, hard, stony to my feet? I do not know. As you have drawn it, there is no sensation."

Leopold de Retz flicked the page dismissively.

"It is texture that your drawing fails to give, mam'selle. Texture. The eye perceives . . . but it is texture alone which informs, enlivens, stimulates."

"It's a pretty picture, nonetheless," Alec said stoutly.

"Pretty? Oh yes, it is that. But what is prettiness? A façade, nothing more. There is no depth to it."

"You think not, sir?"

The other shook his head. "Let me make a comparison. How many of the fair sex attract the eye with prettiness, and yet prove on a closer acquaintance to be shallow, vapid creatures of whom a man soon wearies?"

"*C'est toujours la même rengaine, mes chers!*" Adolphe de Retz had come in at the door in time to overhear his kinsman's observation.

With a bow of acknowledgement to Alec Bethway, he took Isabelle's hand and raised it to his lips, continuing, "It is the old story. A pretty face is like a sugar bonbon. The taste, it cloys quickly. But a woman of intelligent mind is a savoury which lingers and makes a man to taste again."

Still holding her by the hand, the young Frenchman gazed warmly into her eyes.

"You alone, *ma demoiselle* . . . you are the exception. You are *la belle* in name, in visage and also in nature. *Toute belle*."

Some of the pupils exchanged knowing grins.

"Take no note of him, dear," the woman by the dutch stove said humorously, seeing the colour rush into Isabelle's face. "It's only his little way of talking."

De Retz smiled and shook his head. "*Mais c'est vrai.* You will be the adornment of this establishment. Ah – " he checked himself smartly and looked at Leopold. "But perhaps I go ahead too soon? You have made the invitation?"

The other laid Isabelle's sketch-book aside, replying, "I was about to do so. Mam'selle Flynn – "

She released herself awkwardly from de Retz's grasp and moved away.

"Yes, sir?"

"You have, as I say, an obvious gift for art. It would be regrettable to allow such potential talent to be wasted for want of professional direction. Therefore I should be honoured to admit you as a pupil of this academy."

Nothing could have given Isabelle greater pleasure – unless it were a proposal of marriage from Harry Weldrake – than to accept. But the academy was not a charitable institution, offering its services freely: if she became a pupil she would be expected to pay for the privilege. Since she had no personal income of any kind, acceptance was quite out of the question.

Noting her hesitation, Leopold de Retz continued quickly, "I appreciate what is in your mind, mam'selle. Perhaps I may suggest something? If you would consider making yourself available for the life study classes, I should be more than happy to give tuition in return. Does this seem approvable?"

"But . . . what will I be expected to do, sir?"

He spread out work-stained hands. "Nothing more than to sit for your fellow pupils."

"Oh, do say yes, miss!" one of these fellow pupils called out. "It'd make such a change from Clara."

"Aye, we've been drawing Clara nigh on four months," someone else put in; bringing the response from Clara herself – "Is that a complaint I hear?"

"No, no. But we've studied your face and form so often, I swear we each of us could draw you wi' our eyes shut."

"'Tis true," added a third. "We've dissected you on paper from every angle known to man. We've done you in charcoal and in pencil. We've painted you in oil and watercolour both. Speaking for myself, I dare say I could produce a passable likeness with a sausage dipped in gravy."

This provoked some laughter.

"Cheeky young pup," Clara said fondly.

"How often would you want me here, sir?" Isabelle asked Leopold de Retz, still uncertain. "I've not much longer to stay in Lewes. No more'n three weeks, at any rate."

"Oh, that is ample time. If you were to attend the academy, let us say, twice a week? We would arrange the life study for the morning and your tuition for the afternoon."

She nodded. "I'll need to ask my brother first, though."

"Yes, by all means seek your brother's approval," Alec Bethway came in firmly. He was not happy about this suggested arrangement, considering that it placed Isabelle in a somewhat unsavoury position.

"He is, after all, responsible for your welfare whilst you're under his roof—"

"It is not his roof," Adolphe de Retz interrupted smoothly. "It is the roof still of his lady wife, Mademoiselle Rosannah."

"Nonetheless, sir, any decision regarding Miss Flynn's welfare is entirely in the hands of her brother."

"Welfare? What is this welfare?"

Alec sought for an alternative. "Her good . . . her safety."

"Ah? You are suggesting that perhaps *l'académie* would place her in danger?"

"You put words into my mouth. I did not say that."

"*Pardon, je vous en prie.* It is sometimes the tone of voice which speaks more than the words."

Alec frowned.

"*N'importe.* It is no matter," the other went on. "Already I have made the enquiry of my friend Monsieur Weldrake. He expresses himself content with the arrangement."

"Does he, indeed! It is not his duty to express any opinion—"

"You've talked of it to him?" Isabelle asked eagerly before Alec could finish. "He said he approves? Mr Weldrake said that?"

"*Bien sûr.* Of a certainty, he approves."

Alec tried again. "Miss Flynn . . . Isabelle . . . I think you should discuss this with your brother. I urge you most strongly to do so. Surely there's no need for you to lend yourself as a—a sitter? Your brother would not begrudge the fees for a few lessons?"

"Belikes he wouldn't." She glanced around the room, at the attentive faces of the pupils. "But he's not here to ask. And I'd be glad to help wi' the life study class, truly I would."

"*Bravo, ma belle!*" De Retz ignored the curate's obvious reluctance to end the matter there. "It is as Monsieur Weldrake tells me, that you were made to be admired by all.

To gaze upon you, it is a delight which you have not the cruelty to deny to your fellow *artistes*."

Isabelle lowered her head; and by the smile which touched her lips, the Frenchman knew that he was about to score the first small victory in his revenge upon Frank Flynn.

In the bedroom of the alehouse at Weatherfield, Dinah Flynn lay propped against a doubled bolster-pillow, her eyes closed, the lids so sunken with suffering that in the lamplight their hollows showed darkly, as though the shadow of death already touched her face.

She was quiet now, the gnawing agony of the growth in her breast receding to pinpoints of pain as the massive dose of laudanum brought its opiate relief; and the silence in the room was disturbed only by the whisper of sleet against the window, echoed in the whisper of breath between the slackly parted lips.

Someone came in, and Lottie Adams, watching at the sick woman's bedside, turned in her chair. Seeing it was the doctor, she made to get up, but he motioned her with a shake of the head to stay where she was.

"How is she now?" He kept his voice low.

"Peaceful, thank the Lord. She's barely stirred this past half-hour."

"Good."

The neatly bearded man came across to the bed and looked down. There was nothing more he could do here, save continue the laudanum. He had seen death too often to mistake the signs of its advent.

Lifting back the covers a little, he felt the unnatural heat of the body beneath the flannel nightgown. The left breast had been eaten away by a mass of ulcerating abscesses surrounding the site of the tumour, and the left arm was swollen with fluid leaking into the tissue from the affected lymphatic glands of the armpit. How the woman had been able to endure the pain and find strength enough to go about her everyday business these past months, he had no idea.

Replacing the covers, he said, "If she **asks** for anything to drink, give her sips of water. Nothing more."

"Aye, sir."

"I'll come again early tomorrow."

"Aye."

There was a note of weariness in Lottie's voice, and he glanced down at her thin, lined face, noticing the telltale signs of strain.

"Don't overtire yourself sitting up. You need rest, too, Mrs Adams. Surely some other can stay to watch through the night?"

"No . . . I'd rather it's me, doctor. She'd ha' done the same, in my place. I told the rector just now when he come by to pray for her – Mr Howard, I says, she's been like a sister to me all these years, has Dinah. I'd never forgive meself if she was to go wi'out me being wi' her at her passing."

The doctor nodded.

He walked slowly back towards the bedroom door, then paused, asking, "Is there word yet of when her son and daughter will be here?"

Lottie shook her head. "We wrote three days back, an' all, to let 'em know their mother was took worse and as how they should come as quick as they could. But there's nothing been heard from either o' them."

"No doubt they are already on the road."

"Behopes you're right, sir. It'd be a fine thing if their poor dear mam was to breathe her last wi'out the pair o' them here to make their farewells. I blame that Frank for this. He should've sent our Belle back home when she was expected, end o' last month, instead o' letting her stay over in Lewes so long. Art classes, indeed!"

Lottie's voice rose slightly.

"Sitting about in nothing more'n a wrap and allowing strangers to look her all over . . . There's no decency in it, to my thinking. Our Dinah fretted herself sick when she heard of it from Belle's letters. I tell you, sir, it were the worry of it all as brought her to this sorry pass. You mark my words, that Frank and his sister have a lot to gi' answer for, abandoning their own poor mother to her death and grave while they go off gallivanting wi' their fancy friends."

10

"How was I to know she was so bad?"

Frank Flynn looked truculently across the alehouse kitchen where Lottie Adams was standing among the small group of family mourners gathered for the funeral.

"She's been going on by fits and turns these past two years or more. She never let on she was ailing so fast."

He shifted his gaze back to his mother's body inside the open coffin. The ashen-grey features, framed by two plaits of hair upon the satin pillow, wore an expression of serenity, and in the sharp March light shining down on her from the window Dinah Flynn appeared far younger than her two-score years now that death had smoothed the lines of life from her face.

Presently the coffin lid, propped against the trestle legs, would be hammered down to shut her from the world, like a door closing for ever on the cell of her departed soul.

Frank turned to stare out through the window behind, and his lowered glance came to rest on its ledge, where the stone had been worn into a smooth dip. For a moment he was taken back to his infancy, remembering himself watching his grandmother, old Molly Flynn, sharpening the long kitchen knives there on the whetstone; and later, his mother doing likewise, stropping the blade back and forth so fast that the flashes of reflected sunlight had dazzled his young eyes.

After a while he spoke again, a defensive note in his voice.

"Not that it made much difference, Belle and me arriving when we did. She didn't know us. She was too far gone."

"She weren't too far gone the day previous," Lottie Adams answered bitterly. "She were calling out your names all the afternoon, poor woman."

"Oh, mam . . . mam . . ." Isabelle, seated all in black at the kitchen table, buried her face in her hands.

97

Through her tears she sobbed, "If only we'd come home when we first got the news . . . instead o' leaving it . . . we should've come . . . we should've been here wi' her, Frank."

"Now don't start that again," her brother told her curtly over his shoulder. "I've had enough of it. It was you as said to put it off for a day, so you could go off to Brighton wi' your precious Harry Weldrake."

"You said I should go if I wanted! And what about you? What about you wi' that woman?"

"Be quiet, will you. Damn it, we've had that business out already. We don't want it again, not here. Not wi' mam barely cold."

Returning from the excursion to Brighton, Isabelle had gone up to change for dinner. Passing the open door of Rosannah's dressing room, she had overheard Frank and his wife engaged in furious argument. Later she had asked him about it, but he refused to answer; and it was left to the maid to inform her that Master Frank had been seen by one of the Mistress's friends walking arm-in-arm along the bank of the Ouse with some young woman.

What woman?

But the maid had only shrugged awkwardly and looked past her.

"We should've been here quicker," Isabelle repeated brokenly. "If only we'd – " She broke off suddenly, turning her head, her hand going up to her throat.

There was a ring of hob-nailed boots along the stone-flagged passage beyond the kitchen door. Three men came in. Her eyes went quickly to the canvas bag one of them was holding.

"Is it . . . is it time?"

"Aye, miss. 'Tis time."

The other mourners stood back to let the sexton and his two assistants through, watching silently as he took up the coffin lid and set it in place and then bent to take his instruments from the bag at his feet. The sound of the first nail being hammered into the elmwood was unnaturally loud in the stillness: two taps, three harder blows, and a dull thud to drive the head flush with the wooden surface.

When the last nail was knocked home, the sexton replaced his tools and motioned to his assistants to take up the closed coffin on their burly shoulders.

Outside in the lane, Lottie Adams's son Joel was waiting beside his waggon, black ribbons around his hatband and whipstock, black ribbons fluttering from the cheekstraps of his horse's head-stall, making the animal toss nervously as the cold wind blew them about.

The coffin was carried down the alehouse steps and slid over the dropped tail-board on to a pile of straw. Then, followed behind on foot by her son and daughter and the rest of the funeral party, Dinah Flynn made her final journey into Weatherfield, to lie beside her stallion man at last in the long quietness of an earthen bed.

"I presume that you yourself will now be taking charge of the alehouse, Mr Flynn?"

Weatherfield's parish minister, the Reverend Everett Howard, held out his tankard to be replenished. He would have preferred to be drinking port, but since none had been offered, accepted the home-brewed apple cider with good grace.

"Aye, I'm in charge now, I reckon."

"And your wife will be joining you?"

Through his membership of the Eridge Hunt, Mr Howard brushed against the fringe of Lewes society and had some slight acquaintance with Harry Weldrake and his sister. He knew the talk about the family, that its fortunes had seen better days, that there was an aberrant streak in the blood. Somehow, he doubted that such a hot-house bloom as Rosannah would thrive happily in the rustic soil of a wealden cabbage-patch.

Frank Flynn replaced the cider jug on the mahogany counter and cast a glance around the crowded ale-room. The numbers of the funeral party had been swelled by the addition of a dozen or so villagers with wives and children who, having been at St Anne's churchyard to pay their last respects, counted themselves sufficiently in mourning to partake of the funeral feast which followed.

He looked back at Mr Howard before answering, "I've no notion what my wife may want to do. We've not discussed it as yet. Any rate, she won't be wishing to make a move until after the child's arrived."

"Naturally not."

The rector slipped his belt out a notch against the bloating effects of the cider on his already corpulent girth.

"I take it, then, that someone will manage the house in your absence while your domestic affairs are settled?"

Frank nodded.

"Not your sister, surely?" Mr Howard persisted. "It would be too great a responsibility for one so young and tender."

"Aye, you're right, sir. Not Belle. Oh, she'll be living here – it's her home, after all, and I'll expect her to see to the cleaning and cooking for her keep. But I'm leaving a man in charge o' the shop, as you might say."

"A local man?"

"Not local, no. From London way. Palmer's the name. Boaz Palmer."

"Ah, yes. I believe I have heard you speak of him before."

"This kind o' work'll suit him to the ground. I mean to make changes, y'see, Mr Howard."

"Changes to the alehouse?"

"Aye. It's a dead hole as it is. Baccy and beer, and damn all else. A man wants more at the end of his day's labour than swilling his guts."

There was a slight raising of the eyebrow. "As you say. And what manner of change had you in mind, Mr Flynn?"

But Frank would not be drawn. He doubted that the Reverend Everett Howard, sporting gentleman though he was, would approve of his parish's alehouse becoming a venue for entertainment such as bare-knuckle contests, cocking, dog-fights and ratting matches. Better to say nothing and introduce such diversions gradually, one contest a month at first, say, and so whet customers' appetites for more, letting their support speak for him should the parish council start raising objection.

He refilled his own tankard, and noted several quart jugs standing empty on the counter.

"Joel!"

Raising his voice, he called across to his half-brother at a table with a group of womenfolk.

"We're running dry o' cider. Fetch us up another cask from the cellar while I drain this 'un off." He jerked his head towards a barrel at the end of the counter. "And look sharp about it!"

With some remark that made the women laugh, Joel Adams left the table and went up the steps leading from the room into the passage beyond. A short way along, past the door to the snug on the right, was the recessed entrance to the cellar with a shallow ledge at one side for oil lamp and tin box of lucifers.

Lighting the lamp, he pushed open the heavy door with a shove of his broad shoulder and descended into the darkness.

The alehouse cellar smelled of damp brick and earth and rotten wood, overlaid with the sharper odours of fermentation. Age-blackened cobwebs filmed the beams of the low ceiling and hung in thick tangled cords in recesses and corners, undisturbed since first they were spun in that chill, dank place.

Joel reached up and attached the oil lamp to a hook on the centre beam, where the slow circle of its swing sent shadows swaying up and down the walls. Hearing a footfall up at the doorway he turned, thinking that perhaps Frank had sent someone after him to give a hand with the barrel.

The steps came on hesitantly down the shallow stone stairs.

"Is that you down there, our Frank?" a woman's voice called, and he recognised it as Isabelle's. Without answering, he dodged behind a stack of empty crates where she would not see him.

"Frank?" she called again; and as she came past, he jumped out behind her from the shadows.

Isabelle spun round, startled, her hand going to her breast.

"Lord's sake! You give me a fright doing that!"

"Did I?" He grinned at her.

Angrily she said, "I wouldn't have come down if I'd known it was you here."

101

The grin faded.

"Now move out o' the way, will you? I want to come by."

She made to push past to reach the stairs, but he caught her by the arm and held her.

"Let go o' me!" The girl struggled to free herself. "This is no time to be playing daft pranks. Not a day like this. Have some respect, why don't you?"

"Respect? I'm not being disrespectful, am I, talking to you?"

"You know full well what I mean, so stop twisting words."

Joel's hand dropped to his side.

Sullenly he said, "It wouldn't hurt to show me a bit o' kindness, Belle, instead o' treating me so uppish each time I come near you."

"You shouldn't deserve it, then I wouldn't treat you so."

"Deserve it? Why, what have I done?"

When she made no reply, he continued, "I ain't seen you for nigh on two months. It wouldn't have harmed you to write me a little note in all that time."

Her reply pricked him with its scorn.

"Why should I bother, when you can scarce read a primer let alone a joined hand?"

"That's right – make fun o' me again! I can't help it if words muddle me."

He flung himself peevishly away.

"I suppose your friend in Lewes is a reg'lar fine scholard, reading books as fast as eating hot dinners. Lord knows, he seems to've turned your head right enough. It fair made me sick, it did, listening to the letters you sent your mam. If you mentioned the name o' that Harry Weldrake once you must've mentioned it a thousand times. Mr Weldrake this an' Mr Weldrake that – "

"You be quiet, Joel Adams!" Isabelle broke in angrily. "I'll mention him as often as I please, and I don't need permission from you."

"I suppose you fancy yourself in love wi' him."

She started a cutting retort; then checked herself and looked at her half-brother defiantly.

"Since you're so curious to know, you hobbledehoy – yes, I

102

am in love wi' him. He's the finest, most handsome gentleman in all the world."

"An' he loves you in turn, does he?" Joel sneered.

She looked away without reply.

"He's said as much, has he, your fine gentleman?" he persisted.

"Not . . . in so many words, no."

"Nor he won't, neither. That sort never do."

"How would you know?"

"I've got ears and eyes in my head. They're all alike, the bloody gentry – use their own womenfolk for breeding and the rest o' you for bedding. You mind your step wi' that Weldrake, our Belle. He'll only be after you for one thing. Or has he had his hand up your skirts already?"

Isabelle's face flushed scarlet.

"You – " she began. Then, lost for further speech, struck out, catching Joel across the cheek with the flat of her palm. The slap was not painful, but it stung, and he retaliated by grabbing a handful of thick auburn hair and dragging her head sideways.

Isabelle clawed herself away.

"You pig! You disgusting pig!"

She could barely get out the words for the tears of humiliation choking her. She would have run to the cellar steps but her legs were trembling so much she felt she might never reach them.

"That's right – call me names!" her half-brother flung back. "You're very good at that, looking down on folk. Just you let Harry Weldrake have what he wants from you, and see how high and mighty you are then! A few kisses and a bit o' cuddling on the backstairs, and you think he'll marry you . . . There's streets in London full o' girls like you, been led up the garden path. You won't see his heels for dust once he's ruined you, and you won't be too proud then, my lady, to come crawling back here to bear your shame, I don't suppose."

This besmirching of something as pure and beautiful as her love for Harry roused Isabelle to a fury. Throwing herself at Joel, she raked her nails across his face, leaving his cheeks marked with oozing scratches of broken skin.

There was a moment of stunned silence.

Then – "You bitch!"

He went to strike her, but she stepped quickly back and spat at him, "Touch me once more and I'll get Frank on you – and then there'll be another funeral in the family. If it wasn't for my poor mam cold in her grave I'd go straight up this minute and tell him what you've been saying. I would, an' all, but there's been enough sorrow in this house today wi'out causing fresh."

Joel scowled at her and gingerly touched his cheeks. Finding blood on his fingers, he pulled off his neckerchief and used that to dab at the scratches.

"How'm I supposed to explain away this mess?"

Ignoring him, Isabelle went to the stairs; then stopped halfway up and threw back at him over her shoulder, "I'm not staying here in Weatherfield to be abused by the likes o' you. Now our mam's gone there's nothing to keep me from leaving. And that's just what I'm doing, Joel Adams . . . I'm clearing out back to Lewes. And this time for good!"

11

"Your good health, sir."

The Reverend Everett Howard held his glass of port towards the light and examined its ruby contents with a critical eye. Then, satisfied with the appraisal, took a sip.

"Ah . . ."

He transferred his examination to the pleasant-featured young man seated opposite him in the study of Weatherfield rectory. A little earlier he had come upon him in the church, kneeling in private prayer in the side chapel, and recognising a fellow clergyman by his cloth and learning that he was a visitor to the village, had invited him to take a midday meal with Mrs Howard and himself.

"But this is a most happy coincidence!" the rector had exclaimed when the young man introduced himself as Alec Bethway.

"All Souls, in Lewes, you say? Why, I knew your father well when he was vicar of that parish. Yes, indeed. Dear Henry Bethway . . . I remember him very well. And by a further coincidence, d'you know, his curate at that time came to be appointed to the very living I presently hold myself here in Weatherfield."

"Indeed? Is that so?"

The information had intrigued Alec. During the meal he had pursued it further, asking, "In what year, sir, was my father's curate transferred here? Do you recall?"

"I recall it exactly. Will you take a little more vegetable, Mr Bethway? No? Then perhaps another piece of the mutton? That's it. Do help yourself to whatever you please."

He waited until his guest had taken up knife and fork once more.

"Now, where were we. Ah, yes – Mr Bates."

"Mr Bates?"

"Esmond Bates. Your father's curate. He was appointed to this living in 1852. Easter, 1852, I believe. His incumbency lasted no more than half a year, poor fellow . . . a very sudden end, d'you know. But the Lord moves in mysterious ways. I had applied at precisely that time to be moved to a rural parish – for my daughter's health, she required the country air – and so it fell out that I was appointed almost immediately to step into Mr Bates's incumbency here."

The conversation had shifted thereafter to Alec and his years as a student of theology at St Bede's College in Durham, and thence to his ordination and work as curate, and his aspirations for the future of his career in the Church.

Now, sitting in the rectory study and enjoying a pipe of tobacco and a post-prandial glass of Mr Howard's best port, he returned to the subject of his host's predecessor at Weatherfield.

"Was he not trampled to death by a horse at one of the farms hereabouts?"

"Indeed so."

"And his wife – his widow rather – did she not marry again, to a local farmer?"

"That I could not say. There was a widow, yes, a young creature . . . much younger than Mr Bates, I believe. Ah, but wait – " Mr Howard held up a hand. "I do recall something of a marriage, now I think of it. Not at St Anne's, though. The couple had removed from the parish by then. You must forgive my poor memory, Mr Bethway, but all this occurred almost twenty years ago."

"Of course, sir. It is I who should ask pardon for pressing you. It is merely that I already have some slight knowledge of these events through one of your parishioners. She was baptised by Mr Bates here at St Anne's, with his wife as one of the sponsors. By an odd twist of fate, the godfather was a Mr Bashford, the farmer of whom I spoke just now, to whom Mrs Bates was married in her widowhood."

"'There's a providence in it all'," quoted the rector. "And which of my parishioners gave this information?"

"Miss Flynn. Miss Isabelle Flynn."

"Ah. Young Belle from the alehouse. Yes, of course. I knew the name of Bashford seemed familiar. She goes on occasion to stay with the family, does she not?"

Alec confirmed this. "In fact, sir, my purpose in visiting Weatherfield is to persuade Isabelle – Miss Flynn – to visit them again. It would be better if she were at Bonningale for a time."

"In what way, better?"

"Her mother was buried some weeks past – "

Mr Howard nodded.

" – and her brother has returned to his wife in Lewes. When I met him last he told me he's left the alehouse to be managed by his trainer, Mr Palmer."

Mr Howard nodded a second time.

"I will be candid with you, sir," Alec continued, laying aside his pipe to accept a further glass of port. "I admire Miss Flynn very much. Indeed, I must say in all truth that I have an affection for her beyond the ordinary."

"She is a most attractive young person," the rector agreed, "and has much to commend her. Mrs Howard and I always find her very pleasant and agreeably natured. Doubtless she will make some man in the parish a good wife."

He looked across at his guest and smiled indulgently. "You were saying, sir, about Mr Palmer – ?"

A small frown appeared between Alec's deep-set eyes. "Yes, Mr Palmer. He strikes me as a rough type of fellow. I do not think it very right or proper that Isabelle should remain alone with him at the house. It would not matter so much, perhaps, if he were there only during the daytime and slept elsewhere at night. But I gathered from my conversation with Mr Flynn that this man is in full occupancy – and that the room he uses is adjacent to Isabelle's own."

"So you would advise her to remove to the Bashfords for a period?"

"That is what I mean to discuss with her this afternoon."

The rector leaned back in his chair and clasped his hands over his rounded belly.

"She does not expect you?"

"No, she does not. I didn't think it necessary to warn her of such a brief visit."

"Then you will have had a fruitless journey, my dear Mr Bethway."

"Fruitless? I think not, sir. She will listen to my advice, I am sure."

"I do not mean fruitless in that sense. I mean that your journey is in vain. Young Belle is no longer in the village."

Alec looked sharply at his host, and set down his glass on the table beside him.

"She has departed already? To Bonningale?"

"No, not Bonningale."

"Where, then? Do you know?"

"To Lewes. I presume to her brother and his wife."

"But – that is impossible! I was at their house only yesterday. There was no mention of Isabelle being there – not a word." The frown deepened. "Who informed you that she had returned to Lewes?"

"She informed me herself, before she went. I came upon her waiting at the carrier's office in the high street with her box. I enquired where she was going, and she answered me. She also said that she had employment in the town."

"What manner of employment?"

Mr Howard drained the last drop of port from his glass.

"I was not told. But I gather the work had been found for her by some young Frenchman she knew."

On the day following her mother's funeral and the scene with her half-brother Joel in the alehouse cellar, Isabelle had written to Rosannah asking that she might be allowed to return at once to Tea Garden Lane.

The reply, when at last it came, was pointedly brief: Rosannah regretted that it would not be possible to accommodate her sister-in-law again so soon after her recent sojourn.

Isabelle's disappointment was intense. Her immediate reaction had been to appeal to Frank to persuade his wife otherwise; but on reflection she realised it would be an appeal made in vain. Frank would only have told her to bide at the alehouse and stop indulging her idle fancy for life in Lewes.

Already, there had been words between them both over what he derisively called her calf-sickness for Harry Weldrake, telling her that she was throwing away her self-respect by putting herself so much in the man's way and wearing her heart on her sleeve in such a fashion.

Indeed, it was this naive behaviour of Isabelle's that had partly prompted Rosannah's refusal to have her back again. She had only tolerated that first visit because Harry had been so insistent that she honour her wedding-day promise to invite the girl. Knowing her brother as she did, ever ready for any new distraction and quickly tiring once the novelty had faded, she decided there was some kindness in the cruelty of refusing Isabelle's plea.

Harry was not above seducing her, kin or no, and if he ran true to form would discard her almost immediately. The last hopeful little innocent misused in this way had fostered out the baby she bore him and had gone to work in some disreputable tavern in Newhaven. Rosannah had no great affection for Isabelle; but her indifference was beginning to mellow a little with the advancement of pregnancy and she had no desire to see her young sister-in-law inherit a similar fate: one truly worse than death, for working-class girls robbed of their virtue were the raw material from which whores were made.

It was not, however, Isabelle's virtue which gave most cause for concern. It was the fear of what Frank, in his violence, might do against Harry if he discovered him to be his sister's seducer; and, even more disquieting, the probable loss of Miss Adelaide Winter's much-needed fortune, at a time when the betrothal was entering a delicate stage of negotiation.

No date had yet been arranged for the marriage – indeed, the engagement itself had still to be publicly announced – and it would be most regrettable if the lady were given cause to reconsider Harry's proposal on account of some trifling dalliance with a chit like Isabelle Flynn.

"That wretched, silly girl! Dolly, you should not have encouraged her."

Rosannah looked up angrily from the letter Adolphe de Retz had shown her. Her cheeks were flushed, but whether from emotion or from the stifling heat of the coal fire, he could not tell.

"The deceit of the creature . . . After it had been made perfectly clear she shouldn't return to Lewes, to solicit *your* aid in this bold manner. The presumption of it when you are scarcely acquainted!"

"But, *mon ange*, what man could resist so charming a *cri de cœur*?"

Rosannah threw herself fretfully against the pillows on the drawing-room day-bed. The low-cut neckline of the loose gown distracted attention from the disfigurement of her ripening pregnancy, and de Retz's eyes strayed constantly to the enticing curve where neck met shoulder.

"If I had told her no, still she would have come," he said. "She is stubborn, that one."

"Like her brother. Stubborn as mules, the pair of them. And hardly more intelligent."

She flicked irritably at the lace edging of a pillow.

After a while she went on, "Well, she's here now so there's little use in wishing her elsewhere. At least she can't come to much harm lodged with Clara. But for heaven's sake, Dolly, do try to keep her away from my brother, else she'll be trotting about at his heels again like a pet dog."

"I will make it so that she has not the opportunity. Already I explain that if she has the desire to remain with Clara and Leopold, she must work absolutely hard. Otherwise – *adieu, la douce* Belle."

He kissed his fingertips to the window.

"But what work is there for her at the academy?" Rosannah demanded. "Playing the statue for Leopold's drawing class?"

"No, no. She is not to be at the academy."

"Where, then?"

De Retz smiled. "There is another place."

"What place?"

"Oh . . . in the town."

"You're being very obscure! 'A place in the town' could be anything. What is it – one of the hotels, perhaps?"

"One . . . might describe it so, yes."

"Well, she's had experience enough of serving, Lord knows, growing up behind the counter of some rustic pothouse."

He smiled again, his teeth white beneath the dark moustache.

"*S'elle a fait des bêtises qu'elle se débarbouille.*"

Rosannah made a sound of exasperation. "Oh, do speak plainly, Dolly. French I understand perfectly well, but your colloquial cant might just as well be Greek for all I can make of it."

"I mean only to say that she has caused the difficulty for herself, and so she must remove herself from it as best she can. The employment I have found for her, it pays well. The company is – how should I say – amicable. But if the situation does not please her, then she must take for herself the responsibility of finding something other. I have done what I am able."

"You've done enough. More than enough. I should be vexed with you. It is, after all, Frank who should be the one

110

to deal with the problem." The full lips were turned down. "But of course, he's away again . . ."

De Retz got slowly from the armchair in which he had been sitting and straightened himself, the heavy gold watch-chain falling neatly into place across the front of his waistcoat.

Quietly he said, "He leaves you too often."

"Yes. He does."

"He has not the right."

"He has every right if he chooses. There's no law to say that a husband should live with his wife seven days out of seven."

"He has gone to fight?"

She nodded.

"Always the fight! *Quel bondieu d'imbécile*."

"If you are calling Frank a fool — "

"Yes, I call him a fool! He has for wife the most beautiful woman God has made. And what does he do? Does he cherish her, stay at her side, have joy in the child? Is he full of tenderness — "

Rosannah averted her head.

"Stop it, Dolly. You know full well what he is. What I *want* him to be . . ."

She paused, looking round the room, her eyes wandering unseeing over the crowded furniture and picture-cluttered walls.

After a few minutes she went on sullenly, "Though perhaps I should say it was what I used to want him to be. Now . . . now I'm not so certain any more."

"Not certain?"

The young Frenchman crossed the hearth to the day-bed and stared down at her. "How so, you are not certain?"

"I don't know. Oh, I don't know . . . perhaps it's my condition."

"You do not love him any longer?"

There was a raw note of appeal in the question.

Rosannah raised her face and for a long moment they looked at one another. In the silence, the tick of the ormolu clock on the ornate marble mantelpiece sounded unnaturally strident.

Then de Retz asked again, hoarsely, "Do you not love him?" and Rosannah slowly shook her head.

He knelt beside her and took her hands in his.

"What has he done for this to happen?"

"Oh . . . very little. I never realised how fine was the line between my desire for him and my fear of him. Now I'm like this – " her eyes moved down to her child-proud body – "he can't bear me to be near him. He won't touch me, unless it's to thrust me away. If I plead with him for even the least show of interest, it makes him angry and . . . and then he strikes me."

"*Quoi?* Strikes you?" De Retz gripped her hands fiercely and pressed them against his chest.

"He has dared to cause you hurt?"

Instead of answering, she reached up and drew back the heavy ringlets of honey-coloured hair from the nape of her neck; then bent her head forward, disclosing a purpling bruise.

"He made that?"

"Yes."

Until their marriage, Rosannah had always derived a strangely sensuous excitement from her husband's rough handling, feeding her wanton appetite on the pleasurable pain his brutal love-making brought. But since that night at Tunbridge Wells Frank's violence had increased. When he hit her now, it was not in play but as though he seriously intended to inflict real hurt, as though the bruising and degrading of her pregnant body was the only outlet he had for the contempt and frustration and dislike he was beginning openly to show towards her.

And in return, as the all-consuming fire of her passion for him burned lower and lower, Rosannah was becomingly increasingly disillusioned about their future together as man and wife.

She let her hair fall back into place and looked at the Frenchman kneeling beside her. His fists were clenched together, his lips compressed into a thin line, and even without touching him she could sense the tension of his barely contained anger at her ill treatment.

She reached out and brushed his cheek with the back of her hand, feeling a sudden pang of regret for the pleasant hours of friendship they had shared together before her infatuation with Frank Flynn.

Quietly she said, "There's a saying we have. 'Marry in haste, repent at leisure.' Whoever coined it spoke no more than the truth. You know, Dolly, I spend so much time by myself nowadays, resting here in the house or else driving in your carriage out across the Downs . . . so much time to reflect on my mistakes, to tell myself that perhaps I made an unwise choice after all . . . that perhaps I should never have broken off our understanding."

He clasped her hands, pressing them to his lips.

"But it's too late." Wearily she turned her head away, staring into the fire. "We cannot go back and undo the wrongs of the past."

"It is not too late," de Retz said thickly. "Adored one, this marriage, it changes nothing. I love you still with all my heart."

"Dearest Dolly, I've treated you so cruelly – "

"It does not matter! Long ago, when first I saw you, I gave to you all that I am, to be your slave if it please you. You are my life, Rosannah. You are my heart's blood, the air I breathe . . ."

He leaned forward and rested an elbow on the pillow above her reclining head. She continued to gaze towards the fire, and after a few moments he took her chin in his free hand and gently turned her face to his.

"*Ma chérie . . . je t'aime, je t'adore.* Do not be this man's wife. Come with me, yes? We will make the home together in France, in Paris . . . wherever you wish it."

"No, Dolly – "

He silenced her, his mouth warm and firm against hers.

"Yes, Dolly," he murmured.

"But – Frank?"

"He has made the forfeit. *Il paye de sa vie.* I would kill him for his hurt to you, but there are – how do you say? – more ways than one to skin the cat."

He kissed her again, hungrily, exulting in the possession of

113

her lips, his hatred of Frank Flynn transmuting itself into a savage satisfaction at the revenge already being exacted upon that cursed family.

12

The dull smack of Frank Flynn's fist against his opponent's body brought renewed shouts of encouragement from the spectators standing beyond the roped-off fighting area. The bare-knuckle contest had been in progress for a little over two hours, and both men were visibly tiring. A few well-placed punches now would see it finished inside the next round.

Frank danced back a couple of steps and sucked in a deep lungful of air. The match was being fought on Waller's Common, in the neighbourhood of Midhurst, and despite the protection offered by a line of densely knit holly bushes close by, the March wind was still brisk enough to keep the onlookers moving about.

At one side of the ring two large silk handkerchiefs – the fighters' colours – flapped ceaselessly at the end of the stake to which they were tied and every so often would fly out with a sharp double crack as a sudden gust took them.

Frank Flynn's colour was scarlet, repeated in the broad sash he wore round his waist above the tightly fitting breeches. He had adopted it as his own after that first meeting with Lizzie Newbrook a year before in the yard of the inn here at Midhurst, when she had torn off a strip of her petticoat to give him for luck.

His opponent, a blacksmith from Chichester way, wore yellow. Not a shade Frank was especially partial to, but no matter. He meant to have the fellow's colours for his victory trophy even so.

He moved in again, right fist up to protect his head, left fist in front of him to cover the chest area. He fought with his body a little bent, head and shoulders forward, knees well flexed, enabling him to advance or retreat as the quickness of eye and the split-second reaction of muscle dictated.

For much of the match he had adopted a strategy of keeping back, thus forcing his opponent to do the work and come to him so that the man gradually tired himself with repeated charges. There was a further advantage to these tactics: the impetus of the other's own rush lent double force to the blows which Frank was able to land about his body, hitting and stopping with the left and right fists with equal quickness before dancing away from the retaliatory attack.

Steadily he drew in another deep breath; then darted forward. The force of the punch he delivered to the black-smith's midriff drove the air from the man's lungs in an audible gasp and for a moment he dropped his guard, ena-bling Frank to deliver a second telling blow, this time to the side of the head.

The cheers from the spectators increased, interspersed with shouts of advice in the pugilistic slang used by the more dedicated followers of the sport.

"Good fellow! My money's on you – choke him off!"

"That's the go, man! Burst his crust with a chipper and let's see claret flowing."

"Another tap to the brain canister!"

"Rattle his box o' dominoes!"

And then, as he moved in with a flurry of punches that sent his opponent reeling backwards into the ropes, a woman's high voice which he recognised as Lizzie Newbrook's, crying out "Come on, Frank! Come on! Come on!"

Her excitement spurred him into the final punishing attack; and within two minutes the blacksmith lay stretched out upon the turf, the blood from his nose trickling in a crooked stream across the bruise-bright flesh of his cheek.

The referee, a short, bushy-whiskered individual, waved Frank away to his corner, where his second was already crouching down to make a knee for him to sit on. His oppo-nent's two assistants, the bottle-holder and the second, seeing their man unable to rise unaided, hurried to lift him by the arms and drag him, groaning loudly, to his own corner; but it

115

was obvious that he had no more fight left in him, and after the prescribed thirty-second period was up and "Time!" called, only Frank Flynn came out to stand at the scratch-line drawn across the centre of the ring.

The referee looked from one to the other of the pair of umpires on the other side of the ropes.

Then he nodded.

"Your contest, I think, Mr Flynn."

Amid noisy applause and shouts of jubilation from those who had backed him to win, Frank walked over to the stake and untied the two silk handkerchiefs. Waving them triumphantly above his head he turned to look over to where Lizzie Newbrook had been standing.

The smile died from his face. Beside her was a thick-set man of medium height dressed in countryman's corduroy, whom he recognised as her husband, Tom Newbrook.

Frank had seen him on several occasions previously – always from a distance since he had no wish to make himself known – and his unexpected presence here today came as a disagreeable surprise, robbing his moment of triumph of much of its exhilaration. When he had spoken to Lizzie before the start of the contest she had made no mention of her husband, only saying that she'd come from Midhurst in the company of friends.

Tom Newbrook must have joined his wife unexpectedly, while the fight was in progress; and if so, Frank thought irritably, it was silly of her to have called out to him by name the way she had.

He turned away and moved back to his own corner, acknowledging the calls of congratulation with a raised hand. Deliberately keeping his back to the Newbrooks, he took the flask of water held out by his bottle-holder, a tow-haired young lad named Charlie who was Boaz Palmer's nephew, and rinsed his mouth, then spat the water out on to the grass and emptied the remainder over his head and face.

Sam Reaney, who had taken Palmer's place as Frank's second while the latter was managing the alehouse at Weatherfield, had likewise observed the man standing with Lizzie Newbrook.

116

Giving Frank his shirt, he remarked, "Your piece o' fancy's got herself company."

"Aye." The other used the garment to dry himself before pulling it on and fastening the buttons at the neck opening.

"You know him?"

Frank nodded. "Her husband."

"Ah. Trouble, d'you reckon?"

"Does he look like he might be?"

Reaney cast a glance over Frank's shoulder. The Newbrooks had moved a little nearer, away from the shelter of the holly bushes, and it was plain from their expressions as they spoke to one another that their conversation was rather less than amiable.

"Aye, reckon he could be trouble." The second waited while Frank tied his neckerchief and then helped him into jacket and top-coat. "Best we don't enquire his missus's health too closely. Belikes he'd fetch you a stinger for answer."

"What – him? I'd mince his face to bloody pulp!"

The other threw a belligerent look at the couple. Lizzie was shaking her head about something and trying to back away from her husband, who was leaning towards her and gripping her arm.

The spectators had started to disperse now, horse-drawn vehicles already threading their way between those on foot along the rough cart-track crossing the common. Most of them seemed to be heading in the direction of Midhurst, whose distant chimneyed roofs and spires could just be discerned across the open countryside. It was there, at a public house called The Eclipse, that the promoters of the fight would be waiting to give Frank his prize money and the book-makers pay out on winning stakes to the backers.

"Come on – " Sam Reaney slapped him on the shoulder. "This blasted wind's slicing my ribs apart."

He moved out of the way of a couple of men dismantling the ropes, and as he did so, raised his voice to call loudly, "Charlie! You got everything stowed aboard?"

The shout distracted Tom Newbrook's attention. For a moment he turned to watch as fighter and second walked over to a trap and climbed up. Then, when the boy with them had taken the driving seat and flicked the horse forward, his gaze moved back again to focus itself on the face of his wife.

Lizzie was very pale, but quite composed, and there was nothing in her expression now of the animation Newbrook had seen while watching her, unobserved, earlier on. He had thought to give himself a few hours' diversion by attending the prize fight, and had been annoyed at finding himself looking across the ring at his own wife making a spectacle of herself.

She had not told him she'd be coming to watch the contest; but then, she told him very little about anything these days. Not that he much minded her long silences, being himself a man of few words and appreciative of the same quality in others: there were women enough whose tongues seemed never to stay still in their heads for more than a few seconds together and whose constant prattle and tattle wore out a man faster than rain upon sandstone.

Normally he would not have thought much at discovering Lizzie among the crowd at a bare-knuckle fight. It was quite usual for the weaker sex to attend such entertainment; and why not? Such exhibitions of strength, endurance and skill were something to be admired by all. What had galled him today was not her unexpected presence, but her behaviour, the way her attention was fixed upon the fighter in the scarlet colours, the way she covered her face when he took a blow, or else jumped up and down, clapping her hands and shouting, when he delivered one.

Those about her may have been amused by such a conspicuous display of enthusiasm; but her husband was not.

He recognised the name of the fighter: Frank Flynn. He had seen him contest before. As, obviously, had Lizzie. But he knew nothing of the man outside the ring. To judge by appearances, Lizzie did. Watching her across the ropes, it had occurred to Tom Newbrook that his wife was spending rather more time than was nice in gadding about away from the farm. Perhaps it was best she had a child now, something to settle her and keep her occupied at home.

He was not a jealous man. He did not care overmuch that Lizzie so seldom allowed him the satisfaction of his conjugal rights, considering the act of union between man and woman a vastly over-rated business and never being able to understand why folk should make so much fuss of something that was all over and done with between one breath and another.

As for children, well, she was not yet twenty years old, and he hadn't wished to saddle her too early with a family, wearing out her healthy young body with careless pregnancies as many another husband would have done. He'd get a son by her one day, he told himself from time to time; a son to inherit the farm. For generations uncounted there had been Newbrooks in the district, born and reared here, and there was no reason why it should not continue that way.

Well, he'd take her home and get the business started. Good stock required the application of good husbandry.

"But I don't want to go back yet, Tom," Lizzie repeated fretfully in answer to his renewed urging. "How many times d'you need telling?"

She looked up at him, at the brown hair fading to grey on the temples and side-whiskers, at the deep vertical line between the eyes, caused not by temper but by concentration. It was an honest, dull face, and she had loved it once, before she met Frank Flynn.

"I want to go into Midhurst."

"You're going into Midhurst only if you gi' me an account o' what you mean doing there."

"You've had an account."

"What, buying brown sugar and a packet o' pins?"

"Yes."

It was true, she did need the sugar and the pins. She also had an arrangement with Frank to meet him at The Eclipse.

"What's wrong wi' buying the things at Upper Highbury?"

"Don't you listen to what I say? The last lot o' pins I got from Upper Highbury were all rusted. I'm having no more from there."

"Then I'll take you by cart to Midhurst, if your mind's so fixed."

"I don't *want* to go by cart! I feel like the walk, I told you."

He stared at her. The notion of a long walk over Waller's Common in raw March weather, all for to purchase two items before starting another long walk through Upper Highbury to the farm, struck him as ridiculous.

Lizzie pulled her shawl about her shoulders and started to move away, but the wind flapping the dark skirts against her legs impeded her steps as she went and in a few strides her husband overtook her.

Grasping her by the elbow, he said, "I want no more arguing. You're coming along in the cart wi' me."

"No."

"And I tell you, you will."

"I won't! Now stop your pulling at me and leave go my arm."

His hand dropped to his side. Sullenly he said, "It's on a cause o' that bruiser, ain't it? That Frank Flynn?"

"I don't know what you're talking about."

Lizzie began walking on. He'd already asked her earlier about Frank. She pretended that she only knew of him through her friend Martha Izzard, whose brother, a prize-fight devotee, had an admiration for him. At the time, Tom had appeared satisfied with this explanation. It was the Izzards who had brought her along today, and she was to have travelled back into Midhurst with them; but seeing her with her husband, they had started away without her.

As the distance between them increased, Tom Newbrook raised his voice.

"So you're set on going alone?"

She did not pause, merely looked back at him with a brief nod before pulling up her shawl to cover her hair.

"Mind, then, you'd best be home afore dusk, d'you hear?"

There was no response.

He stood where he was, watching her move further off over the tussocks of wind-flattened grass, her slim body bent forward and her head down. In a short while she had over-taken the first knot of stragglers from the fight; and in a while longer had disappeared entirely from his view beyond a slow-moving waggon.

The next time Tom Newbrook saw his wife, she was seated on Frank Flynn's knee in a back room of The Eclipse public house.

It had taken Lizzie rather longer than she thought to walk from Waller's Common into Midhurst and she had run the last half-mile, fearing that her lover might leave before she reached the place of their assignation.

Crossing the busy market square, the worn leather sole of her ankle boot had slipped on the decaying refuse littering the cobbles, sending her sprawling headlong to the ground. The impact had knocked the breath from her. For some seconds she lay without moving; then, with the help of a stall-holder, got unsteadily back to her feet. Fortunately, The Eclipse was not much further on, at the top of a lane leading off the square; but even so, the pain of an ankle twisted in the fall seemed to drag the distance out considerably.

"Well? Aren't you pleased I'm here, Frank?"

She had found him with young Charlie Palmer and two others in the small private room behind the bar.

Pushing aside his pot of brandy and water, he stood up and came towards her.

"Aye, I'm pleased you're here."

"You don't look it."

"It's a wonder I look anything just now!"

Frank touched his face gingerly. The marks caused by his opponent's fists were already darkening to bruises on the jaw and cheekbones, and one eye was enclosed in purpled swollen flesh.

Reaching behind her, he closed the door.

"I wasn't expecting you, that's all. Not wi' your husband keeping you company this afternoon." He jerked his head towards the others. "You know young Charlie, don't you . . . and Harry Walsh and Sam Reaney?"

She nodded to them, and Walsh and Reaney, a brawny tough-looking pair, looked back at her with the kind of knowing familiarity reserved for other men's women.

"Come and sit yourself down, love," Reaney invited, patting the worn plush seat of the chair beside him; and when she moved forward – "What's wrong? You picked up a stone?"

"No. I had a fall backaways a bit. Turned my ankle."

"That was a daft thing to do." Frank took her by the elbow. "Does it pain you much?"

"Aye."

"Then best let Harry look at it. Belikes you'll need a compress."

He swung her up in his strong arms and carried her the few feet across the room to an open window where the raw and colourless light from outside was enough to give illumination.

Seating himself on a bench against the wall and holding her on his knee, one arm about her waist, he unbuttoned the side-fastening of her boot and eased it carefully off.

Harry Walsh leaned over and took her foot in his square, rough hand to examine the swollen ankle.

"You've turned it right enough. You'll not be walking on that for a day or two."

"Oh, but I must! Our Tom's expecting me back by dark. And I've still to go out to buy some'at at the store afore I leave Midhurst."

She turned to Frank, her expression distraught.

"It were the excuse I gi' him, that . . . the excuse for coming into town. He'd have taken me back home hisself, else. He'll suspect some'at's up for sure if he catches me empty-handed."

Frank kissed her lightly on the mouth. "Now don't go working yourself up, girl. What is it needs fetching?"

"Not much – just a packet o' steel pins and a bag o' sugar."

"Young Charlie'll go for you."

"'Course I will!" responded Charlie with a gap-toothed grin. "I'll nip round to the store in North Street. It won't take more'n a minute."

Lizzie went to take her purse from the reticule hanging from her wrist, but Frank forestalled her, leaning over to pull some coins from his breeches pocket and handing them to the boy.

When he had gone from the room he continued, "As for you getting yourself back, Sam here can take you in the trap."

"But what if I'm seen wi' him?"

"What if you are?"

"I told our Tom I wanted the walk."

"You can't walk wi' a twisted ankle, can you now?" observed Sam Reaney. "Who's to know but that I didn't overtake you on the road and out o' kindness of heart take pity on your plight?"

Lizzie's expression lightened.

"You see?" Frank told her, giving her chin a little pinch. "How many times do I have to say it – never worry worry till worry worries you. There's always a bright side to things, my girl, if only you'll trouble to look for it. Now then – " he reached with his free hand inside his jacket – "I promised you some'at, didn't I, if I won that fight?"

She nodded.

"Here you are, then."

He opened his hand. On the palm lay a small box of blue velvet.

Lizzie's dark eyes widened.

"Well, go on . . . open it," he urged, impatient to see her reaction.

Within the box lay a small piece of silver jewelery attached to a fine chain. Lizzie took it out.

"Oh . . . it's a drop!"

She held it up to the daylight, enchanted. Mounted under crystal on a piece of mother-of-pearl no larger than her nail, was a tiny sprig of white heather tied with a thread of ribbon. She turned the drop over. The back had been made from an old silver threepenny piece.

"That's for luck," said Frank. "I got it from a gipsy. D'you like it?"

The pleasure in her young face was answer enough.

Reaching up, he undid the top buttons of her frill-necked blouse, intending to fasten the chain round her neck; then hesitated, seeing she already wore something and remembering that it was a gold cross given as a marriage gift, she had told him, by her husband. He fingered the delicate catch; then, deliberately, gave it a sudden twist so that it broke.

"Oh, that's a pity," he said, drawing out the cross on its parted chain and dangling it in the air. "Just as well you've got this other to wear in its place."

123

Lizzie said nothing; only looked at him and gave a little smile as she took her broken marriage gift and put it away inside the velvet box.

While his wife was thus occupied with her lover, Tom Newbrook was standing less than a hundred yards away in the middle of the market square.

On reflection, he had decided that she should, after all, travel home with him in the cart, and he had brought the vehicle into Midhurst to look for her. There were not many general stores and if he visited each in turn to ask whether a young woman had been in to purchase sugar and pins, then he would know whether or not Lizzie had already passed through the town.

Having tried two of the stores without success, he had walked down to the one in North Street, and had been followed in at the door by a slightly built youth whom he recognised at once as the lad acting as Frank Flynn's bottle-holder at the fight on Waller's Common. Noticing that he seemed in a hurry, Newbrook nodded for him to be served first.

"A packet o' pins, please, missus," Charlie told the woman at the counter. "Steel pins."

Newbrook glanced at him.

"An' a bag o' sugar."

The glance became fixed.

"What kind o' sugar, love?" the woman wanted to know.

Charlie shrugged. "Dunno. The lady didn't say. Pins an' a bag o' sugar was all she told me."

"Well, I'll gi' you the coarse, and if it ain't what she wants, you bring it back directly and I'll change it for t'other."

Deftly she rolled a square of blue paper into a cornet and poured in the measure of sugar, tucking down the flap to form a lid.

Charlie paid for his purchases and left the store.

"Now, sir – "

The woman turned to serve Tom Newbrook; but he was already moving away towards the door, quite certain in his mind that it must have been Lizzie who sent the lad on this errand, and intent on discovering why.

His immediate pursuit was foiled, for he found the door barred by an extremely stout old woman propped on two sticks; and by the time he had stood aside to let her in, young Charlie was already some way across the square.

Newbrook began to run after him between the market stalls, but again his pursuit was impeded, this time by a violet-seller pushing a handcart laden with sweet-smelling bunches of purple flowers. Dodging around the obstacle, he paused in the middle of the square and looked about him; then walked on a short way.

"Have you seen a young lad go by just now?" he enquired of a man smoking a pipe on the corner. "Carrying a blue sugar bag?"

The other removed the stem of the pipe from his mouth and jabbed it to the right.

"Aye, he's gone in The Eclipse."

Newbrook thanked him and continued quickly on.

Failing to see any sign of Lizzie in the public rooms of the house, he went round the side of the building into the stable yard and looked in through the open windows at the rear.

So it was that he found his wife, seated on Frank Flynn's knee and holding out her naked foot to be dressed with a yellow silk handkerchief.

13

"Are you calling me a liar?"

Frank Flynn bunched his fists ominously.

"I tell you, we were doing your wife a kindness, that's all. Helping her out."

"Helping yourself out, more like!" Tom Newbrook retorted furiously. "I'm not soft. I've got eyes in my head."

He switched his gaze to his wife. He was not a man easily roused to anger, but the sight of Lizzie lolling in this fellow's lap with her arms about his neck had incensed him beyond words. Rushing from the stable yard into The Eclipse and pushing aside the landlord who tried to stop him, he had burst into the back room to find her being helped to her feet; and the look on her face when she saw him there in the open doorway had been tantamount to an open confession of guilt.

The fact that he found himself out-numbered four to one by Frank Flynn, Reaney, Walsh and young Charlie Palmer had taken some of the fire from his temper. Even so, there had been a heated exchange of words as he demanded to know what they thought they were about, the lot of them; followed by a scuffle with the landlord, telling him to get out before he caused further trouble, and threatening to have him thrown out if he refused to leave quietly.

"I'm not leaving this place till I know what's been going on wi' my wife!" he had retaliated, pulling the man's hand from his arm.

Harry Walsh, sizing up the situation, spoke reassuringly.

"It's all right, Jack. We'll see to this. It's a domestic matter."

His words did little to placate the landlord, but the man had customers waiting and with a doubtful look and a warning to call in the constable if needs be, he left.

Tom Newbrook glared at his wife.

"Now, then – what's all this about, eh? You told me you wanted to come into Midhurst to buy pins and sugar."

"So I did!" Lizzie protested nervously. "Look, here they are – this lad fetched 'em for me."

She threw out a hand towards young Charlie, standing against the wall still holding his purchases.

"I wasn't able to get 'em for myself, Tom. I twisted my ankle coming across the square."

He glanced at the silk-bound foot she held out beneath her raised skirt, and the vertical line between his eyes deepened with suspicion.

"That's right," Frank came in quickly. "She did. We saw her go, didn't we, Sam – saw her go down on the cobbles?

126

Hurt herself bad for a minute. We brought her along here to make her comfortable and sent young Charlie out to the store. That's right, isn't it, Charlie? You went and got them things for her?"

"Aye," said Charlie. "He saw me there, an' all, he did."

Newbrook snatched the packets away. Turning on his wife again, he said aggressively, "So you hurt yourself, did you, Lizzie? Aye, I've seen your foot, so you needn't put that act on. In a hurry, were you?"

"No . . ."

"Meeting somebody, mebbe?"

"No!"

"You were coming across the square when you took a fall and hurt yourself?"

She nodded.

"And these gentlemen, they helped you up and brought you here?"

Another nod.

"Very obliging o' them, wasn't it?"

"Aye."

"That was the reason you were sitting on Mr Flynn's lap wi' your arms thrown round his neck, was it?"

Blood rushed into Lizzie's pale cheeks. She looked down, biting her lip.

"Well?" her husband demanded. "Aren't you going to gi' me an answer?"

The hectoring manner irritated Frank.

"I took her on my lap to make it easier for Harry here," he interrupted. "She needed getting her ankle up for him to bind."

It was a lame-sounding excuse, and he knew it even as he spoke the words.

"You expect me to believe that?"

"I do."

Newbrook made a sound of derision.

"Are you calling me a liar?" Frank asked in a threatening tone. "I tell you, we were doing your wife a kindness, that's all. Helping her out."

"I've got eyes in my head."

127

"Then take the blinkers off 'em! You saw only what you wanted to see."

Newbrook regarded him steadily. "Mebbe." His gaze switched back to Lizzie. "And mebbe not. Whichever way, I don't want to catch you near my wife again. You hear me? You just keep yourself away from her."

"Are you telling me?"

"Aye. I'm telling you."

Ignoring Walsh and Reaney, Newbrook went over to the bench under the window and snatched up Lizzie's reticule. Opening the drawstring, he pushed the two packets inside, then took his wife firmly by the arm.

"Come on. I've had about enough o' this nonsense. I'm taking you home. And you – " turning round to face Frank – "if I find you sniffing round her again, I warn you, there'll be trouble!"

"Is that so?" sneered the other.

"I may not be as handy wi' my fists, Mr Flynn, but I reckon I could hold my own in a fight wi' you any day."

Frank let out a laugh. "I'd kill you."

"Oh – stop it, stop it, the pair o' you!" Lizzie shouted hysterically. "The way you're both talking . . . fighting each other . . . killing . . ."

Her voice broke, her throat swelling painfully on a knot of tears, and pulling her husband's hand away she began to limp clumsily towards the door.

There she paused and looked back.

"All this over a twisted ankle. I wish to God it'd been my neck . . ."

The sounds of the military band playing on the castle green below were deadened by a barrier of high, creeper-clad wall, reducing the strident music to a series of brassy blarings and drum thumps.

Harry Weldrake leaned back, hands thrust into the thigh pockets of his immaculate breeches, and gazed out over the broken lines of the Lewes roofscape towards the sheer, chalky face of the hill which had given name to the district of Cliffe, away on the opposite side of the Ouse valley. The thin sunshine

128

of early April had warmed the air even here high on the castle mound and he had removed his riding jacket and laid it on the rabbit-cropped grass by the wall.

After a time his eyes moved to the bowed head of the girl sitting beside him. She had stopped crying at last. He noticed that the dried tears had left a glaze on her cheeks, lending the smooth skin a strangely unreal glow from the reflected paleness of her blouse. Some of the pins confining the thick coppery hair had come loose and this untidiness gave her appearance a childlike vulnerability which he found vaguely irritating.

It was the first time he had seen Isabelle since her visit at the beginning of the year. He had been away in London, staying as a guest of Adelaide Winter's family at their town house in Bedford Square. On his return, he had found a number of notes from Isabelle asking that they might meet.

He had ignored them.

Twice she had come in person to Tea Garden Lane; but with her brother Frank absent from Lewes, Rosannah had given the girl short shrift, having her virtually turned from the door before Weldrake was even aware she'd called.

He had discovered from Adolphe de Retz that she was staying with Clara and Leopold at the academy until she moved lodgings to start work at a house in Star Street. Work in Star Street meant only one thing to a man of his experience; and he had felt a slight twinge of conscience on acknowledging to himself that he would not lift a hand to prevent the inevitable soiling and souring which such employment would surely bring.

So it was that when he received a final despairing note from Isabelle pleading to see him, however briefly, and swearing she would die if he refused, that touch of conscience prompted him against his better inclination to grant her request.

The remains of Lewes Castle, ruined not by the neglect of time so much as the wholesale carting away of its stonework in a previous century, were both near enough and private enough to make the ideal spot for their rendezvous, providing seclusion from prying eyes and ears.

Isabelle had been waiting for him.

As he led his horse along the greensward and tethered it to a stout branch of the ivy which smothered the ruins, he'd thought what a little charmer she looked in white tuckered blouse and dark skirt, a chip bonnet perched on the rich red hair.

Then she had spoilt the moment by running to throw her arms about his neck and pressing her hot face against his freshly-starched cravat.

"Don't!" he had said sharply, pulling the clinging arms from him and cutting short her babble of gratitude and joy.

Immediately she had been contrite, asking his forgiveness, clumsily trying to explain how she felt at seeing him again, thanking him for coming, asking why he had not answered her earlier notes, pleading with him to show her a little kindness.

It had all been very irritating.

Putting her away from him, he'd removed his riding jacket and gone to seat himself on a low wall.

"Don't – " he said again when she followed, throwing herself at his feet and attempting to press her head against his knee. "If you cannot control yourself better you give me no choice but to leave."

She drew herself apart a little at that and had had to content herself with stroking the sleeve of the discarded jacket.

"You know that I am to be married, don't you?" he said.

She nodded.

"Then you must understand, surely, why I cannot encourage your affections."

"Yes, I understand. You must think me very forward, the way I've been behaving. But I can't help myself."

"Of course you can. You must put me from your mind."

She made no answer, only gave a sad little smile and a shake of the head.

"I cannot encourage you," he said again. "I am betrothed to another. It would be dishonourable for a gentleman of my standing."

"But you do like me?"

"I like you, yes."

"And you consider me pretty?"

"Very pretty."

She commenced stroking the sleeve of his jacket once more.

Quietly she said, "I love you. I loved you the first moment I set eyes on you."

"You must not say such things."

"But it's true. Why shouldn't I say it? You're so handsome, what girl could help but love you?"

"It is hardly any compliment to me to be loved by a foolish young female. And I do wish you would stop pulling at my jacket – your fingers will mark the cloth."

His uncaring tone stung her, and her hand fell still. Biting her lip she looked away.

After a while she said in a low voice, "You don't care for me in the least. It were all a game you played."

"Nonsense. I have just said that I like you."

"Like. What's liking? You like your horse, an' all, I dare say. It's only a word. It doesn't mean nothing."

Her conversation fed his irritation. He got to his feet.

"Oh – oh, you're not going already, are you?" she cried, reaching out.

"There seems little purpose in my staying. You must understand, Isabelle, I cannot reciprocate your feelings. What more is there to be said?"

"Then why did you kiss me, when I meant so little to you?"

He shrugged, recalling the times he had held her, careful always that no one was about to witness the indiscretion: in deserted passageways, or else up on the Downs; and that afternoon spent together at Brighton when her naivety and gauche behaviour had first begun to cloy.

"Men will always kiss women," he answered lightly. "Unless their intentions are serious, it's a forgettable experience."

"And your intentions were never serious, wi' me?"

"Never."

Tears welled in the lovely grey-green eyes. Those moments she had spent in this man's arms had seemed the fulfilment of her dearest and most cherished hopes. Over and over in her

131

imagination she re-lived each precious second, remembering how he smiled when he looked at her, the touch of his hand on her shoulder, and that heady taste of heaven when his mouth had been pressed upon her lips.

And now – suddenly – to grow so cold and distant, as though those blissful moments had never been: his neglect seemed the greatest cruelty she had ever suffered. From being so totally possessed by happiness, she was now plunged into the very depths of misery and believed herself so trapped by grief that life itself seemed hardly worth the living.

Heart-break is always a most painful experience; but when innocence meets that agony for the first time it becomes wellnigh unbearable, and Isabelle, because of her romantic, affectionate nature, was feeling the pain far more than a less sensitive young woman might have done.

She sat hunched, the small head bowed forward on her knees.

"What's to become o' me, then?" she whispered brokenly. "What else am I but a girl in despair . . . real despair? You led me on to think you had an attachment for me . . . and now you put me off . . . Oh, how can you be so cruel and heartless?"

Weldrake reseated himself on the wall, discomfited by her distress.

"Now, listen," he said. "Stop your crying and listen to me for a moment. Surely you must realise the compromising position I would be placed in by any relationship between us? Would you jeopardise my future – my marriage? If you truly love me, as you say, then do as I ask. Put me from your mind. Believe me, it is the wisest thing. Forget me."

"How can I forget you, Harry? You mean all the world to me."

The eyes she raised to him were haunted with misery.

"If I lost you, I don't know what I'd do. I'd kill myself, I swear I would. I'd swallow poison, or – or cut my throat – "

"That's enough of such talk! What happened between us was a passing fancy, nothing more. You must understand that."

He pressed a hand across his brow.

Lord God, what a fool he'd been to saddle himself with this

132

chit. Had he known what a nuisance she would prove herself to be, he would never have gone near her. Suppose she were serious about ending her life? It seemed unlikely; yet on the other hand these silly hysterical creatures so often lacked self-control when their emotions ruled what little sense they had.

If, indeed, she attempted to injure herself, and his name were to be linked in any way with such a sordid business, the ensuing scandal would be the final ruination of him.

Cautiously he said, "Be sensible now, my dear. Consider how much life has still to offer. You are young, and desirable, and your beauty admired by many – no, don't interrupt – hear me out. Have you not thought that your affection might be more worthily bestowed elsewhere? There must be some young man . . . I know for a certainty that our curate Alec Bethway holds you in warm esteem and only needs some little show of encouragement to make his feelings plainer."

"I'd be doing him no service to encourage him."

"Poor fellow, and he waits with such patience for a word of kindness from you! Would you reward him with the wound of your indifference?"

Isabelle shook her head. In a low voice she said, "Mr Bethway's a fine, good man . . . but it's you I'm in love with, not him."

"Being in love is a fickle state of affairs, my dear. One can fall as easily out as one falls in. It's a thing of the moment. True, lasting affection, if it endures, must be nurtured by the friendship of years."

There was a shallowness about the words which made them sound pompous.

"You think I won't love you always? You think it won't break my heart when you're wed to your rich Miss Adelaide Winter? Oh, I can't bear even to think about it . . . you married to another . . . I'd gi' my immortal soul to be in her place!"

The music from the band below on the green swelled suddenly, as if to emphasise her earnestness.

Weldrake raised an eyebrow.

Mistaking the expression for amusement, Isabelle went on more vehemently, "I mean it. God's truth, I mean it. I'd gi' anything to be yours. You don't believe me, do you? You think I'm making it all up. What can I do to show you? Tell me! I'd do whatever you say. I would, truly I would."

"All I ask is that you put me from your mind and find some other – "

"No! No, that's the one thing I won't do."

"Why can't you understand, girl? I want nothing from you. You *must* forget me."

"But you're my life . . . all I live for."

"This is nonsense – "

"It weren't such nonsense when you kissed me. It weren't nonsense when you had your arms round me, saying how much you liked me!"

He shrugged.

"Don't desert me, Harry," she pleaded. "Gi' me something to hope for. If I thought I was never to see you again, there'd be no point in living. Say you'll let us meet again, please . . . please. If not, it'd be kinder to kill me yourself now and put me out o' my misery."

He remained silent; then, after a while, said slowly and carefully, weighing each word, "Perhaps . . . when you remove to Star Street . . . I may visit you there."

"Oh – ! Oh, will you? Will you?" She could hardly believe it. "You promise?"

"I said only perhaps."

"But you will? Mrs Sullivan won't mind. She's such a kind lady."

"Mrs Sullivan?"

"Aye, she's the lady I'm going to work for."

So he was right: it *was* Fanny Sullivan's.

"I asked if she'd object to callers," Isabelle rushed on blithely. "She said she didn't mind in the least – it was nice to have gentlemen visit. The right kind o' gentlemen, that is. Nothing rough, she said. Hers is a respectable house, after all."

Weldrake looked at the young face raised so innocently to him.

"Didn't she explain the kind of work she expects from you?"

"Oh, Mr Dorrits told me all about that. It'll be like the academy, only more private . . . an art appreciation society, I think he said. The work's nothing hard. There's a big room downstairs wi' a platform at the one end, and curtains, for something called tablocks veevants. That's French. Mr Dorrits wrote it down for me."

The ghost of a smile touched Weldrake's lips.

"*Tableaux vivants*," he corrected softly.

"Yes, that's right, that's what he said it was. It means something ever so pretty . . . living pictures. There's me and some other girls Mrs Sullivan employs, we've to stand on this platform in different classic poses for the gentlemen members to do their figure compositions. Mr Dorrits said it was all in very good taste."

The high note of a trumpet raised stridently for the band's finale sounded almost like a jeer.

14

The house in Star Street had had a chequered history. Built in the reign of Queen Anne for a wealthy seed merchant, its fortunes had thereafter declined, afflicted by the falling social standards of subsequent owners. By the end of the eighteenth century the building had been divided up and its once-gracious rooms become lodgings for a shifting tide of short-term tenantry.

There was a brief return to respectability during the Regency when the place became a hotel to cater for the wives and families of the regiments stationed at out-quarters on the Downs near Lewes; but by 1856 it had once again fallen into a state of disrepair, its roof tiles slipped, gutters leaf-choked, mortar crumbling away between the brickwork, broken windows staring sightlessly down the narrow street towards the smoke-smudged basin of the Ouse.

In that year one Michael Sullivan, a tutor-turned-artillery-man recently returned from the bloody shambles of the Crimea, bought the house with the intention of establishing a boarding school for orphans of the late war.

He had not thought to consider, however, that military widows were seldom in a position to pay high fees for the education of their fatherless children, and it was not long before he and his wife Fanny found themselves rather poorer in pocket than they'd intended.

Fees were lowered to attract impecunious boarders, but the penny-pinching soon showed: food which might hardly have been adequate for twenty young mouths was eked out to fill the thirty-odd in the Sullivans' care. Books were purchased at second or even third-hand to be shared between as many young pupils as could be squeezed together behind a single desk. The dormitory accommodation, in the draughty attics of the house, was pitifully bare of any comfort and a breeding ground for bed-bugs; and the building itself was allowed to fall even further into neglect.

In the summer of 1864 there was an outbreak of typhoid fever. It was swiftly contained, but not before it had claimed the lives not only of three of the boarders but of Michael Sullivan himself. The subsequent public inquiry, blaming the insanitary conditions of the school, forced its closure and recommended that the building should be demolished unless Mr Sullivan's widow attended immediately to its repair and renovation.

In the days before she married, Fanny Sullivan had worked in the Liverpool area, whence she had migrated from her native Ireland at the age of thirteen. An attractively vivacious girl, she soon discovered that a well-managed brothel was far preferable to the sweated labour of dossing rooms and alley-ways, and in a short time had made her way into a superior establishment offering its clients a stimulating choice of tasteful entertainment.

Marriage to Michael Sullivan had brought a halt to her rising career in this oldest of professions.

A distant cousin, he had written to her from the regimental quarters near Lewes and she had travelled south to visit; and, finding her kinsman grown to her liking, had stayed to marry. Her husband remained ignorant of the nature of her employment in Liverpool, for she was careful that no word of it ever passed her lips; not even when she failed to produce a single living child from seven pregnancies and he, despairingly, took the blame upon himself because he had once, as a young soldier, consorted with a whore.

Now he was dead of the typhoid fever and Fanny found herself once again thrown upon her own resources.

Reluctant to give up the house in Star Street – its size and discreet position being ideal for her purpose – she used the money from her late husband's estate to meet the cost of repair and then, leaving the place in charge of a caretaker, disappeared for a time back to Liverpool. She returned months later, subtly altered in manner and looking suddenly older than her thirty-nine years, accompanied by several young girls whom she installed at the house.

It was commonly supposed by her acquaintances that Mrs Sullivan intended to resurrect the boarding school as an academy – a belief she did nothing to discourage.

Indeed, as time went by there were still those in the neighbourhood ready to praise the high standards she set her girls, seeing them always so neatly groomed and nicely behaved whenever they appeared in public: praise which gave cynical amusement to the gentlemen who had penetrated beyond the anterooms of her house and knew precisely to what standards those girls had been trained.

Fanny Sullivan liked her "young ladies" to be as fresh and healthy as possible. For this reason she returned periodically to Liverpool to spend several days at the dockside watching the immigrant boats from her native land disgorge their cargo of inexperienced innocents, destined, most of them, for scullerymaids or streetwalkers.

From this human flotsam she would select some of the more likely, and such was her persuasiveness that she seldom returned to Lewes without at least one bold beauty contracted to work for her.

For the first few weeks they would be required to do no more than pose in the *tableaux vivants* which provided part of the downstairs entertainment for Mrs Sullivan's clients, displaying their veiled charms in such scenes as "Venus Surprised at her Toilette" and "A Maiden's Blushes". Then, a while later, they would be promoted to one of the rooms above where cunningly angled mirrors offered the gentlemen a more intimate view of the forms glimpsed so tantalisingly below.

Even should one of the girls prove reluctant to accept such promotion, the terms of her contract bound her to stay in Mrs Sullivan's employment "as a domestic servant or in whatsoever other form of service as shall be deemed to be in accordance with the conditions of this Contract" for a minimum period of one year; and if, despite her indenture, she should be tempted to think of running away, where would she run to, alone in a strange country and with a brogue that would betray her the instant she opened her mouth?

Isabelle Flynn's first evening in Star Street was spent in the narrow, low-ceilinged attic room she was to share with three other girls.

"'Tis to be hoped ye'll soon feel yeself able to look upon me as a mother," Fanny Sullivan had said after showing her the room, "like all my other young ladies. And why not, when the place is so full as it is of affection each for the other."

Isabelle agreed, looking about her. The flame of the oil lamp on the marble-topped washstand by the window shone brightly against the darkened panes, and in the reflected light she observed how tidied and clean the place was kept. Beside each of the four beds a curtain had been draped from the picture-rail to act as a dust preventer for clothing hung beneath, and for smaller garments there were two chests of drawers opposite.

"I'll be very content here, I'm sure," she had said.

"Tomorrow I'll be having ye down below to start work. But for tonight I want no more than for ye to be making yeself at home here."

"I can't tell you how grateful I am to you, ma'am. And to Mr Dorrits, an' all, for putting me in your way."

"Aye, well, 'tis true I would not have taken ye had he not been telling me what a good girl I'd find ye. Just ye do as ye're bid now, be quick and neat and pleasant, and be having a still tongue in your head and ye'll find yeself fitting in with my young ladies fine."

Yet despite her gladness at the good fortune of finding work so near to Harry Weldrake, Isabelle lay in bed that night feeling alone and suddenly homesick for Weatherfield. She had spent the evening hours making the acquaintance of her three room companions, and though they had treated her in a friendly enough fashion she had yet been made to feel a stranger.

The only thing she appeared to have in common with them was the colour of her hair, for each one was a red-head and the four of them together had made a pretty sight in the looking-glass as they brushed one another's hair, Isabelle's own coppery hue contrasting with the lighter russet of Kate and Bridie and the pale auburn of Tess.

She was not to know that their restraint followed a strict warning from Mrs Sullivan that they were not to discuss with the newcomer anything of the business of her establishment. Now, with the lamp extinguished and only a night-light for illumination, Isabelle lay alone listening to their richly accented voices softly reciting together prayers which to her were totally unfamiliar, directed as they were to the Mother of God.

She turned over, feeling somehow ashamed of her own plain petitions. The curtain drape covering her two gowns on the wall had taken on an almost sinister shape in the flickering light, like a slumped body, and the shadows gave it the impression of being about to fall forward across her bed.

From somewhere below came the sound of a man's voice raised to a shout.

"Bitch!"

Bridie, Tess and Kate fell quiet; then, after a few moments, silence re-established itself in the house and the whispering Irish voices once more took up their repetitive rosary prayer hailing Mary, full of grace and blessed among women.

The following morning Bridie Doyle took Isabelle downstairs to the back kitchen to find them something to eat before the day's work began.

"I trust ye've no grand appetite," she remarked, tearing pieces from a soft white loaf and depositing them, with apples and some stale cheese, within the pouch of her apron skirt.

"Ye'll have to scavenge as best ye can until ye've been here awhiles. 'Tis them upstairs who need the feeding, Madame says – "

She broke off hurriedly.

"Here – " thrusting a quart jug at Isabelle. "Away down to the corner wid ye and fetch us some milk. The cow'll be there already. 'Tis a penny for the milkmaid. Ye have the coin by ye?"

On her return, and having broken her fast with the others in their attic room, Isabelle was set to sweeping the stairs, Mrs Sullivan having decided that her small hands were too coarse for the repairing of the flimsy gauze veils used in the *tableaux vivants*.

"To be sure, there's always one or another of us treading on these blessed things," Kate Brophy commented, busy with needle and thread. "Thin as the web of a spider the stuff is, and all that we have to cover our modesty against the indecency of it all."

"Indecency?" Isabelle asked.

Kate looked down. "Sure but I meant nothing by it. 'Tis art, after all, as Madame is ever after telling us, and to be thinking any different shows a mind like a Ballycarra bog-trotter."

She stood up, draping the wide veil over her shapely arms.

"I'm to be Venus tonight, did ye know that? I've to lie on the couch like so – " casting herself down again on the bed and reclining on one elbow.

"And I've to put on a look as though I've just been after seeing a fellow peeping in at me. Tess Connolly is to stand at my side with a basin o' water, and I hope to God she doesn't slop it . . . these veils cling like skin itself when they're wet."

She rolled over on to her back, petticoats carelessly disordered and showing rumpled black stockings.

"Bridie Doyle will be having the mirror to hold before me.

Though to speak truth, she kneels in such a way 'tis her own long face she can be seeing in it."

Isabelle picked up the veil, remembering the heavy, sweat-stained robe she had had to wear for the life study class at the de Retz academy.

"And what's my part to be, d'you know?"

"Oh, ye'll have nothing a while yet. Not till darlin' Tess moves her bed to join the others. Did Madame not say ye're to be filling her place here?"

"Aye, she did mention something of it."

"Well then, ye'll have time to learn the patience of standing still with that blessed basin o' water."

"What do they do – the other girls?" Isabelle asked curiously.

Kate gave her a sidelong look.

"What they're told to do, to be sure. No more and no less. Ye'll be after finding that out for yeself . . ."

She jumped up from the bed and clapped her hands.

"Now away with ye, before Madame comes in to find us idling!"

There was no time for idleness during the days that followed.

Isabelle did not resent the menial tasks allotted her, having been raised from childhood to domestic work; but there was something about the large old house that affected her sensitive spirits and made her feel constantly uneasy. A depressing atmosphere seemed to cling to the place, particularly in the dimly lit passages that always smelled so heavily of scent and stale cigar smoke.

At times she found herself wondering whether she'd been wise, after all, to come here; wise to have put her signature so readily to that piece of paper of Mrs Sullivan's. Then her thoughts would shift to Harry and his promise to come and see her, turning the doubts into daydreams.

Had it not been for Kate Brophy, always ready to exchange a friendly word, Isabelle would have been quite alone during these first days. Her evenings were spent in virtual confinement in obedience to Mrs Sullivan's request to keep herself to the top floor after the hour of seven; and the girls whom she saw about the place during the day, and took to be boarders or else visiting students of the art appreciation society, passed her with scarcely more than a glance.

Twice she saw Adolphe de Retz at the house, but had no chance of conversation with him.

On both occasions he had been standing a short distance off regarding her at her work, a look on his face as though what he saw amused him vastly; but when she made to move towards him, wanting to ask about Harry Weldrake, he'd deliberately turned on his heel and walked away.

On the morning of the fourth day at Star Street, Kate Brophy went with her to fetch the milk.

The pale grey of the dawn sky above the rooftops was suffused in the east with pink and there was a softness in the air that promised a fine spring day to come. Cocks were crowing in neighbourhood gardens, competing with the monotonous bark of a kennelled dog, and in one of the adjacent streets a fish-seller was already crying his "Fish-o! All fresh-o!" to advertise yesterday's catch.

The milch cow had been led from her pasture by the Pelbrook and tethered on the corner of Star Street, where several women were waiting with jugs and cans. Opposite, observing them, stood a young man in a dark frock-coat.

As Isabelle and Kate came along together he glanced in their direction; then looked again, more intently, and the next moment moved quickly towards them.

"Miss Flynn!"

His sudden call, amplified by the tall houses crowding either side of the narrow street, made the waiting women turn to stare over their shoulders.

Isabelle paused, recognising the young man as Alec Bethway. In the early morning light his unshaven face looked thinner than when she had last seen him and there were lines of tiredness about the eyes.

He came up to her, removing his hat, and reached out a hand to take her arm.

In an agitated voice he said, "Thank God I've found you at last! I've been searching for you everywhere. I've been almost at my wits end wondering what had become of you."

142

"There was no need to worry yourself about me," Isabelle said at once.

"But it's been the best part of a month since I last had word from you! Where on earth have you been hiding yourself?"

He glanced at Kate Brophy.

Kate looked demurely back.

"I must speak with you, Belle," he went on urgently, tightening his hold on her arm. "Will your friend excuse us for a while?"

"We're not supposed to be talking with gentlemen in the street," Kate told him pertly. "Madame is terrible particular about that. Do ye want to be getting us poor girls into trouble, sir?"

Alec looked at her again, and frowned.

"But seeing as how ye're a minister," the Irish girl added, eyeing the white bands of his collar, "sure, 'tis a different matter entirely, so I'll leave ye to your little talk while I'm away to fetch the milk."

Taking the jug, she walked on down the street and went to stand where she would have to wait longest for the milkmaid's service.

"Let's go across here –" Alec guided Isabelle to the mouth of a covered alley.

Once within its shelter he said, "I went out to Weatherfield to see you. You'd already left, they told me. De Retz had found you work of some kind here in Lewes. Is that so?"

She nodded.

"But where?" he wanted to know. "I've seen the fellow several times but he refuses to make me a straight answer when I ask where you are. His behaviour is most odd. And twice I've called at his relative's place on School Hill to make enquiries –"

"Oh? When did you come? I was staying wi' them there till Monday last. They never said a word to me you'd been round."

"Obviously I wasn't intended to see you. But why not? Why all this confounded deception and secrecy? You say you were at the academy till Monday. Where are you now?"

Isabelle leaned from the alley and pointed up the street.

"See that house near the top? The one wi' green shutters and the steps to the door? That's where I am. That's Mrs Sullivan's."

The young curate's expression tightened and the lines of fatigue from sleepless nights of worry made him look suddenly older than his years. This area of the town was outside his own parish and therefore not so familiar to him; but he had heard of a woman named Sullivan living in Star Street, and the kind of house she was rumoured to manage.

Harshly he said, "You are employed *there*?"

"Aye."

The young face turned up to his was open and innocent, the eyes holding no trace of guile. During the course of his ministry Alec had come into contact with all manner of unfortunates – vagrants, drunkards, thieves, whores – and experience had already taught him to ignore the duplicity of words and seek for the truth in the expression of the eyes.

Fearful for her, he demanded, "What manner of work do you do?"

"Oh, cleaning an' that. Washing down the passage floors and the stairs. Sweeping the carpets."

Her gaze remained steady.

"But come next week I'll be helping wi' the life study class, same as I did at Mr Leopold's."

Alec had no idea what form such a class might take, but imagined it must be used as a bizarre device to conceal the sordid business transacted on the premises.

He ran a hand through his thick brown hair.

"Do you know what that house is, Belle?" he asked bluntly.

"What it is?"

"The purpose it's used for."

Still her gaze did not waver. "Why . . . it's an academy."

"Is that what they've told you?"

"Yes."

She paused; then went on hesitantly, "Well, Mrs Sullivan didn't call it that by name as such."

"No, nor would she! Belle, you must leave that place."

"Leave? But why should I?"

144

"It's . . ." Dear God, how was he to explain? "It's not a house for any decent girl to be in."

She stared at him.

"Belle, you must get away!" he persisted. "Today. Now. Come with me – Mrs Kenward will find you a bed at the vicarage, I'm sure. Better yet, I'll take you at once to your sister-in-law."

"Rosannah? She wouldn't have me. Besides – " Isabelle flung herself away – "I don't *want* to go from Mrs Sullivan's. It's not hard work, and she pays me well enough. And if it wasn't a nice house, then Harry . . . Mr Weldrake, that is . . . he'd have tried to stop me when I told him I was going there, wouldn't he?"

"Weldrake knows where you are?" Alec stared at her in perplexity.

"Aye. He's promised to call on me, an' all."

Perplexity deepened to dismay. First there had been de Retz's sinister attitude, and now this . . .

The young curate caught Isabelle by the shoulder and gave her a little shake.

"You *must* leave," he repeated, his voice rising. "You don't know what kind of danger you're exposing yourself to by remaining there. Go away from Lewes, I beg of you, Belle. Look, I have some money by me. Take it. It's enough to buy your ticket to your friends at Bonningale."

"What, go to the Bashfords?"

"Yes, the Bashfords. They'll take care of you. I'll come down to the coaching station with you and see you safely away."

She shook her head.

"Harry's promised to come and see me," she repeated stubbornly. "He wouldn't know where to find me at Bonningale."

Then – "Oh, here's Kate back . . . I'll have to go. I know you mean well, Mr Bethway, but I couldn't leave Mrs Sullivan's service even if I wanted to. Not now."

"Why not, in God's name?"

"Because I've signed to stay wi' her for a year."

"Signed what?"

"Kate's calling me – "

145

"Hang Kate! What did you sign?"

"It was some legal paper. A document, something like that."

Before he could detain her further, Isabelle pulled herself away and walked hurriedly from the alley. Reaching Kate Brophy, waiting in the street, she paused and looked back.

"Behopes I'll see you again soon," she called out. "You can visit me, if you'd like to. Mrs Sullivan won't mind."

15

"What an indelicate sermon Mr Bethway preached this morning," remarked Letty Courthope. "One would hardly think fallen women a fit subject on which to address the congregation of All Souls. Really, there are sufficient tawdry sights about the streets to give offence to our eyes without the Church seeking to offend our ears also."

Cicely Mugridge, seated opposite in the Tea Garden Lane drawing-room, hastened to agree.

"Though I thought his reference to Mary Magdalene rather beautiful, didn't you?" she added, looking to Letty's sister Maud for support. "The way he told her story made it sound exactly like one of dear Miss Braddon's little pieces. A woman of the city of Nain who was a sinner, a harlot – "

"That word should not have been used in the pulpit," said Maud Courthope primly. "And I don't like to hear you repeat it, Cicely."

Cicely Mugridge's pale cheeks took on a pinch of colour.

"But dear Mr Bethway made his point so well! Especially when he said how fitting such a wretched creature should become the first penitent, and how it demonstrated Christ's great mercy that he should forgive someone who had so much to be forgiven."

"We have had quite enough sermonising for one Sunday,

thank you," Rosannah interrupted her tartly. She was lying as usual on the day-bed, now moved into the window embrasure to catch the warmth of the spring sun, and was helping herself from a bowl of grapes.

"What was in Mr Bethway's mind to preach so, I cannot think. He was here again only a few days ago, talking on the same unpleasant subject."

"Perhaps he's considering the raising of funds for a home for these unfortunates?" suggested Letty.

Rosannah gave a shrug and bit into another grape.

The curate's visit had concerned her sister-in-law Isabelle: and she had been forced to make it quite plain that the girl was no responsibility of hers, nor of her brother Harry's, and if the silly creature were in moral danger, as he inferred, then he should apply his complaint to Frank. Though when Frank would be in Lewes again she neither knew nor cared: when last she heard from her insufferable husband, he was at the Weatherfield alehouse to arrange ratting contests, or something equally brutish and nasty.

She changed the subject.

"Doctor Leigh came to see me yesterday. It's his opinion I may be carrying a pair of twins."

"Twins?"

"Heavens above . . ."

"Oh, how novel!"

Three pairs of eyes dropped to the child-swollen body whose thickness not even Miss Perrins the dressmaker's clever drapery could now disguise.

"That would account for your great size, would it not," observed Maud Courthope sagely.

"And twins do come earlier," added her sister, "which should be convenient for you, dear."

Neither would dream of repeating in public what they so often discussed in private: that Rosannah's pregnancy had become obvious rather too soon after her marriage and appeared curiously in advance of itself when the declared date of confinement was not until August.

"How many months is it that you're gone?" enquired Letty after a pause.

"Five. Almost six."

From the way the two Courthope girls were looking at her, Rosannah knew they were thinking seven at least, perhaps almost eight. The guess was accurate enough; but never mind. Doctor Leigh's prognostication of twins would soon put a brake on the wagging tongues of society gossips.

The fact that she would be delivered of two babies and not one, with all the attendant perils such a birth involved, was a worry at the back of her mind which she refused to allow herself to dwell too much on for the present: the time for fear would come with the onset of her labour. What was of more immediate concern was finding an extra nursery-maid to assist the wet-nurse who would be breast-feeding the infants.

"Have you thought what names you'll be giving?" Cicely asked. "It seems all the fashion just now to choose ones with a certain gothicky flavour – Roland, Quentin, and the like."

"And very vulgar they are, too, in my opinion," commented Maud. "Why people must burden their offspring with clumsy names copied from Tennyson and Sir Walter Scott, I really can't say. There was one poor little creature – wasn't it you told me, Letty? – recently baptised Ivanhoe Lancelot Galahad."

"Oh, but how imaginative!" Cicely cried.

"But scarcely in good taste. Especially when the family name was Codling."

Rosannah gave an odd laugh.

"Ivanhoe Codling? I'm surprised the minister allowed such a freak," she said, handing Maud the bowl of grapes to put back among the ferns on the chiffonier. "My own preference would be for something slightly more dignified. If one must be swayed by literary influence, why not choose a name that won't bring ridicule on the child. Like Ralph, perhaps. Or Eleanor – "

A knock at the door made her pause and turn her head to see what was wanted.

"Yes, Minnie?"

The little maid gave a bob in the doorway.

"Mr de Retz is here, ma'am."

"Thank you." There was no change in the tone of her voice. "Ask him to come up."

"Now, Rosannah dear, you don't want to tire yourself with too much company," Cicely Mugridge said, jumping from her seat. "Perhaps you'd prefer us to leave you to your little tête-à-tête."

"Not at all." The words were spoken blandly. "There's no need to rush away."

"Well, if you're sure . . ." Cicely made to reseat herself.

"No, it's quite time we made our farewells," Letty Courthope said, taking her firmly by the elbow. "We promised Mr Kenward we'd visit a poor family in Pinwell Street, and we mustn't neglect our charitable duty."

She looked round as Adolphe de Retz entered the drawing-room; and after greetings had been exchanged, went on casually, "Do remember us to your husband, Rosannah. We see him so very infrequently these days."

"Bitch," Rosannah said lightly when the door had closed behind the three. "It's a pity you had to find them here, Dolly."

The Frenchman shrugged.

She smiled at him and held out her arms.

"Not that I care in the least what they think. They seem to regard me as another of their unfortunates to visit out of charity."

He came across to the window embrasure and seated himself beside her on the day-bed, the sunlight picking out the sleek macassar gleam of his blue-black hair.

"Why else did *le bon Dieu* give women the tongues if not to wag?"

Taking her hand, he turned it over and raised the soft palm to his lips, murmuring, "And why else did he give us the hearts, if not to love?"

Rosannah threw her arm about his neck and clung to him.

"Do you love me, Dolly? Truly?"

For reply he covered her upturned face with kisses, on the eyes, the tip of her nose, her mouth, whispering between each caress, "*Je t'aime . . . je t'adore . . . je soupire après toi . . .*"

She moved her face away, and there was a strangely hungry look in her expression.

"But do you *love* me?"

"With all my heart and soul. Each day that passes makes me to love you stronger."

"I'm glad. Oh, I'm glad. It makes me feel so . . . safe."

"Safe?"

"Yes. Protected."

He smiled indulgently. "And you also, *ma chérie*? You love me in return?"

Rosannah leaned forward to press her full mouth hard upon his.

"Always!"

"Then I, as you, am content."

He held her tightly against him, and for a while they were silent, arms entwined, bodies awkwardly separated by the unborn forms which were the only barrier to the completeness of their love.

Then de Retz asked suddenly, "You will not leave me, will you?"

"Leave you?"

"Grow weary of me as before . . . want not to be with me any longer."

"Never – oh, never! I have learnt my lesson. Don't you know that yet?"

"That is the truth?"

"I swear it."

He drew her close again and buried his face in her hair.

"Then listen to me. I must return tomorrow to Paris – no, do not move, *ma douce chérie*. Hear me. It is because of the war since last year with Prussia. A stupid war. *Une folie!* The Empress, she thought to make secure her son's inheritance – and for what? *Eh bien*, now *la France* is a country humiliated. No more an empire, even, since they have removed the little Louis-Napoleon and he comes now to live in England. At Chislehurst in Kent, I read. But no matter. I will not wish to present my compliments to this *ci-devant* emperor however close he comes. His *faux pas* to make the war against Prussia, it has cost my family much business . . .

it takes me from you . . . it makes necessary my return to Paris to give assistance to my father."

"Do you know how long you will be gone?" Rosannah asked dully.

"No. It may be it is for several months."

She raised her head, staring at him, eyes widening, not wanting to believe.

"What – *months*?"

"Do not look so distrait!"

"But to be alone all that time! Oh, no . . . no!"

"There is not the need for us to be parted. Listen to me."

He took both her hands in his and held them tightly.

"I have thought about this well. I have made the decision. You will come with me, Rosannah. It is as we have said already, that we wish to be together. *Alors*, I will take you from this town and make for you a new home in Paris."

"Go away with you, Dolly? Now?" Again there was that unbelieving stare.

"*Mais oui*. It is what I want."

Her gaze fell. "But what about my condition?"

De Retz made a gesture of dismissal.

"It is the child of your body. What is of you is of me also."

They had talked of this before, and he had always assured her that her pregnancy was no impediment to his love; but while never doubting his sincerity, Rosannah had instinctively felt it might be wiser to wait until after the birth before making any move towards a permanent separation from her husband.

"What do you say? You will come with me, yes?" de Retz urged her.

For a time she remained silent, her head bowed, turning over in her mind all the implications of his proposal, desperately wanting to free herself from the shackles of a dying marriage and find fresh happiness in a new life with Dolly; and yet . . .

She looked up at him again.

"Yes, I will come with you. But not immediately. I cannot simply leave . . . abandon everything. You understand that,

151

don't you? My affairs will have to be put in order. I'll need to consult my banker, my solicitor – "

"But then your husband will suspect – *je te demande*!"

"No. It will be done discreetly. Don't worry, Dolly, he'll know nothing. Everything will appear to be as normal until my confinement. After that, as soon as I'm able, I will join you in Paris."

De Retz drew her back into his arms; and had started to speak when he was suddenly interrupted by a knock at the door. There was no time to move away before it opened to admit the maid.

"How dare you enter without permission!" Rosannah cried out furiously. "You knew I had company. What do you mean by not waiting?"

The young girl stood in the doorway, her face reddening under the white lace cap.

"Beg pardon, ma'am, I'm sure. I – I only come up to see if you wanted tea served yet."

"Your mistress will ring the bell when she wishes for tea," de Retz said calmly, rising to his feet as though nothing in the world were amiss.

Minnie bobbed a curtsey.

"Can't keep his hands to hisself even for a minute," she remarked afterwards in the servants' kitchen belowstairs.

"And her – letting herself be mauled about like that! It ain't right, is it, Mr Osborne?"

Osborne, a bent-shouldered individual with thinning grey hair, winked at her across the scrubbed-top table.

"They're all of a piece, them froggies. Females, it's all they ever thinks about."

"Aye, but with her the way she is . . ."

"What's in the blood shows out in the flesh, Minnie. Takes after her mother, does that 'un."

He looked down at his thick rough hands and smiled reminiscently.

"But Miss Rosannah, having him mauling at her . . ."

"Let that husband of her'n catch 'em together at it and there'll be more'n mauling going on. Aye, he'll croak loud enough then, will our Monsewer Froggie. Once Frank's done learning him, he'll be lucky to crawl, let alone hop."

Osborne smiled again at his own crude humour, showing stumps of blackened teeth.

At the further end of the kitchen the short, dumpy figure of Mrs Jenkins the cook emerged from the scullery.

"Behopes it don't come to that, Mr Osborne," she said, wiping her hands on her apron skirt. "Behopes it don't. There's been enough nastiness, one way and t'other, in this house wi'out looking for further."

"You say what you like, but he's bringing it on his own head wi' his warm ways."

"Warm ways . . . 'tis only nature! He's as devoted as a dog to her. Whyever she had to go and marry that Frank Flynn when she could've wed this other, I'll never know."

"She wed Frank on account o' him getting a child on her," Osborne said bluntly. "I've heard him say wi' my own ears it were the only way she could catch him, she were that hot-arsed for him."

Minnie's eyes widened.

"You'll mind your language in my kitchen, if you please, Mr Osborne!" Mrs Jenkins said indignantly.

The manservant shrugged.

"I was no more'n repeating what he did say hisself."

"'Tis no excuse for using such vulgar words afore children."

"Minnie's no child –"

"Indeed I'm not! I'll be fourteen years come August," the girl declared roundly.

Then, as though to stress her precocious maturity – "I overheard some'at upstairs as would astonish you both to know."

"Oh?" Mrs Jenkins, her attention turned to the steaming pans on the kitchen range, glanced over her shoulder. "What was that, then?"

"I don't know as I should tell you."

Silence.

Osborne got up from the table and stretched himself.

"Wouldn't you like to know what it was?" Minnie asked quickly, sensing her moment slipping away.

"Aye."

"Well, then—" She turned herself in her chair to face them both, slipping an arm over the backrest.

"The drawing-room door were open a crack . . . and just afore I went to knock, I overheard Miss Rosannah saying some'at to Mr Dolly, some'at about going away to Paris wi' him after her baby's born."

Osborne exchanged glances with Mrs Jenkins.

"And what then?"

"That's all. Oh, except that Frank—Mr Frank—weren't to know anything of it."

The cook set down her saucepan with a thump, sending sparks showering into the cinders under the fire bars.

"Well! Here's a fine how-d'you-do! Running off wi' him now, is she? Whatever next!"

"God help us, has she no sense o' shame?"

Minnie looked from one to the other, enjoying their consternation.

"You can wipe that smile off your face, my girl," Osborne rounded on her sharply. "It's you who'll be the first to go."

"Go? Go where?"

He jerked a thumb. "Out on the street. If the trollop takes herself off to foreign parts wi' her fancy man, it's us below stairs who'll be the ones to suffer for it. Mr Harry will reduce the household, you'll see."

"Not if he weds Miss Adelaide Winter, he won't."

Osborne made an impatient gesture.

"*If* he weds Miss Winter. That business has been hanging fire too long, to my mind. Besides, I had it from Mr Ambrose Foster's man that it's more'n likely she'd want to stay on in London to live, not remove herself into Sussex."

Minnie's head drooped.

"Be that as it may, he won't be turning me and Mr Jenkins out, surely," said Mrs Jenkins fretfully. "Nigh on thirty years we've been in this household, ever since old Mr Weldrake, God rest his soul, took my Tom on as gardener. And you yourself, Mr Osborne, I mind when you first come here, and that's been a good time back."

"Aye, eighteen years come Christmas."

Minnie's head drooped further. She had counted herself

fortunate to find domestic work with the Weldrakes when her two older sisters, both at home still with their widowed mother, were employed as labour at the iron foundry down by the river. The sight of their dirt-grained hands and broken nails and the sharp metallic smell that always seemed to cling to their hair and skin had caused her to take a smug pride in her own fresh cleanliness.

The thought now of being forced to join them in the heat and grime of the foundry with rats running underfoot and some of the men unable to keep their hands from the bare flesh of the women beneath their sacking skirts, was suddenly too much.

"You reckon Mr Harry'll dismiss me, then?" she asked tremulously.

"Aye, if Miss Rosannah leaves him wi' an empty house."

Minnie burst into noisy sobs.

"Oh – there now. Don't take on so!" Mrs Jenkins put her arms about the thin little shoulders and began rocking the girl back and forth. "There's no need for it, I'm sure. Why, none o' this may ever come to pass . . . 'tis all conjecture."

Shaking his head, Osborne reseated himself and placed his clasped hands on the table.

After a moment he said, "There's one way o' making certain it'll never come to pass. One way o' keeping her upstairs from her shameless folly."

Minnie's sobs turned to hiccoughs.

"Frank's one of us. Now, just supposing," Osborne went on slowly, "just supposing he were somehow to hear o' the business. He's in Weatherfield just now, am I right, Mrs Jenkins? At that alehouse of his'n? Just supposing he were to get a message . . . a letter . . . acquainting him wi' his wife's misdeedious conduct. That'd stop her, don't you reckon?"

Minnie gave a loud sniff.

"But who'd send such a letter?" she asked tearfully. "There's only us as knows."

Osborne smiled.

"Dear Mr Flynn, solicitous of your reputation I write to inform you that your good lady wife in your absence has

155

cuckolded you with a certain foreign personage, further she plans on desertion to set up with him where you wont be able to reach them, I am sir one concerned for your welfare."

The letter, crumpled and torn now where Frank had vented his fury on its brief contents, had the desired result. This revelation of Rosannah's misbehaviour had come at a time when the tide of his fortunes seemed to be turning against him.

His plans to make of the alehouse a sporting venue had been thwarted by the local authorities, who had despatched a group of constables to close his cock-pit and confiscate his baiting equipment; and then struck at him again by revoking his licence for fist-fighting contests after a series of particularly bloody encounters which had ended in near-riots among the spectators.

His own fighting career had fallen into the doldrums since his manager, Boaz Palmer, plainly preferred the management of the alehouse tap-room; and the purses earned from the few bouts Frank himself had arranged had been thin enough to hurt his self-esteem.

That anonymous letter had been the final straw: his mood was savagely close to murder as he lashed his horse mercilessly through the dust of the road to Lewes to confront his pregnant wife with her unfaithfulness.

16

It would never have occurred to Frank Flynn that his reaction to Rosannah's infidelity was grossly hypocritical, since infidelity was something he himself had constantly pursued with Lizzie Newbrook throughout the months of his marriage.

Even had he paused in his anger to give the matter a little consideration, he would have rejected it out of hand. This was an age when men were the undisputed masters of their womenfolk, with powers over them of only slightly less than life and death; and whereas it was perfectly acceptable for a husband to indulge himself outside marriage (provided he behaved circumspectly), for a wife to act in like manner was regarded as outright betrayal of all social and moral decency, an attack upon that most sacrosanct of Victorian values, family unity.

Moreover, Rosannah had pedigree and she had money. Marriage to her had elevated Frank to the ranks of the middle-class, and he was damned if he was going to allow his wife's misconduct to affect his social status. It was her background and breeding he had made his church vows to, not her; it was her background and breeding that had kept him with her once the pleasure of her body palled.

Had Rosannah been some penniless drab, doubtless he would have been heartily glad to see the back of her, despising her as he did; but the point did not arise. She was his wife, his property, she bore his name and his child. She had no right to any existence that was not controlled by her husband.

Frank would have brushed aside the argument that Lizzie Newbrook, by the same token, belonged to another. Lizzie he regarded as his only true wife in the eyes of heaven, and the man she had wed a mere provider of bed and board, a gutless, spiritless poor creature who chose to turn a blind eye to the obvious flaws of his own marriage.

Tom Newbrook had hesitated to pursue the matter of Lizzie's behaviour at the public house in Midhurst where he'd discovered her with Frank Flynn.

He was a man who preferred to let sleeping dogs lie undisturbed; and there was harboured in his mind the fear that he might lose her affection completely were he to keep harping on his suspicions. Better to say no more and avoid further mischief by seeing she was kept well occupied at home.

Since that day in March their life on the farm at Upper Highbury had resumed an even course. With one difference. Whereas before, he had seldom troubled her in their bed,

Newbrook now made a twice-weekly ritual of his conjugal rights; and being a methodical man, he took his pleasure each Wednesday and Saturday night.

It was this very methodicalness which denied success to his efforts and kept his child from being conceived: Lizzie had learnt from Frank a way of guarding herself by using a ball of sheep's wool soaked in vinegar, and always prepared herself with this in advance of her husband's attentions.

If Tom Newbrook noticed the sharp odour permeating his marriage bed he gave it scant thought, being more concerned for the performance of his own body.

His behaviour never varied. Blowing out the candle on the chair beside the bed, he would lie on his back to say his prayers, then turn on to his side, put an arm about Lizzie's waist and kiss her on the cheek. Then his hand would move to her breast and his lips to her mouth; and after a few minutes more he would pull up his nightshirt and shift himself on top of her.

The entire business was so lacking in all that she enjoyed with Frank that Lizzie was left feeling used and humiliated. Finally, after enduring some half dozen or so repetitions, she was resolved the following Wednesday night to endure no more.

Considering they were no further into the year than April, the day had been unnaturally close and even though the dormer in the bedroom had been open, the air felt heavy and stagnant.

"Don't you want the window shutting?" Newbrook asked when he came up.

Lizzie rolled over. "No, leave it."

"I'd best shut it, I think. There's thunder about – the cows are restless. Belikes we'll be in for a storm afore morning."

He moved across the room, bare boards creaking underfoot, the candlelight casting his shadow hugely against white-washed wall and ceiling. There were no curtains at the window: none were ever needed, except in winter to keep out the worst of the cold, for Newbrook, like all countrymen, relied on the morning light to rouse him.

He pulled off his neckerchief and dragged his shirt over his head. The heavy leather belt was unbuckled and his trousers hung over the brass rail at the foot of the bed.

"I swilled myself in the yard."

"Oh."

"Aye. The pumpwater livened me a bit."

Pulling on his nightshirt he climbed into bed and blew out the candle.

After a while Lizzie said sharply, "Don't!" and pushed his hand away.

"What did you do that for? My hands aren't cold."

"I don't want you touching me tonight."

"Why not?"

"I don't fancy it."

"But I'm ready for it."

"Then you'll just have to unready yourself, won't you."

His voice in the darkness took on an angry note.

"What's the matter wi' you? And don't keep pushing me off, neither. I'll fondle you if I wish, I've got the right."

"Mebbe."

For a few minutes they lay side by side in silence. Then Lizzie sat up suddenly.

"If you won't leave me be, I'll go downstairs and sleep in the chair."

"What for?"

"To get some peace . . . I won't be misused against my will."

"It's not misusing you! You've never had cause to complain o' my attentions afore. I've not been like some husbands, at you every night. I've barely laid a finger on you since I wed you."

"Then why start now?"

"It's time we had a child."

Lizzie bit her lip.

"Come on, lay yourself down again," her husband said patiently.

"No."

He pulled himself up and rested against the bedhead.

"Well, tomorrow night, then, seeing you're in a poor mood."

"Not tomorrow night, neither."

His temper quickened again. "No, nor next week, I suppose!"

She made no answer.

"D'you think I enjoy what has to be done?" he asked. "You're like a blasted corpse, for all the response I get from you."

"Then take your pleasure elsewhere, why don't you?"

"I'll not go fathering come-by-chance bastards. I want children born in wedlock. Born of you. You're my wife, it's your bounden duty to give me a child."

"You'll never get one by me, Tom Newbrook."

"Damn it, but I will an' all!"

"No, never. I've seen to it you won't."

He stared at her in the darkness. "What d'you mean — you've seen to it?"

Again, there was no answer.

He leaned across his own side of the bed and fumbled about to re-light the candle, coughing as the acrid fumes of sulphur from the burning match-head caught his throat.

"You've done some'at to yourself?" he demanded hoarsely. "You've been interfering wi' yourself so you won't conceive?"

Lizzie nodded.

Slowly Newbrook said, "I've never yet raised my hand to a woman, but by God I'm tempted now."

She shrugged. "Hitting me won't alter things."

"It might knock some o' that contrariness out o' you! Meddling wi' yourself to cheat nature . . . that's sinful wickedness, that is. Why did you do it?"

No reply.

"Why, Lizzie? You've always liked children well enough. You've always been pleased to have my sister Annie's little 'uns to stop."

He paused; then — "Is it that you're frightened o' giving birth? Is that it?"

"No."

"No? Then what?"

"I don't want any child o' yourn, that's all. So I'd rather you left off pestering me."

160

Goaded by the indifference in her tone, he reached out and seized her by the arm.

"You needn't think you can fool me. It's that Frank Flynn, isn't it? Aye, you may well look away, my girl. I've held my peace these last weeks, but if it's him that's come atween us to make you act so cold, you'd best be honest and say so."

Lizzie pulled her arm back, but he tightened his grip.

"You're hurting me!"

"I'll hurt you still more if I don't have the truth from you."

"Truth about what?"

"That Frank Flynn."

"What about him?"

"What you and him have been getting up to together."

"I told you last time you started on about him – "

"That was all lies."

"You said you believed me."

"I *wanted* to believe you. A man'll swallow anything to save his pride."

Lizzie picked fretfully at the counterpane, the dark hair falling forward and hiding her expression.

He gave her arm a shake. "Come on, let's have it. There *is* some'at atween you and him, isn't there?"

Sullenly she answered, "I'm not saying anything."

"It was him as give that trinket you've taken to wearing, I suppose? In place o' my poor mother's gold cross?"

"The chain broke."

"Never mind that! It was him as gi' you that other thing, weren't it?"

Another shake, rougher this time.

"Aye . . . it was."

"And what you been letting him have in return, eh?"

"Leave go o' me! You're hurting, I tell you."

"You're lucky I don't knock you from pillar to post! Any other husband would, finding his wife's been giving her favours so freely elsewhere."

Lizzie flung the hair back from her face.

"But you're not any other husband, are you? If you'd

161

been more of a man in the past : . . if you'd paid me more attention . . ."

"Oh, so that's it, is it? Just because I've shown a bit o' respect for you, not been mucking about wi' you night after night, you go running off like some bloody bitch on heat to the first man that whistles you – "

"It wasn't like that!"

Newbrook flung her from him and threw aside the bed-clothes.

"I'll kill him when I catch hold of him. I'll knock the living daylight out of him!"

He got out of bed and walked a little way across the room, then swung back to face his wife.

"I can see what's been happening. You made yourself easy bait and he's not been slow to take advantage, helping hisself to all he can get. Well, not any more he won't."

Lizzie burst into tears.

"Aye, you do well to snivel, you faithless madam! I've been too soft wi' you by half, letting you gallivant about the place as you please, fobbing me off wi' your lies and pretences. There's going to be no more o' that. I'll be watching you from now on like a cat wi' a mouse . . ."

He began dragging on his clothes.

". . . and as for that blasted Frank Flynn, bruiser or no, I'll make him sorry he ever so much as heard the name o' Lizzie Newbrook!"

Rosannah screamed again.

It was four o'clock in the morning and she seemed to have been screaming for ever, though it was actually little more than twelve hours since Frank's terrible beating had brought on her labour.

He was out of the house now, forcibly removed by a pair of burly, frock-coated constables called in when the sounds of Rosannah's ill-treatment grew disturbingly loud enough to be heard two floors below in the servants' kitchen.

Strapped down in the handcart normally used to carry violent drunks, he had been taken off to the police station and put to cool his heels in a cell overnight, to face a charge next morning of causing a disturbance of the peace by using threatening behaviour towards members of Her Majesty's Constabulary.

No mention was made on the charge sheet of assault. Wife-battering was regarded purely as a domestic dispute unless evidence was forthcoming of intention to endanger life.

Rosannah was in no state to provide evidence of any kind just now, beyond her ability to suffer. She had been found crawling about the room like a sick animal, barely coherent, her face disfigured from blows; and upon Doctor Leigh being fetched to attend her, had been discovered to be in the early stages of premature labour.

Now she lay in bed, fists clenched on the sheet which the attendant midwife had tucked around her to contain her wilder movements, leaving only the bottom loose to allow the doctor's examinations without exposing more of his patient's nakedness than was decently necessary.

At first the pain had seemed bearable, compared with the throbbing ache of her bruised flesh. But gradually, insidiously, it increased, gripping her a little harder each time it came; seeming to expand in a burning blood-red ball inside her body until, just when she thought she must burst apart with the agony, the ball would shrink again, recede into distance, almost, before slowly beginning its next unbearable expansion.

Chloroform, administered drop by drop on to a pad of cloth covering her mouth and nose, had done little more than dull the sharp needle edge of pain, replacing it with the sensation of drowning in a web of greyness shot through with searing flashes of light.

For short intervals she was aware of the bed, the room, the people with her; the leaden thud of her heart, the hoarse gasp of her breathing, the groans which seemed to come from some huge throat stripped raw by screams.

And then once more would come the merciful suffocation to blanket her senses.

Her labour lasted eighteen hours. At the end of that time Rosannah was delivered of her twin children. A living daughter, and a son, born of her dead.

17

Since that early morning meeting in Star Street with Isabelle, Alec Bethway had been considerably anxious for her well-being. Seeing himself in the role of protector, his first impulse had been to go straight away to the house which the girl, in her innocent naivety, believed to be an academy, and demand of its proprietor that she be released at once from her terms of service.

Then prudence urged caution, and sent the young curate instead to his vicar, Robert Kenward.

After a lengthy consultation he was advised to approach Isabelle's brother, for Mrs Sullivan's sinister deed of contract was not legally binding unless signed by Frank Flynn, as closest relative. Isabelle was not yet twenty-one years of age and was therefore still a minor in the eyes of the law.

Learning that Frank was at Weatherfield, Alec travelled immediately to see him; only to find, on arriving in the village, that he had missed his man by no more than a few hours. Vexed, he spent the night at the rectory as guest of the Reverend Everett Howard; and then, at the rector's urging, reluctantly agreed to stay a further day to participate in the parish's May Day celebrations.

He was standing with Mr Howard and his wife on the edge of the green to watch the children's maypole dance, when a rider came by at a gallop along the verge, spattering the three of them with a shower of mud droplets.

Mr Howard gave a snort of annoyance. Brushing his sleeve with his hand, he motioned in the direction of the departing horseman.

"Fortune has favoured you, Alec, my boy. 'If the hill will not come to Mahomet, Mahomet will go to the hill.' Your diligence is rewarded. As you see, Master Frank has returned to Weatherfield."

After a luncheon which he had not been allowed to refuse, Alec drove his trap to the alehouse. In the three hours or so since his own arrival there Frank had been drinking steadily, and by the time the curate found him he had reached that stage of lucid inebriation when all sense of judgement and proportion had become dangerously distorted.

Entering the taproom, Alec discovered him with his boots up on a settle beside the cold, ash-choked hearth, a half-empty bottle tilted to his mouth. There was no one else in the room except two old shepherds in creamy-grey embroidered smocks, who remained silent and impassive over their pots of husser-and-squencher.

"Good afternoon to you, Mr Flynn."

Alec removed his round black hat and placed it on the counter.

Frank's eyes swivelled towards him. Recognising his visitor, he said belligerently, "You can put that back on your head and get yourself off my premises. And you can say to whoever sent you I'm not finished wi' them yet, not by long chalks I'm not."

The curate remained where he was.

"No one has sent me. I come on no errand but my own."

Frank squinted up at him over the neck of the bottle.

"He thinks he's safe, running off to France. But he's not, you know. I'll get him. I'll deaden his daylights for him, I will. I'll see him inside a cold-meat box if it's the last thing I do."

"We seem to be speaking at cross-purposes –"

"I suppose you've come to whine at me, have you? Tell me I ought never have laid into her? Well, she only got what she asked for, carrying on wi' him behind my back. I only wish I could've found 'em at it, her and that bloody Frenchman . . . I'd have brained 'em both together."

This statement was delivered in a flat monotone which had the effect of increasing its menace.

Alec's expression reflected his sudden unease as he asked, "You are referring to Mrs Flynn? To your wife?"

165

"Aye. Her and that Dolly de Retz, damn them. And you can wipe that silly look off your face! Coming here wi' your snivelling sanctimony when you must've known all along what was going on."

"Nothing was going on that I knew of!"

"Oh, don't gi' me that. You're as thick as gutter mud, the lot o' you. Always round supping cups o' tea in that blasted drawing-room. It wasn't you as wrote the letter, was it?"

"Letter? What letter?"

Frank motioned vaguely with his bottle. "Just a letter I got."

He slumped back against the settle.

Then, suddenly – "You know the bitch has paid me out, don't you? She's dropped a boy. A dead son. My son . . ."

Alec moved from the counter. His hands gripped the back of a chair.

"What? Your wife has had her child? Is that what you're saying?"

"Aye. You could almost say I knocked it out of her."

"Dear God above . . . And the child – the child's dead?"

"The boy is. The other won't last long, neither, so they told me at the station this morning."

He gave a mirthless laugh and slopped more brandy into his mouth. Coughing, he went on, "All I've got out o' that damn' marriage is a sickly useless daughter."

The other could say nothing. The import of what he had just heard made his stomach churn in disgust. How in the name of heaven could such a violent young brute as this be brother to Isabelle . . . Isabelle, that sweet and lovely girl . . .

Frank coughed again. "You tell your friend de Retz it's one more score against him. If he hadn't come sniffing round Rosannah again none o' this would ever have happened."

"Your wife has been delivered of a dead son," Alec said slowly, "because you ill-treated her on discovering some – indiscretion with Adolphe de Retz?"

Frank turned on him, the handsome dark features contorted, guilt fuelling his sullen anger.

"She had him dead to pay me out!"

166

"May God forgive you, that's wicked nonsense, and you know it."

"It's the truth as I see it."

The other thrust aside the chair he had been grasping. Heatedly he said, "Then your conception of truth is woefully amiss. What kind of man do you show yourself to be, to commit violence upon a helpless woman so near her time and then accuse her of deliberately bringing forth a stillborn child? What kind of man do you show yourself to be, sir, leaving her alone in her grief and weakness, to desert her at such a time when it is a husband's duty to be there with his wife to give her strength and encouragement?"

"Damn what kind of man it shows me!" Frank shouted. "I'll have no woman making a fool o' me. Let her look to her blasted Dolly for strength and encouragement, the faithless bitch!"

Alec made a gesture of angry impatience and turned away. For a moment or two he closed his eyes. When he spoke again it was in a more controlled manner.

"Do you plan to return to your wife?"

"What's that to you?"

"She resides within my parish. Her welfare is my concern."

Frank shrugged. Taking another swig from the bottle, he wiped the back of his hand across his mouth.

"I can't go back to her yet," he said after several seconds silence, "even had I a mind to go. I've been warned to stay clear of her for a bit."

"Warned?"

"Aye. The bloody peelers. They let me go this morning wi'out charging me on a condition I keep away from Lewes."

Alec digested this information. Then, to his great disquiet, was suddenly struck by its implications. If Frank Flynn were barred by the town constabulary from returning . . .

"Isabelle!" He spoke her name involuntarily.

"Leave our Belle out of it. She's got nothing to do wi' this business."

"Not with the business of your wife, no. But Isabelle's trouble is as serious – if not more so. It's on her behalf I'm here to see you."

The other's dark eyes fixed themselves upon the curate, comprehension hampered by the liquor fogging his wits.

"Trouble? Our Belle? What trouble?"

"Do you know a house in Star Street? Managed by a woman called Sullivan?"

"Fanny Sullivan? Aye."

"Your sister has been employed by her these past weeks."

Frank's gaze hardened to a stare. He swung his feet down from the settle.

"Employed at Fanny Sullivan's place?"

"Yes."

"But – it's a knocking house!"

Alec was unfamiliar with the term, but grasped its meaning.

"Precisely."

"In God's name . . . what's our Belle doing there? She was lodged at that fancy academy the last I heard, prinking herself up as some dummy."

"She's come to no harm as yet," the other hastened to assure him. "At least, I pray not. But we must act with the utmost speed to get her away as soon as we can."

"De Retz . . ."

Frank rose unsteadily to his feet, supporting himself on the arm of the settle.

"It's de Retz has done this."

"We have no proof of his involvement, Mr Flynn. None at all. Unless – "

Alec wavered, a frown creasing the smooth brow. He suddenly recalled to mind his conversation with Mr Everett Howard the last time he had visited Weatherfield, following the death of Isabelle's mother. Something had been said then about the girl being found employment – what were the rector's words? – "by some young Frenchman she knew."

He looked up. Frank Flynn was staring at him. The expression in the man's eyes caused a chill of alarm.

"You did it together," Frank said thickly. "You and that de Retz. Aye, and Harry Weldrake, an' all. He's always hated me, has Harry . . . never forgiven me for getting atween his sister's bedsheets. It was you lot did this to our Belle – "

"You drunken sot! Do you think I'd be a party to such a

168

thing?" Alec responded angrily. "I, of all men? There's no creature alive more precious to me than Isabelle. Do you imagine I would lend myself to cause her injury? Dear God in heaven, I'd sacrifice everything I had to save her from coming to harm!"

Frank's knuckles, clenched on the bottle neck, showed white.

"Don't you come that wi' me . . . it won't wash. I know what's been happening . . . you an' Weldrake an' that bloody de Retz . . . reckoning to take advantage . . ."

He swayed backwards on his heels and almost lost his balance.

Alec took a deep breath. It was useless trying to talk some sense while the fellow was in this state. He went over and seated himself on a chair at the other side of the empty hearth and leaned forward, hands clasped between his knees. A strand of hair fell into his eyes and he tossed it back.

They were both young men of almost identical age, yet how very differently life had treated them: one born into the respectability of the Church of England, the other working his way up from labouring stock by the useless violence of the prize ring.

After several minutes' reflection, he said slowly and carefully, as though addressing a child, "There is a paper. A document of some kind. Isabelle has signed it – something to do with her terms of service in Star Street, do you follow? The point is, she is under age and so this document has no worth. It isn't binding on her. You understand? There is nothing to keep her employed there."

"Then get her away!" Frank said harshly.

"You must act with me."

"Damn you, don't you listen? I can't go back to Lewes, not inside a month. I'll be in contempt if I do . . . I've no wish t'find myself lodged in a gaol cell . . . if the peelers lock me up . . . I'd be no use t'Belle . . . no, nor my Lizzie, neither . . ."

All the fight seemed to drain away from him. In a voice suddenly thick with weariness he went on, "You bring her home, Mr Bethway . . . bring Belle home . . . don't let them hurt her."

Even as he spoke, the legs went from under him and he fell clumsily against the settle, the bottle still clutched in his hand.

On their bench beside the window the two elderly shepherds maintained an impassive silence, weatherbeaten faces devoid of all expression as they gazed with faded blue eyes into their pots of husser-and-squencher.

The room which Mrs Sullivan liked to describe as her salon had in the days of Queen Anne been the main reception area of the house in Star Street.

Anyone now entering its double doors from the spacious hall beyond might be excused from thinking themselves within the sanctum of some wealthy exclusive fraternity; which was precisely the impression Fanny Sullivan intended.

Flock-papered walls were hung with pictures painted on glass, depicting the female form in assorted classical poses, and the same rich crimson pattern was repeated in the deep Turkey carpets underfoot. Gas brackets shed a roseate glow upon the mahogany sheen of tables and chairs, all turned to face one end of the room where velvet curtains hung from ceiling to floor to conceal a small stage.

Standing there behind them, Isabelle Flynn was nervously aware of an atmosphere of expectancy within the room. There were a dozen or more gentlemen, Bridie Doyle had told her – a good number for a Thursday evening – and a party expected to arrive later in time for the *tableau vivant*.

"'Tis all the way from London, no less, they've travelled," said Bridie, to whom London was the capital city of the world, "so Madame wants us to be giving them a fine night's entertainment."

Earlier in the day, it had seemed very exciting; but now, draped in nothing but the sheerest of fine gauze, Isabelle was beginning to wish herself back in the lonely garret where she had spent so many other evenings since coming to work at Mrs Sullivan's.

This was the first time she had been required to pose. Tess Connolly, whose role in the tableau she was taking, had moved a few days ago from their attic room to join Madame's young ladies on the floor beneath, and Kate Brophy had since been rehearsing her in her part as Venus's water carrier.

In their rehearsals she'd played the part to perfection, and Kate had praised her ability to hold her pose without moving.

"Just ye be remembering now, 'tis a whole bowl of water ye have there in your hands, and I'll not be thanking ye for spilling the cold stuff upon me while we're posing for the gentlemen below."

She had proved herself a sincere friend during these past weeks in the unfamiliar surroundings of Star Street. Of the three red-haired Irish girls with whom Isabelle shared the garret, Kate Brophy alone had shown her genuine affection and interest; and her ready wit and spontaneous acts of kindness had more than once lightened the dark times of home-sickness.

One early evening alone together, the Irish girl had confided some of her own fears.

"I'm not entirely happy in this place," she had said. "I miss the old country. Though to be sure, it was no comfort to be caring for six brothers and know I was planned for feeding them bread and broth till the last of them married. And what was I to be fitted for then, I ask ye? There was only old Michael Byrne away down the village, and him so bowed in the legs he wasn't after stopping a pig in an alley. What kind of a husband would he be for a healthy young creature?"

"But you could go back to your home, even so," Isabelle told her. "Not the same village, mebbe. I've heard of a city called Dublin there – bigger than Lewes, even. You'd find a situation that'd suit you, surely."

But Kate had only laughed and called her a sweet darling innocent, and sworn in jest to rescue them both from something she called a fate worse even than Michael Byrne.

A voice was raised above the rumble of conversation in the room beyond the closed curtains. Then the sound of men's laughter in response.

Isabelle shivered.

171

Unhappily conscious in her present state of nerves that the line of her breasts showed clearly through the thin material covering them, she fingered the wispy gauze, wishing that Mrs Sullivan had not insisted upon her wearing it quite so immodestly low. Surely it wouldn't matter, since the gentlemen would be viewing her only in profile as she knelt beside Kate's couch with the basin of water?

Beside her, Bridie Doyle hugged the mirror which was to reflect Venus-Kate's alarmed expression as she caught sight of the admirer (invisible) spying upon her toilette. Someone at the side of the stage turned up the gas jets, flooding the small area with yellow light. An acrid aroma of cigar smoke hung on the air.

"Have yeselves ready now," directed Kate, already seated on the painted leopard-skin draped over her couch. "'Tis time we were taking up our poses."

Stretching out her bared legs, she pushed aside the folds of gauze covering her shoulders and settled herself sideways on one elbow, the filmy material falling away to expose her rounded breasts.

"Kate – Kate . . ." Isabelle stared at her.

"D'ye think the gentlemen pay to see us clothed entirely?" the other hissed. "Just ye be holding still with that water!"

She bit her lip and stood aside, the bowl heavy between her hands. Bridie Doyle went down upon one knee, holding the mirror up to Venus. After a few moments the curtains drew apart, moving in a series of quick jerks along the pulley.

Isabelle closed her eyes. She heard a sound, a drawn-out sigh that was not quite a groan, as though the waiting audience had released its breath in a single exhalation of pleasure.

"Ye're spilling the water," Bridie muttered between teeth clenched rigidly on a smile.

She steadied herself and opened her eyes again, turning her head a fraction to see out into the room. The contrast between the bright stage lights and the subdued glow beyond made it impossible to pick out anything but the smoke-wreathed outlines of seated figures.

She looked down.

172

At the nearest table three men were leaning back in their chairs, faces turned up towards her; and one of them was Harry Weldrake.

Weldrake had been staying as a guest of the Winters when, on the eve of his official engagement to Adelaide Winter, he received news sent post-haste from Lewes of his sister's confinement. The tone of the message was urgent enough to warrant his immediate return, travelling by railway that he might arrive the quicker.

He had found Rosannah weak and very distressed and still bearing the vivid bruises of her husband's violence. Though barely coherent from the effects of her gruelling labour, she was able to whisper a halting account of what had happened.

Weldrake's anger was coldly, frighteningly, intense.

The surviving infant had been removed to the nursery along the corridor. He visited it briefly, watching with distaste as it suckled weakly at the wet-nurse's breast. Aimée. That was the name Rosannah wished for it since Adolphe de Retz, in bidding her farewell, had referred to the unborn child as *la petite aimée* – the tiny beloved.

The milky blue eyes and pale wisps of down promised a fair-skinned child should it survive. Thank God, at least the sickly creature bore no trace of its wretched father. The other infant, the dead boy, had been the image of him, they said, all covered in black hair like a little monkey.

Weldrake would very much have liked to have Frank Flynn tied up in the privacy of his stables and methodically flogged to a bloodied pulp at the end of a rope. But the coward had fled, so Osborne informed him, with his tail between his legs back to the village midden he had come from.

But (Osborne again) there was his young sister, still in Star Street.

Only a week or so past, Weldrake had been discussing the girl with his friend de Retz and had been cynically amused to learn of the Frenchman's reason for placing her there, to pay out her brother.

Now Dolly had had to leave Lewes, his "cold dish of revenge" only half-consumed. A pity to waste it, decided Harry Weldrake. It was a dish he himself now intended tasting to the full. Any passing interest he may have shown in Isabelle had long since faded to indifference. He had not even troubled to avail himself of her sweet young charms, tempting though they were, not with his engagement to Adelaide Winter so near.

But honour now demanded that Frank Flynn's ill-usage of Rosannah must not be allowed to go unpunished; and what could be more aptly fitting than that a brother should avenge his sister's wrong upon the sister of her wrongdoer?

18

Often, during their conversations together, Isabelle had spoken to Kate Brophy about her unrequited affection for Harry Weldrake. Kate had listened sympathetically, while urging caution. Though they were of the same age, life at Star Street had made her wiser by far in the ways of the world than the girl she had befriended, and she recognised only too well what kind of "handsome young gentleman" this Weldrake might prove to be.

Her repeated warnings had fallen upon deaf ears. And now he was here among Mrs Sullivan's visitors, confirming her judgement.

"He's come to see me at last, like he promised he would," Isabelle said breathlessly when the tableau performance was finished. "Didn't I tell you, Kate? He swore when last we met he'd come soon as ever he had chance, and now he has!"

There was an edgy nervousness to her excitement.

Bridie Doyle, putting her head in at the door of the little anteroom leading to the stage, said, "Madame wants ye up directly, Belle Flynn. Ye're to go as ye are, she says, and not to keep the gentleman waiting."

"Which room?" Kate asked quickly, before Isabelle could answer.

Bridie smirked. "She's in luck the night. 'Tis the one at the end. Number seven."

Room number seven, at the far end of the first-floor corridor, had been furnished for the use of those gentlemen able to take their pleasure without the need of any other stimulation than a good firm bed and a willing girl. There was nothing here to suggest anything more than the cosily intimate boudoir of a young lady.

Visitors whose enjoyment needed to be encouraged by unnatural means would be directed to rooms two or three, where cunningly angled mirrors offered unlimited view of the proceedings; or else to room one – known among Mrs Sullivan's young ladies as "the black hole" – where every possible surface including the bed was so hung with the sombre hue of mourning that the place resembled a funeral parlour.

The remaining rooms were not dissimilar to that in which Isabelle was to spend her fateful evening with Harry Weldrake, except that one of them contained a wardrobe full of feminine garments for temporary guests whose chief source of pleasure was to be had in attiring themselves in lace-trimmed drawers, petticoats and tightly laced corsets.

Those whose gratification could only be gained from the sharp edge of pain were accommodated in a chamber in the basement at the back of the house, where their muffled shrieks would not disturb the neighbours.

Isabelle stood outside the closed door of room seven, a hand on the brass knob, the other still clasped tightly in Kate's.

She was aware how much her naked limbs were trembling beneath the diaphanous wrap, how dry her throat had grown, at the prospect of being alone in private with Harry Weldrake. This moment was the culmination of all the hopes and dreams and wishes she had nursed since first seeing him at Frank and Rosannah's wedding . . . how strange, then, that she found herself now longing suddenly to be able to walk away from that door and what was waiting for her beyond.

Recently there had begun to grow in Isabelle's mind a strange fancy that the house in Star Street was not what it seemed, that what she had so readily accepted for the truth was in reality all a pretence. Her doubts had been fed by snatches of overheard conversation, sentences broken off or subjects hurriedly changed when she entered a room; an uneasy feeling that she was being deliberately misled for some reason.

If this place were a real academy, why did she never see any of Mrs Sullivan's lady boarders engaged in the pursuit of their studies? Not once had she so much as noticed a single sketch-book, nor anywhere about the house caught the distinctive odours of turpentine and oil which clung so persistently wherever paint was used.

And if the *tableau vivant* in which she had just played her part were in truth for the artistic appreciation of Madame's gentlemen visitors, why had there been such a tense and hungry atmosphere in that room below?

Her hand dropped from the doorknob and she turned and flung her arm about Kate's neck.

"Remember ye love him," Kate said abruptly, pushing her away. "It'll make it easier."

"But . . . I'm not so sure any more . . ."

"I'll be in the back scullery if ye're needing me after."

For a long moment the two looked at one another; then the Irish girl swung round and walked quickly away down the dimly lit corridor.

Isabelle bit her lip nervously.

"I trust you don't intend I should spend the entire evening waiting here for you?" The door was opened before she could summon fresh courage to turn the knob. Harry Weldrake stood outlined against the soft yellow gaslight beyond.

Isabelle cast one last despairing glance after her friend.

"No. I'm sorry . . ." She felt timorous, fearful almost.

"Apologies so soon? Do come inside, my dear, before you catch your death of cold from a draught."

176

He held the door wider and she moved reluctantly past him into the room.

"Face around. Let me see you."

There was the sound of a key turned in the lock behind her.

"Come, Belle, no need to play the coy maiden with me here, admirable though your performance was tonight. Face around!"

She did as she was bid, taking in the opened wine bottle on a side table, the chaise longue with his evening jacket flung across it, the curtained bed against the wall.

He came towards her and she was conscious of the smell of alcohol and cigar smoke tainting his breath as he leaned down to press his mouth against her bared shoulder. When she tried to draw back he pulled her roughly against him.

"What's the matter? Aren't you pleased I'm here? Isn't it what you've wanted?"

He kissed her hard on the lips.

"Isn't it what you've been begging me for?"

"No!"

This was not how she had imagined being with him in her dreams, not like this, alone in a locked room having him fumble at her half-naked body. This was not the Harry Weldrake she had loved. This was a stranger.

"It was your affection I wanted, Harry . . . your love!"

His laughter silenced her cry.

"Love? Love? Come, dear Belle, that is hardly a word fitted for use in a place such as this."

Miserably she said, "I don't know what it is – this place."

"Of course you don't. You were not intended to know. Oh, but it was not difficult to play that little deception on you, not difficult at all."

"What – what deception?"

"You thought this was some respectable institution for ladies, did you not? No – don't struggle so, I shall kiss you if I wish! What a simpleton you are. Shall I tell you what this place is, my dear? You wish to be enlightened? Very well. It is, among other things, a house of assignation. You don't understand what that means? No, I can see you don't by the dull look upon your face. Come – "

He pulled her by the hand to a chair at the table and seated himself, forcing her down upon his knee.

"Take a glass of wine and I'll explain."

Numbly she watched him fill the glass, too dazed by a growing sense of shock to comprehend quite what he had been saying.

"There. Drink it."

The glass was forced against her mouth, but her throat was so tight it made her choke.

"Swallow it, you stupid girl, not dribble it down yourself! Good. That's better. Now, I will describe precisely what is a house of assignation. Are you attending? It is a place where gentlemen may come to be entertained by a woman of their choice. No, choice is not perhaps the right word. A woman they require to satisfy their necessary appetites. That dull look again? You fail to understand me? Then I see I must resort to demonstration?"

"No! Harry – please – don't!"

Before she could stop him, Weldrake dragged at the gauze. The thin material tore like tissue, exposing her breast. He fastened his mouth on the bare flesh and Isabelle cried out again, pulling at his hair with all her strength.

He shook himself free. Pinioning her against him, he took her chin in his hand and smiled savagely.

"Don't you like my lovemaking? A little rough, maybe? Not quite as you fondly imagined? What did you expect, I wonder – that I should go down on my knees before you and stammer out my devotion like some callow youth? You chose the wrong man, my dear! Gentlemen of my station do not behave like gentlemen with girls of your kind. But then I warned you, did I not? Far better that you'd heeded my advice and bestowed your pretty favours on the Reverend Mr Bethway. What's this now – tears?"

He squeezed her chin cruelly.

"Excellent! The sight of your distress will increase my enjoyment of this evening immensely. For I mean to make you suffer, you know. You will not find me at all the tender lover you had thought."

All this was uttered in a sibilant hiss between clenched

178

teeth; and the expression on that handsome young face was so distorted that it seemed to Isabelle she was staring at some hideous travesty of the man she had so hopelessly adored.

"What have I done . . ." she whispered. "What have I done to you . . . to make you misuse me so . . ."

He kissed her brutally.

"Done? Oh, it's not what *you* have done."

"Then – what?"

He released her chin and leaned back. In a more conversational tone he said, "You have not heard the news? Of the outcome of your brother's recent show of fisticuffs?"

She looked at him, uncomprehending.

"You have not heard?" he repeated more sharply.

She shook her head.

"It makes no difference. A little more wine?"

"No – no."

"But you must. I insist."

He refilled the glass and held it up.

"To Aimée."

Isabelle's bewildered, fearful face provoked a fresh burst of anger.

"To Aimée. Say it, damn you!"

"To – to Amy."

"Good. Now drink. Again. And again."

She obeyed, the tears running unchecked down her cheeks.

"Who is Aimée, you are doubtless wondering? I will tell you. She is your niece. Your niece and mine. Born yesterday. A trifle before time. Hurried into the world by your brother's less than tender use of his fists upon the mother. The name means 'beloved'. Charming, is it not? Though why the brat should be in any way beloved, sired by such a father – "

He stopped; then, after a moment continued viciously, "So you see, my dear Belle, you must forgive me if I'm about to treat you unkindly. There is a certain principle of honour at stake."

She cringed away.

"What . . . what d'you mean to do wi' me?"

"No more than your brother did with my sister. Be consoled that you, at least, are not with child."

"You'll not hurt me, Harry? For God's sake, please don't hurt me. It weren't my fault what Frank's done!"

"Perhaps not. But I mean to make you pay for it, even so. Come – "

Weldrake got to his feet, his arms gripped round the girl's half-naked body.

"Oh, you intend to struggle, do you?" he said between his teeth. "Then I see I must administer a taste of the family medicine!"

The slap was delivered with such force that Isabelle's head jerked backwards. She let out a scream, instantly cut short by a second blow.

There was a moment of numbed paralysis; and then, as he grabbed at her again to throw her down upon the bed, she began to fight back, terror lending her a sudden and unexpected strength.

The tussle was short and violent. As they reeled together about the room Weldrake crashed up against the chair, and in trying to keep his balance, loosened his grip. Breaking free, Isabelle made a snatch at the wine bottle on the table beside her. He lunged for it; and in self-defence she struck out wildly, the thick glass base catching him with a sickening crack across the temple.

Weldrake made an inarticulate sound and half-raised a hand to his head. Then, stunned, crumpled to his knees, swayed for a moment, and slowly toppled face-forward on the carpet.

He lay there quite motionless, a trickle of blood oozing over one cheek.

Sobbing with terror, Isabelle backed away, the bottle dropping from her nerveless fingers. Without taking her eyes from him she felt behind her for the door, her only thought one of instant flight. The key was not in the lock. Oh God, hadn't he put it in one of his pockets? Not the jacket – that had already been discarded on the chaise longue. It must be somewhere on him still.

She moved hesitantly forward again, willing herself to

approach that recumbent figure and kneel beside it, half-faint with the fear that he was only shamming unconsciousness and would suddenly reach out and seize her.

There was no movement. Harry Weldrake lay as though dead.

She clenched her lower lip between her teeth and touched him, running her hand beneath his thigh. Then, finding what she sought, cautiously inserted her fingers into the trouser fob pocket and drew out the key.

In a moment she was on her feet and back at the door, fumbling to unlock it, the knob slipping on the sweat of her palms and refusing to turn.

There was a sudden hoarse groan behind her. Panic-stricken, she wrestled to open the door and, succeeding, threw herself frantically into the corridor and ran down it as fast as she could, heedless of where she was going so long as she could put as much distance between herself and that room.

There were voices on the lower landing, a man and woman talking. Hardly pausing in her flight, Isabelle made towards them, thinking to beg their protection. Then, realising in the next instant that they might turn her over to Mrs Sullivan, hastily checked her steps and turned instead in the direction of the back stairway leading to the garret.

In all that dreadful, deceptive place there was only one person she could trust. Kate Brophy. Kate, who had befriended and protected her. Kate, who might have opened her eyes to the truth had she not been so blind, so besotted with Harry Weldrake. Kate, who had gone with her to room seven, who had told her, "Remember ye love him, it will make it easier."

Love him!

Halfway up the garret stairs Isabelle stumbled to a halt, remembering something else. Of course. Kate Brophy wouldn't be there. She was at the other end of the house, four floors below, keeping a watch for her in the back scullery.

With a cry of despair she flung herself about and began breathlessly retracing her steps.

It was possible to descend all the way to the basement level by this back stairway; but it was steep and unlit and closed off from the corridors by doors at top and bottom. Without a lamp Isabelle had to go slowly, holding fast to the handrail and feeling for each step with her naked foot, her heart pounding its fear and its exhaustion so strongly in her ears that the hammer-thump of blood was all she could hear.

Several times on the way down she trod on something that squirmed and cracked under her weight, for the stairs crawled with cockroaches and beetles, and in that ghostly dimness her revulsion and horror were so intensified that it was all she could do to keep herself from screaming.

Kate Brophy was waiting, as she had promised.

After changing out of her tableau wraps she'd been occupying herself in the scullery scraping carrots, reason enough for her to be there should anyone come through. The sight of Isabelle, appearing suddenly at the open stair door, made her throw aside the scraping knife and spring to her feet.

"Mother o' God — Belle!"

Isabelle ran across and flung herself into the other's arms, giving way to uncontrollable anguish.

"Hush now . . . hush," said Kate softly, holding the trembling body against her and rocking from side to side. "Oh, but there was no need for the devil to tear off the very clothes from your back. Was he not gentle with ye, then?"

Isabelle made no answer.

"Sure, but they're terrible hard creatures, are the men. 'Tis a distressing thing, it is, the first time for a poor girl, yet they never think to be a little kind and easy. Their own quick pleasure, it makes brute beasts of them till they've done."

"He took no pleasure from me," Isabelle wept against her shoulder.

"What's that ye say?"

"Harry Weldrake . . . took no pleasure from me."

She lifted her head, strands of auburn hair stuck to her wet cheeks.

"Oh, Kate . . . Kate. I must get away from this house! Tonight, now, afore he finds me. If he catches me, he'll kill me for sure. I know he will. He don't love me at all . . . not a bit . . ."

182

She burst into fresh sobs.

"He wanted to misuse me, to spite my brother. Oh, I must get away! He's up in that room still . . . lying on the floor. I never meant to hurt him, but oh, I had to stop him hitting me . . ."

"Ye've hurt the gentleman?" Kate looked at her sharply. "What is it ye've done?"

"I . . . I caught him wi' the bottle . . . cut his head."

"Did ye, an' all!"

"He fell down . . . I thought he were dead. Oh, God, what shall I do? What's to become o' me? I thought he loved me . . . I'd never have gone near him tonight if I'd known what he wanted. He talked so strange . . . he hurt me . . . I had to stop him, Kate. Oh, help me, please help me! They'll find him there and come looking for me. Tell me what to do!"

The other took her firmly by the shoulders and pushed her back at arm's length, holding her there.

"I'll help ye. Hush now, stop your noise. I'll help ye, so I will." There was a long pause. "But ye've to promise me something first."

"Anything – oh, anything!"

"We'll get out together, the pair of us. To speak truth, I've no more stomach for this house than ye have yeself. But I'll be needing somewhere to go, Belle, d'ye understand that? I've no people of my own here to shelter me, and 'tis for sure Fanny Sullivan will be having the officers out to fetch me back. I've been thinking, watching for ye here tonight. If we went directly to your young minister friend's house, would ye speak for me and have him find me a place outside the town where I'd be safe from her?"

Isabelle sniffed convulsively, wiping the tears from her face with the back of a hand.

"I'd speak for you . . . I swear I would. Mr Bethway'll find you somewhere. Only for pity's sake, Kate, help me get away from here."

The other looked at her in silence for several moments more; then, her decision made, gave her a little push backwards towards the scullery door.

"I have the plan already – one I was keeping for myself

some day. 'Tis into the coal hole with ye. They'll not think to search there, not till they've looked in every other part of the house. I'll away up and fetch ye something decent to wear, for ye can hardly walk the streets dressed in the few poor rags that ye are."

The coal hole, down a flight of brick steps at the end of the scullery passage, was darker and more unpleasant even than the cockroach-infested stairway; and when Kate returned long minutes later, her lamp sent ruby-eyed vermin scurrying away into corners.

"Oh, don't worry yeself for the rats!" she said breathlessly, thrusting a bundle of clothing into Isabelle's hands.

"The place is in a terrible stir above. Your fine gentleman's taken himself to Mrs Sullivan and is treating his head with best French brandy while Madame swears to have the hide from your back when she finds ye. 'Twas Tess Connolly told me that. She stopped to ask had I seen ye. I wonder I did not blush for the lies I gave her! So make haste now and dress yeself before the silly creature thinks to wonder why I should be taking clothes to the wash-copper this hour o' the night."

While Isabelle fumbled hurriedly with buttons and hooks, Kate carried the lamp over to the foot of the coal shoot and peered up.

"'Tis our best way out, I'm thinking. We'll not be too clean for the taking of it, but we durstn't risk being seen about the house. They'll be watching the doors for sure."

She turned back, the lamp held high.

"Are ye ready, Belle? Aye? Then hold this steady – and pray with me the coal-heaver hasn't set down the cover too tight."

Putting her foot on the first of the metal brackets in the wall of the shoot, Kate started upwards, guided by the lamplight which Isabelle directed from below.

Towards the top she paused and felt about with a hand for the round cast-iron cover sealing the mouth. It was an awkward position to work in; but after several strong thrusts she succeeded in dislodging it, and pushed it aside to clamber out into the alley running behind Star Street.

The night was clear and the light of a full moon washed the backs of the houses in silver.

Giving a quick glance to left and right to make sure no one was about, Kate knelt beside the mouth of the shoot, whispering to Isabelle to leave the lamp on the coal hole floor and follow up after her.

"They'll find it there, no doubt, when they come to look," she laughed softly, reaching a hand to help the other complete the precarious ascent, "and let them make of it what they will. Bad cess to all in that house."

Replacing the shoot cover and seizing Isabelle by the arm, she led her along the alley to the end, where an arched entry opened on to the next street.

During nights of a full moon the gas-lamps were not lit in the town, and the only illumination came from squares of uncurtained windows whose yellow light fell brazenly upon the silvered cobbles.

Keeping well into the shadows, the two girls were able to make their way in safety towards the further end of Lewes; and within less than half an hour of their escape had arrived without any sign of pursuit at the door of All Souls vicarage.

Late though the hour was, Mrs Kenward, the vicar's wife, had taken the two girls in when she heard their plight. Showing them to the study, she sent at once to have her husband's curate told.

Having returned that day from Weatherfield and being fatigued by the journey, Alec Bethway had already retired to bed. The housemaid's insistent knocking roused him. It took only a moment after hearing her message to throw on his clothes again and hasten downstairs to the study.

Seeing Isabelle there, grimy and dishevelled, head bowed in such a dispirited fashion, his heart had leapt into his mouth; and he listened grimly to Kate Brophy's stark account of what had taken place in Star Street.

Not until both girls were refreshed and arrangements made with Mrs Kenward that they should spend what remained of the night there at the vicarage, did he attempt to question Isabelle.

The marks left by Weldrake's blows bore their own mute testimony to the ill-usage she had suffered, and moved Alec to bitter anger. He reproached her for not heeding his advice to go to Bonningale, to her godparents the Bashfords, instead of remaining in Lewes; and when she tearfully reminded him of the document Mrs Sullivan had made her sign, told her bluntly it was not worth the paper it was written on.

"You are under age, Belle! I have here a witnessed testimony from your own parish minister to that effect. The wretched woman would never dare instigate action against you! Nor against you, Miss Brophy. That document was tantamount to selling you into prostitution, if you will forgive my speaking so plainly, and constitutes an offence against the law."

The following afternoon, having sent a message ahead to the Bashfords, Alec accompanied Isabelle to the coaching station and saw her safely started on her journey to Bonningale.

He had readily promised his help to Kate Brophy. After consultation with Mr Kenward, it had been decided to send her to the shelter of the Reverend Everett Howard at Weatherfield, where she would be far enough removed from Lewes to be beyond the reach of Fanny Sullivan.

"It's an ideal arrangement," Alec assured Isabelle when she asked why Kate could not go with her instead. "Mrs Howard, as I learned while staying there, needs a suitable girl to replace a maid at the rectory. Miss Brophy goes with my full recommendation."

He had not intended to mention Harry Weldrake; but at the coaching station, their farewells and promises of letters made, was unable to resist asking her quietly, "I hope your infatuation for Mr Weldrake is cured now, Belle?"

And had been half-gratified, half-wounded to hear her answer, "Aye, it's cured . . . it's finished. Love's a thing for fools. I'll never trust myself wi' another man again."

19

Joel Adams reached inside the rusty wire cage and pulled out the last of the barn rats; then, leaning over the wooden barrier surrounding the ratting pit, flung it by its tail on to the white-painted floor.

"Twenty!" came a concluding chorus of voices from those around.

Most of the rats already in the pit had gathered themselves in a closely packed mound at one end, while a few others, bolder than the rest, ran about the circular space in an aimless fashion, frequently pausing with noses raised and whiskers quivering to sniff the smoke-fumed air.

The number of rats was only slightly less than the number of men who had paid their shilling to watch them die. Farm-workers mostly, crowding beside each other to rest their elbows on top of the pit barrier, their faces shadowed under wide-brimmed hats from the light of lamps hanging from nails in the low roof.

Since the suppression of cock-fighting, ratting had greatly increased in popularity and hardly a week elapsed at the Weatherfield alehouse without contests being held in the wooden shed Frank Flynn had put up on the site of the old orchard.

After the threat of arrest if he allowed illegal prize fights to take place on his property, Frank had lost much interest in the idea of making the alehouse into a sporting venue; and though the occasional sparring match brought in spectators, it lacked the excitement of a proper prize meeting and attracted few supporters outside the immediate neighbourhood. Ratting contests, badger baiting and the like he considered scarcely sport at all, and had tended to leave their supervision in the hands of his erstwhile trainer, Boaz Palmer.

This evening, though, he had come across from the tap-room to watch what promised to be a lively contest, between the dogs of two local farmers, a prize of ten guineas to be given to whichever animal succeeded in killing twenty rats in the fastest time.

The first to go was a fierce-looking little terrier which had been held at the barrier in its owner's arms, shivering with excitement, its eyes fixed intently upon the occupants of the pit.

Boaz Palmer checked his timepiece; and at the command to "chuck him in" the dog was released.

At once it rushed at the mound of rats and seized one in its mouth, giving it a violent shake by the neck. This action was repeated rapidly several times more, to the accompanying shouts of the spectators.

"Dead 'un! Leave it!" cried the owner, beating with his fists upon the barrier wall as the dog paused to sniff at one that lay still kicking in its death throes.

A fresh assault broke up the mound and rats scurried away in every direction, their little thin squeals adding to the noise as the terrier pursued them about the pit.

In a short while the floor was strewn with grey bodies and the owner, well pleased with the performance, jumped in to retrieve his dog.

"Three minutes and forty seconds for Mr Beatup's animal," announced Boaz Palmer above the hubbub of voices.

"A good time, I think you will agree, gentlemen. Mr Lambe will have his work cut out to better that."

The pit was cleared of carcasses and a further twenty victims counted from Joel Adams's cage.

"This next dog is a good 'un, though," Frank Flynn remarked over his shoulder to a man behind, his eyes on the white bull-terrier struggling to be released.

His words proved true, for no sooner was it thrown in than it laid about it in a frenzy, biting the rats so viciously that the white-painted floor was soon flecked with their blood.

Just when it seemed that the prize was already won, one

creature, evading the snapping jaws, fastened its needle-sharp teeth into the dog's nose and hung there tenaciously despite the wild attempts to shake it loose.

This unlooked-for turn of events provoked a fresh hubbub in the small room, with cries of "hi up there!" and "kill 'un!" and not a few cheers for the plucky rat from Farmer Beatup's faction.

The bull-terrier dashed about the pit flailing its tormentor against the walls in an effort to dislodge it; and eventually succeeded, leaving blood dripping down its muzzle. But the setback had used valuable time, and lost it the contest by half a minute.

"The purse goes to Mr Beatup," called Boaz Palmer, indicating the perspiring owner; and, when the noise had abated a little, "Gentlemen, I give you a further prize of guineas to be killed for Thursday next. All comers, provided they be novice dogs. We shall have plenty of sport to offer and a pit o' fresh clean rats."

He put away his timepiece and looked around.

"And now, gentlemen all, if you will give up your minds to drinking there's orders waiting to be taken at the alehouse. Those wanting carcasses may remove what they will from the pit."

There were several who acted on this offer of rat meat to bait their traps. Tying the limp little bodies by the tail, they flung them across their shoulder and went off to join the rest of the company in the ale-room, where the dogs' owners were rinsing out their animals' mouths with peppermint water as a guard against infection, before similarly serving their own throats with porter.

Frank Flynn had remained behind to extinguish the lamps in the shed, and was alone when he came out a while later. The moon, which had been full a week before, was now on the wane and its pallid light gave only faint illumination to the path leading back to the alehouse. Consequently it was not until a voice spoke that he realised someone was standing waiting for him.

"Aye, that's me. I'm Frank Flynn," he said in response. "Who is it wants me?"

A figure moved from the shadows.

"Thomas Newbrook. From Upper Highbury."

"Ah." A pause. "I've been expecting you. Your wife sent a message you were coming."

"I thought she might. She likewise told you my purpose, I hope?"

"She did."

"Then she's saved me breath."

"You'll need it, Mr Newbrook, if you propose raising your fists in any fight wi' me."

There was a note of contemptuous humour in Frank's voice. Lizzie's letter had reached him from her mother's farm at Barkham, warning that her husband had uncovered the truth of their relationship and intended finding him "to offer you violence on account of it".

This had struck Frank as almost comical foolhardiness in the circumstances, and he was inclined to treat the whole business as something of a jest despite Boaz Palmer's urging of caution.

"You've been cuckolding me wi' Lizzie, Mr Flynn. I've had it as fact from her own lips," Tom Newbrook stated bluntly, his face glistening with sweat in the thin moonlight.

"So it's only right I should ask you to gi' me satisfaction. I could've acted different. I could've put a knife atween your ribs while I was standing at the back o' you in there – " he gestured with his head towards the ratting shed – "but that's not my way. I'm a fair-minded man and I like things to be done in fair fashion."

The smile died on Frank's lips.

"You won't find it so easy, killing me."

"Oh, it's not my intention. Leastways, I hope it don't come to that. Killing's not in my nature. A good thrashing, that's all I mean to gi' you."

"The devil you do! And I'm expected to stand and let you?"

"No, Mr Flynn, we'll do the thing properly, wi' others present to see we fight clean. This is no hole and corner affair. I've spoken openly to others o' the matter, so there's witnesses already that I mean to challenge you."

190

"Witnesses, eh? I hope they're backing you to win."

"Belikes they are. I passed through Lewes on my way here, d'you see, thinking to find you at your wife's. My name was no stranger's, as I learned. It seems Lizzie and you have been common knowledge to the house a while or more. But they treated me very civil, did Mr Weldrake and his sister – which is more than I can say for the things they spoke o' you. Oh aye, you needs laugh! Mebbe you don't know it, sir, but there's a one or two there would gi' thanks to see you dead afore your time."

"Is that so?" sneered the other.

Newbrook disregarded him. Stolidly he went on, "So I'm here in a manner o' speaking to settle more debts than my own. The last words your wife spoke to me, such as she was able, she said, 'I'm done wi' him, me and the child both. He can go to the devil for all I care, and the day can't be too soon a-coming'."

Frank shrugged.

"We'll have it finished then, here and now," he said, starting to take off his jacket.

"No, we'll see the thing through properly, Mr Flynn. We'll follow the rules o' the game. I'll be back come the morning at ten o'clock sharp, so mind you're ready for me."

Without another word Tom Newbrook turned on his heels and started away into the darkness.

The other watched him go, debating whether to go after him and give him a short taste of what was to come; then, deciding it might spoil the morrow's entertainment, hitched his jacket back on his shoulders and with a few whistled bars of "Sweet Lemeney" sauntered off towards the ale-house.

"Oh, stop your weeping, do," said Lizzie Newbrook's mother, working vigorously at a lump of floured dough on the kitchen table at Barkham.

"Tom's well within his rights to act as he has, and there's few as would blame him. Behopes he don't get a broken head to add to his woes, that's all I pray."

She sprinkled some water from a basin.

"Hush now, Lizzie. Get on wi' what you're doing and dry your tears. The dough's salted sufficient wi'out you adding more."

Her daughter gave a loud sniff and wiped her wet cheeks with her apron skirt before returning to her kneading.

After a while she said sorrowfully, "It's all my fault. I should never have took up wi' Frank in the first place. But I couldn't help myself, mam . . . I don't know why, but I couldn't help myself."

"Aye, well, we've had it out already. These things do happen," her mother answered patiently.

There was a time before she faded and aged when she, too, had been captured by a pair of dark eyes and a few kind words of flattery. Her husband, God rest him, had suspected nothing of the brief, fierce love she bore another those long summers ago; and she had carried its mark in secret ever since, forgetting nothing, neither the passion nor how tempted she'd been to give up the security of marriage for a few short months of pleasure.

"It's not that I don't understand, Lizzie," she began again, wiping wisps of grey hair from her forehead with the back of a floured hand.

"You must think o' the future, though. Tom's a good man. He's kind and he's considerate. And when you've seen as much o' life as me, you'll know it's suchlike qualities as they as makes a woman's happiness. A handsome face and a handsome manner, they're all very well when you're young. But youth don't last. The things a girl admires in a man at twenty have faded away by forty and it's what he's like beneath as shows then . . . the hasty temper and the tight fist and the roving eye. No, Lizzie, you be advised by me. Give up this other and stay wi' Tom Newbrook. He's dull, mebbe, but you'll never want for aught. And in time, when patience and prayer have mended your heart, you'll look back on all this and thank the good Lord you chose the best o' the two."

"But it's Frank I want, mam!" her daughter burst out. "It's him I love, not Tom. When I'm with him I feel so belonging . . . so complete. It's as if we were always meant to be for one another, him and me. There's some'at atween the two of us that goes so deep, it's – oh, I can't put it in words. I wish to God it hadn't had to end this way. If anything bad happens on a cause o' me, I'll never forgive myself . . . never to my dying day."

"Now we'll keep this a clean contest, gentlemen, if you please," Boaz Palmer announced in a professional manner, looking from Tom Newbrook to Frank Flynn.

"You've both agreed to a fair stand-up fight, and there's me and these few others present to see you keep it that way."

The little trainer gestured towards the four men standing behind by the alehouse wall. One of them, Joel Adams, Newbrook remembered from the previous night at the rat-pit. The three others he recognised as the men who had been in company with his wife at the public house in Midhurst: Harry Walsh, Sam Reaney, and the young lad Charlie Palmer. Hangers-on, every one of them, he thought grimly; toadying to Frank Flynn in return for free beer and lodging. They were hardly likely to prove themselves impartial witnesses.

There was no one else in the alehouse garden. It was too early yet for customers. In the May morning sunlight the place looked shabby and neglected, a few scattered tables and benches, banks of nettles blurring the outline of flower-beds; and over by the ratting shed, mounds of rubble and a dusty chicken-run.

By contrast, the fields beyond the garden wall stretched neat and green beneath a clear-washed sky to the distant wooded horizon.

Newbrook looked back towards the alehouse, flexing the remains of night stiffness from his shoulders. At one of the upper windows a woman stood watching, her face a pale oval behind the glass.

"Shall we make a beginning, gentlemen?" suggested Palmer.

"Aye. Let's have this nonsense over," Frank Flynn said curtly.

Now that he had taken stock of his opponent the contest appeared rather less one-sided than he had thought. Both men were stripped to the waist and Newbrook proved in good condition for a man approaching middle-age, the muscles of his arms and chest rock-firm, hardened by years of working the land. True, he had no skill in the art of fighting, but Frank had grudgingly to warn himself that a well-delivered blow from one of those fists could have him in serious trouble.

Boaz Palmer stepped away.

For a brief moment the two antagonists stood facing each other across the space he had left. Then they closed together; and Tom Newbrook went down almost at once, floored by a right hand to the pit of the stomach.

There was laughter from Joel Adams and the rest.

Grimacing, he hoisted himself back to his feet.

"First point to you, I reckon," he said thickly, raising his fists again.

Frank grinned. Moving in, he shot out a second right hand, but this time the blow was carried on the other's forearm and a quick flurry of punches was exchanged before Newbrook went down once more.

It took him a little longer to get up.

"Stir yourself, now," Frank jeered. "This is only practice. Let's have some fight from you!"

They closed again and in the tense stillness the smack of fist against bare flesh sounded like pistol shots. Countering a jab, Newbrook managed to return a strong punch through the defence, catching his opponent over the heart and winding him badly. He followed up with a second blow; but was then sent staggering back in turn, blood welling from a split lip.

"Better . . ." said Frank, breathing heavily. "But still not good enough."

That blow to the heart had hurt him and he meant to return interest for it. Moving quickly, he landed three fast left-hand jabs to the other's body and then brought up his right in a swinging hook to the chin.

Tom Newbrook seemed to rise into the air on the balls of his feet before crashing over backwards to the hard-packed earth.

"That's done for the beggar!" shouted Harry Walsh enthusiastically, swinging a fist in imitation of the blow.

"Come on now, Frank – finish him!"

Frank showed no response. Finish him he meant to, but not yet; not so easily. He intended administering the full quantum of punishment before he was done with him.

His own body was already marked from the punches the other had landed; but Newbrook presented by far the more pitiable sight as he lay groaning on the ground, blood from the split lip smeared on his chin, one eye starting to close and the flesh of his ribs blotched red with incipient bruising.

Boaz Palmer walked over and made a cursory examination, then moved away again, leaving Newbrook to clamber dizzily to his feet.

The world seemed to be swinging in slow circles . . . sounds around him coming as if from a long distance.

He shook his head to clear his blurred vision and squinted across at his opponent. Then, arms half-raised, advanced unsteadily towards him.

"So you'd thrash me, would you?" Frank goaded him. "Get on with it, then. I'll stand here and let you throw a few at me, just to even things up a bit."

He thrust out his jaw and pointed at it, then dropped his hands to his sides.

It proved an over-confident gesture. Punch-mazed though Tom Newbrook was, he did not lack in courage and tenacity. Sucking in a lungful of air between bloodied lips, he drew back his right arm; and then, suddenly, unleashed it with all the force he had left in him, driving his bunched knuckles into the other's face and splitting the flesh of the cheek to the bone.

Frank Flynn's eyes widened with pain. A split second later he went down, and as he lay there looking up into a sky that had turned as black as ink, heard Newbrook say hoarsely, "I don't think you'll be trying that again."

Frank rolled over on to his side and got slowly up, waving Palmer away. Narrowly he looked his opponent up and down, raised his guard and came forward.

For several minutes the only sound in the alehouse garden was the laboured breathing of the two men as they half-circled warily around each other. There was some light sparring;

then Frank feinted rapidly with his left, blocked a return punch to the head, shifted his weight, and sent the wind whistling from the other's lungs with a piston-rod punch to the midriff.

Newbrook doubled over in two, legs buckling under him, yet somehow managed to stay on his feet. Staggering drunkenly, he half-fell, half-threw himself forward and clasped his assailant round the body. He was immediately attacked with a rain of close blows, but held desperately on, hugging the other to him so that they strained together breast to breast, teeth clenched, eyes staring, in a deadly embrace of blood and sweat.

Then Frank broke away with a stinging crack to the side of the head, followed up with a flurry of quick jabs to the heart.

Newbrook reeled, driving his collapsing muscles to the last ounce of their strength, gamely offering the pathetic defiance of his useless fists against that punishing attack.

Frank danced away; then came in again, knuckles skidding each time they battered at their bloodied target. Blindly the other swung about him in a futile attempt to hold off his attacker, both eyes now swollen to mere slits in the puffed flesh of his face.

"God's sake – !" came a woman's shrill voice above the shouts of the onlookers. "Leave off afore you kill him!"

It was Joel Adams's mother, at the upper window where she had been watching.

Her cry went unheard. Frank was going in to finish it.

Tom Newbrook swayed in front of him, unconscious on his feet almost, arms dangling, a string of red saliva running from his mouth. Slowly, deliberately, Frank placed his right fist into the palm of the left, half-turned, gathered himself, and let fly straight from the shoulder.

The violence of the blow snapped Newbrook's head backwards with force enough, it seemed, to tear it from its neck.

He dropped like a pole-axed ox. For several seconds his body lay twitching convulsively; then there was a final spasm and he rolled on to his side and lay still.

Dashing up, Boaz Palmer knelt to raise the battered head, putting his face close to feel for the warmth of breath. There was none. He laid an ear against the naked, bloody chest and listened intently, motioning to the men now crowding round to keep silent.

Lottie Adams came running across from the alehouse door, her skirts flying.

"Be quick and fetch us a looking-glass!" Palmer snapped up at her.

When she hastily brought one, he held it in front of the swollen mouth, looking in vain for the clouding that betokened life.

"One of you'd best ride for the doctor," said Lottie agitatedly.

The little trainer shook his head and slowly got to his feet.

"A doctor's no use here."

Frank stared at him.

"This man's a dead 'un," Boaz Palmer told him.

20

Lottie Adams had never liked Frank Flynn. He was his father all over again; and every time she looked at him she was reminded of Morgan the stallion leader.

Not that she had known Morgan all that well. She'd only laid eyes on him twice, the first time when she'd met him one Sunday in Lewes and let him seduce her with his flattery and lies, the second when she found she was carrying his child and had gone looking for him to help her in her trouble.

She could have spared herself the journey. His help had amounted to nothing more than a handful of coins, as if she were some common whore he'd been pleasuring himself with; and if it hadn't been for young Jack Adams rescuing her from the gutter almost and making her respectable, her son Joel would have been born a bastard in the workhouse.

No, maybe she hadn't known Frank Morgan well; but

she'd known enough to see the spit of him in the come-by-chance namesake Dinah Flynn had borne. Thank God her Joel was different and took after her own side instead of favouring the father.

Lottie had been very close to young Frank's mother and knew from hard experience what a despair he'd been to her, right up to the day she lay on her deathbed. It was a mercy the poor woman had been spared this at least, to see her own son take the life of an innocent man – and, worse, a man he'd been wronging this past year or more (so Boaz Palmer told her in his cups) by carrying on behind his back with his wife.

Well, Frank Flynn had gone a step too far this time. No use him and Palmer and the others trying to cover up the misdeed, thinking they could get away with it, telling her and Joel that if anyone came enquiring, Mr Newbrook had left the alehouse that day none the worse for wear, when in truth his dead body lay stiffening under a mound of rubble at the back of the ratting shed.

Lottie Adams had no intention of becoming party to such deception. She knew where her duty lay; and it was not in helping the guilty to escape the consequences of their wickedness.

While Frank and his troubled friends sought the sanctuary of the ale-room to blunt the sharpness of panic with beer and brave words, she slipped away with her son and made directly for Weatherfield rectory, going up the holloway and across the top of the hill pastures rather than risk the road.

The door was opened to them by the Howards' new maid, a friendly red-haired Irish girl; and within half an hour of the rector hearing their disconcerting news, the parish constable was on his way out to the alehouse.

When questioned, Frank and Palmer and the three others stuck to their story.

Yes, there had been a fight that morning – no use denying that, when Frank's face carried the proof of it – but none of them had the least idea of Tom Newbrook's present where-abouts. The last they'd seen of him was when he left the place shortly after midday. On horseback, yes. (Newbrook's horse, left tethered by its owner at the side-gate, had already been turned loose and the saddle and pack thrown into a water-logged ditch.)

The constable noted down the answers and departed; but their relief was premature. He was back a short while later with reinforcements and a search in the area of the ratting shed uncovered all the evidence he required to apply to the magistrate at East Grinstead for a warrant for arrest.

In the homely parlour of her godparents' farmhouse at Bonningale, Isabelle re-read Alec Bethway's letter for the dozenth time.

". . . taken before the coroner, your brother charged with the unlawful killing of Mr Newbrook and attempting to pervert the course of justice by concealing the body, and the other, Boaz Palmer, on a similar charge of concealment and with aiding and abetting your brother in the matter of Mr Newbrook's most unfortunate death.

"I am reliably informed of this by your minister, Mr Everett Howard, who was called to attend the hearing as a witness. He has been so good as to acquaint me at once with details . . ."

Dispiritedly she turned the pages, understanding little of the working of a coroner's court and its business of viewing bodies, hearing evidence, the returning of verdicts, and committals for trial.

". . . and upon the jury bringing in their verdict of man-slaughter against your brother, and of the lesser charge of aiding and abetting against Mr Palmer, the inquest was adjourned until after the conclusion of criminal proceedings. It is my painful task to inform you, my dear, that bail being refused him, your brother was ordered to be conveyed to Lewes Gaol, to be held in detention there until the case against him is brought before the county court . . ."

Isabelle laid the letter miserably aside, too low in heart to appreciate the tender sentiments and assurances of support with which Alec had ended it.

"What they going to do wi' our Frank, Aunt Rachael?" she asked yet again. "Will they hang him, d'you suppose?"

Rachael Bashford, sitting with one of the children in her lap, tried to keep the anxious concern from her voice as she answered, "You mustn't let yourself dwell on such thoughts, Belle dear."

"But if he killed that man . . . that Mr Newbrook?"

"It was an accident, surely. It must have been."

"Yes, you keep saying that. But there's so much as needs explaining. Who was he, that poor man? What was he doing fighting wi' Frank? Oh – "

Isabelle flung herself to her feet and began pacing about the room, her restless shadow silhouetted by the afternoon light which streamed in at the windows from the western Downs, burnishing the glow of beeswaxed floorboards and warm mahogany surfaces.

"Mamma," said the small child on her mother's knee, "mamma, why is Belle so sad? Did Ellis do it?"

"No, my pet, it wasn't Ellis."

"Who was it, then, made Belle sad?"

"Oh . . . someone a long, long way away."

"I don't like them."

Her mother gave her a little hug.

"Go and look for Henry to play," she said, lifting the child down.

"I don't like Henry. He pulls my hair."

"Now, Mary . . ."

"He did, he did! I hate him worse'n Ellis even."

Rachael Bashford sighed.

"I'll take her," offered Isabelle, glad of some distraction. "Mebbe a game wi' her might cheer me a bit."

She held out a hand. "Here, Mary – come and show me the house for your dolls that you had for your birthday."

The child caught at the hand and broke at once into a bright chatter as she tugged her away to the nursery.

At five years of age, Mary was the youngest of the six children Rachael had had from her marriage to George Bashford. Her eldest child, posthumously borne to her first husband, the Reverend Esmond Bates, in 1853, was Ellis, who would be eighteen in two months' time. In between came fifteen-year-old George, Richard a year younger, Phyllis who was ten, and eight-year-old Henry, now quite recovered from his Christmas cough.

Of her seven pregnancies, Rachael Bashford had lost only one child, a girl, who had lived no more than three days. She had grieved deeply over that baby, blaming herself for its loss, convinced she was being punished for the many times she had wished Ellis dead; miscarried before his birth or else stillborn.

She could never bring herself to love her eldest son. He had been the fruit of fear and madness, conceived on the last night of his father's life; and as he grew up, it was as though the seed planted in such bitter darkness had somehow been tainted by the father's corruption.

George Bashford, whom Rachael had married at Christmas-time in 1853 when Ellis was five months old, had brought the boy up as his own son. Yet he had always remained a cuckoo in the nest – jealous of his young half-brothers and sisters, possessive of his own belongings, indulging in wild outbursts of temper when thwarted of anything on which he had set his mind.

There had been many occasions when his step-father was forced to chastise him in an effort to correct his character, especially when it manifested itself in vindictive tendencies: never anything open or healthily naughty, but always spiteful and secret and sly.

The boy had shown not the slightest interest in working the farm or engaging himself in outdoor pursuits. Books and learning were his sole passion, and he had excelled so well in his studies at the grammar school in Arundel that he was expected to gain a place at one of the university colleges at Cambridge.

Apart from the honour of the achievement, this was something greatly to be desired, for it would effectively remove him from the Bashford household, and with him the uneasy atmosphere his presence had always generated.

Ellis's future doubtless lay in an academic career. In any case, he had no claim to his step-father's property. When the time came, the farm itself would pass to the eldest Bashford boy, George, who was born to the land and loved it with all his generous young heart.

The other side of the family business, in agricultural machinery, begun some years ago when Mr Bashford gave up the breeding of Shire horses, would eventually be inherited by the second eldest boy, Richard, whose aptitude for engineering was already marked.

Apart from the difficulty of Ellis and the loss of that little child, there had been no other shadow to mar the happiness of their life at Bonningale, Rachael reflected. Her marriage to George Bashford had proved a loving and contented one and she had every reason to thank God for such a husband, remembering in darker moments the strange, tormented man with whom she had briefly shared her life so many years before.

Child-bearing had thickened the once-slender figure and the chestnut hair was touched with grey, but the passing of time had lent serenity to her face and she was lovelier now, at forty, than she had ever been.

Rising gracefully to her feet, she went over to the parlour table with its handsome aspidistra plant and picked up the letter which Isabelle had left lying there.

The name of Alec Bethway was already familiar to her, for there had been several times in the recent months when he had written to her husband to express concern for their god-daughter's welfare.

George Bashford had been very willing to accept the curate's suggestion that she should live permanently with them here.

"But it's a fair old distance between Bonningale and Lewes, and Mr Bethway will be hard put to it if he wants to keep up acquaintance," he had added with good humour.

Certainly, the young minister gave every appearance of being warmly disposed towards Isabelle, Rachel thought, glancing at the final page of his letter.

". . . whatever our troubles may be, we must bow with submission to the will of the Almighty, who alone knows what is the most proper for us. It is this confidence which must be our support under the affliction of these terrible events . . . Dearest girl, you are continually in my thoughts and in my prayers. Be assured, nothing can change the sincerity of my heart and you will always possess my faithful friendship.

"Anxiously awaiting your reply, I have the honour to subscribe myself, yours, most truly, Alex^r Bethway."

A small, sad smile touched Rachael Bashford's lips.

When she had first read the letter aloud, Isabelle had distractedly commented that it was nice of Mr Bethway to concern himself so on her behalf. That she should appear so insensible of his regard was hardly to be wondered at, Rachael thought, when one considered the great unhappiness the girl had been forced to suffer — her mother's death, her deplorable mistreatment in Lewes, and now this dreadful business with Frank.

Love, however, was the kindest and most gentle of healers, as Rachael had learnt for herself. She had no doubt that Alec Bethway's constancy would eventually enkindle an answering response: the more tenderly affection was nurtured, the more stable and wise it would prove with maturity.

She folded the pages thoughtfully away; then, hearing voices out in the hallway, turned.

"George?"

"Aye, it's me, my love."

George Bashford came through into the parlour, young Phyllis and Henry clinging each to an arm and clamouring to know what he had brought them from his visit on business to Tonbridge.

"'I want' doesn't get," their father told them, setting them firmly aside.

He bent to kiss his wife affectionately, glancing briefly at the letter in her hand.

"But if your mother says you've been well-mannered and helpful while I've been away — "

"We have! We have!" Henry declared.

"Indeed, we have," echoed Phyllis. "Haven't we, mamma?"

Rachael gathered them both to her.

"As good as gold."

Mr Bashford's weathered, bearded face warmed into a smile.

"Then I believe I may have brought you something after all."

"Oh – what, pappa? Where?"

For a moment he pretended to forget; then, laughing at their noisy impatience, told them there was a labelled packet for each of them in his riding-coat pocket.

"Now be off, the pair of you. I want to speak to your mother."

He closed the door on them.

When he turned back to Rachael his expression had grown serious. Indicating the letter he said, "You've had the news from Lewes?"

"Yes, from Alec Bethway. You've seen him, then?"

"Aye. I was with him yesterday. He said he'd written. It's a bad business, and no mistake."

"It could hardly be worse."

"How has she taken it?"

"She's very shocked. We all are . . ."

"Poor girl. I knew nothing of it, of course, till I called on Mr Bethway to collect her box of belongings as we'd arranged. He told me there'd been some trouble getting it from that place where she'd been kept. But they let it go in the finish. Threw it out at him in the street, almost."

George Bashford put an arm round his wife's shoulders and led her over to the couch by the window. Outside, in the sunlit garden, Henry was already playing with his new battledore and shuttlecock.

"I tried to see that Harry Weldrake yesterday," he went on, watching his son. "Ask him what he meant by treating Belle as he did. Perhaps it was as well for him he wasn't there – he's gone back to stay in London, they told me. I had a word or two with his sister instead."

"Oh? You saw Frank's wife?"

"Aye. Briefly."

"How did you find her?"

"Poorly still. She's slow to recover from her confinement."

"And the baby?"

"A little scrap of a thing, and ugly as a monkey. But it's thriving."

204

"She knew about Frank . . . about his arrest?"

"Oh, yes. The news is all over Lewes. He'll get no help from her, though. Rosannah may be weak in body still, but the tonguing she gave him – ! I'm afraid that marriage is finished and done with. She'll not have him back, she says, no matter what the outcome of the trial. As soon as she's recovered enough, she'll be leaving Lewes and settling herself and the child elsewhere."

"She told you that?"

"Aye."

Rachael shook her head.

"And there's more to come," her husband continued, seating himself beside her.

"I rode back this morning by way of Coldwaltham – you recall they'd a thresher there I'd talked of looking at? Well, that's by the by. The machine wasn't what I wanted, as it happens. But I thought while I was in the district, I'd call over at Upper Highbury – "

"Upper Highbury? Isn't that where – ?"

"Aye, it's the place that poor devil Newbrook has his farm. I took it in mind to ask after the family's wellbeing."

"That was considerate of you, George." Rachael pressed his hand.

"Well . . ."

He looked away; then, after a pause, went on, "It was a wasted journey, as it turned out. There was nobody there but the foreman. But while I was resting the horse he invited me to take a drink with him, and told me a thing or two. The man had no children, it seems, only a young wife. And she'd been going behind his back a year or more with some other man. The fact was common knowledge to them all. All, that is, but Newbrook himself, and he didn't appear to want to know about it, according to the foreman. Turned a blind eye to her gadding about, belikes in hope she'd come to her senses faster if he kept his peace. At least, that's how the tale goes in Upper Highbury. Then, about a fortnight back, he sent her off to her mother's at Barkham, and a few days after that, told the foreman he was going away himself for a bit, but to expect him back again within the week."

"But he never went back," Rachael said softly.

"No. He didn't."

There was a long silence.

"It was Frank, wasn't it? The man Mrs Newbrook had been seeing?" she forced herself to say at last.

"That's what I heard."

"Dear God . . . And Mrs Newbrook? Is she still with her mother?"

"No, she's gone. Left directly she heard what had happened. Never said where she was going, either. They'd sent from Barkham to know if she'd come back to the farm at all."

"And had she?"

George Bashford shook his head.

"It seems nobody's set eyes on her from that day to this, so the foreman told me. But word's going about that she's made her way to Lewes. To be near Frank."

Rumour, for once, was true.

Lizzie Newbrook had been beside herself with grief and – worse – with guilt when the news of her husband's death and the manner of his dying was broken to her.

Ever since that first meeting with Frank Flynn she had been a woman torn in two, one half of her struggling to keep her head in control of her heart, knowing it was her duty to obey the conventions of respectability and remain a loyal wife to Tom Newbrook; the other half hungering constantly for Frank and too weak to resist the ungovernable passion he aroused in her.

She no longer loved her husband. Cared for him, yes; but nothing deeper than that. Frank had exposed their marriage for what it was – a union between an older man wanting a young wife, and a girl needing direction and security. Such matches were made the world over, but without the vital spark of love they could never grow beyond mutual toleration and force of habit.

There were times when she had pitied Tom with all her heart. And now he was dead, cruelly, uselessly, needlessly dead; and all because of her.

Lizzie's sense of guilt had been so overwhelming that she'd

considered ending her own life, unable to face the knowledge that but for her wilful betrayal of her marriage her husband might yet be alive.

Her conscience-stricken remorse had so tormented her in the dark hours of that first night that she had deliberately left her mother's house and gone down to the farm pond, intending to drown herself.

Instead, she had stood there in the moonlight with the cold water numbing her legs, looking at the distortions of her shadow in the rippled glassy surface and weeping bitterly because as long as Frank was still alive, she too had to live.

Some long while later she returned to the sleeping house and packed what she needed; and then had taken her way eastward in the first pink flush of dawn along the distant, lonely miles to Lewes.

21

Harry Weldrake gazed stonily at the solitaire diamond adorning Adelaide Winter's left hand. It had taken him long hard hours of concentration at the gaming table to raise enough money to buy her that ring; but anything less would not have done. It was necessary that he maintain the pretence of affluence right up to the very moment of their wedding.

The ring flashed in arcs of brilliant light as Miss Winter's long fingers swooped up and down the keys of the pianoforte in the drawing-room of her father's house in Bedford Square. At precisely timed intervals she would give a brisk nod of the head and Weldrake dutifully turned the page of music, his handsome features frozen into a smiling mask.

". . . and I heard it float farther and farther
In sounds more perfect than speech,
Farther than sight can follow,
Farther than soul can reach . . ."

Her voice, too, swooped up and down, cracking a little on the high notes.

". . . and I know that at last my message
Has passed through the golden gate,
So my heart is no longer restless
And I am content . . . and I am content . . . and I am content to wait."

Oh God, let the sacrifice be worth it, Weldrake thought to himself; and the bland smile slipped a fraction.

"That was most exquisitely rendered, my love," he said when the last sobbing note had been wrung of all its pathos and Miss Winter's fingers had fluttered away from the keys to rest in her lap.

She smiled up at him, the pale cheeks colouring at the compliment.

Adelaide Winter had never been an attractive woman, and at thirty-one her features had already lost the softness of youth and acquired an angularity which unfortunately emphasised the long lines of nose and jaw. Her complexion was clear but lacked tone, and was not flattered by an invariable choice in attire of sages and sepias which, with her mousy hair, made her appearance insipidly dull.

Her one good point, she knew, was her eyes, large and grey and expressive; and since her suitors, needing something of which to write in honest praise, had tended to concentrate their poetic efforts solely upon these features, Miss Winter was inclined to make great play with her glances and the fluttering of her eyelashes.

However plain her looks, she had never lacked for proposals of marriage. The eldest child of a City banker, she had been reared amidst all the trappings of wealth and its attendant comforts, and at the age of twenty-one had been provided with an independent income of her own from an uncle's generous legacy.

Adelaide Winter was intelligent enough to entertain no false illusions. She was perfectly aware it was her fortune and not herself which inspired those proposals; and therefore declined them.

"When a woman marries, she exchanges the attention of

many men for the inattention of one," she averred. "I prefer to live as a maiden lady and be reasonably content, than be married and discover myself utterly discontent."

This had always been her view; until she met Harry Weldrake.

He had been introduced by one of her younger brothers, whose leisurely involvement with the racing fraternity, where the name of Weldrake still carried weight, had led him to cultivate the other's friendship.

Miss Winter had been inclined not to trust her brother's new acquaintance when he was first brought to the house, instinctively feeling that a man as handsome and charming and apparently wealthy as this had no need to exercise his attentions on a plain, dull woman who was several years his senior.

Weldrake was prepared to be patient.

During the course of further visits he set himself to discover her personal interests and amusements. Thus armed, he was careful in the course of conversation to keep to those topics which he knew would animate her; and his compliments, when he paid any, were directed rather at her intelligence than at her appearance.

She enjoyed walking; therefore many hours were spent together in the parks of London and its environs. She liked riding. A skilled horseman, he excelled himself in her company. Botany interested her: Kew Gardens saw them often there. She had a passion for music, and in particular German sonatas, so he attended her frequently to the concert halls.

Never, at any time, did Weldrake mention the subject of Miss Winter's money. Instead, he took pains to infer that he was himself in receipt of a comfortable income and that any lady fortunate enough to become his wife could expect to live free from all financial care.

When he (very reluctantly) announced his sister Rosannah's marriage, it was supposed from what he said that her husband was a man of property. Which was truth enough, even if that property amounted to no more than an alehouse in a small Sussex village.

By the end of 1870, Adelaide Winter was deeply and devotedly in love with her constant companion of that year. Her family, too, after some initial reserve, had accepted him; and when Weldrake judged the time was ripe to approach Sir Horace Winter to ask for his daughter's hand in marriage, the answer he received was entirely favourable.

All had gone as smoothly for his schemes as he could have wished.

Then, just as the prize for which he had worked with such assiduous care was ready to drop into his outstretched hand, fate gave one of its sudden contradictory twists.

Frank Flynn had been a painful thorn in Harry Weldrake's side ever since Rosannah, in the blindness of her unnatural passion, had got herself with child by him. He had proved a thorn which obstinately refused to be plucked free, working his way deeper and deeper into the flesh of Weldrake's pride until his presence had become an unbearable irritation.

His ill-breeding, his presumptive manner, his barbarous treatment of his wife, had rubbed salt into the wound; but the worst smart had come from that night at Fanny Sullivan's in Star Street. Weldrake had intended the humiliation of Flynn's young sister to be the cautery of his revenge. Instead, it was he himself who had been made to feel humiliated, and that had exacerbated the sense of injury even further.

Now had come the deepest prick of all, and one which threatened to cause the greatest harm.

So far, the Winters knew nothing of Frank Flynn's arrest. Coroners' inquests, unless there were some special feature of national interest attached, seldom attracted other than local report, and the household was unlikely to see the copy of the *Sussex County Advertiser* which had made the tragedy at Weatherfield a front-page item.

Even so, the trial itself was bound to be carried by the London newspapers, and Weldrake could well imagine Sir Horace Winter's reaction upon learning that his future son-in-law's family bore the foul taint of murder.

He had spent hours debating with himself what course of action he should take: whether it might not stand him in better light to make an open admission of the case at once, washing his hands in public, as it were. Or whether he should remain silent and hope that the trial would not be heard until after his marriage to Adelaide.

Either course carried great risk and Weldrake was still, after almost a fortnight in London, uncertain which to take.

Again, the blue-white blaze of the diamond flashed in the light of the pianoforte candles as Miss Winter reached out her hand for a fresh sheet of music.

"'Be Always Mine', Harry?" she enquired archly, "or do you prefer 'Ah, Would that I could Love Thee Less'?"

"Whichever pleases you, dearest one," he responded, adjusting the mask of his expression.

The devil take Frank Flynn to hell. But not just yet awhile. Fervently as Harry Weldrake desired to see his brother-in-law hanged by the neck, for the sake of his own salvation it seemed he had no choice but to hope for an acquittal.

Lying on her sick-bed in Lewes, Rosannah Flynn hoped otherwise. Hoped and prayed for a verdict of guilty which would set her free to marry Adolphe de Retz.

She could think of little else. Whatever taste for violence she had inherited from her mother was channelled now against her husband, the passion soured to utter loathing.

She would not have thought it possible to feel such hatred. Only a year, a brief year, ago she had been so besottedly infatuated with Frank that she couldn't bear him out of her sight; couldn't bear him near her unless he was touching her, his rough hands upon her skin the most sensual intoxication she had ever known.

The memory of that time now filled her with repugnance and self-disgust.

They had been little better than two animals together: no love, no dignity, no respect; nothing but the slaking of greedy lust as each took their own indulgent pleasure and called it happiness.

The only happiness Frank Flynn could give her now would be by making her a widow.

"Beg pardon, ma'am."

There was a tap at the half-open door.

Rosannah turned her head on the pillow.

"I'm awake, Minnie. What is it?"

"Are you receiving this afternoon, ma'am? Miss Mugridge and the Misses Courthope have called."

"Oh . . . very well, I'll see them for a while."

"Would you like me to open the curtains a way?"

She raised herself weakly on an elbow and nodded.

"It's a lovely day outside," Minnie said from the window. "What a shame you can't go and sit in the garden, ma'am. It'd do you a power o' good 'stead o' being cooped up here indoors. Shall I gi' you the extra pillow for your back?"

"Yes." Rosannah leaned forward. "And my hair – it needs tidying. Is baby home from her walk yet?"

"Mrs Bennett's not long brought her in," the maid replied, fetching silver-backed brush and handmirror from the toilet case on the washstand. Mrs Bennett was the wet-nurse hired to feed Aimée, and for two shillings more a week, took her out with her own infant every afternoon.

"She pushed the perambulator as far as Castle Mound, so she tells me, and sat in the sun on the green to hear the band."

"I hope she didn't let baby get too hot?"

"Oh, no, ma'am. A bit o' fresh air and warm can do the little mite no harm. She'll sleep all the sounder for it. There – " handing her mistress the mirror – "is that to your satisfaction, ma'am?"

"Thank you."

"Will there be anything else you need afore I show the ladies up?"

"Only the wrap for my shoulders. Oh – and bring baby in from the nursery."

"She'll be asleep, ma'am. Mrs Bennett's only this minute put her down."

"I want her with me here. Please fetch her, Minnie."

It was strange, Rosannah reflected, gazing down at the infant lying in her arms, how very much she loved this child, hating its father as she did. Unnatural, almost, to cherish so dearly something which was as much a part of him as of herself and which had cost such terrible suffering to bring into the world.

Yet love and cherish this little life she did, fiercely, jealously, exulting in the feeling of unique possession which motherhood had brought.

It mattered not at all that the child was not pretty. She would grow into a beauty, of that Rosannah was instinctively sure. In a year or two, the pale, sparse hair would have thickened and ripened to her own corn colour, and the milky eyes darkened and the flat monkey nose become small and straight.

Whenever Rosannah held her baby daughter she was overcome by the same tenderness, the same feelings of need and protectiveness and security which her deepening love for Dolly de Retz had stirred. How sweetly precious to share them both together.

A smile touched the drawn features as she whispered to the ugly little scrap in her arms, "You are beautiful, Aimée . . . beautiful."

The other child, the boy, had he survived his birth, would have been a very handsome baby; but he could never, for all his physical favour, have aroused in Rosannah the same measure of affection. Just as Aimée was solely her own, so that boy would always have been Frank's; and as a scapegoat for his father, his young life would almost certainly have been crippled by his mother's hatred.

She did not like to think of his tiny body in its grave in All Souls churchyard. Yet some perverse, macabre impulse sometimes tempted her to imagine the baby flesh and bone, created within the warm darkness of her womb, now mouldering away in the cold unloving darkness of the earth. That little coffin with its shroud-swaddled occupant seemed to symbolise the end not only to life but to so much else: as though there'd been buried with it all the mistakes, the follies and misdeeds of her own past.

"Oooh . . . she's smiling for me!"

Cicely Mugridge poked a finger at Aimée and clucked again.

"'As 'oo another smile for auntie, 'as 'oo?" she cooed.

"She isn't smiling," Rosannah said, irritated. "It's wind that makes her grimace so. And please don't lean over her in that fashion. You'll draw her breath away."

213

"Lord, what a notion!" declared Letty Courthope. "Wherever did you hear that?"

"Mrs Bennett told me."

Letty exchanged a glance with her sister, and both smiled.

"Has Doctor Leigh seen you today?" Maud enquired.

"Yes. This morning."

"And he's pleased with your progress?"

There was a nod. "With baby, too. A period of recuperation abroad in a warmer clime is all we require to restore us both to full health, he says."

"Abroad? Oh, where will you go? Have you thought?"

Rosannah observed the expressions of the two Courthope girls.

"To France," she answered; and saw, as she expected, a sudden sharpening of interest in their eyes.

"Certainly, the weather in France is most beneficial," said Maud at once. "And how convenient that Monsieur de Retz has returned to Paris."

"Most convenient!" echoed her sister. "He will be able to offer his assistance, will he not?"

Weak though she was still, Rosannah's answer was sharp enough to silence this artificially bright chatter.

"It is not my intention to go to Paris! That would be the last place on earth I'd take Aimée, in view of the dreadful things happening. Surely you must have heard of the troubles there?"

"Oh – " cried Maud, "you mean this business of setting up a . . . what are they calling it, Letty? Papa read it out from his newspaper after dinner the other evening. Some political rebellion or other. A commune – was that the word?"

"*The* Commune," her sister corrected. "But I confess I wasn't paying much heed. I never follow any news from France other than the latest mode in gowns."

Tiresome, silly, empty-headed creatures, thought Rosannah wearily. Thank God Dolly had managed to leave Paris while he was still able.

He had written to her on the twenty-third of May from his brother's house a safe distance away, telling her of the worsening conditions within the city since it came under siege from Thiers's troops. Food supplies were rapidly running short and he had heard the people were reduced to such a level of starvation that they were killing dogs and cats, and even hunting vermin from the sewers.

"These are terrible times for us, *chérie*. I cannot ask you to come to me yet, the danger is so great. But patience. I am making the arrangement that you stay a time with the cousin of my brother's wife, at Mirandol le Château in the Dordogne. There it will be very safe for you and *la petite aimée*."

That letter, and the few others Rosannah had received from de Retz, were all she had had to comfort her since he went away. She had read each line so often that she knew every word by heart, and slept with the letters beneath her pillow at night so that she might feel a little closer to him.

"There is always trouble in Paris," Letty Courthope said lightly. "What difference does it make whether a few people are killed every now and again?"

Little more than a week later she would listen, and this time pay heed, as her father read from his newspaper after dinner that on the twenty-ninth of May the Commune had been overthrown, and some twenty thousand Parisians were believed to have perished at the hands of their fellow-countrymen.

Among them was Adolphe de Retz.

He had returned to the city with his brother to ensure that the offices of the family business were not looted by Thiers's victorious troops. It was a foolhardy risk to take. France had learnt from the days of her Revolution that mass arrest and execution was a most effective, albeit bloody, answer to civil disobedience.

Together with innumerable others plucked at random from the streets without regard to age or sex or political affiliation, he had been thrown into one of the already over-flowing, stinking prisons and held there without food or water, protesting his innocence to deaf ears while his brother tried desperately to obtain his release.

To no avail.

On the first day of June, early in the morning, Adolphe de

215

Retz – "dearest Dolly" – was bound and blinded and herded out to take his turn against a bullet-scarred, flesh-spattered wall in Père Lachaise cemetery.

22

Except at night, All Souls church was never locked. A house of God, its doors stood open to any who might wish to enter its peaceful stillness and lay aside for a while the burden of their cares in private prayer and contemplation.

It was the lament of its vicar Robert Kenward, however, that not all who came did so for the easement of their souls.

The disused part of the churchyard had long been a trysting place for lovers, and in inclement weather young couples were apt to take advantage of the poorly lit pews beneath the gallery for the pursuit of devotions more physical than spiritual.

Neither was the quietness always appreciated for its proper purpose. There were some who interpreted too literally the Gospel words "Come unto Me all ye who labour and are heavy burdened and I will give you rest", and caused complaints of disturbance with their snoring, slumbering presence.

Vagrants, too, were inclined to prove a nuisance, tainting the place with a malodorous reek and pestering parishioners for money; but Mr Kenward had been quick to decide that the young woman recently appearing at All Souls each day was no vagrant.

True, there was about her that air of impermanence which he had come to recognise in those who must needs make shift to find themselves a bed at night, yet it seemed she was not there to beg for charity: neither he himself, nor the verger, nor the ladies who cleaned the altar brass and changed the flowers, had ever observed her speak to a soul.

If she were waiting for someone then she waited in vain, for she invariably sat alone, staring ahead of her, quite still except for the constant agitated twisting of her hands in her lap.

As a rule, Mr Kenward preferred not to interfere; but there was something about this young woman which stirred curiosity as well as pity.

A week after her first appearance he went and seated himself beside her in her solitary pew, and after introducing himself, enquired gently whether she might be in need of assistance.

Lizzie Newbrook shook her head.

"Thank you, sir, but there's none can help me now," she answered in a low voice. "I'd rather be left alone."

"But there is something which troubles you, I feel. Will you not tell me?"

No reply.

"You have suffered a bereavement, perhaps?"

Again a shake of the head.

Mr Kenward was undeterred.

"It may be I can offer you spiritual comfort. Will you allow me to pray with you?"

She raised her eyes to his for a moment, then looked down again.

"I don't pray, sir."

"Then what is it you seek here?"

"I don't know."

It was true, she didn't know.

Every day since coming to Lewes Lizzie had been to see Frank Flynn at the county prison on the western outskirts of the town. She had found him subdued and withdrawn, alternating between bouts of remorse for Tom's death and a self-pitying despondency over his own plight.

"It's done for us, Lizzie," he kept telling her. "Best you go away and forget me. Make a new life for yourself if you can."

But how could she make a new life when she loved him still, needed him still, wanted him still, despite everything that had happened?

"Don't come any more to see me . . . it'll do you no good."

Each day she'd gone back, and each day he repeated the same words, lately adding his argument to that of the counsel engaged to defend him at his trial.

Mr Digby Mayhew, a senior partner in the Lewes firm of Jones, Mayhew, Morris and Jones, was inclined to be long-winded with his advice.

"As you are doubtless aware, madam," he told Lizzie when she came at his request to see him in his chambers, "my client has been charged under the Offences Against the Person Act of 1869 with the unlawful taking of another's life, to wit, that of your husband, Mr Thomas Newbrook. Now, the law of the land as it presently stands presumes all homicide to be – and I will quote to you – 'malicious, and therefore murder, unless it is either justified by the command or permission of the law, excused on the ground of accident or self-preservation, or alleviated into manslaughter by being the involuntary consequence of some act not strictly lawful or occasioned by some sudden and sufficiently violent provocation.' I trust you follow me so far."

He glanced at her over the top of his steel-rimmed spectacles.

"The case for the defence rests upon this last clause, that of provocation, in that the deceased – your late husband, madam – approached my client of his own volition with threats to cause him injury, and that in the course of defending his person, Mr Flynn, whether accidentally or in self-preservation, struck a blow which resulted in Mr Newbrook's death. Now, the prosecution in the case will seek to prove otherwise, that cause for provocation was given not *to* my client, but *by* my client, in consequence of his admitted intimacy with the deceased's wife – yourself, madam. Therefore, to speak plainly, you are prejudicing Mr Flynn's case. That is to say, you but arm the prosecution with their proof if you are seen to be openly pursuing a relationship still by visiting my client during the period of his detention. My advice to you, madam, is to remove yourself forthwith from Lewes and cease all connection until this case has been tried."

Lizzie received his advice reluctantly. Finally, for Frank's

218

sake, she had given her promise; but only to keep away from the prison. Nothing would induce her to leave Lewes: in that she was adamant. She could bear not seeing Frank, she said, but only so long as she could be somewhere close by him.

With that, Mr Mayhew had to be content.

To support herself, she had found work at a tavern down by the wharves, lodging at night in a common dossing-house in the next street. Used as she was to the wholesome freshness of the country, this miserable neighbourhood increased her lowness of spirit with its poky atmosphere of poverty and dirt; and the nauseous fumes from the gasworks so soured her stomach that she had no appetite for the little food she could afford to buy.

After a fortnight of this depressing existence Lizzie's life had settled into a routine of a kind.

Her work at the tavern occupied the whole of her mornings and evenings, and often half the night too when the place was crowded with freightermen from the Newhaven docks.

In the free hours of the afternoon she had taken to escaping up on to the Downs above Lewes, where the fresh, sweet air carried away the taint of the town and she could sit and watch the windmills turning on Cranedown in the distance beyond the river valley.

Then, before returning to the drudgery of the tap-room, she was in the habit now of going to sit for a while in All Souls church. There was a peace and quietness in that place which, although she could not pray, somehow seemed to ease the anguish of her mind. Brought up a regular church-attender, Lizzie had never given much thought to religion, taking it for granted as a Sunday ritual, the services a boring duty to be endured an hour or so each week on a stomach grumbling to be fed.

God, to her, was a totally impersonal deity, too remote for any feeling of attachment; and if He did exist, she thought, then He had surely abandoned her now for what she and Frank had done.

Indeed, she would not have gone into All Souls in the first place had it not been for the fact that Frank had been married here, and she had wanted, just briefly, to touch the nerve of her own unhappy memory in recalling how she had stood on that cold November morning to hear him plight his troth to another.

It was a strange impulse which had prompted her to enter the church again. Once inside, though, seated alone in the empty silence, she had fallen into a reverie; and in that reverie experienced a temporary lightening of her burdened spirit, as though all the sadness and misery and grief of her life were slowly draining away.

It was this respite, this relief, which had drawn Lizzie so often back to the place; but today, with the Reverend Mr Kenward disturbing her with his persistent questions, she merely felt tired and ill, far rather that he leave her alone however genuine his wish to be of help.

"Excuse me, sir."

She rose to her feet.

"I'll be late for my work if I stay any longer."

He followed her along the aisle to the porch door, his boots squeaking plaintively.

"May I enquire where it is you work, my dear?"

"The Shades in Stanley Street."

She turned back for a moment to answer.

In the daylight Robert Kenward was able to see her face more clearly. She was young, much younger than he had taken her to be; and yet there was nothing of the healthy bloom of youth about her. The dark eyes were lifeless, the features pinched, the skin pallid and with a sallow tinge telling of an inadequate diet.

The girl's waif-like appearance stirred his compassion, and as she walked away towards the church gate he called after her.

"We shall see you here tomorrow, hopefully?"

She raised her shoulders in a little gesture of uncertainty; and then, dragging her shawl about her, hurried out into the busy street.

The next day, when she did not reappear, Mr Kenward feared that his solicitude had frightened her away; and was relieved, therefore, to find her again in church the afternoon following. If anything, she looked more tired and drawn than before, he thought pityingly, and the thin material of her gown was dark with damp from the steady drizzle through which she had walked.

With this as his excuse, the minister waited until she was leaving before approaching to greet her and suggest she might wish to come across to the vicarage to dry herself, and perhaps take a little refreshment with his wife and himself.

Lizzie's immediate thought was to refuse, politely.

Then again, it would seem rude to throw the man's kindness back into his face; and besides, she had only the one change of clothing and could ill afford to have the gown she was wearing stolen – as would be bound to happen were she to leave it hanging to dry at the dossing-house.

"Well . . . thank you, sir," she said hesitantly. "If it's not too much trouble."

"No trouble, no trouble at all, I do assure you."

She was directed along the gravelled path which ran beside the churchyard to the vicarage, and there made comfortable before a fire in Mr Kenward's study.

"This, my dear," he introduced Lizzie to his wife, "is the young lady of whom I've recently spoken. Let me see, it is Miss – ?"

"Mrs. Mrs Newbrook, sir."

"Newbrook?" The tone sharpened with sudden interest. "Newbrook, you say?"

"Yes, sir. Elizabeth Newbrook."

Her awkwardness was evident, and Mrs Kenward, a plump grey-haired little woman, gave a comforting smile as she took her hand.

"I'm pleased to make your acquaintance. Do sit down, won't you, and warm yourself at the fire."

She indicated an armchair and took a seat herself opposite.

There was a perceptible pause.

Then, as Mrs Kenward was about to say something more, the study door was opened and a young man looked in.

"No – don't go, Alec!" Robert Kenward called hurriedly as the other went to withdraw again on seeing him occupied. "We have Mrs Newbrook here with us. This gentleman," he went on, turning to Lizzie, "is my curate, Mr Bethway."

She recognised the pleasant young man immediately as the minister who had assisted at Frank's wedding; but it was the name which caused her to stare so openly. She had heard it mentioned frequently on her visits to the prison, but until this moment had failed to connect it in any way with the face.

Before she could stop herself, she cried, "Oh – have you been to see Frank? For God's sake tell me how he is! They won't let me near him – "

Then, falling abruptly silent and biting her lip at having spoken out in such a fashion, collected herself, and after a pause went on, "I'm sorry . . . It's just that I've not had a word of him this past week. I know as how you go up there, sir. He's told me hisself of your kindness."

Alec Bethway closed the door behind him and moved towards her.

So this is Lizzie Newbrook, he thought. This shabby, colourless, wretched young thing. There was nothing of the Salome or Jezebel about her, as imagination had led him to conjure. Had he passed her on the street he would certainly not have singled her out as being a wanton or harlot.

"Mr Flynn's as well as we can hope for, in the circumstances," he told her, glancing across at Mr Kenward. The two of them had held several discussions about Frank's arrest and detention and the misguided actions which had led him to such a serious strait; but it was Lizzie herself who had been giving most concern.

"We must thank the good Lord in his mercy that he has directed Mrs Newbrook to us," Robert Kenward told his curate.

"Indeed we must!"

His gaze fixed upon that unhappy face, Alec seated himself by her.

"And now that we've so fortunately found you, ma'am, we should inform your mother at once. She's been most concerned for your whereabouts."

Lizzie's head drooped.

"I kept meaning to write," she said in a low voice. "But what wi' one thing and another . . ."

"Of course," Alec responded. "You must appreciate,

though, that your sudden disappearance, coming so soon after the news of Mr Newbrook's tragic end – "

He made a little gesture of the hand.

"I've been in correspondence with your mother through the good services of Mr George Bashford, of Bonningale. You may know of him, perhaps?"

"Bashford? Aye. Frank . . . Frank's mentioned the name. Some connection of his sister's."

"Yes, her godparent. He's been kind enough to take Isabelle into his house. You have met Isabelle – Miss Flynn, that is?"

There was a shake of the head.

"Ah. I thought maybe – but no matter. It's possible you will make her acquaintance quite soon. She'll be here in Lewes. I understand she wishes to be present at her brother's trial. Naturally, it will comfort him greatly to have her in court – a friendly, sympathetic presence to support him. Though my own personal opinion is against putting Isabelle to such a distressing experience."

"There speaks your fondness for the girl, Alec," Mr Kenward observed.

He was answered with a slightly rueful smile.

"If she *is* there," said Lizzie, before he could speak again, "then that'll be two of us alongside o' Frank."

Mr Kenward looked at her, surprised.

"But surely, you do not intend to be at the trial yourself?"

"Aye, I do. I owe it to him."

"With respect, Mrs Newbrook, you are in mourning, and you owe more, I should have thought, to your late husband's memory. It is hardly proper in such circumstances for a widow to attend a court hearing. Especially when she does so to give succour to the man charged with the death of her spouse!"

Lizzie hunched herself forward, and made no answer.

"Perhaps she's obliged to be present, sir," Alec said in defence. Leaning towards her, he asked gently, "Have you been called to give evidence?"

Still she remained silent, and he saw that she was close to tears. Her damp clothes had begun to steam a little in the warmth from the fire, and this, together with her wan expression, gave her a look of such pathos that compassion made him forget for a moment that it was the girl's own wrongdoing which had reduced her to this state, and that her wilful misconduct made her almost as equally culpable as her lover for what had happened at Weatherfield.

In fact, Lizzie had learned only the previous day that it was likely she'd be required to testify at the trial, and that she should therefore hold herself in readiness to be called.

The information had come not from Mr Digby Mayhew, but from an officer of the court.

"But what will they want wi' me?" she had asked, bewildered.

"Merely to answer truthfully the questions which may be put to you."

"Questions? What questions? I'll not say anything against Frank!"

She repeated those words now, bunching her fists in her lap, not looking at Alec Bethway or the Kenwards but staring fixedly at the coal flames in the grate.

"They'll never get me to say anything in that court against Frank. Not a word. They can do what they like, but they'll not make me answer their questions to harm him."

"We must pray such an ordeal won't be necessary," Alec said quietly; and then, referring their conversation back a little, "Where are you lodged in the town, Mrs Newbrook? Is it close by?"

She sniffed, wiping away her tears with the flat of her hand.

"Down by the wharves."

"Is there an address I may send to your mother?"

"Aye. Number twelve, Flood Street. She'd best not write to me there, though. I wouldn't get her letter, the place it is. Tell her . . . tell her she'll find me at The Shades, in Stanley Street."

"The Shades?"

"It's a tavern, sir."

"Yes, I know."

"I earn a living there, if you can call it a living. Mostly

224

pot-washing. Be hopes not for much longer . . . it's work to break your back, and the money they gi' me scarce pays for a bed in the dossing-house. I'll be glad to leave the place."

"You've been offered better employment?"

Lizzie sniffed again, and shrugged.

"Whereabouts?" Alec prompted her. "Having found you, ma'am, we are not about to lose you again!"

She made an effort to return his smile.

"Well . . . nothing's been settled, sir. Not for certain. But there was a gentleman come into The Shades a couple o' nights back. He knows of a place the other end o' town, he says. They're looking for clean, obliging girls to do light work."

"What kind of establishment might this be, my dear?" Mrs Kenward came in.

"Establishment, ma'am?"

"Yes – is it a shop, or a manufactory? Or a place of domestic employment, perhaps?"

"I don't know. I didn't think to ask. The gentleman seemed sure I'd be well suited to the work, though. He's promised to speak for me to the lady."

"Did he give the lady a name, I wonder?" Alec asked sharply.

She shook her head.

"It wasn't by chance a Mrs Sullivan, was it?"

"Sullivan? No, not Sullivan. I can't recall the gentleman making mention o' names. Oh – is that five o'clock chiming?"

Lizzie stopped to listen, her head turned towards the rain-spattered window where the clock on All Souls tower was just visible above the churchyard trees.

"I must be getting along to Stanley Street afore they open."

Rising to her feet, she shook out the skirts of her gown to remove the worst of the creasing, and then, somewhat diffidently, thanked the Kenwards for the kindness of their hospitality.

"Remember to let us know immediately if you decide to take up this offer of other work," Alec said, getting up and taking her hand in both of his.

"In fact, we would all feel easier were you to make enquiry first, and let us know what manner of work it is. And where. I myself will be only too happy to help you in whatever way I'm able, Mrs Newbrook, so please don't hesitate to seek my advice at any time."

"Thank you, sir."

Lizzie withdrew her hand.

"I feel I should warn you – " the young curate went on. Then hesitated, thinking how best to put what he wished to say.

After a moment he began again, "I feel I should warn you, ma'am, that there are several places in this town where it would be – unwise, shall we say, for a young lady in your present unhappy situation to take work."

She looked at him.

"I mean, if you will pardon my speaking so bluntly – and you also, Mrs Kenward – I mean houses of assignation. In particular I must mention one in Star Street which conceals its true purpose behind a curtain of deceit by purporting to be some kind of academy for the gentler sex."

Lizzie's sudden burst of laughter had an edge of hysteria to it.

"By the time Frank's trial's over and done with, somewhere like that will be the only place anxious to take me! I don't reckon to come out o' this business wi' much of a reputation left me, Mr Bethway. A woman of ill-repute, that's what they'll brand me as. A woman of ill-repute . . . fit for nothing but a house o' the same name."

23

"I suppose," said Joel Adams mournfully, "it's on account o' this trouble o' Frank Flynn's that you won't walk out wi' me."

"Oh, I'll not be saying that."

Kate Brophy tossed him a glance over her shoulder and continued on her way across Weatherfield green.

"Sure, but 'tis no fault of yeself that ye're kin to the man. And if ye're to carry that basket for me, then see ye hold it straight. I'll not be thanking ye for tumbling the minister's groceries upon the ground."

Joel blew out his cheeks and hoisted the handle of the heavy wicker basket further up his arm before following.

Ever since meeting the red-haired Irish girl and liking her at once for her manner and her bold good looks, he had dogged her footsteps about the village, seizing every excuse he could to speak to her.

Kate had turned a blind eye and a deaf ear for a week or so. Then, seeing that he was not to be put off, had finally deigned to acknowledge his existence, even if only to make him the butt of her caustic humour.

Discovering his new love to be several months older than himself, Joel had been making great efforts to act the man, smoking a clay pipe (though it sickened him to the stomach to do so) and letting his beard grow in the hope that a set of whiskers would lend maturity to his juvenile appearance.

But Kate disliked the stink of tobacco, she said; and had laughed at the sparse wisps on his chin and called him "a darling boy", uttering the words with such mockery that he had snapped the stem of the pipe in his mortification, and had seized upon soap, strop and razor the moment he reached home.

Since Boaz Palmer's removal under arrest from Weatherfield, Joel's mother Lottie had taken the management of the alehouse entirely upon her own shoulders, leaving her son to work the carrier business and shift for himself at their cottage in the high street.

Sometimes, alone late at night, he would sit with his hobnail boots upon the polished brass fender and ruminate about his half-brother, and how convenient it would be were Frank to be put away somewhere for life. Then his mother could become licencee of the alehouse and supply him with all the free ale he could drink; and he'd be master of his own

227

hearth before the age of twenty-one and able to ask Kate Brophy to marry him soon as ever they'd cried the banns in church.

Such idle fancies served to while away the dark and lonely hours; but as his mother was fond of saying, "if wishes were horses, beggars would ride."

Hoisting the laden basket higher, Joel quickened his pace.

"Why d'you have to walk so quick?" he demanded.

"Why d'ye walk so slow?"

"I don't."

"Ye do, an' all."

He stared vexedly past Kate's shoulder. They were almost at the rectory gate already and had scarcely exchanged more than half a dozen sentences.

"I'll come round the back wi' you," he said.

"Oh, will ye now? And what if Mrs Howard chances to look out and see us there? I'm not allowed gentlemen callers."

"She can't complain. I'm only helping wi' her blasted groceries. Leastways she knows me well enough not to take me for any gentleman caller."

"'Tis right ye are there!"

Kate turned by the gate and stood looking up at him, laughter in the dark blue Irish eyes.

"Sure, but ye're no gentleman, Joel Adams."

He coloured up.

"Now why d'you go saying a thing like that? I've treated you civil enough. I've minded my manners. And you can stop pulling at that basket – I said I'd come round the back wi' it, didn't I?"

Indifferently, the girl let her hand drop and turned away along the brick path running beside the churchyard wall. Joel's eyes followed her. She had put on a little weight since coming to work at the rectory, and it suited her, rounding out the curves of her body beneath the calico print gown.

"You may think what you like," he said warmly, catching up, "but I'm as well bred as any hereabouts."

"Ye say so?"

"Aye, I do. My father was one o' the best-respected men in Weatherfield."

228

"Is that a fact now? And how many fathers did ye have, pray?"

He frowned at the ambiguous note in her voice.

"Only the one."

"Ah, but which one? There's tongues in this village that wag a long way back, to be sure. I've heard tell there was a stallion man here upon a time – "

"Who've you been a-listening to?" Joel demanded angrily.

"Oh, a sweet creature of a lady I visit to pass the time o' day."

"Some blasted old nabble-trap, you mean! Poking their nose where it don't concern 'em. Which one's this 'un?"

"If ye're asking after her name, 'tis Charity Poole, and she lives away down the lane past the store."

"I know where Charity Poole lives – "

"Sure, she's been here since your father even, whichever he was."

Kate smiled at the expression of sullen confusion her teasing provoked.

She enjoyed her conversations with old Miss Poole. There had once been two sisters living, but the other had died three winters ago after breaking a hip on the children's ice-slide in the lane. Since then the other had occupied the cottage alone, with her cats and her memories: mostly of the kind her neighbours would much rather she forgot, being family skeletons whose desiccated bones provided the old lady with many hours of nourishment.

The Irish girl visited twice a week to take charitable provisions from the rectory – a few eggs, or a cheese, a card of thread, some vegetables from the garden – and in return was entertained to the gossip of days long past.

Much of it meant nothing and only interested her because of the drama or the humour it contained; but she had pricked up her ears at mention of the Flynns and their tangled background. While they were together in Star Street, she had often heard Isabelle talk about her brother Frank, and her half-brother Joel, and her godparents the Bashfords; so she had been curious to discover this other, slightly tarnished, side of the family coin.

By far the most favoured of Miss Poole's topics of remembrance was the former village priest, the Reverend Esmond Bates, whose history the old lady recounted frequently and with great relish.

Kate had heard of him already from conversation at the rectory. There was even supposed to be a room there – the front bedroom above the porch – which was haunted by his ghost. Having been brought up with a firm belief in the presence of the unseen, she entered that part of the house as seldom as possible, fearful of seeing his shade materialise from behind the hangings of the old bed, as one of the other maids had described.

It would be her duty later this morning to dust those upper floors. Reminded of this, she cast a hurried glance over the churchyard wall at the grave mound of the late Mr Bates, and crossed herself.

"You'd best not let them in the village catch you doing that," said Joel truculently, still smarting at her jibes at his paternity.

"Oh?"

"They don't hold wi' papists in these parts, you'll find."

"And to think I never knew it."

"There's no cause to answer me so sarcastical. It ain't natural, all that bending and bobbing and kissing o' crosses."

Kate shrugged.

"Ye'd prefer we worshipped plain and to the purpose as protestants do, I suppose?"

"I dunno about that. It's just that folk here don't hold wi' queer foreign ways. Aye, you needs laugh! I'll tell you this much, Kate Brophy – if I'm to wed you, you'll have to alter your romish notions – "

He stopped abruptly, silently cursing his tongue for having run away with him.

"Oh? Ye're very bold, to be sure. What makes ye think I'd have ye?"

"Because I want you to."

"And that's enough is it now? Mother o' God – men, ye're all of a kind. Better for me, I'm thinking, if I'd stayed behind in my own land and married Michael Byrne for all his poor bowed legs."

The two of them had now reached the rectory yard and were standing facing each other. Kate turned her head surreptitiously to make sure no one was about to see them together; then swiftly raised herself on her toes and kissed Joel on the cheek.

"But I thank ye, even so. 'Tis not often a girl is asked to be wed on such short acquaintance."

He grinned. At least she had not laughed in his face, or flown into a temper, or turned indignant, as he had feared she might.

Putting the basket down by the wash-house wall, he went to take her by the hand.

"Will you walk out wi' me, then?"

She touched his palm with her fingertips and moved back a step or two.

"What a fickle creature ye are, to be sure," she began to tease again. "And I thought it was some other girl ye hankered for."

The grin faded.

"Charity Poole told you that an' all, did she?"

"Indeed not. 'Twas Belle Flynn herself. There was time for talking of such things whilst we were together, the pair of us, in Lewes."

Kate had been careful since coming to Weatherfield to refer as seldom as possible to the circumstances of her previous situation. The rector, Mr Everett Howard, knew something of her history from Alec Bethway; but everyone else in the village, including old Miss Poole, believed she had been in ordinary domestic employment, forming a friendship with Isabelle Flynn when the latter came to work at the same house.

Nothing would have induced the Irish girl to identify that house, however, nor the nature of its business. Having tasted a little of freedom and respectability, she had no wish to jeopardise either.

"And what else did our Belle say?" Joel demanded to know.

231

"Oh, that ye were ever after pestering this other – "

"I was not! Belle shouldn't be saying such lies!"

"Whisht, now. Ye'll have the house all ears with your noise."

He looked down. Sullenly he kicked a pebble away with his boot.

"I like you far better'n ever I liked the village girls," he said at length.

"Is that so?"

"Aye."

Kate smiled; and gave a shake of the head.

"It's the truth!" he protested. "I've not given one o' them another thought since you come here. Why won't you believe me?"

She smiled again.

"Oh, I believe you – though thousands would not. Now will ye hand me up that basket."

He did as she asked; and then went on in a pleading tone, "I wish you'd say as how you liked me, Kate . . . leastways, you don't *mis*like me."

"I like ye fine, Joel Adams."

"And you will walk out wi' me, then?"

"I will. Even though 'tis sore against my papist principles."

"Keep your principles. I'll not let that come atween us," Joel said hastily, his face brightening. "When can I see you next?"

Kate put both arms through the basket handle and hugged it against her.

"Sunday. Ye may offer me a ride in that handsome cart ye have. There's a mission run by the Jesuit Fathers, I hear, over at Shatterford. I've a mind to travel there and hear holy mass."

Every day for over a week now there had been masses for the repose of the soul of Adolphe de Retz offered in the newly opened Roman Catholic church of St Pancras, tucked away at the furthest end of Lewes high street. And every day for over a week Leopold de Retz and his wife Clara had been accompanied to the church by Rosannah Flynn.

This questionable behaviour of Rosannah's fanned afresh the idle speculation which had long padded conversation about her among the town's society.

Lewes had been rabidly anti-Catholic in sentiment ever since the days of the Marian persecutions, when a number of its men and women were burnt to death in the marketplace for their protestant convictions. Each fifth of November this local martyrdom was vociferously celebrated by the "Bonfire Boys" in torchlight processions through the narrow cobbled streets amid the crackle and bang and roar of giant rockets known as "rousers", with a chaired effigy of a pope-guy and the waving of banners which were defiantly anti-papist, anti-Irish and, in more recent years, anti-Pusey.

Catholics were still, even in these more enlightened days, regarded with feelings of mistrust; and in Lewes itself there had been an outbreak of mob violence earlier in 1871 when St Pancras first opened its doors for worship.

It was, therefore, with a mixture of scorn and derision and downright indignity that the tea-parties and soirées received the news that Rosannah had been seen on several occasions going into that den of idolatry – and worse, being fawned upon by its priest as though he already had his hooks into her income.

They could only surmise that their suspicions had been right all along about her illicit relationship with Adolphe de Retz; that the pair had continued as lovers throughout her brief and disreputable marriage to Frank Flynn; and that there were now plans of some kind afoot to leave Lewes with her child (Dolly's child, said some, citing Aimée's name) and make a new life elsewhere as Rosannah de Retz.

Rumour is seldom without a core of truth. For Rosannah's detractors, however, that core proved a hollow thing indeed when the *County Advertiser*, somewhat belatedly, published a highly coloured account of Dolly's summary arrest and execution, embroidered from details reluctantly given to the newspaper by Leopold de Retz.

The elderly academy proprietor would far rather have preferred to keep his loss a personal one and be left alone to mourn in private with his family and friends than to have their sorrow cheapened by such front-page sensationalism. It had been Osborne, the Weldrakes' manservant, who was responsible for alerting the *Advertiser*'s interest, hoping thereby to line his own pocket at the expense of their grief.

Among the letters from France bearing tidings of the cruel fate suffered by his young kinsman, Leopold had received one for Rosannah personally, sent to her from Dolly's brother. Sensible of their love, he had written a few lines telling her of the devotion she had inspired even unto death.

Rosannah's broken-hearted desolation had been so terrible that it was feared the shock might unhinge her mind.

The sounds of her anguish could be heard in every part of the house, rising and falling in a harrowing litany of lamentation that went on hour after hour until she was finally exhausted; and slept, only to wake again to another dawn of despair.

She talked of nothing but Dolly, his affection, his attentiveness, his appearance, what he had said, what he had done, what they had planned together: a breathless, feverish monologue that poured ceaselessly from her lips as though the very frenzy of her words could blot out the pain of his death. And when she had drained herself of the strength to go on, she lay dark-eyed and wasted against the pillows, hugging her infant daughter to her breast.

It was Clara de Retz, a warm-natured yet shrewd woman, born the daughter of a cabinet-maker at the back of Bear Yard, who persuaded Rosannah at length to leave her bed and attempt the rebuilding of her life.

"Do it for Dolly," she urged each time the other gave in to grief, crying out that she did not want to be bathed, did not want to be dressed, did not want to be taken down to the drawing-room, or into the garden; wanted nothing, only to be left alone to follow her love into the stilly silence of the grave.

"Do it for Dolly, my pet. He wouldn't want you to be moping behind closed curtains a-spoiling that pretty face wi' tears. All the crying in the world won't bring him back, you must make up your mind to that. Take a leaf from his own book, my pet, and be brave and learn to live wi'out him."

Such homely encouragement saved Rosannah from slipping altogether into a permanent state of nervous derangement. Slowly she began once more to take some slight interest in life; and with Doctor Leigh's cautious permission left the house for the first time since Aimée's birth when she drove with the de Retzes to St Pancras's church to attend the services of requiem for their deceased kinsman.

Harry Weldrake, who had returned earlier that week from London, remonstrated strongly with his sister in the privacy of her bedroom when he learned of these outings. His aggressive show of displeasure was both thoughtless and unwise, for it served to rekindle her morbid hysteria and work her once more into a dangerously volatile state.

"Why should I care what people are saying!" she screamed at him. "Let them talk, let them point the finger! My life is my own. I'll conduct it as I please. So long as my behaviour causes harm to no other, they have no right to judge me with their tittle-tattling!"

"Rosannah – "

"What have they to hold against me? That I dare to violate their petty provincial standards by going into some church of which they disapprove? What bigotry! Oh, I can't wait to see the looks upon their faces when they discover what I've done – "

There was a strange glitter in her eyes, and she began to laugh suddenly.

"That I've paid for Dolly's memorial in St Pancras's . . . that I'm having Aimée baptised there with Clara and Leopold as sponsors . . ."

"Are you quite out of your mind?" her brother stormed at her, outrage robbing him of the sense to see that her sanity was indeed very near to breaking point.

"God knows, the reputation of our name has already been sullied enough by your behaviour!"

"Who are you to talk of reputation! You successfully managed to gamble and whore and squander away every shilling Father left you – and now you must needs play the pander to some old maid to leech off her for your livelihood."

"It is not my intention to leech off Adelaide – "

"Liar!"

"Damn it, Rosannah, whatever chance I had of bringing off that match may well have been ruined for good by the drunken, murdering brute you insisted on marrying."

"Yes – blame me! Blame me!"

She threw herself across the bed, beating with clenched fists at the pillows.

"Blame me – just as you've always done! Oh God, can't you for once remember your own mistakes? Why turn on me? Haven't I suffered enough from that marriage?"

"I warned you!" Weldrake came back at her furiously. "I warned you what would become of it all. If you'd listened to sense and married Dolly de Retz, none of this would have happened. Dolly needn't have died, even. It's your fault he's dead, Rosannah . . . as surely as if you'd killed him yourself. It's all your fault!"

"No – no – no – no –"

"Yes! De Retz would still be alive but for you."

She covered her ears with her hands and screamed. This was too much; this was more than her fragile sanity could bear.

Leaping suddenly like a mad thing from the bed, she flung herself across the room at her brother, the screams rising to piercing shrieks of hysteria. He caught her by the arm, but her frenzy lent her wild strength as she kicked and clawed and scratched.

Grabbing her by her dishevelled hair, Weldrake managed to drag her head away and slapped her hard across the face.

A thunderous knocking came at the bedroom door. A moment later it was thrown open and he saw the manservants Osborne and Jenkins there.

"Fetch Doctor Leigh!" he shouted at them. "And hurry. For God's sake, hurry!"

24

"Take the Bible in your right hand and say after me: I, Francis Patrick Flynn, do solemnly swear that the evidence which I am about to give . . ."

Sitting in the public gallery above, Isabelle listened to her brother repeat from the witness box the words of the clerk of the court.

". . . and nothing but the truth. So help me, God."

She had arrived with George Bashford from Bonningale two days before the opening of Frank's trial, in the final week of September, at the Lewes Quarter Sessions. It was one of fate's wry little twists that her godfather should have taken rooms for them both at The White Hart Hotel and that Isabelle's should be neighbour to the one she had shared with her mother ten months earlier, when they had stayed here those few days before Frank's wedding.

"May the court know how old you are, Mr Flynn?"

The question was put by counsel for the prosecution, Mr Henry Winthrop, an intimidating figure in long black gown and barrister's wig.

"I was twenty-two this birthday just gone."

Mr Winthrop glanced at the paper in his hand.

"Twenty-two. And we have heard that the deceased, Thomas Newbrook, was more than twice that age. Forty-seven."

He pronounced the words with emphasis, his eyes moving to the jury seated within their boxed enclosure across the well of the court.

"And what is your profession, sir?"

"I work as a groom."

"Ah, yes. Formerly in the employment of your brother-in-law, Mr Harry Weldrake."

"Aye."

The Recorder, Mr Cunningham Bruce, the circuit judge presiding at the trial, leaned forward in his high seat with a clearing of the throat.

"Defendant will kindly address counsel as sir."

". . . sir."

He looked pale, Isabelle thought, and thinner from the enforced inactivity of his detention, the muscular build of his frame wasted a little for want of accustomed exercise. The checked coat he wore over the freshly-laundered shirt she'd sent seemed to hang slackly on the shoulders as he stood below in the witness box, hands resting tensely on the ledge in front.

"And at what date did you cease to work as Mr Weldrake's groom, Mr Flynn?"

Counsel for the prosecution did not look up as he put this next question, but turned instead to take a document handed to him from behind by his clerk.

"It was when I married his sister . . . sir."

"And that was?"

"In November o' last year."

Alec Bethway had visited Isabelle several times at The White Hart. Her brother's spirits had become noticeably lowered, he reported, after Boaz Palmer's sentencing: at his own trial at the intermediate sessions earlier in the summer, Frank's former manager had received eighteen months in prison for his part in the Newbrook affair. If that was the punishment meted out for hindering the course of justice by helping to conceal the body, then what possible leniency could Frank himself, on a much graver charge, hope for?

"But you continued still to pursue an activity of another kind, did you not, Mr Flynn? One which you had been engaged in for some years previous to that date?"

This time Mr Winthrop fixed his glance directly.

"You mean my fighting?"

It was not, perhaps, the most prudent word to use in the circumstances, and Mr Winthrop seized upon it with relish.

"Indeed, sir, I mean precisely that. Your fighting. Your prize fighting, sir. Your bare-knuckle fighting, sir. It is true, is it not, that since your seventeenth year you have partici-pated in some thirty-two contests of a pugilistic nature – that is, something approaching a half dozen contests a year from 1866 until the present time?"

"I don't fight to a regular number every year," Frank countered. "It might be eight, like it was in '69. Other times it's been no more than four."

"But you would describe yourself, would you not, Mr Flynn, as an experienced fighter?"

Again, the significant stress on the word.

Isabelle had been forewarned that the prosecution would make great capital of her brother's proficiency and skill in the professional ring, and the considerable advantage this would have given him over the unhandy and skill-less Newbrook. Mr Digby Mayhew, appearing for the defence, had at the previous day's hearing attempted to shift the emphasis to Newbrook's lust for revenge, seeking to show that it was the deceased man's determination to settle his quarrel by violent means that had led to the fight, rather than that the defendant had goaded and provoked him.

"Aye, sir. I'd say I was an experienced fighter."

"And a good one?"

Frank's chin went up a fraction.

"I'm reckoned about one o' the best bare-knucklers in southern England."

"You are justifiably proud to hold that reputation, sir?"

"I am, sir."

"Was it not, then, an act of great cowardice and brutality to use your superior strength and expertise against a man who had virtually – "

"Your Honour, I must protest!" counsel for the defence intervened sharply, rising to his feet.

He was overruled by the Recorder.

"Counsel may put the question again."

Counsel did so.

". . . against a man who had virtually no means of self-defence and who was, moreover, already disadvantaged by a considerable difference in agility and age?"

Any expression on Frank's swarthy features was concealed

239

by the thick beard grown during his detention; but the anger in his voice was plain enough.

"Newbrook come looking for trouble! It was him wanted a fight, not me. I'd have had no truck wi' him, left to myself, but there was no talking sense to the man. He was eaten up wi' what he thought had been going on atween me and his wife."

Two rows from the front of the public gallery sat a young woman in a shabby black tuckered gown and black chip bonnet. Isabelle knew already who she was: Lizzie Newbrook.

They had met very briefly on the first morning of the trial, when Alec Bethway introduced them outside the courtroom. Isabelle's reaction had been one of resentment at his lack of sensitivity; but this proved short-lived when, at their next meeting, Lizzie explained something of her situation, that she was lodged in reduced circumstances at the bottom end of the town and working in a wharf-side tavern.

The initial resentment had softened to curiosity; and curiosity had led to interest; and from interest had grown sympathy.

"What he *thought* had been going on between you and his wife, Mr Flynn?"

Counsel allowed a note of disbelief to creep into the question.

"Come, sir, there was a great deal more to it than mere thinking, surely? This court has heard from a previous witness that Mr Newbrook had, some weeks earlier, discovered you with his wife in the private room of a hostelry, in circumstances suggesting far more than casual acquaintance. Are we to believe that when a man comes upon his wife seated upon the knee of another, it would be an error of judgement to see this as proof of her unfaithfulness?"

That previous witness had been Boaz Palmer, brought from Lewes Gaol to testify on Frank's behalf. Under the cut and thrust of Mr Winthrop's interrogation he had proved of far greater value to the prosecution. Perhaps it was just as well, Mr Mayhew remarked gloomily afterwards, that the two other witnesses he had hoped to call for the defence, Sam Reaney and Harry Walsh, had both of them shown such a

240

clean pair of heels it had been impossible to trace either in time for the start of the trial.

"Mrs Newbrook was on my knee so as I could attend to her strained ankle," Frank said tersely.

His answer provoked a burst of laughter, silenced only after several repeated warnings from the bench.

"I would suggest to you, sir," put in Mr Winthrop, "that Mrs Newbrook had been upon your knee a few times more before that occasion, and not always to receive such – ah, tender ministrations for her little aches and strains."

Defence counsel rose smartly to his feet a second time.

"Your Honour, is such facetiousness on the part of my learned friend really necessary to his questions?"

The protest was allowed.

Mr Winthrop redirected his line of fire.

"Were you aware, Mr Flynn, when you first made Mrs Newbrook's acquaintance, that she was already a married woman?"

"Aye, sir. She told me that."

"Nevertheless, a relationship of some intimacy developed between you both?"

"We became . . . close."

"Very close?"

"Aye."

"She was your mistress."

"That's not a word I'd care to use."

"What word *would* you use, Mr Flynn?"

Frank's gaze dropped.

After several moments' silence he said, "Lizzie was my wife. In the sight o' God, she was my true wife."

"Your *wife*, sir? When you were each legally bound to another partner?"

"Aye. To my mind, marriage means a long shot more than a man and woman standing up together afore some minister and parroting the words he tells 'em. There's been many a one I know that's lasted well enough wi'out all the blessing and blether o' the church. And there's others as had no more meaning to 'em than some'at acted out on a stage."

Mr Winthrop cupped his chin in his hand and appeared to

241

give earnest consideration to this piece of homespun philosophy.

"Your own marriage, Mr Flynn," he said finally, dropping his hand to rest upon his hip, "to the former Miss Rosannah Weldrake. How do you view that?"

"Stage-acting."

"Stage-acting?"

"It was a sham, the whole damn' thing."

"Defendant will kindly avoid the use of irreverent speech in his replies to counsel," the bench admonished sharply.

"So it would be true to say," prosecution continued, "that you felt no compunction – no pricking of conscience – at continuing your irregular association with Mrs Newbrook after your own marriage had taken place?"

The weather outside was sunny and warm, and the atmosphere within the crowded courtroom was becoming uncomfortably stuffy as the morning drew on. Ushers had opened the high sash windows, but the closeness of bodies packed into the public gallery created a stale heat which the currents of air failed to penetrate.

There was a constant ripple of movement back and forth along the rows of seats caused by the discarding of outer garments, the mopping of perspiring brows and the fanning of newspapers and handkerchiefs.

"Conscience had nothing to do wi' it," said Frank. "I never had any intention o' giving up Lizzie Newbrook. I had no reason to. My wife knew well enough what was going on atween us."

"And she offered no objection?"

"Oh, aye, she'd say her piece from time to time. But she'd no room for complaint. She'd a fancy man of her own to keep her company, had Rosannah."

A buzz of interest rose from the gallery.

"A fancy man, Mr Flynn? You are saying that your wife, also, was engaged in an intimate relationship?"

"Aye, sir. I'm saying that."

"Mrs Flynn has not been called upon to give evidence before this court, but I have here a letter written to her solicitor."

Mr Winthrop held aloft several pages of notepaper containing a statement which Rosannah had made before the final breakdown of her mental health.

"Exhibit three, Your Honour. With the permission of the court I will read out the contents."

"May I beg leave to enquire of my learned friend," came in Mr Digby Mayhew, "to what end he purposes this examination?"

"Your Honour, it is my intention to show that the defendant is a man of such violent temperament that not even his own wife has been spared the infliction of repeated acts of physical abuse and ill-treatment."

"Counsel has the court's permission to continue."

The Recorder waved Mr Winthrop on; and Mr Mayhew, somewhat discomfited, reseated himself and sat with his face in his hands, steel-rimmed spectacles pushed up to his forehead, seeing the cracks in the defence he had built widening into gaping fissures.

"Mrs Flynn's letter is addressed to Mr Thomas Fowler, of Nixon, Fowler and Toft, at chambers in Southgate Street.

"'My dear Tom, I am truly obliged to you for your correspondence concerning the forthcoming trial of my husband, Francis Flynn. The testimony which you request can do nothing but add to that black name which he has so fully deserved for himself.

"'In the short space of our marriage, my husband has used me with great cruelty and ill temper and has at several times offered violence which occasioned me physical injury. My medical adviser, Doctor William Leigh, will readily confirm should there be need that the early confinement which resulted in the still-birth of my son and which so nearly proved fatal to my own life, was directly induced by the brutality of a sustained assault suffered at Mr Flynn's hands. Indeed, you will recall that my servants deemed it urgent to summon the aid of officers of the law to prevent my further injury.

"'Not content only to treat me in so ill a fashion, Mr Flynn has not troubled to hide his adulterous connection with a Mrs Elizabeth Newbrook. Indeed, it has pleased him to

243

acquaint me with details of their meetings and the affection he claims to have for this person, comparing it at every opportunity with the detestation and revulsion of feeling which he bears towards me, his wife.'"

Mr Winthrop lowered Rosannah's letter and looked for a moment about the hushed court before addressing himself to the jury.

"Gentlemen, I would draw your attention in particular to the final paragraph of this damning indictment:

"'It is my firm conviction that in the matter of Mr Thomas Newbrook's death, my husband fully intended to offer him sufficient violence to occasion grave injury, and that blame for the unfortunate outcome of their meeting may be laid solely and surely upon that cruel and bullying nature which Mr Flynn is ever wont to demonstrate towards those weaker than himself.'"

Slowly, with the deliberation almost of ritual, counsel for the prosecution folded the pages and, replacing them within their envelope, handed them to the usher to be laid upon the exhibit table in front of the bench.

Every eye in the courtroom followed his action before moving to fix once more upon Frank Flynn where he stood in the witness box, quite motionless except for a discernible working of his jaw muscle.

Isabelle felt her godfather stir at her side; and his hand came over to cover hers and give it a small squeeze of comfort. Mr Bashford had been with her in court every day since the start of the trial, and but for his presence she did not think she could have endured to watch her brother put on public display, like a bull to be baited, and have to hear things about his life causing her so much distress.

She had always known that Frank was quick-tempered, inclined to lash out at the least provocation. He had been so ever since childhood. But Rosannah's letter shocked her with its bluntness. She felt suddenly much older, as though the events of this cruel year had forced an untimely maturity upon her.

Her gaze moved along the crowded seats and came to rest on Lizzie Newbrook. Someone was there beside her, a

lump, middle-aged woman, grey hair pinned tidily under a
onnet, who had first appeared in the public gallery the
revious morning. Alec Bethway, briefly present at the hear-
ng before going to minister at a funeral, had pointed her out
to Isabelle as Lizzie's widowed mother, Mrs Copper, from
Barkham.

She seemed a quietly dignified, respectable person. What
must she be feeling, Isabelle wondered – what must any
mother feel – to have to sit in this place and listen to the
sordid details of her daughter's adultery made public knowledge?

"Do you have any comment to make upon your wife's
letter, Mr Flynn?"

Mr Winthrop could afford to sound condescending now.
He had won the case for the prosecution and he knew it: the
jury's verdict of guilty would be a mere formality after the
evidence of the next witness, the final one to be called.

Frank made no immediate response to the question.

"Mr Flynn? I ask again – "

"I heard you plain enough the first time – sir," the other
came in truculently. "And aye, I've some'at to say about it.
She's a woman wi'out shame, her who wrote that letter . . . a
woman wi' morals no better than a common whore. No –
worse, even, for a whore at least has some spark o' decency in
her, and Rosannah Weldrake has none. The act o' pleasure
for her – "

"Defendant will kindly call to mind that he is in a public
place," the Recorder interrupted as the buzz of interest started
afresh, "and will moderate his speech accordingly."

"I was asked for a comment – and by God I'll gi' you one!"
Frank retorted bitterly. "She cozened and connived to lure
me atween her bed-sheets, did that bitch. Nothing would
satisfy her but that she got herself wi' child by me. She knew I
didn't love her . . . she knew about Lizzie . . . Did it matter to
her? Not a bit! And then, once she'd hooked me into that
farce of a marriage and her belly started swelling, oh, it was a
different tune she sang . . . her and her blasted French
dandiprat – "

The volume of background murmurs increased rapidly as

Frank continued to speak, and the Recorder was forced to raise his voice in order to ask, "Are there any further questions counsel wishes to put to the defendant?"

"No, Your Honour, none."

"Then he may stand down. Silence!" The hammer was banged forcefully. "Silence in this court!"

The two officers who had escorted Frank from the dock to the witness box stepped forward.

". . . she deserved every blow I give her!" he shouted as he was led down. "I wish to God I'd broken her blasted neck while I'd the chance . . ."

It was several minutes before order was sufficiently restored for the final witness to be called.

She came hesitantly behind the usher across the floor of the court, casting quick, nervous glances at the jury, at the bewigged and gowned counsels with their attendant clerks, at the bench where Mr Cunningham Bruce sat robed in all the majesty of the Law beneath a large, ornately gilded coat of arms.

"It's Aunt Lottie. Lottie Adams," Isabelle said quickly in response to Mr Bashford's question.

"Lottie . . . of course."

She had been Charlotte Smith, this thin, faded woman, when George Bashford had seen her last, years before in Weatherfield. He had offered her shelter at one of his farm cottages, pitying her wretched condition; but he had already removed to Bonningale at the time of her marriage to Jack Adams and had heard nothing more of her, save that she had given birth to a son.

Once she had taken the oath, Lottie's apprehension receded a little. She knew already what questions she'd be asked, and the answers she was expected to give: that she had witnessed the fight between Frank and Tom Newbrook from an upper window of the alehouse, that she had seen Frank deliberately beat down a man already unconscious on his feet, had watched him and Palmer carry the body to the end of the garden and conceal it under a mound of rubble, had been told what lies to say if she were asked about Mr Newbrook; and that not wishing to be a party to any of this, she had

246

sought out the village rector, Mr Everett Howard, and informed him of all that had taken place.

Lottie Adams was the prosecution's last card; but not even the confident Mr Winthrop, as he rose to put his opening question, could have guessed at the trump about to be turned up.

"Would you be good enough, ma'am, to tell the court in what relation you stand to the defendant?"

"He's blood kin to my son, sir. My son Joel. Him and Frank, they're half-brothers."

Desire to say the right thing made her garrulous.

"They had the selfsame father, sir. Both of 'em. Frank Morgan, his name was. Aye, Frank Morgan. He were a stallion man by occupation."

This unsolicited detail caused titters of laughter.

"Thank you, Mrs Adams," counsel responded. "And you – "

"What did she say?" Someone – a woman – shouted out from the public gallery, checking his words.

"What name did she say?"

"Silence!" called the Recorder, growing impatient. "I will not have this hearing continually interrupted."

Isabelle saw Lizzie Newbrook's mother get to her feet and turn round, her face working with emotion as she repeated her plea.

"For God's sake," she cried piteously to the crowded gallery, "won't somebody tell me what name that woman gave? Was it Morgan? Frank Morgan?"

Several voices were raised in answer.

"Aye, Frank Morgan it were."

"Some'at about horses – a stallion man, she said."

The call for silence rang out across the courtroom again; but Betty Copper was deaf to the entreaty. Swinging back, she stared down towards the dock where the defendant sat flanked by his two guardian officers.

"Is it true?" she cried out to him. "Is it true Frank Morgan was your father?"

"Usher, remove that person!" Mr Cunningham Bruce ordered, pointing his hammer.

247

Frank raised his head to look up at the distraught woman in the gallery, and saw Lizzie's pale face there beside her.

"Aye. He was," he shouted back defiantly, before being restrained.

"Oh God . . . oh God, what a thing . . ."

The wailing cry echoed around the hushed courtroom. Everyone waited, silent; every face turned to watch the off-stage drama being played out above them.

Frank Morgan . . . the man she had given her heart to those twenty years ago. Betty Copper gripped her hands together and pressed them to her breast.

In the late spring of 1851 Frank Morgan had brought his horse to her husband's farm to cover one of the mares. Hungry from the emptiness of a barren marriage, she had fallen an easy victim to his seductive ways. He had proved faithless in the end; that kind always did, leaving the woman to carry the burden alone.

But at least she had had his child to remember him by . . . his daughter.

"Morgan . . . Morgan was Lizzie's father, an' all," she wept, her voice cracking in the stillness, so overwhelmed by shock that she did not shrink from revealing her own shame to the world.

"He was her father, an' all. And all this time, you and her . . . you and her, together . . . the same blood and flesh . . . oh God, what a wicked, dreadful thing."

25

Lizzie Newbrook's cheeks burned afresh with shame. The scene in that courtroom would remain imprinted on her mind for as long as she still had life within her to remember it.

"But we didn't know! How was we to know?" she had cried repeatedly at the mass of staring, accusing faces.

"Nobody told us . . . how was we to know?"

What had followed after, she was unable to recall clearly. Everything grew suddenly so disjointed . . . Frank being taken, shouting and struggling, down to the cells, her mother weeping, herself being questioned again and again, Frank's young sister – her own half-sister, God help her – in tears beside her; someone else, a man, a gentleman, taking her and her mother to a hotel along the street, and the crowd following, gathering outside below the window, whistling and calling out names that made her choke to hear them.

Then the minister from the church had come, and a doctor who gave her something that had made her sleep like one dead.

When she woke again, long hours later, her eyes were so blurred it was some little while before she realised that the copper-red flame burning against the bed-head was the glow of Belle Flynn's hair in the light of an oil lamp.

She heard her mother's voice, full of sadness, from somewhere close saying, "Sup this down you, if you can, Lizzie . . . sup it down;" and the bitter-sweetness in her mouth once more, the lead weight of her limbs as the voice receded into echoing distance.

It seemed after a time that Frank himself was there beside her, his rough, strong hand gripping hers; and though it was only a dream, she had cried out to him in her need and her love and her terrible guilt.

"Don't fret yourself about it, Lizzie," she thought she heard him answer. "We're one flesh, you and me. One in body and one in blood. We belong together now more than we ever did. We're the same breed . . . the same stock."

She had been excused from giving any further evidence at his trial, they told her later. She was obviously unwell and not in her right mind, and the bench in its mercy had spared her the ordeal of having to appear on display to a pruriently curious public.

The jury, responding to a clarifying point in the final summing-up that the death of Thomas Newbrook, though neither justifiable nor excusable, had been attended by alleviating circumstances which brought it short of wilful homicide, had, after a lengthy deliberation, returned a verdict of not guilty to murder but guilty to the lesser indictment of manslaughter.

There had been loud applause from the gallery as the Recorder passed sentence of seven years' imprisonment with hard labour, though whether it came in support of Frank, or whether in approval of his punishment, no one was sure.

"At least they've spared him his life," George Bashford commented, bringing news of the judgement to the three women waiting in a private sitting-room at The White Hart Hotel.

"For that, I suppose we must be grateful."

"Better they'd hanged him," Betty Copper said bitterly.

"I almost wish to God they had," wept Isabelle. "It would've been kinder. What sort of a life will he lead these next seven years? Caged up like some brute creature . . . breaking his flesh on stones and cranks and treadmills . . ."

Her godfather laid a comforting hand on her shoulder.

"He's a strong young man. He'll survive. And let's remember, my dear, when he's served his sentence he'll still be less than thirty years of age. Time enough to make a new life for himself."

"A new life for himself—"

Lizzie Newbrook repeated the words, her voice choked with despair.

" — but I won't be there to share it wi' him. They've sentenced me, an' all. Better they'd taken *me* and put a hempen rope round my neck, for all the life I've got left me now."

No one made an answer.

Something she had said at All Souls vicarage those long weeks past came back to her.

"A woman of ill-repute, that's what they'll brand me as. Fit for nothing but a house o' the same name."

The way those eyes had looked at her in the courtroom . . . Her face burned with the memory of it as she stood in the dank early morning mist at the foot of Star Street.

She had taught herself how to live with the pain and the guilt of Tom's death; she had learned how to hide the shame of her adultery. But she had no strength to bear the disgust, the revulsion, the contempt she had seen in those faces as they silently damned her with the word incest.

Lizzie pulled her paisley shawl further over her head and began walking slowly on. A pallid light filtered down between the rooftops from the shrouded sun, and sounds in the wakening neighbourhood were deadened by a blanket of damp river air that hugged itself to walls and windows and alley openings on either side of the narrow street.

Reaching her destination, she paused for a moment; then, suddenly resolute, went up the three stone steps and raised her hand to the ornate brass knocker on the panelled door. She knew what this house was. The customer at The Shades in Stanley Street had left her in no doubt about the services it offered.

Several minutes passed without any sign of answer to her knock. She tried again, louder; and when, finally, the door was opened, did not know which emotion was stronger, her relief or her regret.

"Can I have a word wi' Mrs Sullivan?" she asked the blowsy-faced girl who stood there.

"'Tis too early for Madame to be receiving. Best ye come back later."

The door began to close again.

"Please – I must see her now. I can't come back."

The desperate urgency in her voice made the other pause.

"Well . . . come away in, then."

She slipped inside, casting a last backward glance down the empty street as the door was shut behind her.

"If ye'll wait here I'll find where Madame is. Ye've a name I can give?"

"Name? Oh, oh yes. It's Mrs Newbrook, tell her."

A flicker of recognition showed in the sleep-swollen eyes before the girl turned away, clattering in unlaced shoes across the entrance hall to a door at the far end.

Mrs Sullivan's reception of her caller proved a chilly one. She had not long risen from bed when Lizzie was shown into

251

her, and the sour consequence of last night's pleasure was showing its effect on both temper and stomach.

"Of course I know who it is ye are," she said curtly in response to the question. "Was I not sitting not a dozen seats from ye in the court gallery?"

She did not need to say on which occasion.

Fanny Sullivan had not missed a single day of the trial, arriving each morning early at the courtroom to secure the most advantageous viewpoint. Heavily veiled, she had not been particularly noticed among the crowd, and had found amusing diversion in observing her fellow occupants of the gallery, including among them a number of her own clientele, some with their wives, others with females who were not their wives but behaved as though they wished others to believe they were.

Also, it had assuaged her bitterness somewhat to be able to watch the snivellings and grizzlings of her erstwhile "young lady", Isabelle Flynn, as the wretched chit's family skeletons were exposed in all their ugly nastiness and the lowly circumstances of an illegitimate background were picked over by counsel in the nicest detail.

"I wonder ye have the audacity to come showing your face in my establishment," Mrs Sullivan went on acidly, setting down the measure of brandy and hot water she had been nursing among the cushions of her chaise longue, "when there's hardly a soul in the entire town can be ignorant now of who ye are."

"There was nowhere else I felt I could come," said Lizzie.

"Nowhere else? Nowhere else, indeed? I'll have ye know, Mrs Newbrook, this academy is one of the best-respected places of education for young ladies of breeding between here and Tunbridge Wells! What makes ye have a right to come here and – "

"This place is a house for whores," Lizzie interrupted in a colourless voice. "And it's whore's work I've come here to do, if you'll take me."

Mrs Sullivan's crayoned eyebrows rose a fraction.

"Ye're a very bold-spoken young woman. And who was it told ye that, now?"

"Mr Bethway, from All Souls. He warned me against you, thinking to do me a kindness."

"He did, did he? He knew it was in your mind to pay me this visit?"

"No. Nobody knows of it. I slipped away afore they were awake."

Fanny Sullivan took up the brandy glass again and slowly drained it. She admired openness and honesty, but not when such qualities were motivated by the strong desire for self-abasement which she sensed lay behind this pitiable creature's behaviour.

After a few moments' silence she said carefully, "And what makes ye think I'd want to employ ye, Mrs Newbrook? Why come looking to me for work?"

Lizzie bowed her head. She was trembling noticeably, but her voice when she spoke was quite without emotion.

"There's nothing else left for me but a place like this. I've lost everything . . . my home, my good character. It's all over the country what I am. Wherever I go, there'll be fingers pointed at me, skirts twitched aside, names flung . . . What am I fit for now but selling myself to whoever's willing to pay?"

"Ye'd be useless to me," Mrs Sullivan said bluntly.

"But – why? I've a nice enough face. I'm young. I don't carry any sickness."

The other made a gesture of impatience and got to her feet.

"Not in your body, maybe. The sickness is in your head, I'm thinking. And ye'll find no cure for it in this house, Mrs Newbrook, so I'll thank ye to take your leave."

Lizzie made no move.

"Did ye not hear me?" Fanny Sullivan asked impatiently. Then, "Oh God – " as the other suddenly crumpled forward and slid to her knees – "what's wrong with ye? Are ye not well?"

There was an inaudible reply.

Cursing beneath her breath, Mrs Sullivan moved round the huddled figure and threw back the door.

"Kathleen!" she called out into the hall. "Kathleen!"

And when the blowsy-faced girl came clattering to see

253

what was amiss — "Help me on to the chaise with Mrs Newbrook. I think she's taken a faint. And then be off with ye to the minister's house at All Souls and tell that Mr Bethway he's to fetch the woman away from here directly!"

"Oh Lizzie, what on earth possessed you to steal off like that?" her mother chided tearfully. "I took it in my head you'd run away again, like last time."

Her pale, sleep-starved face turned to Alec Bethway, standing looking out from the window of the room at The White Hart where she and her daughter were temporarily lodged.

"A lucky thing you happened across her in the street, sir. She might've wandered anywhere, the state she's in. It was kind of you to see her safely back."

"I was glad to do so."

Far better for the time being, Alec had decided after coming away with Lizzie from Star Street, that nothing was said of the foolish prompting which had driven the girl to that house. Plainly, she was not to be held responsible for her actions while yet in such a distressed state of mind.

She had made an oblique response to his word of advice as he conveyed her in the Reverend Kenward's trap to the hotel.

"She didn't want me, neither, that Mrs Sullivan. There's nobody wants me. Not now."

He had done his best to comfort and encourage her, but to little avail.

"Thank the Lord this is our last day in Lewes," Mrs Copper said, brushing the tears from her cheek. "I was never so glad to see the back of a place, I can tell you, sir."

"Mrs Newbrook is going home with you to Barkham?"

"Aye, she is. There's a railway carriage leaves for Keymer Junction ten minutes to seven in the morning."

"I don't want to leave," Lizzie said dully. She had hardly spoken a word since coming back to the hotel.

"Oh, now, pet," her mother reproached her, "we've had this over before. You're not going back to that public house. I won't let you. You're coming along home wi' me."

She turned again to Alec.

"She thinks she should stay on at The Shades, sir. But I ask you, what life would that be for her? I've seen the place for myself, and a dirtier, dingier hole it'd be hard to find anywhere."

It was not The Shades Lizzie had intended returning to, as Alec realised; but he said nothing, asking instead, "What's to be done with the farm at Upper Highbury? Will it be kept on, do you think?"

"I don't know. That's for Lizzie to say. It's her property now, sir, according to Tom's will. Though there's a sister of his arguing whether she should by rights be left it, seeing as how poor Tom would never have died but for . . ."

Mrs Copper left the rest of the sentence dangling awkwardly.

"I don't want to go back to Barkham," Lizzie repeated in her flat voice. "I want to stay here, in Lewes."

"Why?" Alec wanted to know, watching her carefully.

She shook her head.

"Why?" he said again, more firmly.

Her lips trembled. "Frank . . ."

"There you go again – that dratted Frank!" her mother cried. "As if he hasn't done enough damage. You tell her, sir, do. I can't seem to make her see reason. You tell her. She might listen to you. Tell her it's no use her pining still for him."

Alec's deep-set gaze moved over the bowed shoulders, the tightly clasped hands.

"Do you pine for him still, Mrs Newbrook?"

There was a silence.

Then she nodded.

"It's a wickedness, that's what it is!" Fresh tears brimmed in her mother's eyes and spilled down the plump cheeks.

"Grieving like that . . . it's against all the laws o' nature."

A tap at the door interrupted whatever she was about to say next.

"Shall I – ?" Alec asked.

"Oh, if you would, sir. Thank you."

He went over and opened it.

"Isabelle!" The quick pleasure in his voice was evident. "And Mr Bashford. Good morning to you, sir."

"May we come in?"

George Bashford removed his hat and looked from the doorway across at Mrs Copper; then, seeing her distressed state, added hastily, "Though if it's not convenient, ma'am – "

"No, no, sir, you're welcome to come in." She sniffed back the tears.

"Sit down, both of you."

Mr Bashford stood aside to allow Isabelle in before him, then closed the door.

"I'm glad to find you here, Mr Bethway," he said. "My news will concern you, too. We have just come from seeing Mr Flynn's representative."

He looked at Lizzie Newbrook, and saw the quick expression of hope leap in her eyes.

"I'm sorry, ma'am. Frank's application for leave to appeal has been refused."

The hope faded.

Isabelle removed her gloves and sat down on a chair beside the window. Carefully smoothing the creased kid leather, she said without looking up, "Mr Digby Mayhew told us he's to be sent away to serve his sentence – "

"Sent away?" Lizzie cried out. "What . . . you mean they're not keeping him here at Lewes?"

"No. He's being shifted to Maidstone."

Lizzie's head sunk to her breast. In a low voice she asked, "Why couldn't they let him stop? Why send him over to Kent?"

George Bashford knew the answer, though he would be loath to reveal it in such circumstances as these.

Maidstone Gaol had better facilities by far for the serving of a sentence with hard labour. Better facilities from authority's point of view, that was, though infinitely worse from the viewpoint of those forced to use them.

There was shot-drill exercise – considered so taxing that men over forty-five years of age were generally excused it – in which a circle of prisoners stood paced out at three yards from one another, and for periods often exceeding well over

256

an hour were made to lift, carry, and deposit between their own place and that of their neighbour, cannon balls of lead shot twenty-four pounds in weight.

Of rather shorter duration, but no less exhausting, were the treadmills, each housed within its own cramped compartment, revolving at a carefully measured speed which denied the prisoner proper support as the steps sank away beneath his tread. By the end of even fifteen minutes the air within the narrow box had grown so hot and fouled that breathing became an agony to match that of the aching leg muscles.

For those who shirked hard labour and could not be persuaded by flogging or birching, there was the crank, a heavy drum of sand turned by a crank handle requiring back-breaking effort to move it.

"At least they are not sending him to one of the London prisons," said George Bashford. "Conditions in the capital beggar all description. The overcrowding is appalling, I'm told."

"And Maidstone is not so very far, no more than half a day's journey," Isabelle added optimistically.

Lizzie slowly raised her head and looked across at her; and for a moment, watching them both, Alec Bethway caught a fleeting glimpse of their shared sisterhood.

The experience of discovering, in such a cruel manner, that this dark-haired stranger was her own blood kin had, after the shock of the first days, given Isabelle an inner strength and maturity which she never imagined she possessed.

"She's as much our father's flesh as Frank and me – aye, and Joel Adams back in Weatherfield," she had responded when Alec spoke warmly of her charity in helping at Lizzie Newbrook's sickbed.

"She's my sister, for all she's done. Who am I to turn my back on her? Or on Frank, come to that? We all of us need one another."

"Promise me you'll go back to Barkham wi' your mam," Isabelle said now, getting up and going to kneel beside Lizzie's chair. "There's no use you staying here in Lewes."

257

She took the other's clenched hands within her own and held them tightly.

"Promise me! You remember I told you as how I'm going to live at Bonningale now? Wi' Mrs Bashford and the children? Well, Bonningale's handy enough for Barkham – only the other side the Downs. I thought mebbe we could meet to see each other. And I'll be needing company travelling to Maidstone to visit our Frank. I can't expect the Bashfords to put themselves out to do that. So you will go back to Barkham, won't you, Lizzie? It'd make me so content, knowing you're there whenever I need you."

Isabelle looked pleadingly into her sister's face, and felt the cold hands tremble.

Mrs Copper began to say something; but George Bashford checked her with a touch on the arm.

Minutes of silence passed.

Then Lizzie drew in a long, uneven breath.

"I'll go back to Barkham," she whispered.

26

"Lord help us!"

Mrs Jenkins set down a dish of peeled potatoes on the kitchen table at Tea Garden Lane and stared in consternation at young Minnie.

"Mr Osborne told you *what?*"

Excitement had robbed Minnie of breath. Pressing her hands to her apron bib she repeated what she had said, the sentences coming in gulps.

"Mr Harry . . . he's run off to Scotland wi' that Miss Winter . . . and wedded her there! Mr Osborne's just this minute had word . . . Mr Harry's bringing her back wi' him here . . . and we're to have the house opened up ready."

"Lord help us!" said Mrs Jenkins again.

"They'll be here the day after tomorrow," Minnie went on. "Mr Osborne said to tell you . . . he'll be down directly hisself to show you the letter."

"And what am I supposed to gi' them to eat when we've hardly a crumb for ourselves in the place, and no wages nor nothing paid us for nigh on three weeks?" cried the cook. "You'll have to go down the high street, my girl, and ask if they'll let Mr Harry's credit run a few days longer. I'd pay out o' my own pocket – "

"Aye, as I dare say we're expected to."

The stoop-shouldered figure of Osborne appeared from the direction of the stairs.

"Leastways, there's no sign of a promissory note wi' Mr Harry's letter," he went on caustically, holding out the envelope. "Nor no mention o' payment for the wet-nurse to farm out his sister's poor child. Seemingly the small matter o' money slipped his mind, what wi' one thing and another. Or mebbe he thinks his household should live off air and water?"

Mrs Jenkins shook her grey head in resignation.

"It'll soon be coming to that, an' all, the way things are going."

Taking the envelope, she produced a pair of spectacles from a pocket in the voluminous skirt of her apron, placed them carefully upon her nose and seated herself at the table before withdrawing the letter.

There followed a short perusal.

"It has here, written from Dumfries-shire. That's somewhere in the north, is it, Mr Osborne? Oh, yes, so it is. Away up in Scotland. Mr Harry says so hisself . . ."

She read on.

Then – "Well!" – putting the page down in her lap.

"What's it say?" demanded Minnie, whose own ability with the printed word was sadly wanting. "Read it out for us, do."

Mrs Jenkins obliged.

"'Annan, in the county of Dumfries, the seventh day of October'," she announced, taking the paper up again.

"'My dear Osborne, I am this day returning from Scotland in company with my wife, the former Miss Adelaide Winter,

259

to whom I was married here Tuesday last. I shall desire you to have the house prepared in readiness for our arrival at the week's end. Yours, & etc.'"

"And that's all?"

Disappointed, the little maid leaned over the other's shoulder to peer at the scrawl of words.

"It's enough," said Osborne, sniffing. "Reading atween those lines, I reckon Mr Harry has had to act hasty. That marriage weren't set to take place till the spring. He's jumped afore the gun were fired, that's what he's done."

"And on account o' Frank Flynn's trial, I shouldn't wonder," Mrs Jenkins observed.

"Aye. On account o' that . . . and his sister being taken off to a bedlam. I thought mebbe he might. I mind some'at Mr Ambrose Foster's man told me, a month or so back. He'd overheard Mr Harry tell his master he was tempted to make a run for it wi' the lady if ever news was to reach her family in London."

"Well, leastways thank the Lord it seems we shan't need to trouble ourselves further for a roof above our heads. When poor Miss Rosannah went into that institution, I thought Mr Harry might shut up the house for good."

Putting away her spectacles, the cook got to her feet again and retrieved the dish of potatoes.

"There's a silver lining to every cloud that passes, as I always say . . . Hand me down that pan o' boiled cabbage from the pantry shelf, Minnie. I'll heat it wi' the cold mutton from yesterday's nuncheon. And don't pull your face, neither! It's all I can gi' you both for the present. Just you be thankful you've not been put out o' work altogether, my girl."

"You reckon for sure Mr Harry'll be keeping us on, Mr Osborne?" Minnie asked hopefully, reaching up in the pantry for the black enamelled pan put well out of the way of cockroaches.

She had not forgotten the bitter tears wept at the thought of being given notice and having to leave this employment to share the dirt and drudgery of her sisters' lives in the foundry.

Osborne, too, had been concerned for his own future. It

was all very well for Mrs Jenkins and her husband: they had grown sons and daughters to provide for them. But he was alone; and what prospect was there for a man of his age, entering his declining years, but inferior domestic work and the constant overshadowing threat of the poor-house waiting at the end of it?

Now, however, he was prepared to be optimistic.

"We'll be kept on, Minnie, don't you fret. Mr Harry and his good lady will be making this their residence. Marrying so hasty the way they have, they'll not be welcome at her father's in London, and where else are they to live if not here? It's Mr Harry's house now, when all's said and done. Miss Rosannah won't likely be needing it further for a good while, not where she is. You mark me, Minnie, it'll be like the olden days come back again, wi' a master and mistress in the place – "

He grinned, displaying his blackened stumps of teeth.

"Us below stairs, we'll be happy as pigs in summer."

The solitaire diamond adorning the former Miss Winter's left hand was partnered now by a heavy gold band a shade too large for the finger it encircled. In years gone by, it had been worn by Harry Weldrake's grandmother; and though gambling debts had swallowed everything else bequeathed him, for reasons of sentiment he had held on to this one particular piece of family jewellery.

Weldrake was far from being a superstitious man, yet it had been his grandmother's ring which decided him finally to anticipate events and hurry Adelaide into marriage.

He had been in his dressing room to change one evening soon after the start of his brother-in-law's trial, and, cursing fate and Frank Flynn alike for the imminent downfall of his plans, had flung open the ebony box containing his few remaining sets of studs and cuff-links and spied the ring lying there among them.

Snatching it up, he began hefting it from one hand to the other; and then, quite suddenly, in the desperation born of despair, had decided that he must stake everything on a final gamble.

He had not, after all, gone out that evening.

Instead, he had sat up far into the night composing a letter to Miss Winter which hinted subtly at a family matter which might possibly result in her father wishing to have the date of their wedding postponed, and beseeching her, therefore, to marry him immediately.

". . . I have no alternative but to entreat of you to consent to an elopement. This proposal may startle your delicacy, yet, for heaven's sake, do not suffer its impulse to induce you to reject the ardent prayers of your affectionate lover, who can no longer exist without you. Consider, we may return again in a short while united beyond the power of any to separate us.

"Reflect, my adored one, upon what I have written, throw yourself upon my protection, confide in my honour, remember we have perhaps no choice but this, and the alternative is to be parted for ever. I trust my dearest Adelaide is not afraid to confide in him whose most desired object is to become her protector through life . . ."

There had followed two days of unbearable waiting; and then had come Miss Winter's reply.

"Your letter has agitated me greatly, indeed I know not how to conduct myself. The situation in which we are placed is so unusual, I am fearful the world may judge harshly of us: and it would make me wretched for life, were you to be considered a guilty creature with your kinsman, even though conscious of your own innocence.

"You desire me to reflect – alas! I cannot. My reason condemns the step you are so anxious for us to take; but my heart decides in your favour. I am sensible that I may trust myself to your affectionate protection, nor can I for a moment doubt the honour of him whom I so tenderly love.

"Do then with me as you will. Whatever your determination may be, I will consent, and by so doing resign my eternal happiness to your care. May heaven grant that nothing unpleasant may attend upon our rash expedition.

"Let me be informed when and where I am to meet you, and depend upon your Adelaide's punctuality.

"I am, dear Harry, ever yours."

Weldrake's relief at her acceptance was tempered slightly by the oblique reference to "guilty creature", but he had to let that pass for the moment: time enough for quibbles once his ring was safely upon her finger.

Somewhat belatedly it had occurred to him that an elopement might be prejudicial to his gaining control of his fiancée's money, in view of the recent legislation relating to married women's property; and upon making discreet enquiry, he had been advised that in order to circumvent possible penalties and expedite the wedding with all speed, the ceremony should take place in Scotland.

Fifteen years earlier it would have sufficed for Weldrake and Miss Winter to travel to one of the border villages and there, in the presence of witnesses, declare their wish to marry, for the wedding to be carried out immediately. Anyone of local standing, not necessarily a minister of religion, was empowered to officiate at such a service and it was not uncommon for "runaway" marriages to be performed by an alehouse keeper, ferryman or blacksmith.

The traffic was virtually ended in 1856, however, when a change in Scottish law required one of the contracting parties to have resided in the parish for at least three weeks before the event.

Accordingly, Weldrake travelled north alone and settled himself at a hotel in the border town of Annan, writing to inform Miss Winter that she should join him there at the end of the required period.

His boredom during this time of voluntary exile was such that her arrival, two days before their wedding, aroused the strongest feelings of thankfulness and he found himself almost enjoying his role of guide to the Roman remains outside the town, which was all the diversion the neighbourhood had to offer.

The marriage of Harry Weldrake and Adelaide Winter was duly solemnised on a windy, grey October morning by a minister of the Scottish Presbyterian Church in the presence of the minister's housekeeper and two guests from the hotel, a commercial traveller and an antiquarian, acting as witnesses.

It was remarked that the bride's wedding gown, of heavy

vhite silk, was much creased and hung very loosely upon her, :specially about the waist.

Not wishing to arouse her family's suspicions by bringing away too much baggage on her supposed "visit to friends at Oxford", Miss Winter had readily agreed to her fiancé's suggestion that he take it upon himself to provide her wedding outfit.

He had brought it with him, packed with his own wear, from Lewes: the discarded gown in which his sister Rosannah had married Frank Flynn.

"Why," enquired the new Mrs Weldrake some weeks after taking up residence at Tea Garden Lane, "do you suppose Cook ignores the menus I prepare, and continues to serve us each evening with hashed meat or else plain boiled fish?"

Weldrake raised his eyes from the newspaper he was reading at the dinner table; then gave a shrug and looked down at his plate.

"I have not the slightest notion," he said, jabbing his fork into the mashed remains of his meal.

Adelaide Weldrake pushed her own plate away.

"This evening, had my instructions been heeded, we should have dined on mock turtle soup, followed by brill with oyster sauce, roast mutton for the main course with turnips, and charlotte russe with a compote of peaches to finish."

"Indeed?"

"Yes, Harry, indeed. I was brought up to appreciate that the dishes of a meal should be both nourishing and complementary."

"I found nothing wrong with what we've just eaten."

"It was not what I asked Mrs Jenkins to prepare."

"Then you must speak to her on the matter, my dear."

"I have done so already."

"And what is her answer?"

Adelaide Weldrake smoothed out a crease in the napkin covering the lap of her moss-green gown.

"That she is given insufficient housekeeping money to buy other than the very cheapest cuts."

Weldrake folded his paper and tossed it aside.

"I give her enough. If I want to eat in style, I dine out."

"And I must be content with . . . hashed meat and boiled fish?"

"If that is what is served at your husband's table."

He pushed back his chair and got up.

Some nights ago he had used almost the same words, when Adelaide complained of the lack of affection he showed her in their moments of intimacy. Loving him as she did, she had not found the act between husband and wife repugnant, but surely it should be more than this swift, selfish, loveless taking of physical gratification?

"A wife is in no position to demand anything when she is in her husband's bed," he had said stingingly in answer to her complaint.

Leaving the table, Weldrake went over to the fireplace and stood there with his back to the flames, coat tails raised to warm his immaculately trousered legs.

"If you wish us to keep an elaborate table, my dear Adelaide, I suggest you augment the housekeeping from your own purse."

Two small red spots appeared on the sallow cheeks.

Diffidently she replied, "I have no money of my own at present. My allowance for the month went on the expenses of our . . . marriage."

"Oh, come now, dearest. What allowance is this? The income you receive from your uncle's estate is paid directly to your account with Coutts. You may draw upon it at any time."

"Not any longer, Harry."

He let the coat tails fall, and his tone sharpened as he faced his wife.

"You mean your arrangement with your bank has been altered?"

Adelaide lifted her napkin and placed it carefully beside her plate.

"I mean, the income from my uncle's legacy has been made over to my brother Augustus, by a deed of transfer – "

"The devil it has!"

" – which gives Augustus the control of my money. In

265

future I am to receive a monthly allowance, sufficient to meet personal expenses."

Weldrake went white to the lips.

Striding across the room, he struck the tabletop with his clenched fist, making dishes and cutlery rattle.

"That income became mine on our marriage! How dare you and your conniving brother try to swindle me out of it!"

Adelaide cringed away.

"The transfer was made before our marriage – "

"Then perhaps you should have done me the courtesy of consulting me earlier!"

"Augustus said it would not affect you . . ."

She bowed her head.

Her banker brother Augustus had also said that Harry Weldrake was a fortune-hunter, a cheat and a liar; and when she had vigorously defended her fiancé against those charges, had further warned her that she was allowing her heart to rule her head.

It had been the certainty of her belief rather than the dictates of caution which made her agree to Augustus's suggestion that she transfer the income from her inheritance into his name, that he might set up a trust fund which Harry Weldrake, should he become her husband, would be power-less to touch.

"You had told me yourself, Harry, and often, that your own income was more than adequate to support a wife and family," she went on unhappily.

"And so it is, provided my creditors do not require too frequently to see the colour of my money," he snapped back.

Pulling out his chair from the table, he seated himself heavily and leaned forward, elbows on knees, his head between his hands.

How life liked to hit at him, he thought resentfully.

Fearful that the wretched Flynn affair would damage his standing with the Winters and prevent him espousing Adelaide's fortune and family connections, he had hurried her into this marriage. Only to discover too late, it seemed, that he'd merely succeeded in exchanging the frying pan for the fire: not only had the connections with her family been wellnigh severed, but the fortune was apparently now placed well beyond his grasp.

Sir Horace Winter's reaction to the news of his daughter's elopement was predictably one of outraged indignation; and his unwelcome son-in-law's letters of apology and explanation had done very little to mollify his temper in view of the lurid details which had emerged from Frank Flynn's trial and been splashed in the sensationalist London press while Weldrake was away north of the border at Annan.

Adelaide herself, learning something of these details, had chided her bridegroom for his fears that the trial might have prejudiced her affections. He was not to be held responsible, she assured him fondly, for the ill-conduct of a relative.

Weldrake had been greatly cheered by this sympathetic response, and demonstrated his relief by the attention he had paid his bride during the first days of their marriage. Adelaide, too, had rejoiced that her brother Augustus's warnings were proved so groundless.

Since their homecoming to Lewes, however, the first slight misgiving had crept into her mind. Why had Harry not been open from the start, taken her into his confidence and explained this dreadful business fully and frankly? He told her he'd feared to lose her esteem . . . but perhaps, the little voice of doubt whispered, it was her fortune he'd feared to lose more?

She had willingly paid the hotel bill and the cost of their railway travel from Scotland, accepting his explanation that he had misjudged his own expenses. At the time it seemed mere forgetfulness. Now, though, she was not so certain.

There was another thing. During their courtship, Harry's kindly nature had made a warm impression, and so it was difficult to excuse his present cruel-hearted attitude towards his sister's child.

Adelaide had been told that the sudden tragic loss of a dear friend so soon after the still-birth of her son had caused Rosannah to fall ill; and her illness, taking the form of a violent hysteria, had required her confinement in a Bethlehem Hospital – a bedlam – which was an institution for the medical treatment of mental sickness.

Her infant daughter, scarcely more than five months old, had been farmed out with a wet-nurse in some nearby village; and when Adelaide suggested she herself might care for the motherless little creature, Harry had adamantly refused, saying the child was well enough placed where it was.

She looked across the littered dining table at the handsome head bowed between the hands, and ran her tongue nervously over her lips. If this marriage were to succeed, she must act contrary to her nature and become more boldly insistent.

"Harry . . . You love me, Harry, do you not?"

"I suppose that I do." He did not look up.

"Only suppose?"

"Oh God, Adelaide, do we have to have this yet again? Would I have wed you had I not loved you?"

She made no answer.

Weldrake straightened himself. Getting up, he went towards the door.

"Where are you going?"

"To my club."

"Your club? Again? You went there yesterday in the evening. And the evening before."

"And I intend to go this evening also."

Adelaide pushed back her chair and rose to her feet, the light from the gas chandelier reflecting dully on the mousy hair Minnie had tried to tease into ringlets with a curling-iron before dinner.

"I do not wish it, Harry."

He swung back towards her and answered savagely, "Your wishes, dear heart, would be my command were it not for the fact that I am virtually bankrupt unless I make a good killing."

"A . . . killing?"

"Yes. A killing. A gambler's term. It's the only way of making money I know – apart from marriage."

She turned away, the plain, ageing face furrowed with hurt.

After a few moments' silence she said, "You must not leave me alone again tonight, Harry. Papa would not like it were he to learn of your cruel neglect."

"I would not need to neglect you, Adelaide, had you not allowed your family to cozen you into entrusting them with your wealth."

From the door, Weldrake stared at her angrily.

"If your papa is so concerned for your happiness, perhaps you should write to request he show a little leniency towards his impecunious son-in-law."

She flinched at the tone. The sallow features were mottled with a red stain.

"He would not give you a penny-piece if he knew how miserable you have made me this evening! It might be in your best interest . . . to treat me with kindness and consideration. I know papa will come round in time to accepting our marriage. But unless you are prepared to prove yourself a loyal and loving husband, Harry, I fear you can expect no financial assistance from any of my family."

For a while there was no sound in the room other than the soft hiss of the gas jets.

"I think . . ." Weldrake said at length, quietly, "I think I understand."

Moving away from the door he came slowly to Adelaide's side, and reaching out, took her hand and raised it to his lips.

"Upon reflection, there is no need after all to deprive myself of your company this evening, dearest wife."

27

It had frozen hard during the night. The points of pick-axes slipped treacherously on the surfaces of frost-whitened stone and already one man in the gang had had a leg gashed open from a glancing blow. A couple of the guards had released him from the chain and carted him, groaning, from the site to be returned in one of the horse-drawn vans to Maidstone Gaol.

Frank Flynn did not mind the cold too much: it numbed

his feet inside the ill-fitting boots and deadened the pain of broken chilblains and the constant chafing rub of the leg iron which, like the rest of the gang, he wore to hobble him and prevent possible flight.

To give some respite to the aching muscles of his back he straightened himself for a moment and stood resting on his pick handle, looking out from the quarry towards the spires and towers of distant Rochester and the wide grey waters of the Medway estuary. Nearer at hand, the wintry Kentish countryside spread away below the North Downs, each feature and shape and colour of the landscape clearly defined in the sharp air.

Frank bent again to the pick-axe, his breath cloudy white as he blew out his cheeks and set himself once more to stone-breaking. In the four months since his transfer to Maidstone Gaol he had quickly learnt that the appearance of idleness attracted a truncheon about one's shoulders.

Though his body had retained its strength, the poor prison diet showed in the clammy greyish pallor of his skin, and was especially noticeable now that the beard grown during his detention and trial had been shaven and his head cropped to the bone.

Her brother's changed appearance had caused great concern to Isabelle Flynn when she came to visit him. She had sat leaning a little forward on a wooden chair at the other side of the grille, a prison warder standing at the door behind her. When she spoke, her light voice echoed slightly in the emptiness of the narrow room.

"Are you all right, Frank? Have they been treating you well? Are you being fed enough?"

He had smiled grimly.

"You don't come to a place like this to be treated well and fed enough. But the devils ain't done for me yet, not by long chalks."

There was a pause.

"I stayed at the alehouse last night," Isabelle began again quickly, "to break the journey from Bonningale. Aunt Lottie's got the licence now. She wrote saying she'd applied. You should see the changes she's made, Frank. All the garden's been cleared up and laid afresh wi' turf and flowerbeds. Oh, and you'll never guess, but our Joel's got hisself betrothed to marry – "

"Are the Bashfords looking after you sufficient?" Frank had interrupted tersely, not wanting to hear how the fortunes of others had prospered since the decline of his own.

"Don't you want to know who it is he's to wed? Though she's no one from Weatherfield, so belikes you wouldn't know her. Her name's Kate, Kate Brophy. I met her in Lewes, but she's at the rectory now, and Joel says – "

"Joel can go hang! I asked if the Bashfords were looking after you properly."

Vexed by his rudeness, she gave a little nod.

"And that blasted curate – what's his name – Bethway. He's still dancing attendance on you, is he?"

Isabelle's cheeks flamed and she lowered her eyes.

"He's not dancing attendance, Frank. I – I've only seen him the once, and that was when he come over at Christmastime. It's not likely I'll see him again, I don't suppose . . . he's leaving Lewes the start o' March. They've given him a parish of his own now, somewhere away up in the Midlands."

She fell silent; and then, in a soft voice, "He's been real kind to me, Alec has. I shall miss him when he's gone . . . but he'll never know it."

"They're too pious for their own good, that sort," Frank had said churlishly. "You're well rid of him. Anyway, where's Lizzie? Why hasn't she been to see me yet? She got my letters, didn't she? You said she promised to come over wi' you. Where is she? What's going on?"

"Nothing's going on!" Isabelle protested. "It's on account of her having her work taken up wi' the farm. Now she's made up her mind to keep the place on and not sell it, she hasn't got time to come traipsing all this long distance."

"No, nor time to put pen to paper, seemingly. I haven't had a word from her, even."

"It's for the best, Frank. She's learning to make a fresh life for herself . . ."

Isabelle had looked at her brother through the grille, leaving the rest of the sentence unspoken.

He stared miserably back, hunched inside the coarse grey prison clothing.

"You tell her from me, she's to come. You understand, our Belle? You tell her she's to answer when I write. I want word from her. I want to see her . . . even if it's only the once. You tell her. Or God help me, I think I'll go mad in here, not knowing what's going on, what she's doing, how things are wi' her . . ."

"I *would* have come afore, Frank," Lizzie Newbrook said awkwardly. "I'd have come wi' Belle at the new year. But you know how it is. I've got the farm to manage all alone now – "

"What d'you want to keep that place on for? I thought you were all set on moving back to Barkham wi' your mother."

The two looked at one another through the meshes of the grille, Lizzie fidgeting uncomfortably with the fringes of her shawl, Frank Flynn staring at her as though he would imprint for ever the sight of her pale face on his mind, to be remembered in the bitter wasted days of his confinement.

"You *told* me you were going back to Barkham!"

"Aye, I know I did, Frank. But that was . . . that was afore you were tried . . . afore I knew . . ."

Her voice trailed into silence. She made a gesture with her hand.

Lizzie Newbrook had altered in the months since that moment of terrible discovery in the Lewes courtroom; altered not so much in appearance (though those who knew her well had noticed her glance was not so bold as it used to be, and she had developed a nervous habit of touching her fingers to her face when spoken to, as though wishing to hide something) as altered from within, in those attitudes and reflections which shape the future outlook.

She had loved Frank Flynn; of that there could not be the slightest doubt. She had surrendered herself completely, to the point where emotion had blinded her to his defects.

No matter that he'd destroyed her marriage; who was to say that it might not have destroyed itself in time, through indifference and monotony. No matter that he was responsible for her husband's death; she would have taken that guilt upon herself and suffered it for the sake of her love. No matter that her relationship with Frank had brought distress to his wife, and concern to her own mother, and branded Lizzie herself an adulteress and a slut in the eyes of all. For his sake, she would willingly have continued to endure all this, and more.

She had thought, too, that she could learn to live with the knowledge that he was her own half-brother. Now she knew she could not.

In the beginning, she pined for him day and night, missing his physical presence so much she thought her heart would break with longing. Over and over she relived in her thoughts all those times they had shared together, the stolen meetings, the words of tenderness, the passion that had fired their loving; and then she had tried to look ahead, to the day when Frank would be released from imprisonment and they could be once more together as in the old days.

But Lizzie could not see ahead: the way had closed itself off to her. The man she'd loved so desperately belonged now in her past, like a dead man. He had died on that day of the trial in Lewes. The Frank Flynn she had known and needed was not the same as the Frank Flynn serving seven years with hard labour in Maidstone Gaol for the manslaughter of her husband. This was her own flesh and blood, fathered like her by some itinerant stallion leader whose face and voice and character lived on still in his bastard children.

Lizzie could no longer even tolerate the memory of giving herself as a woman to Frank: it was akin to mating with that unknown father. God forbid that they should ever come together again, for each time Frank caressed her she'd be thinking of that other, wondering if his hands had touched her mother as Frank's touched her; wondering if his lips had been as warmly demanding, his body as strong, even the smell of his skin as exciting.

She had gone home to Barkham with her mother after the trial, not knowing what her future must be, and hardly caring. When the question of her late husband's place at

Upper Highbury was raised, her first response was that it should be sold, house, land and stock together.

She had returned there for the first time since Tom's death, to collect what there was of her own personal things; and standing in the doorway of the kitchen, looking out across the flat expanse of snow-levelled fields towards distant Highbury Mill, had at last allowed herself to break through the self-imposed barrier of guilt, and remember her husband as he had been during the first months of their marriage, before she met Frank Flynn.

In her mind's eye she saw Tom again, working this land, labouring from sunrise to dusk that he might make of it a home and inheritance for his wife and the children he hoped she would bear him. The image was too poignantly strong to resist: before the day's end Lizzie had decided she would not sell this place, she would stay, and with the hire of day labour try to work it herself. It was the only way she knew to make amends for the bitter wrongs of the past.

Hesitantly, she tried now to explain to Frank what she had thought she might do with the property, increase its income by renting the outlying pasture to a neighbouring dairy farmer, turn the home fields over to market gardening and grow produce to sell locally.

He listened with impatience.

"It sounds as though you're not allowing yourself much time to miss me."

"It's not a matter o' missing you, Frank," she answered defensively. "If I don't do the work, who else will?"

"I wish to God I was out o' this damn' place!"

He stared angrily round, at the bare brick walls, the single unlit gas lamp, the narrow barred windows overlooking the dark well between this block of the prison and the next.

"You don't know what it's like . . . day in, day out, nothing but the same cell to wake up in, the same faces to look at, the same voices saying the same blasted things all the while, the same work breaking your back – "

"But you're strong. You can do it."

"Oh, aye. I can do it. I've got to do it, haven't I? Every

274

single day for the next seven years of my life. The only thing that keeps me going is the thought o' you."

Lizzie looked down.

Behind her, the attendant warder at the door sneezed loudly, then blew his nose before folding his arms again and shifting his weight to the other foot.

"The food they shovel at you isn't fit for pigswill," Frank went on peevishly. "I wouldn't mind that, even, if there was some'at to wash the taste of it down. But there's nothing except watered ale of a Saturday, and what use is that to a man who likes his drink? When I get out of here, Lizzie, the first thing I'm going to do is find the nearest grog shop. And the second thing . . ."

He paused, gazing at her through the grille in a way that was almost pleading.

"The second thing I'm going to do – is find you."

"No!"

Her cry of rejection echoed in the emptiness, causing the pleading expression to change at once to one of bewilderment.

"But, Lizzie – "

"No, I said! I don't want you come looking for me, Frank."

"Why not, in God's name? What's wrong wi' doing that?"

"You know what's wrong. It's not right . . . not any more. Best we put all that behind us."

Bewilderment was succeeded by a suspicious anger.

"Who's been having a go at you, Lizzie? Eh? When you visited me that time in Lewes you seemed happy enough to let things go on as they had. You said it'd make no difference. We had none o' this talk o' putting things behind us."

"I was upset . . . everything was such a muddle . . . I didn't know *what* I was saying."

"Has that Bethway been meddling again?"

"No."

"Who, then? Tell me!"

"It's no use, Frank. It's over atween us, and that's that. There's no more to be said."

"Oh, but I think there is! You've got yourself somebody else, is that it? Some other's come sniffing round you?"

"No!"

275

"A comely young widow wi' a place all her own, and not a man's risen to take her bait? I'll not believe it. Who's put you up to this change of heart, my girl? Eh?"

His tone of anger sharpened.

"You don't come near me for months, no word from you. I might've been dead – aye, hanged – for all you've damn' well cared. Did you ever stop for a minute to think how it is wi' me here? Wellnigh going out o' my mind just wi' the thought o' you? The nights I've laid awake aching wi' the need o' you? Well, did you? And now – now you tell me it's all over and done with atween us, you don't want any more to do wi' me. You, who said countless times you'd rather die than lose me! God knows, but I wish I could be out o' this place so's to find out for myself what's going on!"

The warder in the background spoke up sharply.

"Keep your voice down, there. If you can't talk without shouting I'll have you taken back."

Frank glowered at him from behind the grille, biting back a retort that might have brought further, harsher reprimand. In the pallid light from the window a film of sweat glistened on the shaven skin of hairline and upper lip.

He passed a hand over his face, and when he spoke to Lizzie again his voice was more controlled.

"Somebody's helping you, are they, wi' the farm and so on?"

"I don't want to talk about it, Frank. I think it's best I went now."

"No – no, sit yourself down. Don't go just yet awhile . . . please. I'm sorry I let my temper get the better of me. Sit down again, will you?"

Reluctantly, she obliged him.

There was a silence; then she said, "The foreman at the next farm – Everdene's – he's lending a hand for a bit. And Mr Bashford's been over a time or two from Bonningale. His eldest boy, Ellis – "

"That's none o' Bashford's, that's the step-son," Frank interrupted pettily.

"Well, his step-son, then. He's stayed on and off over the new year while he's been on holiday from his college."

"What, stayed wi' you?"

"Aye. Not in the house – at the cottage the other side."

"He likes you, does he, this Ellis?"

"Oh . . . don't start again. He's only eighteen. He's three years younger than me. Four, almost."

"But he's good wi' his hands."

She flushed at the coarse implication.

"He's been going through Tom's account books for me, that's all. He's got a good head for figures."

Since he first came to Upper Highbury with his step-father, in the first week of 1872, Ellis Bates had returned alone on several subsequent occasions. Lizzie raised no objection. She was grateful for someone to sort through the accumulated litter of farm accounts and put the books in order, a task which the young student seemed clearly to relish.

They had little conversation together. He showed himself to be a quiet, private individual who preferred his own company to any other, and apart from their shared meals in the kitchen she saw him rarely. When he was not occupying himself with the ledgers, he would be out walking the country-side alone, or else reading: something he frequently did late into the night, for Lizzie, a poor sleeper herself, had sometimes seen the lamp still burning in the cottage window.

Before returning to Cambridge for the new term, Ellis had asked if he might come back to Upper Highbury during the next holiday – it was quieter for his studies than the family home at Bonningale, he explained – and had made Lizzie promise to write to him with news of herself.

She had not resisted.

"Visiting time's up, ma'am." The warder consulted his timepiece.

Lizzie acknowledged him with a nod of the head and got to her feet.

"Well, Frank . . ."

It was a difficult moment, and she could think of nothing to say in parting.

Frank leaned forward at the other side of the partition and thrust his fingers through the meshes of the grille.

"You'll come again — won't you, Lizzie?"

"I don't know. I'm not sure."

"But you'll keep in touch? Please?"

Without meeting his eyes, she answered, "I might write and let you know how I'm doing wi' the farm. I suppose we should stay friends. You're . . . family, after all."

She took something from her reticule and laid it down. It was the gipsy jewel he'd given her that day at The Eclipse in Midhurst, all those long, long months ago.

Dumbly he watched her turn away and go out through the door held open for her. She did not look back. Her footsteps echoed lightly in the corridor beyond and then gradually faded.

Frank slumped against the grille, head bowed between his shoulders. He had lost everything, he told himself despairingly. His livelihood, his freedom, the respect of his fellows, his chance ever of becoming a gentleman . . . and now, his woman.

The following afternoon, when shot-drill exercise ended, he went missing.

There had been an ugly fight between two other prisoners, and in the rumpus no one saw him slip away. His absence was not discovered until the men were counted back into their cells. A thin powdery snow had fallen, sufficient to coat the ground, and searching warders came upon a track of boot-prints leading to a store shed.

The padlock had been forced and the door stood slightly ajar.

Inside, they found Frank Flynn. He had hanged himself with a hempen rope from a rafter crossbar; and though they cut him down at once, it was already too late to save his life.

28

Winter passed, slowly giving way to spring of 1872, and then to early summer; and the sharpness of bereavement faded a little, itself giving way to the soft ache of remembered sorrow.

Already green spears of bramble and nettle were starting to cover the mound of raw earth in St Anne's churchyard at Weatherfield, where Frank Flynn had been laid to rest beside his mother and father. In another month or so, as summer drew on and the earth settled more firmly within the grave, the mound would be dug over and levelled, and the border of limed cockleshells edging the burial place of Dinah Flynn and her stallion man Frank Morgan would be extended to enfold their son.

Being at Bonningale, Isabelle was spared the full hurt she might otherwise have suffered from the blow of Frank's suicide. The Bashfords drew themselves around her, giving her the strength of their close family unity, and she had been greatly solaced by their comfort and compassion.

Her own developing maturity, too, stood her in good stead at this time of fresh trial, enabling her to accept her loss with a dignity which would not have been possible for the ingenuous girl of only twelve months earlier.

"Weatherfield's changed. I don't feel as if I belong there any more," she had said to Rachael Bashford when she returned to Bonningale after Frank's funeral.

"It's not home to me now. My home's here, wi' you and the family."

Rachael had understood. "You'll go back, though, to visit, won't you?"

"I don't know that I will. There's nothing left for me there. I'd rather remember it the way it was, when mam was alive and we had the running o' the alehouse, and our Frank . . . Frank was living wi' us still.''

But though she had not gone back, Isabelle was not forgotten in Weatherfield. Towards the end of May, a few days before her twentieth birthday, her aunt Lottie Adams wrote enclosing anniversary greetings in a querulous letter of news from the village.

Joel was home again from Ireland, thank the Lord, and safe. Though why he'd had to go all that long distance out of the shire merely to marry, she was blessed if she could understand, when Weatherfield church had been considered good enough for Weatherfield weddings since time out of mind.

Not that she had anything against her new daughter, she wrote – a cleanly girl, albeit tempersome. But foreign folk had foreign ways, and it was sad to see the needlework pictures stitched by some old granny Adams thrown out for no better reason than the moth in them, and the prints of the crossing-sweep and lavender-seller taken down from the cottage wall and images of martyred saints and other such truck put up to take their place.

The letter ended on a happier note, however, for since Lottie had started providing overnight accommodation for passing carriage trade, business at the alehouse had picked up considerably and she could now afford to have the gas laid on for lighting, and a proper stove in the kitchen instead of the old range.

There was a letter, too, from Lizzie Newbrook at Upper Highbury; but far briefer and saying only that she was well and thanked Isabelle for the invitation to attend her birthday celebration.

"I'll come with Ellis if I'm able," she had ended cryptically.

From Alec Bethway, there was no word at all.

Two months earlier the young minister had ridden over from Lewes to spend a day at Bonningale. It had proved an enjoyable visit for them all, and he confessed on making his farewell that his pleasure was now tinged the more with regret that he must depart from Sussex to take up his new incumbency in the diocese of Worcester.

At the end of the day, she had walked with him in the fading light of evening as far as the river bridge; and before mounting his horse to leave her, Alec had taken her hand and held it to his lips.

"Do you still think at all of Harry Weldrake?" he asked quietly.

She shook her head.

"I'm glad. He was never worthy of you."

"Perhaps not." She withdrew her hand. "I hear tell he's married now. Behopes his wife will find him kinder than I ever did."

"Indeed. And you, Belle – shall *I* find you kinder, in time?"

"I . . . I don't know what you mean."

"I think you do."

She had turned away, looking out across the water-meadows to where the last faint bars of sunset touched the haze-heavy hills in the west.

"I'll write to you, if I may – " Alec had said; and then, swinging himself lithely into the saddle, had touched his crop to the horse's flank and circled round.

" – otherwise I fear you may forget me."

"Oh, no – I'll not forget you! Likely it'll be you forgets me first."

He shook his head and smiled; and Isabelle had stood watching him ride away across the bridge and along the road that would take him eastward over the uplands to Lewes.

Only when horse and rider had gone from her sight into the thickening shadows did she pull her shawl around her suddenly chilled shoulders and start walking slowly back towards the house.

Since then, she had had no word from him; and pride and reticence had held her back from being the first to break the continuing silence.

It is often the way that when a woman fears she has lost the admiration of a man, she begins to yearn after him, no matter how distantly she may have treated him while she still had his affection. So it was now with Isabelle.

Believing herself neglected by Alec Bethway, not a day

went by but that she did not think of him and wonder why he had failed to keep his word; not a day went by but that she did not reproach herself for her own indifferent manner, blame herself for her coolness, realising too late that she might have kept his regard had she but shown herself more responsive in the past.

She sought solace in explanations. He's been too preoccupied with his new parish to find time for trifling messages, she told herself . . . he may have fallen ill and be so weak he's unable even to lift pen to paper.

But less comforting and more frequent was the refrain that faithless Alec had become acquainted with some other, better-bred young woman and had forsaken Isabelle entirely.

Rachael Bashford, watching her god-daughter grow more and more disconsolate, and guessing the cause, spoke reassuringly and encouraged her to busy herself helping with the preparations for the birthday celebration, to be held on the last day of May.

The Bashfords were determined this should be an especially joyous occasion, a day of happiness and good cheer to wipe away the memory of the recent past and its attendant sorrows. If the weather were clement, it was planned to set out trestle tables on the large lawn behind the farmhouse, so that guests might sit in the open to eat; and afterwards, there would be entertainments and dancing to the music of the Bonningale church orchestra, comprising clarinet, hautboy, tenor-viol, double-bass and tambourine.

As the event drew nearer, excitement among the younger Bashford children mounted infectiously; and despite her melancholy humour, Isabelle found herself responding. Three days before, she travelled with Rachael into Arundel for the final fitting of her godparents' gift, an evening gown of pale green taffeta whose wide skirts were trimmed with tiers of narrow frills and looped at the side to reveal an underskirt of emerald.

The effect, with Isabelle's auburn hair drawn back into a chignon and bound with matching ribbons, was utterly enchanting; and the sight of her at the house porch beneath the blossoming lilacs, welcoming well-wishers to celebrate her birthday, drew compliments from them all on the day itself.

Of the many who had been invited, only Lizzie Newbrook and Ellis Bates were missing. Their absence, and particularly her half-sister's, was a little hurtful.

"She could have sent a note, at least," Isabelle said fretfully. "I wouldn't expect anything from Ellis, but I thought better o' Lizzie than have her treat me so neglectful."

"She's busy with the farm, I dare say, and can't get away to join us," Rachael consoled her.

"Aye, that's what it is. She wouldn't want my birthday spoiled, I know. I'll write tomorrow and tell her all about it, so's she won't feel she missed it."

Apart from this one small cloud, it was a perfect evening. Coloured lanterns had been lit for supper and hung in the trees surrounding the lawn; and as daylight began to fade their candleglow shed a soft radiance among the foliage, producing an impression of jewels glowing between the blue shadows of the trunks and sending ripples of colour floating across the grass beneath.

Supper being finished and the tables removed, the little orchestra took its place under the trees. Isabelle's card for the dancing was filled already with partners, and the first, a glossy-haired young man in tweed knickerbockers and Norfolk shirt, stepped forward to lead her into the opening waltz.

The waltz gave way to a schottische, followed by a clumsy galop. Then, wearying of these modish figurings, the dancers called for the orchestra to play a Sir Roger de Coverley, and formed themselves into two lines across the softly lit grass, ladies facing gentlemen.

As soon as the music struck up, the couples began one by one to advance diagonally to the centre, where they saluted each other with curtsey and bow before retiring backwards. Both lines then promenaded, the ladies turning off to the right down the lawn, the gentlemen to the left, meeting again at the bottom and so returning side by side to their places.

This sequence of movements continued at a graceful pace until every couple had taken their turn at the head of the line.

Isabelle and her partner were the last to go. Releasing hands, she turned away and went down the outside of the line to re-join him at the foot for their dance together up the middle. But as she reached out her hands again, she saw her partner had exchanged places during the gentlemen's promenade and was no longer the same as before.

The man now moving forward to take her in his arms was Alec Bethway.

"But I did write," he said quietly. "Every day, without fail, I wrote to you."

"Then why did I never get any of your letters?"

"Because, dearest Belle, I never posted them."

They had left the noise of music and dancers behind and moved away together into the shadows under the trees, where the pale green hue of a lantern's glow shone like moonlight upon their faces through the leaves.

Alec had left his Midland parish at dawn, travelling from Worcester by railway carriage and completing the journey by stage-coach and horseback. It was a long distance to cover in one day, but he was determined to reach Bonningale in time to share a few hours at least of Isabelle's anniversary.

"You never posted them?" she exclaimed. "But – why? I thought, when there was no word from you, you'd likely forgotten all about me."

"Forgotten you? You've been in my thoughts every waking moment!"

He turned to her, the light reflecting on the white bands at his throat, and took both her small hands in his.

"Let me explain . . . if I am able. You must surely be aware of the great regard I have you, my dear. Since I saw you first, my heart has not been my own. No – let me speak . . . I have wanted to say this for so long. In the beginning, I was determined to put you from my thoughts. Plainly, I told myself, you could feel no answering attraction while your affection was given so openly to Harry Weldrake. But nothing could cause an alteration in my sentiments, and being able to render you what service I could during your many sufferings brought me closer to you still. During all the months I have

284

known you, Belle, I've observed you change from a hapless innocent creature to a young woman of dignity and virtue . . . and beautiful as you were when first I beheld you, you have grown more beautiful yet. I've waited in patience for a sign that your regard for me may have matured also. No, no, please say nothing – hear me out. You have blessed me with your friendship, I know, but your manner has always remained . . . polite, almost careless. When I went away to my own parish I'd already decided I would no longer pester you with my attentions. That is why I didn't post those letters – letters which would have revealed the true depth of my feelings. I would withdraw myself from your notice for a time, I thought, and see what effect my silence might have upon you. I confess, dearest, I was tortured with ten thousand anxious doubts, and under constant apprehension that you might forget me entirely – "

Too agitated for a moment to say anything more, he fell abruptly silent and stood looking into her face.

Tears glistened in Isabelle's eyes.

"I never forgot you, Alec," she said softly. "All this time I've been hoping and praying I'd hear from you. But . . ."

"What is it? Why are you drawing away?"

"Your friendship . . . it's more than I deserve. I'm not worthy of such affection from a man like you."

"In heaven's name, why not?"

She flung back her head and stared up at him, holding him firmly from her.

"You're a gentleman by birth. Placed in a most respectable situation. I wouldn't for the world bring harm on you, let anything atween us give rise to gossip. Folk know the name o' Flynn well enough by now – "

"A name is soon altered by marriage."

His hands gripped hers tighter and he pulled her against him, pressing his face into the soft thickness of her hair.

"Do you understand what I'm saying, Belle – beloved Belle? I am asking you to marry me."

A tremor ran through her slender body.

"No! I can't!"

"You don't care enough for me to be my wife?"

"Oh yes, Alec . . . God knows I care for you."

"Then what?"

In a low voice, she said against his shoulder, "I'm no good for you. What would folk say? The daughter o' poor parents. Not wed, even. Raised in an alehouse. Bad blood in the family – "

"Listen to me. If I'd remained ministering in Lewes, such things might be said, I agree. Even so, I'd have been more than prepared to brave such shallow spite. There are people there, and elsewhere, who class their fellow men as they do their horses, rating stock above everything. I thank the good Lord I've been given a parish where there is true respect shown for the dignity of human nature."

He released her, but only to place his hands gently on either side of her face.

Earnestly he went on, "You have experienced much in your short life, my love. You've known hardship, betrayal, misery . . . you've seen the darker side of man's condition, you've witnessed the ignoble face behind the mask of respectability which so many choose to wear. A priest in his ministry needs a wife who can feel true sympathy for the distress of others, having endured it for herself. He needs a helpmate who can look with tenderness upon poverty and suffering and rejection, knowing that but for the grace of God, she might herself have sunk to such a plight. My parish is a poor one, Belle. Its people live in conditions of great want. I need you with me to help me – to give me strength – so that together we can help them in the Lord's name to find some dignity in life."

Isabelle closed her eyes.

Never before had she felt so humbled, and yet so fiercely proud. After all that had gone before, surely it was the destiny intended, that she should give herself in the service of others at the side of a loyal and loving man.

She opened her eyes again to look up at him, and tears spilled over and ran unheeded down her cheeks into the cup of his palms.

Tremulously she whispered, "If you truly need me . . . then yes, Alec . . . yes, I will marry you."

286

He murmured something as he kissed her, but she did not hear it, so loud was the beat of her blood as the warm, strong lips upon hers betrayed the force of a passion he had for so long denied himself.

Voices sounded somewhere, calling Isabelle's name, and in the lantern glow beneath the trees the little orchestra was striking up another traditional country tune; but neither was sensible of anything but their own joy in each other.

At last, releasing her with great reluctance, Alec said, "No one will be more pleased for my good fortune, I know, than George Bashford. He and his family will be the first to share our happiness, my sweet. And with you as my wife, that happiness is only the beginning of so much more we're going to have in life together."

ALSO AVAILABLE IN CORONET BOOKS